CUSTOM TRANSPORT...

The anguLord's eyes burned a

Vows wit—————————ly, and asked Tairyn, ——————————will return me to this ————————done?"

The Faerie Lord dipped his head in the curtest nod. "My word on it."

Bound by my vow to him, I could do nothing else after that but say, "I will come. But how—"

"Call." With that, Tairyn's image flickered and was gone. *"Call,"* one last mind-whisper told me.

Call. Call for what? Couldn't Tairyn do *anything* without mystery? What manner of ride had he arranged for me?

But before I did any riding at all, I detoured hastily down to the kitchen for a flask of water and a carrying-bag of food. Tairyn might need me right now, but that didn't mean I could trust him; I was *not* going to risk being ensorcelled by Faerie food or drink. Just in case, I also stopped in my chambers long enough to snatch up my Faerie sword and belt it about my waist. But you didn't keep an Otherly being waiting, so I raced down from my tower and back up the winding stairs to the other tower's flat roof, where I stood panting and wondering.

Call, Tairyn had said, and call, once I had breath, I did, trying not to mind that I had no idea what I might be summoning.

And something came, great-winged and huge against the fading sunset.

"Gallu..."

Tairyn had sent me a griffin.

BAEN BOOKS BY JOSEPHA SHERMAN

KING'S SON MAGIC'S SON

JOSEPHA SHERMAN

BAEN

KING'S SON, MAGIC'S SON

Copyright © 1994 by Josepha Sherman

A Baen Books Original

Baen Publishing Enterprises
P.O. Box 1403
Riverdale, NY 10471

ISBN: 0-671-87602-3

Cover art by Clyde Caldwell

First printing, June 1994

Distributed by Paramount
1230 Avenue of the Americas
New York, NY 10020

Printed in the United States of America

CHAPTER I

BEGINNINGS

I am Aidan ap Nia, Aidan, Nia's son, and I am brother to a king.

Half-brother. My mother was no queen nor fine court lady, but Nia, a wild witch-woman of Cymra, that you beyond our borders call the West Country. And the way of my begetting was this:

King Estmere, the first of his name, was a widower, his wife the queen having died in the bearing of his son and heir. And even after a year had passed, the king still mourned that poor lady greatly. At last, desperately hoping to beat down his grief, he wildly went hunting in the secret forests and ancient downs of Cymra, that stubborn, independent land between his kingdom and the Great Sea, went all heedless of the legendry that placed a shimmering of old, old magic there.

And as he rode with reckless haste, a thick gray mist arose about King Estmere, soft as silk, chill as the death of hope. The king lost all trace of his hunting companions, lost indeed all traces of the warm and living world.

How long he wandered in that soft gray twin to death, I don't know. But at last the king stumbled onto my

1

mother's hut. And by then that simple hut must have seemed a palace to him in his relief, and its black-eyed owner a queen.

So King Estmere stayed with her that night while the mist lapped close about the hut like a blanket to shut out the world. And he forgot his sorrow for a time. . . .

But in the morning, his companions came hunting for him. And Nia sent him away.

So, in the due course of things I was born, a babe with the black hair and tapering black eyes of my mother, though with little else of her in my features.

It was a good place, that small corner of the west lands. There was my mother's thatched-roof hut itself, with its earthen floor hard-packed and smooth as stone and its scents of clean herbs and spices. Outside the hut, there was the ancient woodland, with trees so old and mighty my young arms couldn't span their rough-barked trunks. There was dim green forest light and golden dapplings of sunshine, there were birds and beasts and none to harm me. For the early years of life I ran wild in wood and down as any happy, healthy young creature, secure in my witch-mother's love, safe under the mantle of her spells.

I learned much in those youthful days without realizing I was being taught (all but magic; I wasn't old enough yet to be trusted with Power), hungrily absorbing the ways and lore of our land. Though we led a solitary life, seldom seeing other folk, I knew the names and ways of every ceremony of the turning year, knew the proper way to honor the spirit of an apple tree with food and drink or keep evil from the door with rosemary and garlic. I learned tales from the first coming of humanity to the West Country in the long-ago-that-was. A small, dark, mystic folk, those, whose origin is lost in time but whose blood ran in my mother's veins and in my own. They and all successive waves had come, in peace or violence, determined to master the land. All in turn had been mastered by it, settling into that ancient place, living by its rhythm, worshipping *y Duwies*, the Goddess, which means worshipping the fierce, wondrous All that is Creation.

I learned speech, too, of course, not merely Cymraeth, our native tongue, but Anglic, that newer language common to the lands lying just to the east (where, it was rumored, men no longer worshipped the Goddess but followed a triple male deity), brought by merchants and the last, failed wave of invaders into the region five generations back. Anglic was a language less melodic, maybe, than our own, but simpler in the speaking: Cymraeth has twenty words for "yes" alone, each with its own shade of meaning. At the time I did wonder a little at my mother's insistence I become fluent in both languages, since the only other humans I saw were farm folk, set in their ways and speaking only the old tongue. But learning languages has never been too difficult a chore to me, and I quickly grew as comfortably bilingual as any other Cymraen child, though I thought (and think) in Cymraeth.

Easy lessons, those. But as I grew older and began to show some signs of reason, Nia took me in hand as her apprentice. It began like this:

I was home with a runny nose and a scratchy throat—even magic has no power over the mundane little illnesses—and feeling very sorry for myself. My mother was gone off to tend a farmer with a badly broken leg; at the time, I had waved her away, feeling very manly, insisting he needed her help more than I. But now I was only a lonely little boy. Worse, the fire in our central hearth wasn't burning hotly enough. Get up and gather more firewood? I didn't want to leave my warm bed. But when I reached out and tried to poke the fire up with a stick, I prodded so enthusiastically that the fading flame went out altogether.

For a moment I just stared in horror. Then I scrambled to the hearth and began blowing frantically at the last embers.

Nothing. The fire was good and truly dead.

Shivering in the rapidly growing chill, I hugged my arms to me and looked helplessly about. What now? I couldn't simply relight the fire with flint and steel; there weren't any. When one has a magical mother, one gets used to seeing fires lit with no more than a flash of will: will that I didn't yet know how to control.

The hut grew colder. I snatched a blanket about me, heart pounding. My mother would return before night; she'd promised me that, and Cymraen folk never lie. But the day was chill, and I had heard stories about folks dying from exposure. Here I was, already weakened by illness . . . Suddenly overwhelmed by the specters of my own imaginings, I nearly sobbed aloud. Would she return to find nothing but a pathetic, blanket-wrapped corpse?

I never did have much patience for self-pitying folk, even then. All at once I was so angry at myself for this silliness that I forgot to be afraid. Was I nothing but a helpless babe wailing for his mother? No!

"I won't give up like this! I won't!"

A surge of sheer, stubborn energy raced through me. And I felt something stir deep within my being, a new, hot, dazzling strength like nothing I had ever felt before. I stared at the dead fire and said, with perfect certainty:

"You—will—*light*!"

The dazzling power flashed from me to the wood. It blazed up into a blinding fountain of wild flame, and I fell back, tangled in the blanket, staring at what I'd just done in sheer disbelief. Then, with a yelp of alarm, I untangled myself and set about hastily beating out the flames before they could set the whole hut burning.

Just when I'd gotten them back under control, I heard the faintest chuckle from the doorway. My mother had returned, blue woolen cloak and gown fluttering about her in the wind, black hair loose and wild. Her eyes fairly glowed with eerie Power. "You are my son more than his after all," she murmured.

"I . . . don't understand."

"Your father was a good man, but he was no magician. I wasn't sure you had inherited anything more than scraps of my magic. But now your own Power has come on you, and even sooner than mine with me." She shook her head, smiling faintly. "I couldn't even begin to focus such a blast of will till sometime after my first bleeding. You do know what all this means, boy?"

I shivered with a delicious mixture of excitement and fear. "That I'm going to be a witch, too?"

She stirred impatiently. "The farm folk placed that name on me. Witch, wizard, magician: those are only names. You shall be a wielder of magic."

Just then I sneezed. The arcane light left her eyes, forced out by maternal concern. "Enough, Aidan. Back to bed with you."

And for a time I was glad to still be young enough to be tucked into bed and fussed over. But I couldn't forget what had happened, and at last had to ask:

"Does this mean I'll have to go off by myself and live in my own hut?"

My mother laughed. "Bless you, child, no. Not unless you wish it." She sat beside me. "I chose this solitude because I enjoy it. I find living close to other folk too disturbing, because I'm forever sensing their emotions quivering through my mind. But your magic will be shaped by you, to you. Who knows? There's a wide and wondrous world out there beyond the forest, and one day you may find yourself preferring to live in a village, even a city."

Of course I started to swear a boy's light, thoughtless oath that I would never leave her, but Nia waved me to silence.

"A vow once spoken is sacred, not to be broken. You know that."

"Yes, but—"

"I know you mean well. But I won't have you forswear yourself. No human can truly see the future, boy. But I suspect your destiny just may take you far from here."

"But . . ."

"Hush." She pulled the blankets up about my throat. "Enough talking, now. Go to sleep."

*   *   *

The next day my lessons in the ways of magic began in earnest. They weren't easy. Nor was my mother a gentle teacher.

"What is the true source of our Power, Aidan?"

"I ... uh ..."

"Come, boy, think! Some fools say magic only comes from Evil, from the sacrifice of innocents or studying grimoires bound in human skin."

I winced. "That's sick!"

Nia gave me a hint of a dour smile. "It is, indeed. But there really are some people who, though born without a spark of true magic, are still so hungry for power *and* Power that they're willing to try such obscenities. Book-sorcerers, learning their spells by rote." Her voice dripped contempt. "Forget about them. They aren't worth our thoughts. Now come, Aidan. Name the true source of our Power."

I hesitated. "*Y Duwies?*"

"*Och*, yes, of course, the Goddess is the source of everything that exists. That's not what I meant. Most of the force behind our magic comes from within, from our own minds, our own life-forces, shaped into useful form by will and inner strength."

"But I've seen you use potions for some of your spells," I argued. "Yes, and I've watched you work some of them standing barefoot on bare earth, too."

"Of course. It would be the worst conceit to think ourselves the only source of magic. There's Power to be had in anything of nature, most surely in the immense life-force that is our world. Assuming," she added drily, "you have the skill and humility that lets you tap into that boundless force of Earth without burning out your mind. Remember that point, boy: wielding Power is intoxicating, but calling up too much Earth-force is suicide. One small, mortal magician can't fight the Earth Herself and survive."

I had no intention of ever playing with anything so perilous. "But what happens if you rely only on your own inner strength? That could still be dangerous, couldn't it? I mean, if you got too tired."

"Exactly. Draw out too much of your inner force, deplete your body's strength too far and ..." She shrugged expressively. "Nobody ever said our Art was without its perils. A wielder of magic must never ever lose control if he would live. It's as simple as that."

Did her warnings frighten me? Of course. Did they discourage me? Of course not! In the years that followed, I devoured knowledge as a wolf devours meat, learning the proper names of things, the languages of bird and beast, what it is the trees are singing when the breeze stirs them, and what news the wild winds bear. Many a night I went to my bed weary to the heart with the weight of learning—but so filled with wonder I couldn't sleep.

Of course some spells came more easily than others. The charm for invisibility, for instance (or rather, for the illusion of invisibility), is a fairly simple one, once the mind is trained, a trick of will that lets the untrained glance slide blindly past you as though your flesh had genuinely turned to air. The charm for shape-shifting is another matter, since what you're trying to achieve isn't illusion but true physical change. It demands fine control of strength and will.

Of course, in my young pride I thought nothing of that. After all, hadn't I watched my mother slide smoothly from woman to beast to bird till I burned with envy? But when I tried the spell, fire blazed down every nerve and muscle till I lost my hold on magic and fell helplessly to the ground, sobbing for breath.

"It *hurts*!"

"Of course it does." My mother's voice was annoyingly calm. "The greater spells always do. The trick of it is to ignore the pain."

But try and try though I did, I couldn't manage that.

"Ah well," my mother murmured as I gnawed my lip in frustration. "You'll learn with time. At least you know the way of the spell should you ever need it. Hey now, don't sulk! You're mastering enough other magics. Forget about this one for now."

That, of course, was all I needed to hear to make me swear to master it. Aching with wounded pride, insecure as only a half-grown boy could be, I went off into the forest so she wouldn't see me fail. Watching a small herd of deer browsing unconcernedly, I set about trying to imitate their shapes till I was too sore and exhausted to think straight and sat down despondent in the middle of the field.

And felt someone watching me. I looked sharply up from the crumpled, miserable heap into which I'd fallen to find a young stag staring down at me. In my over-wrought state, I could have sworn he was mocking me. That was the final blow to my damaged pride, that even an animal should laugh at me— "I'll teach you!" I hissed. "You're coming home with me, stag—for dinner!"

And I sent the full surge of my will out to snare the animal mind and control it. For a moment, savage delight in my own magic blazed through me, overwhelming all else. As I pulled the stag forward with my mind, step by helpless step, I felt the cruel, horrible joy the strong can feel in abusing the weak.

But then something seemed to crumple within me. All at once I was flooded by the stag's emotion: terror, an agony of terror that burned from the wild, white-rimmed eyes, the bewildered, heartrending terror of an innocent creature caught by—

By evil. Evil knowingly, wantonly done.

"No! *Duwies glân*, no! What am I doing?" The sadistic joy fled. Shaking with self-disgust, I let my net of will fall. "Get out of here!" I shouted at the dazed stag.

He didn't move.

"Go on, get out of here!" I hurled pebbles, twigs, any-thing I could snatch from the forest floor. "Oh please, I'm sorry . . . I didn't mean . . . go away . . ."

He was never going to move. I had damaged his mind, and now I would have to kill him out of mercy, and bear the weight of his death forever. . . .

But then, to my breathless relief, the stag shook himself, blinked, and bounded away, leaving behind him only the stench of his fear. Sobbing, I turned and ran for home. There my mother found me, dry-eyed by that point but still sick at heart, and sat by my side. Shaking, not daring to look her in the face, I told her what I'd done.

There was a long silence. Bewildered, I glanced at her.

"Aren't you going to punish me?"

"No. Your own heart did that."

"But . . ."

"Think of the Threefold Law, Aidan. What does it say?"

It was one of the first rules I had learned. "That all good a magician does is returned to him threefold. All evil, too. . . ." I remembered how I'd been flooded with the stag's terror, and buried my face in my hands. *"Duwies glân. . . ."*

What if I had killed the stag?

What if the stag had been a man? What if I had killed *him*? I groaned. "Am I damned?"

"Och, Aidan." My mother's hand ruffled my hair. "You did a cruel, thoughtless thing, but that doesn't turn you into something demonic! Love, listen to me. True Evil takes delight in torment, with never a qualm of guilt. Are you like that?"

"No, but I . . ."

"Learned a painful lesson. Power must not be misused." There was a sudden sharpness to her gaze. "You were fortunate enough to learn that without lasting harm. You won't forget it."

"Never."

Nia sighed. "I've been wrong to keep you isolated here. I do think it's time you see other folk, meet youngsters your own age. Tomorrow, you know, I meant to travel to Pentref to see how Elin-the-baker is recovering—you remember that she burned her leg—and give her a new salve. But you've learned to treat burns as well as I, and you already have a skillful healing touch. Will you go in my stead?"

Pentref was the small village that lay a day's walking away. I had been there before, as a small boy with my mother, and found no great delight there. The children had shied away from me. Worse, considering a boy's fierce self-consciousness, I'd caught the adults making furtive good luck signs when they realized I was the witch-woman's son.

I sniffed. Did I really need the company of my own kind? Maybe I didn't have human friends, but up to this point I'd been quite content with the Others to be found in the woods, strange, lovely forest sprites and gnarled, wry-humored earth-folk who were occasionally friendly to a budding magician. There were the shy, wild confidences of bird and beast, and in the deepest, oldest groves glimpses of such wonders as unicorns, swift and shining as white flame.

Still, it *was* the first time my mother had entrusted me with such an important errand. Drawing myself up to my full height (at my young age, I was already nigh as tall as she), I said as proudly as any hero accepting a quest, "Yes, Mother. I will go."

CHAPTER II

HUMANS

I wasn't so confident once I'd reached Pentref. Passing within the rickety wooden palisade that surrounded the village, I shuddered to feel it psychically and physically cut me off from the forest.

Don't be a fool. If Mother can endure this, so can you.

With that, I started boldly forward, only to stop in confusion, facing what to me was a vast confusion of houses, squat, graceless things with smoke-darkened thatching and thick, wattle-and-daub walls set seemingly at random around a central, grassless square. All of them looked exactly alike to me. Which was the home of Elin-the-baker? I took a tentative sniff, hoping for the aroma of baking bread, and coughed. Looking back, I suspect Pentref's smell wasn't all that unpleasant, but used as I was to the clean forest air, the combination of close-packed humanity, refuse, and *y Duwies* knew what else was enough to make me choke.

There was a well in the square, and people around it. I decided to ask them which was Elin-the-baker's home and get this over with as soon as I could.

But my confident strides slowed as I saw all those

heads turn to stare at me. These were mostly young people, boys and girls together, a few years older than myself, snatching a few moments from their daily chores to chat and flirt. But I was unnerved by the open hostility to me that I read in the boys' eyes.

"Good day to you," I said carefully in Cymraeth. "Can anyone tell me which is the house of Elin-the-baker?"

One rawboned, fair-haired youngster took a swaggering step forward. "Who is it wants to know?"

He was speaking the clipped, curt language of the east. Later, I came to realize the young folk saw Anglic as more fashionable than Cymraeth because it was new and foreign—but spoke it primarily because (being, after all, like younglings the world over) it annoyed their elders.

Just then, I was simply grateful to my mother for insisting I learn both languages.

But why was this boy so rude? My tunic and cloak were of good weave, taken as trade goods by my mother from a weaver in exchange for her having magically strengthened the poles of a loom for him, and if I was barefoot, why, so were they all. "My name is not your concern," I said shortly in Anglic. "Just tell me which house belongs to Elin-the-baker and I'll not disturb you further."

A second boy moved lazily forward to join the first. "Maybe Elin-the-baker doesn't want to be bothered. Not by one like you."

Light dawned. These were all stocky, powerfully built youngsters, fair of hair and skin, while I was tall for my age, and slender, black of hair and eye: alien. "*Duwies glân*, do you think me something out of the Hollow Hills? I'm here to help the woman, not harm her!"

"Are you, now?"

There was an unspoken threat behind the simple words. The boy who had first spoken took another step forward, crowding me, trying to force me to move back, studying me through half-lidded, contemptuous eyes. Alarmed Power stirred in me, swirling hotly through my veins. I could make this idiot cringe! I could make him kneel in the dirt and wet himself in fear—

As I'd done with the stag.

No!

"Look you," I said, struggling for calm, "I'm Aidan ap Nia, son of the ... ah ... witch-woman."

Someone drew in his breath in a sharp hiss of alarm, and I saw several hands steal surreptitiously to hidden amulets. I saw something else: some of the girls, lingering warily by the wall, were giving me quick, hot, intrigued glances, speculative glances that disturbed me even though I was just a little too young yet to fully interpret them. The boys were old enough, though, and not too pleased at what they must have seen as a betrayal. But before anyone could say anything, one of the girls pushed her way boldly through the crowd to my side.

"Wanted Elin-the-baker's house did you? I'm going that way. Come on."

I was busy staring at her, taking in the broad, cheerful, blue-eyed face (those blue eyes so strange to me, so exotic), the healthy, warmly curved figure. I felt my face begin to redden at the sight of those curves, felt the first bewildering flickerings of an inner fire that had nothing to do with Power, at least not magical Power. I glanced hastily up again in confusion, still too young, as I've said, to quite understand all that was being offered to me and managed to stammer out:

"Thank you. That—that would be very kind."

She reached out and took my arm; the touch seemed to burn right through the good wool sleeve of my tunic. As we walked away from the well, I heard one of the boys mutter, not quite under his breath, "Fatherless witch-boy."

Fatherless. That wasn't quite the epithet you might think it. Granted, you may be puzzling that I haven't mentioned my father again—or rather, my wondering about the apparent lack of one. Well, of course I wondered, and of course I wove romantic stories for myself of whom he might be, making him now hero, now minstrel, now enchanted wanderer. But after that one mention of him having been a good man but no magician, my mother had never spoken of him again, and I—why, I never asked her.

Does that surprise you? Ah, but you must remember I am of Cymra, where the old ways still linger, and where a woman need not bind herself to a husband. If it was sufficient to my mother that she had found a man fair enough to want to create a child with him, that was her right. And if she then hadn't wished to cleave to him— why, that was her right, too, and no shame or strangeness about it, or reason for me to want a father's name to add to my own.

But I certainly wasn't thinking of my father just then, not with my buxom escort leaning on my arm and giving me quick, sly glances. Her name, I learned, was Nona, and I suspect that she couldn't have been much more than fifteen, ripe for marriage. Or mischief.

"Here we are, Aidan."

"Uh . . . thank you."

"Is that all?" She moved closer to me, so close that I could smell the healthy young female scent of her. "Don't you want anything else of me?"

"No, I—I don't think so."

She hesitated, then backed off with a reluctant sigh. "No. I can see you don't." Nona shrugged. "Come back to see me again, Aidan ap Nia. When you're a little older."

Heart racing, I bowed my politest bow, and hurried into the house of Elin-the-baker.

She turned out to be a chubby, middle-aged woman limping about spryly enough with the aid of a forked stick crutch. "Eh, you're not the witch-woman. Her son, though, with that black hair and those eyes."

"Ah. Yes. Aidan ap Nia, at your service, ma'am. She sent me in her place."

Elin-the-baker was a polite woman. She must have been doubtful about letting a raw boy treat her, but she never uttered a word of complaint. Even so, I felt awkward as any farmboy at first.

But as soon as I saw the half-healed, ugly burn and gingerly reached out to touch the skin around it, I forgot my unease and her skepticism, aware only of the *feel* of wrongness that was damaged flesh like a shiver of pain along my own nerves. For the first time I understood why my mother, otherwise such a private, solitary soul, was driven out of her way to heal: it wasn't from any Anglic sense of saintly goodness, but out of sheer discomfort.

Doggedly I began to murmur the intricate words of healing my mother had taught me. But my Power stirred within me of its own accord, rising up and up like waves of ever brightening flame. And I couldn't deny it. Nothing else was real. There was only the magic quivering through my fingertips to the wound, there was only the indescribable sensation, not pain, not pleasure, as delicate layer by layer the burned skin sloughed aside at my will and fresh, healthy flesh grew and joined to take its place. Intoxicated by the wonder of what was happening, I fed more and more strength into the healing. . . .

All at once it was done. The burn was healed. And I was toppling over sideways into exhausted slumber.

I woke, weak as a new fawn, back in my mother's hut. As I looked up at her in confusion, she smiled slightly.

"Yes. You're home. I brought you here myself, after what I'd seen in my scrying pool."

I stretched tired muscles, too worn to be angry that she'd spied on me, and blinked at the light filtering into the hut. "Morning? I slept the day around?"

"Aidan, love, you've been asleep for nearly two days! Not surprisingly," she added with a touch of wry humor. "I did warn you about drawing out too much inner strength, didn't I?"

"Sorry . . ."

"I'm not scolding you. Far from it." Nia shook her head in amazement. "The healing you worked . . . I never taught you that. How did you know what to do?"

"I—I don't know. It just . . . felt right." I stared up at her in alarm. "I didn't do anything wrong, did I?"

"Not at all." My mother hesitated, as though trying to decide whether or not I was up to a lesson, then added gently, "Of course, if you're to be a successful healer, you do need to learn something about priorities."

She sighed at my blank look. "Why do you think I hadn't worked my own magics on the woman? First, the burn, ugly though it might have looked to you, wasn't much worse than a scorching from too much sun. It wasn't even paining her any longer. Second, it was well along the way to healing. One more application of the salve, and I doubt there would even have been a scar."

"Oh."

"You see? You didn't need to squander your strength like that. A good many wounds and illnesses heal very nicely with nothing more than rest, cleanliness, and the proper medication. That's a fortunate thing, believe me!" she added with a laugh. "It's much less wearing on the healer!"

"I guess so."

"Hey now, don't sulk. I didn't mean to insult you." Before I could turn away, she reached out to ruffle my hair. "You acted out of a good heart, and that's the most important thing." Her eyes were thoughtful. "And I'm still impressed by your skill. You do seem to be developing your own unique Power."

That idea was both exciting and a little frightening. Seeing the unease that must surely have shown on my face, my mother grinned at me.

"*Och fi,*" she murmured, which is our Cymraeth way of expressing a whole world of meaning—everything from "alas" to "oh my"—in only two words. "All in all, your trip to Pentref didn't work out exactly the way either of us had planned."

I thought of the hostile youngsters, and the bewilderingly friendly Nona, and the healing I'd worked. "No," I agreed. "I guess it didn't."

*   *   *

So the seasons passed. I was sixteen, and finding a new restlessness within me. Understanding, my mother helped me build my own hut so we'd both have our privacy.

Not that I was home very often. No, that restlessness made me wander far afield, seeking in wood and down I didn't know what, dreaming dreams without names, comfortable only with my Power, vaguely discontent with all else though I didn't know why.

Nona, I thought, remembering sly blue eyes, the promise of that warmly curved body—a promise I was now old enough to understand. I wasn't quite an innocent by that point: there were forest sprites delighted to counterfeit a woman's form and tarry with the young magician. But they were light and soulless as mist, forgetting me between one moment and the next, leaving me with an aching loneliness they couldn't understand.

But Nona was human.

In my restlessness, I set out for Pentref once more.

I arrived on a night of celebration, not one of the four Great Solstices but one of the lesser, when everyone in the village was out in the fields, feasting about a blazing bonfire, enjoying mead and song. It was a warm night, heavy with the intoxicating scents of forest in late summer, rich, almost overripe yet with that first faint, sharp undertone that hinted of the coming autumn.

At first no one noticed me. But it wasn't long before the young men of the village, my less-than-friends of my last visit, now nearly fully grown, realized I was wandering among them.

"What're you doing here, witch-boy?"

"You're not welcome here, witch-boy."

They were ringing me round, full of the courage that comes with mead and companionship. But I had come a long way in just the few years since my last visit, and now I could see with a magician's clear sight, looking past the façade of bravado to the fear of the unknown quivering in their minds.

Puppies, I thought, for all that they were a few years

my senior, *just puppies trying to drag down a wolf. Be
wary, pups. This wolf has fangs.*

And I put just enough magical will into that thought
to make them move out of my way, still muttering their
brave words but no longer daring at all to back the words
with anything stronger. I couldn't really be angry with
them. They were only fools, and I was seeking something
warmer than a fight—

"Nona."

She was plumper than I had remembered, and there
was a coarseness to the cheerful face, but still . . .

Nona stared at me blankly.

"Don't you remember me, Nona? I'm Aidan, Aidan
ap Nia."

"The witch-boy!" Blue eyes looked me up and down.
"Not quite a boy anymore."

"Eh, Nona!" called a man's laughing voice, and she
grinned and yelled back, "Rein in your team, Tomos,
I'm coming!"

"Nona, I—"

"Nice seeing you again, Aidan. Happy times to you."

"But—"

"That's my husband calling, love. Got to go."

Her husband. I should have realized.

With a sigh, I turned to leave. But now there were
other girls gathering about me, drawn by the intrigue of
magic. And if they weren't Nona, if they were plump
and healthy rather than pretty, at least there was pleasure
in learning they didn't find me at all fearsome or unat-
tractive. For a time, being young, I enjoyed that night,
enjoyed awing and delighting them with little tricks of
mildest magic. Enjoyed, too, being human, the nervous
hoverings of the young men in the shadows, desperately
trying to pretend they didn't see me. Who knew? Maybe
I would pick one of these cheerful, silly girls and praise
y Duwies with her this night, as the country saying goes.

And yet . . .

I had magician's sight. I saw past their flirtings and
found nothing save that childish awe, and behind it,

shallowness. For them, joy was this: food and drink and couplings, warmth in the winter, the security of knowing life was and would forever remain the same. And I realized that for all our shared humanity, we were alien to each other, very alien indeed. At last, confused and lonely, I went my way, trying not to notice the young men swaggering forward to their girls, pretending that no, of course they hadn't been afraid.

Och, but they were glad to see me go.

So the slow days passed and I still found myself forlorn and frustrated, searching for the unknown.

And then, walking by myself one night beneath a radiant moon, I found the answer to my search.

CHAPTER III

SO FAIR BY
MOONLIGHT ...

It was the sound of the music that drew me, music so
fair it filled me with a joy nigh sharp as pain. Entranced,
amazed, care and caution gone, I wandered nearer.

And I saw them there in the moonlight.

Of course I knew the theory that Cymra was a land
where the veils between our human realm and that realm
of fear and wonder we call Faerie grew thin, permit-
ting—if one has the eyes and skill to see the way—
passage from one to the other. Now, trembling with
terrified delight, I watched that theory proven true.

Why should any of the proud Faerie Folk deign to
cross into merely mortal woodland? Are you thinking of
invasion, cruel conquest of the magickless by those who
are the very heart of Power? I don't doubt it might
amuse them for a time to appear as warriors, to ride out
all fierce and splendid in their shining armor, perhaps
even hunting down or enslaving any human foolish
enough to attract their fancy. But conquest of a realm
of sun and iron—no. Sunlight is a purely mortal thing,

20

unknown in Faerie, fatally burning unadapted Faerie skin. Iron is utterly a metal of the mortal earth, more so than moon-linked silver or sun-loving gold, so alien in essence to those never-human Folk it destroys Faerie magic, Faerie life, at the touch.

And yet, I was to learn, for all its perils, the mortal world is fascinating to the near-immortal Folk, intriguing in the swiftness of its seasons, its cycle of birth and death and birth. This elegant, perilous company before me had come on nothing stronger than a whim to dance amid the ever-changing woodland beneath the ever-changing moon.

Elegant, *och*, yes. They were tall and slim in tunics and gowns of green or silver or colors of which I knew no names, proud of eye and keen of face in a fierce, sharp, alien way that shook my ideas of beauty to the heart. As I watched, nearly forgetting to breathe for sheer wonder, I saw two Faerie men sport with slender silver swords. The grace, the cold, clear beauty of that swordplay pierced me to the soul, drew me helplessly forward.

They saw me then. Cool green eyes, glowing and opaque, watched me without blinking, the proud, sharp, fine-featured faces cold and hard as stone.

And the moonlight turned chill about me. Foolish, foolish, to forget all my caution. . . . As changing as the patterns of light on wind-tossed leaves are Faerie whims and fancies, and there is true danger for unwary mortals in those fancies, for the minds that think them are never human minds. As my thoughts fluttered about like frightened butterflies, I sought in vain for the words of apology that just might get me out of this whole, in body and spirit.

But as I stood frozen in growing panic, I heard the faintest gasp, almost a soft cry of wonder. A small, slim form slipped through the crowd, and I forgot anything so small and foolish as fear. For me it was as though my heart had stopped and then begun again in a finer, fairer song.

How shall I describe my first sight of Ailanna? I am

no poet. If I say she was fairer than the moonlight ...
No, that is stale, cold imagery, fit only for some minstrel
who has never loved. I will say only this: she was reed-
slender, reed-graceful in her soft, green gown, her long,
silken hair—so beautiful!—like a pale, pale golden cloak.
The Faerie lines of her face were proud, yet, I thought,
entranced, not quite as sharply cut, as fiercely inhuman,
as those of her companions. In her clear green eyes was
a light of warmth and humor and a touch of shyness that
told me she could only be young as me.

She is mine, I thought, *she is mine and I am hers ...
I am complete at last.*

"Human? Why are you here?"

Wonderstruck as I was, it's a marvel I didn't gasp and
stammer like a fool. But no, I heard my voice, though it
sounded as though it belonged to another, say almost
calmly, "The beauty of your music drew me."

Fool, fool, say something else! Praise her beauty.

But I was no trained courtier. The words just wouldn't
come, and I could only stare.

She understood. Faerie or human, some things are the
same. The color rose in her cheeks, and she turned aside
to speak softly and quickly to the others in the lilting
Faerie tongue. They, too, understood what was happening, and if they didn't approve, at least there was a certain tolerant—almost resigned—amusement hinting on
the proud faces as they answered her.

Ailanna turned to me again, joy in her eyes. "Now that
you've come this far, will you dare stay with us a while?"

I stumbled over my words in eagerness. "Oh, n-need
you ask? I would, I would indeed!"

Try though I will, I can remember little of that night.
All that remains in my memory is Ailanna, only Ailanna,
and the two of us shy and wondering and joyous in each
other's company as though within our own small, private
world. Had she asked me then and there to go with her
to Faerie as a slave forever, I don't doubt I would have
agreed without a moment's thought.

But she asked nothing of me. And the night, being only a mortal night, passed too swiftly.

Ailanna sighed. "We must go. The dawn is nearly here."

"But—no! I mean, you will return? *Och,* you will return?"

For answer, her sweet lips brushed mine in a quick, shy caress.

Dazed and wonderstruck, staggering as though I'd drunk too much rich mead, I wound my way back home through forest so dark with the death of night that only my magician's sight and knowledge of the path let me continue.

The path? I knew every step of it, and yet all at once I couldn't seem to move. . . . Something was drawn in the earth before me, glowing faintly in the darkness by its own faint light, soft as starlight, a twisting, turning design I must follow and follow with my gaze. . . .

My own magic woke within me, and all at once I knew what was being done to me. With an angry little cry, I tore my glance away, blindly reaching out a foot to erase the carefully drawn lines and break the spell. This was a Rune of Entanglement I was destroying, a charm meant to bind and confuse the will, though one more intricately and beautifully drawn than any I had ever seen.

The spell dissolved, and the faint glow with it. Someone laughed without humor.

"He knows that much, at least," said a cool male voice.

Darkness seemed to condense itself into a shrouded shape. The shape took a step forward, tossing back the folds of its black cloak, and revealed itself as a man of Faerie, too tall, too lithely slim ever to have been mistaken for humanity. Magic played about him as it had about the rune, casting its own soft glow, revealing him as elegant from the sleek fall of his long silver hair to the sharp, fierce, refined planes of his narrow face to the folds of his fine green silken tunic richly embroidered in silvery thread in a design more intricate even than the

Rune of Entanglement. There was nothing at all to be read in his sharply slanted eyes of flat smoky green, but silent strength and menace was in every supple line of him. My Power stirred uneasily in response to his presence, the call of magic to magic, but I knew I wouldn't stand a chance in combat against a being of Faerie.

He doesn't like a human daring to love a woman of his race, I thought, quite calmly. *Now I'm going to die.* I suddenly recognized the man as the Faerie group's leader, and added with desperate humor, *At least I'll have the honor of dying at the hand of a Lord of Faerie.*

Because I had nothing to lose, I asked boldly, "You set that rune for me, my lord? Why?"

"So-o! The boy has courage, too." He spoke Cymraeth with a lack of accent that was somehow alarming in its perfection. Clinging for straws of comfort, I wondered if there could have been the faintest glimmer of amusement in that clear voice. "Or is it foolhardiness," he continued, "to dare woo such as Ailanna?"

"I love Ailanna!" The shock of actually saying it out loud nearly staggered me, but I repeated defiantly, "I love Ailanna—and she loves me."

Now go ahead and kill me, I added silently. *I've told you the truth.*

But to my amazement, he waved my outburst aside impatiently. "Of course you do. We all saw it happen. It could be no other way."

"I'm ... afraid you've lost me."

His stare was contemptuous. "I did not come here to lecture a raw human boy on the subject of matching auras. I wished the chance to study you, alone."

Without any by-your-leave, the strange green eyes were burning into my own, the cold, quicksilver, alien mind was beating at mine, trying to learn who I was, what I was. For a bare flicker of time I was too stunned with outrage to resist. Then I angrily slammed down every barrier of will my mother had ever taught me, and felt the Faerie presence shy away. But no barrier I could ever hope to create was going to repel a determined Lord for very long. That realization frightened and angered me so much I forgot caution. My voice as cold as his, or as nearly so as I could manage, I told him:

"No, my lord. Not at your demand. With my permission."

And as he stared at me, astonished that a mortal should dare reproach him, I deliberately let my barriers fall.

I had shaken that inhuman calm. Though the frozen mask of his face never thawed, this time his mental touch was almost gentle, almost ... apologetic. The contact lasted for perhaps five heartbeats. Then he withdrew, and though there was still no softening of his proud bearing, I sensed I'd passed some arcane test.

"Satisfied, my lord?" I asked daringly.

"As much as I can be with one of your kind." A corner of that thin, elegant mouth quirked up in a grim imitation of a smile. "Were I not, you would be dead."

"Look you, if that was supposed to scare me, you're wasting your time. I'm already scared, my lord—"

"Tairyn. Call me Tairyn."

The Faerie Folk never lie. But since he hadn't actually said his name was Tairyn, this was almost certainly nothing more than a powerless use-name. Still, that he'd granted me that much was a concession. It also meant, I realized with a blazing of hope, that I probably wasn't going to die that night.

"As you will it, my Lord Tairyn," I said carefully, then added even more carefully, "Are you Ailanna's ... father?"

He looked barely old enough for it, perhaps a score and five years at the most—except for those ageless Faerie eyes. Tairyn laughed, this time with genuine humor. "Youngling, mortal youngling, I am the father of Ailanna's mother's father." As I stared, speechless, he continued softly, "Ailanna's mother's mother was of your kind. She aged and died too swiftly, a brief blaze of fire, then ... nothing. But you, with the magic in your blood, should last somewhat longer. Particularly in Faerie."

"Your pardon," I cut in hastily, "but I haven't quite finished with this world yet."

His smile was sharp. "I wasn't planning to steal you away. You are already too old and stubborn to make a fitting changeling." Faerie humor. The cool green eyes narrowed in sudden speculation. "Can you ride?"

The question caught me by surprise. "Uh . . . no."

"Use a sword?"

"Sorry, no."

"Sing? Dance?"

"I . . . no."

Tairyn's quick glance said plainly, *Human dolt!* But then he gave me his cold flash of a smile. "No matter. The capability is there. You will learn. And," he added mildly, "you may, with time, actually become something near to a fitting mate for Ailanna. If you survive the learning."

I wasn't sure if that was meant as a compliment or a threat. "Ah—thank you."

He stared at me. If there wasn't anything remotely resembling friendliness in his gaze, at least there wasn't open hostility, either. "Make no mistake, human. I am not at all pleased with what has happened this night. I could find it in me to wish Ailanna had never strayed into mortal lands. But things are the way they are, and only a fool would deny it." Tairyn paused, and now his glance was coolly speculative, full of chill, ageless wisdom that summed me up yet again, what I was, what I might be. "And," he added slowly, "it just may be that someday you might be of use to us. Will you swear with me, human?"

"Uh . . . swear *what*, my Lord Tairyn?"

"We will give you the learning to be a fitting mate to Ailanna—as far as such is possible for one of your race—if you will agree to come when we have need of you."

What need could the Faerie Folk possibly have of me? Uneasily, aware that I was very much out of my realm, I said warily, "If it's nothing that will endanger or enslave my soul or honor, Lord Tairyn, I do, indeed, so swear."

He gave me the barest hint of a gracious bow. "So be it." Tairyn glanced up at the brightening sky. "The dawn is near. You will return here tomorrow night for the first of your lessons. Perhaps we can make you just a little bit less blatantly ... human." He swept his cloak regally about himself. "You will, of course, say nothing of this to your own kind."

If he was trying to cow me, Tairyn was succeeding nicely. But I refused to grant him the satisfaction of knowing it. Bowing my most courtly bow, I said sweetly, "Good night to you, my Lord Tairyn."

When I straightened, he was gone.

"*Duwies glân,*" I said aloud. "What a night. What a wonderful, terrible, amazing night."

Not certain whether I wanted to laugh about it, or shudder, or weep, I set out for home.

It was full morning by the time I reached my home, and by then wonder and joy and sheer exhaustion had won out over fear. With Ailanna's love to shield me, I told myself, how could I ever possibly be afraid of anything ever again?

My mother showed no surprise at my having been away all night. She asked no questions. But the corners of her mouth hinted at a smile, so that I wondered if she did not, indeed, know perfectly well where I had been.

But all she said was:

"New wisdoms are often the sweetest."

CHAPTER IV

THE RELUCTANT PRINCE

"Aidan? Aidan!"

I had been lying flat at the edge of a deep, clear, swift-flowing brook, idly watching the small fish dart about, idly catching the echoes of what thoughts fish may have: simple, half-formed things of bugs and grubs and the like. But Ailanna's voice pulled me from that silly reverie, and I turned gladly to look at her where she sat comfortably curled in the tall grass. The stirrings of leaves overhead dappled my sweet lady with sun and shadow, changing her cloud of hair now to glowing silver, now to palest, warmest gold, changing her silky gown to a subtle rainbow of blues and grays and greens.

And I, entranced, stared, just stared, even now scarce believing the wonder that had happened between us, even after four years.

Four years. It hardly seemed possible. Surely the time had been much shorter; surely I had only known Ailanna for the barest blink of time. Yet, at the same time, hadn't I known my love forever?

Och, and hadn't I been under Tairyn's unforgiving tutelage not for four little years but for an eternity? The Faerie Lord hadn't been trying to frighten me away with empty words when he had mentioned the rigor of his training, and there hadn't been anything of human gentleness or pity about it. But I had survived, I had learned from him all that haughty lord had deigned to teach me. My body still bore the marks of his blade—Tairyn and his fellows did *not* believe in wasting precious training time with unedged weapons—and my mind still ached from all the knowledge I'd struggled to assimilate in such a short time. Never in all that time had I won the slightest hint of liking from the Faerie Folk; whether I lived or died meant nothing to them. But at least I had the satisfaction of knowing I'd forced grudging approval from them. I had become reasonably fluent in the Faerie language (blessing the Goddess for my gift for tongues). After those initial painful lessons, I had taken to the sword with an ease that secretly delighted me. And I was at least mostly at ease with Faerie song and magics.

Love and sheer terror mixed together make wondrous motivators!

But then, how could I have been anything *but* a good student with Ailanna beside me? Ailanna, my heart, my life . . .

Ailanna, who had just now had enough of my calf-eyed gazings. "How pensive you are. For a . . . mere human."

She had mimicked Tairyn's tone perfectly. I sat up in mock indignation. "Such scorn from someone whose own family line isn't exactly . . . untainted." I could imitate the man, too.

Ailanna gave a delicious little chuckle. "I yield! Without some human blood in my veins, I could never endure this lovely sunlight, and we would have only half our already too brief time together." She hesitated, and I saw a softness come into her glowing eyes. "I don't begrudge my mother's mother her humanity, love. Without something of what she was within me, there might never have been so strong a bond between you and me."

For a moment we were both silent. Then Ailanna threw herself full-length in the tall grass, pulling up a stem for dainty nibbling. "I do love this mortal world! The forest with all its secret green life, the downs with all that wide, free space under the golden sunlight— Do you know what daylight is like in the Faerie realm?"

"Only from what the old tales tell: there's no sun, of course, and the light is supposed to 'seemeth always afternoon,' like a perpetual twilight."

"No, it's not like that at all! The air glows, love, full of clear light, so beautiful. . . ." She sighed, then sat up suddenly, smiling, as somewhere in a treetop high above us, a thrush began to sing. "But it's so beautiful here, too. I think I would like to build a little hut right in the middle of the forest, and live just like a mortal woman."

"What, and cook and clean and spin? You'd be bored to tears in a week!"

"Why, then I would go back to Faerie for a time." Ailanna straightened. "We could do that, you know. We could live in both our worlds, now this one, now that, and be happy."

"Ailanna, that's a wonderful—no. It's not. You're forgetting the differences between Faerie and mortal time."

"Oh, that."

"Yes, that! I don't want to spend a day in your Realm, then return to mine to find a hundred mortal years have passed and I'm dying of sudden old age!"

"If Tairyn can play tricks with time, matching the Realms, so can we. You wouldn't age a moment more than the norm, I promise." She shivered with excitement. "Come with me, love, come to Faerie now."

Och, I wanted it! To be with Ailanna in a Realm of pure magic—

"I . . . can't. My mother—"

"You don't live with her any more. And she's hardly the sort who needs your care. And besides, she doesn't even know about us!"

"Hey now, that's not *my* fault, is it? If your so proud and noble Tairyn hadn't put a ban on me, I would have told her everything, and delighted her heart. But no, he wouldn't trust me! And so, every time I try to tell my mother where I spend most of my nights, every time I try to even mention your name, I start gagging and sputtering like some poor, weak-witted fool!"

"Aidan, love, I'm sorry. Please, let's not quarrel. I—I love you so much I ache."

We fell silent once more, gazing deeply into each other's eyes as lovers have done since the Beginning.

"Ailanna," I said, "we belong together, in this or any of the Realms. There's no life for me without you."

"Nor for me without you." Then Ailanna's eyes widened in horror. "What ill-omened words! Say simply, we *will* stay together."

But not even the Faerie Folk can know what lies ahead. There was sorrow, and great change, though the beginning of it was simple enough: my mother fell ill. It seemed so impossible, my dear witch-mother who was so full of life, and at first we laughed, and thought it nothing but some small, passing fever.

But as the days passed, my mother grew weaker, while the fever lingered on. As the strength of the year waned, so did hers, while I, heartsick, tried spell after spell, human and Faerie, potion after potion, all without success, refusing to admit that there are some things without cure, refusing to admit the truth:

She was dying.

But at last, when the springtime had come again, and all the world was bright with new life, she called me to her bedside, and I could no longer pretend all would be well.

I looked down at my mother where she lay uncomplaining. Her hair, untouched by time, was blacker than the heart of night, her face unlined and smooth. And yet it came to me suddenly, for the first time—we are so unobservant about those we love—that she was far older than I'd ever realized, that it was only by her magic that she had ever been able to bear a child.

She smiled up at me, eyes tranquil. "Don't mourn, lad."

"But—"

"No. I've lived long, but now *y Duwies* calls me, and I must return to her. You know that." She sighed. "But there is something you don't yet know. First, you must not stay here in the woodland after I am gone."

"I—"

"No. Hear me out." Her eyes were troubled now. "I've never spoken much of your father. Perhaps I was wrong. But I loved you dearly, my son. I . . . feared I might lose you if you knew the truth."

"Never that!" I said sharply, and she laughed.

"*Och*, Aidan, so firm, so sure of yourself! Like your father, indeed."

And she told me then what you already know, of King Estmere and my begetting, nor did she stop at my open-mouthed amazement.

"I wanted a child, Aidan. And he was a good, kind man, for all the weight of the crown on him." A ghost of humor flickered across her face. "I do think he wanted to bring me back to court with him. But his ways were not my ways, and we never could have—" She stopped, then added softly, "But he's dead now."

A thought penetrated my stunned brain. "Mother . . . are you . . . surely you're not trying to say I'm heir to a throne."

She laughed, but her black eyes studied me with something of their old strength. "Would you want that to be so?"

"*Duwies glân*, no!" The words burst from me without thought, but they were true ones, and my mother laughed again.

"Now, that's most fortunate, because there is already a king! You have a brother, a half-brother nigh two years your senior. And he, too, is called Estmere, the second of his line. I've studied him through my mirror, and found him a fine young man and an honest ruler." Almost to herself, she murmured, a dreamy, sensual smile on her lips, "What else, with such a sire?"

But then she roused herself, fixing her gaze on me. "He's lonely, Aidan. It hurt my heart to see young Estmere so in need of a friend. A brother. And you . . . it is in my mind that I've been wrong to keep you here."

"No."

"Yes. Your blood is half of the realm of court and throne, your very name is Anglic in your father's honor, yet you know almost nothing of the ways of the human world! Go to your brother. Offer him your friendship."

No! I wanted to cry. *No! Ailanna!* Ah, Tairyn, Tairyn, why did you do that to me? Why deny me that final chance to tell my mother of my love? How it would have comforted her to know I wasn't alone, how she would have smiled to see Ailanna at my side—

But Tairyn's will bound me. Faerie pride proved stronger than my merely human Power, and though I fought till my head blazed with pain, no words came.

My mother must have thought I was merely fighting back grief. I didn't argue with her. *Duwies glân*, I couldn't argue with her, not at such a time.

And in the end she won from me this vow, though it wrung my heart to swear it:

I would go to the royal court and seek out King Estmere, my brother.

I would stay by him till the day came when he no longer needed me at his side.

Now, perhaps you don't understand what a vow means to one of the West Country. It isn't just a light speaking of words. It's a duty, an unbreakable obligation—in short, the sworn word is sacred, it's as simple as that.

Once I had sworn that unbreakable vow, my mother smiled in satisfaction. And then, quite peacefully, she died and I was alone.

Of that time I will not speak.

When all was done that needs must be done, I took up those few possessions I wished to keep, and left forever the hut that had been my childhood home, and sought out Ailanna.

She knew what had happened ere I spoke. I saw my sorrow reflected in her eyes, and we wept together without shame.

After a time, Ailanna asked softly, "What will you do now?"

"I ... don't know." I did know; I couldn't say the words.

Ailanna was wiser. "You swore a vow, love. You must go."

"Come with me."

"No!" Fear blazed up in her eyes. "That is a world of stone walls and iron!"

"I would shield you."

"How?" she asked fiercely. "Being surrounded by so much of that cruel, cruel metal would kill me, no matter what you did!"

I winced. Iron is, just as the tales tell, most deadly to all Faerie kin. "Forgive me. I wasn't thinking clearly. But—*och*, my love, how can I ever leave you?"

"You can. You shall." Ailanna suddenly smiled. "What, do you think me a mere human, to be frightened by the passing of a little time?"

"It may be more than a little time."

"What of that? Aidan, what am I to you?"

"*Och*, Ailanna, you know! My lady, my love, my wife-to-someday-be—my very soul, Ailanna."

"So," she said with wry humor. "After that outburst, are you afraid you might forget me? And I certainly won't forget you, either." She cupped my face in her cool hands. "You'll return when the One wills it, Aidan ap Nia, and I'll be waiting."

The Folk cannot lie. And despite myself, I felt the burden of grief lessen just a bit, and my spirits lift. I was young, after all, and new to the promise of adventure. "So be it. I'll go forth and conquer worlds for you, my lady, like some hero of the sagas."

"Ah, but a hero needs a sword." It was all at once

there in her arms, a fine, slim Faerie blade in a scabbard of pale, soft leather. "Tairyn left this for you, when you should be ready for it. But it was forged at my request."

My hand itched to hold it. The hilt, wound about with silver wire to provide a better grip, slipped into my palm as though it belonged there. Wondering, I drew the sword free, seeing how the guard curved towards the blade as sweetly as the bow of the crescent moon. And ah, the blade was fiercely beautiful, not gaudy-bright as swords of mortal forging but sleek and clean and coolly shining, Faerie metal, with runes for strength upon it.

Reluctantly, I resheathed the sword, reminding myself I was a healer, not a warrior. "But this is a princely gift, Ailanna."

"And are you not a prince?"

That gave me pause. "Prince Aidan," I said experimentally in Anglic, "Prince Aidan ap Nia," and had to laugh. "Doesn't sound quite right, does it? Doesn't sound like *me*." My hand caressed the smooth softness of the scabbard. "But I do thank you for this gift."

Her eyes were all at once strange, very Faerie and farseeing. "It will serve you well," she said in a cool, clear tone totally unlike her norm. But then Ailanna shivered, and the strangeness was gone. She gave an awkward little laugh. "Come, my hero. It's time you set forth."

We both knew I dared not wait. A moment's hesitation more, and I might not be able to keep my sacred vow. So, without another word, she fastened the swordbelt about my waist, as tradition demands human ladies do for their knights.

We embraced.

And then, tearing myself away, not daring to look back, I set out eastward for the world of men.

CHAPTER V

FAMILY REUNION

King Estmere's lands are broad and fertile: rolling hills and healthy farms, and over all the scent of prosperity. Queen of these lands is the ancient capital, Lundinia, that mighty walled city on the River Taemese. Nine gates has Lundinia, and nine bridges over the Taemese, and all of these are usually well-crowded with merchants and farmers, peasants and nobles, with wanderers and traders and just plain curious visitors from all over the kingdom—yes, even from all over the known world.

Now, in my travels eastward, I had come to consider myself cosmopolitan enough, easily accepting that the folk I met wouldn't be speaking Cymraeth, attuning my ear instead to the clipped sounds of Anglic (no easy thing; no one had ever warned me just how many dialects had arisen from the basic form) and being careful not to mention *y Duwies* just in case. I had passed through villages and towns in plenty, some of them large enough to make simple Pentref look like a poor little huddling of huts. After the first shock of seeing so many folk living crowded together had worn off, I had become almost blasé about such things, sure that Lundinia would prove to be nothing more than a slightly bigger town.

My initial view of the city, from the far end of a vast, grassy field, did nothing to change my mind. At that range, the bridges and the famous stone walls looked scarcely more impressive than the wooden palisade about Pentref.

But as I came closer, the walls began to tower and tower over me till I had to tip my head back to see the top of them. For a confused moment, it seemed that the law governing the proper proportions of things had vanished, and I had shrunk to the size of a cat. Then the confusion cleared, and I realized that the walls really *were* that tall, and winced at the sheer cold strength of them. Had I blithely thought to trap my dear Ailanna behind *that*? Overwhelmed by the sudden terror of a wild thing being driven into a snare, I paused nervously by the side of the road, unable to take another step.

This is ridiculous! Do you want to meet your brother or not?

Or not. But I had given my word, and so ... gritting my teeth, I forced myself forward.

I entered Lundinia by the West Gate, a massive affair fully twenty feet thick and guarded by two stone watch-towers from which guards peered down through narrow arrow-slits of windows. I entered wonderstruck and dazed, gawking like any peasant, the sights and scents and bustle hitting me like a blow.

I have no idea how long I stood staring like a fool, eyes dazzled by the colors, reds, blues, golds, flashing bravely in the bright sunlight from cloaks and gowns and banners, ears ringing with shouts and laughs and the squawking of chickens, nostrils filled with the scents of cinnamon and roses, horse sweat and human sweat and dung. But I was shaken from my trance by the curses of the driver of a wagonload of vegetables, telling me in no uncertain terms what he thought of idiots who blocked the road, and I set out to find the palace of the king.

My brother.

Westgate Street is broad and smoothly paved with cobblestones, swept reasonably clean. Faced on either side with houses of wood and plaster two and sometimes even three stories high, some of them with ground floor shopfronts unfolding out onto the street to catch the eye and narrow the roadway, it slopes gently up into the city to the great marketplace, the true hub of Lundinia, with the nine main streets radiating from that vast open square like the spokes of a wheel.

And here in the market I was temporarily lured aside from my mission, fascinated by the riches for sale: not just the wealth of forest and field so familiar to me, but silver and gold and gems (flash of ruby, glint of pearl), thick piles of furs blue-black or dull gold from the chill northern lands, perfumes with the memory of a hundred springtimes in them, even carved ivory and rare silks almost fine as Faerie weave—and almost as costly—from the lands that lie so many months' journeying to the east.

And the people! In the space of perhaps twenty heartbeats, I noted broad-faced farmers in sensible brown homespun, sharp-eyed, gaily clad merchants, northerners thick-bearded as bears, dark-skinned southerners, supple and quick to laugh or curse: a true tangle of humanity. In the air clashed such a jangling of tongues (a flash of Cymraeth here and there to make me homesick) as was a confusion to the ear and a bewilderment to the mind. The wild variety of human essences beat dizzyingly against my senses till I slammed shut every psychic wall I could muster, understanding in that moment why my mother had chosen to live in solitude.

But it was the citizens of Lundinia who disturbed me the most. Many of them would glance casually at me, then glance again, sharply, almost staring. I would read puzzlement in their eyes, then comprehension and alarm or, sometimes, what might have been amusement. And yet I had done no magic, drawn no attention to myself, and though the city folk tended towards blond or reddish hair, there were enough black-haired foreigners about for me not to be outstanding.

Then why in the name of Power are they all staring?

Almost, I decided to catch myself a townsman, to ask him pointblank what he found so amazing about my appearance, and if he refused, to put a truth-telling spell on him! But no, that wasn't a wise idea. It seemed that wizardry was frowned upon in these more ... modern lands. I had discovered it the hard way during my travels, having nearly gotten myself burned at the stake by some terrified villagers for passing the time of day with some-one's cat. I certainly didn't want these folk thinking their king's brother was in league with Evil!

The amusements of the marketplace had palled. I pulled up the hood of my cloak to hide my face and put an end to staring, and set out once more upon my quest.

The royal castle of Lundinia stands on a high, craggy hill overlooking the River Taemese. And a fine, proud, forbidding old fortress it is, all curving towers and sharp-angled walls, home to who knew how many generations of kings.

And now home to one King Estmere.

There is a custom at the royal court old as the castle itself of once a month allowing into the royal presence anyone, noble or peasant, who would petition the king. And I, who'd chanced to arrive on that very day, saw here the easiest way possible to meet my brother.

Short of magic, of course.

Getting myself admitted into the castle was no prob-lem. I merely followed the crowd up the steep ramp, across the wide moat, past the heavy, brass-bound doors and under that alarming, spear-pointed contraption known as a portcullis, then made eye contact with a guard and willed him to let me pass into the great audi-ence hall beyond.

"Your sword."

"Eh?" I turned, startled.

"Surrender your sword." There was no emotion on the guard's weatherworn face; he had plainly been through the routine countless times before. "Look, man, you didn't expect to go into the royal presence armed, did you?"

"Oh. No. Of course not." Reluctant though I was to part even temporarily with Ailanna's gift, I obeyed. "Be careful with it." And I put just the smallest touch of Power behind the words.

"Heathenish-looking thing," the guard muttered, eyeing the crescent-curved hilt. But I saw how gingerly he was handling it, and I smiled to myself. While undergoing a quick, professional search for concealed weapons, I asked the man:

"How long do you think it will take before I can speak with the king?"

"How should I know? Don't you see the crowd ahead of you?"

He couldn't have seen much of my face, not with my hood so far forward, but he must have belatedly responded to the uncertainty in my voice, because he added, not unkindly, "Don't worry. If you really need to see him, you'll see him. Our king may be young, God bless him, but he cares about us common folk. Just like his father, God rest him." Then, brusquely, "Hurry up, now. There's others behind you."

The hall was vast indeed, the sharply peaked roof so high overhead its color was hidden by shadow, its timbers supported by rows of tall, slender stone columns. The furthest end of the hall, like the roof, was shadow-shrouded. In fact, the entire room was shadowy, poorly lit by window slits set high in the walls and by a profusion of torches that sputtered and swayed in the occasional breeze. The air reeked of smoke and too many not quite cleanly folk crowded in together. By peering over the heads of the throng ahead of me, glad of my height, I could just make out the shape of a tall, richly dressed young man, golden crown glinting on golden hair, though I was still too far from him to make out detail.

Estmere, I thought, and then, *of course it's Estmere, you idiot! Who else would be wearing a crown?*

I was nervous, no denying it, and dizzy from the

massed emotions surrounding me, the petitioners' unconscious sendings of fear, hope, desire. I turned my mind inward, silently repeating disciplines for calm, succeeding so well that it was a shock to realize time had passed and there was no longer anyone ahead of me.

So I came before my brother like any other petitioner, going down on one knee as I'd seen was proper. A strong, clear young voice bade me rise, and I did, rather bemused at hearing curt Anglic turned into something more pleasant by a melodic, aristocratic accent. My hood was blinding me, and I quickly pushed it back out of my way.

Our eyes met for the first time.

And what a shock that was! Now I knew why the city folk had stared. For though Estmere's hair is gold, his eyes sky-blue, while mine are, as I've said, black as night, the likeness between us, feature for feature, was so strong that anyone who saw us must name us kin.

There was a long silence during which we were both too stunned to speak. But then Estmere found his voice. My brother's first words to me were a stumbling, "I—I didn't know—I did not know my father had . . . wandered so far afield."

"Don't blame him for that!" I felt a sudden irrational need to protect the man I had never known. "It was a full year after your royal mother's death that he met my mother, and him full of grief and lonely. . . ."

My words trailed off. Again we stood staring at each other, awkward as two young stags come face to face in a forest. At last Estmere said, "An audience hall is a poor place for . . . kin to talk. Have you any belongings?"

"My sword."

"It will be brought to you."

He signalled a little page, who took me away from the court's buzzings of excitement to rooms within the castle where I could bathe and change into fresh clothing. Princely clothing, I suppose, but truth to tell, my mind was so awhirl I couldn't have described it.

Estmere, King Estmere. "*Fy brawd*," I said experimentally in Cymraeth, and then again, in Anglic, "my brother."

Duwies, yes! My brother, no denying that.

But . . . Estmere. Until that brief meeting in the audience hall, he had been only a name to me, hardly more real than someone in a tale. Now I had to face a living, breathing man, one about whom I knew nothing save our relationship by accident of birth. Yes, the vow had forced me to come. But was I right to upset my brother's life, and my own?

It was on these troubled thoughts that Estmere entered. Alone. Which wasn't quite as trusting as it sounds: I was still weaponless, and of course guards were right outside the chamber door. I hesitated, uncertain, then started to bow. Estmere waved that off.

"There's no need, ah . . ."

"Aidan," I supplied. "Aidan ap Nia."

"Aidan ap Nia. Why have you come here, Aidan ap Nia?"

I couldn't, by the wording of the vow I'd sworn, tell him about that vow. "I wanted to see what you looked like," I said, which was, when I thought about it, quite true.

He gave an involuntary little laugh. "So! I trust you approve of what you see?"

"Yes." It wasn't empty flattery, because I was looking at him with magician's eyes, and my gaze was going beyond the physical. "I see a young man as honest and just as is wise for him to be." The rest came tumbling forth without conscious thought; a magician engrossed in truesight can't always control his words. "Ahh, and I see the strain . . . the strain of never daring to trust . . . hiding honesty for diplomacy's sake . . . keeping to justice and never, never yielding to the endless seduction of power."

He certainly hadn't expected such an answer. For perhaps two heartbeats' time Estmere was too surprised to hide his emotions. I read loneliness there like a quick cry of pain—how very alone he was!—and a weariness of spirit that didn't belong in so young a man. Shaken by sudden fierce pity, I almost said that aloud, too. But Estmere had turned away.

"You speak strangely, Aidan."

Didn't I know it! "I'm unfamiliar with court speech," I hedged. "I didn't mean to offend you."

"No offence taken." He shot me a wary little sideways glance. "Are you always so . . . blunt?"

"I fear so! You see, I grew up in Cymra, and the—Folk I know there just—do not lie."

"And now that you've satisfied your curiosity about me, what will you do?"

What, indeed? I stared at him blankly. "Frankly, I'd made no plans beyond this point."

"I see." Estmere studied me, eyes guarded, and this time I could read nothing of his emotions. "Well, Aidan ap Nia of Cymra," he said suddenly, "it would be a novelty to have someone at this court who just—does not lie." It was an excellent imitation of my voice, Cymraeth accent and all. "Will you stay?"

Was that kindly meant? Or did he simply want to keep this unexpected and potentially perilous relative safely under his eye? "If you will it," I answered cautiously, "I'll stay, ah—I fear I don't know what to call you."

The boyish flash of his grin surprised me. "Look in your mirror, man. Call me 'brother,' of course!"

CHAPTER VI

BROTHERS

What can I say of my entrance into the court of His Most Gracious Majesty, King Estmere II? Of course my mother had taught me manners, and the Faerie Folk, under Tairyn's stern eye, something of their elegant graces, but this . . .

First, understand that the palace was a separate small city in itself, housing not only the king and his advisors, servants, and the like, but the various smiths, weavers, bakers—in short, the whole population of Pentref could have fit amid the maze of walls and outbuildings. Despite the crowding, I think I would have been much happier down there with the common folk, even if few of them spoke Cymraeth. At least I would have understood how their minds worked!

Instead, Estmere swept me through a dizzying crowd of nobles, introducing me hastily to this lord or this lady (almost as if he still wasn't quite sure what to do with me), all of them splendid in their fur-trimmed gowns and cloaks and tunics glinting with gems—all of them fairly blazing with curiosity about me.

Not that they had a chance to satisfy that curiosity.

No sooner was I being greeted by Sir Verrin, Estmere's seneschal, a pompous, efficient little man with a smile that didn't include his wary eyes, than I was coming face-to-face with such courtiers as Baron Aldingar, a fine, elegant, auburn-haired fellow with the *feel* of a ferret to him, or with the whole covey of royal advisors, shrewd, well-settled noblemen, not one of them young (indeed most of them looked old enough to have served Estmere's—and my—father) all of them quite polite to me with proper, surface courtesy. The impact of so many very human, very unmagical minds against mine, particularly when I was so used to the totally magical, quicksilver wits of Faerie, was enough to leave me dazed.

And what a tight little artificial world was in that palace! Convention would not allow for anyone of noble blood to actually *do* anything, not even take up a craft. That left too many noble folk with too little for them to do. Save pick at each other and play with elaborate rules of order.

Still, I told myself, a magician was supposed to welcome any form of knowledge. At least I was gradually getting the trick of inuring myself a bit to being surrounded by so many emotions of so many ever-present courtiers.

So I endured, though my mind winced from the sheer triviality; I learned what there was to be learned: the proper style of dress and address (*y Duwies* help the poor soul who dared wear ermine when his rank entitled him only to vair, or who called a male bird of prey a falcon, not a tercel!), the ways to deal with noble and favor seeker, saying much and promising nothing.

It was a learning more tiring than any swordplay or magic. And, *och*, it suffered so much by comparison to the cool, clean elegance of the Faerie Folk! There were times when I would have welcomed even Tairyn at his sardonic, perilous worst.

And what of the court's reaction to me? I've already mentioned that initial burst of curiosity. As the saying goes, I was a "seven-day wonder," with everyone staring at the king's mysterious half-brother, whispering behind my back (not always complimentary things, either; these people of the newer ways have some very uncharitable names for the son of an unwed mother), and waiting for me to do something extraordinary. But when I neither overthrew my brother nor grew fur and fangs when the moon was full—I hadn't the slightest intention of revealing a hint of magic, see you!—and when I, with my unfashionable Cymraen ways and accent, proved most shockingly innocent of court intrigues (deliberately innocent, I need not say), they lost all interest in me.

"A peasant," I heard one nobleman whisper condemningly. "Royal blood or no, he's nothing but a peasant."

So be it, fool, I thought. *At least that keeps me out of your silly status games.*

And I? I was bored. And very, very lonely: *hiraeth,* we call it in my land, that wistful, bittersweet, painful longing that is so much more than the simple Anglic word "homesick." Grief for my mother had died to a dull ache by now, but—*Duwies,* how I hungered for the sound of Cymraeth, for the feel of clean, spicy woodland air about me once more. And Ailanna . . . my longing for Ailanna was sharp and fierce as flame.

They had no true idea of privacy at Estmere's court. But when I, half-mad with the need for solitude, had begged the favor of chambers in an isolated tower top, my brother had ceded them to me without a moment's pause. It was, I realize now, done as much out of caution as kindness; he must surely have been thinking that, stuck up there, I could work no plots against the throne.

I didn't much care. Sitting in my tower's window one night (since the window was high enough to be out of bowshot, it was agreeably wide), listening to the small winds bring me tales of my homeland, I was aching with *hiraeth.*

What did I know about Estmere? Really know? Other than that he made a fine, handsome picture of a king who took his royal job very seriously. *Pw!* Any courtier with an eye in his head could have told me that much.

I looked moodily out over the night-dark city, then gradually let myself slip into trance, just as I'd done every night when I'd felt myself safe enough. Magicians have, of course, their means of seeing and speaking from afar. Almost at once I felt Ailanna's mind brush mine, and laughed for joy. We made our usual happy, frenzied greetings, aching to hold each other in the flesh. And then my love asked the same question she'd asked ever since I'd entered the palace:

"Have you befriended your brother yet?"

"You make it sound so simple! I've tried—no, I'll be more honest, I don't know *how* to try! Ailanna, love, I've spent too much time in Cymra. I don't even know how these folk think."

"Nonsense. If you can understand my people—"

"As much as they'll allow."

"Well yes," she admitted wryly, "there is that. But you're among humankind now, your own kind. They *must* be simpler to understand! Surely your brother—"

"Surely my brother has no need of me! Ha, he doesn't just have no need of me, he out-and-out avoids me!"

"But the vow—"

"The vow, the vow!" I snapped, nearly shaking myself out of trance. "My poor mother was wrong, Ailanna. Estmere doesn't need me at all. We might chance to be brothers, but *y Duwies glân* knows we're as remote as any strangers."

In my innocence, it never occurred to me that Estmere might have his reasons for keeping things like that.

"That's it, Ailanna," I decided. "I've been apart from you for far too long for nothing. Good night, love."

"Wait! Where are you going?"

"Why, to find the king, offer him my farewells, and end this ridiculous exile!"

"I don't think it will be so easy," she murmured.

But I was already shaking myself out of trance. Blinking groggily as mind and body reunited, I got to my feet, stretching stiff muscles, and left my chambers.

Now, I had flatly refused the normal thing of allowing

servants to share my quarters: sleeping at the foot of my bed, fussing over me, prying into my every move. Estmere already thought me eccentric; let him accept this as just one more bit of proof. But of course I wasn't completely free of attendants; I had been watched and followed from the moment I'd first entered the palace. As soon as I opened the door (thanking *y Duwies* my chambers *had* a door; not all castle rooms did), the little cluster of servants waiting outside roused themselves from what looked like a hot game of dice, springing to their feet in a flurry of nervous motion, frantically smoothing red and gold royal livery, hastily bowing.

"My . . . ah . . . lord?" No one at court had quite decided what my proper title should be. "Is there aught we can do for you?"

"No. Go back to your game. Let me pass."

They continued to block my path, very obsequious, very determined. "Ah, no, my lord, we can't just let you wander about by yourself."

"Really? Why not?"

"Why it . . . it just isn't done. You might get yourself lost or something."

I snorted. "I might spy on my brother, you mean. Look you, I mean him no harm. Stay here."

"But—"

My nerves were beginning to tighten. "*Will* you leave me alone?"

Wait, now. Gently. Faerie spells, I had already discovered, worked not at all during daylight hours, their Power cancelled by mortal sunlight. But the sun had already set. And Tairyn had taught me a subtle, harmless charm, smoother and more effective than any human magic. I had made use of it more than once back in Cymra, finding it the quickest, kindest way to soothe an injured patient.

"Listen," I told the servants, and softly recited the elegant, twisting words, putting the proper touch of will behind them. One by one, the men blinked and yawned, sliding down into sleep. I smiled.

Thank you, Tairyn. Not that you would appreciate my thanks.

I slipped past the softly snoring servants and set out to find my brother. But as I passed the doorway to a small, tranquil cloister, I was stopped and held by a lovely, silvery waterfall of music. A figure was seated alone there in the semidarkness, bent over a small harp. A court minstrel? A singularly fine one, then; only a true poet could create beauty to so touch the heart.

It was Estmere. Estmere for once, amazingly, free of servants and courtiers. Estmere letting his harp say for him what he could not, singing of gentleness and poetry and love. The music he coaxed from that small harp nearly made me forget the hard reality of the castle around us and see only the play of leaves beneath a radiant Cymraen moon.

Almost without willing it, I moved to his side, silently, not wanting to break the thread of his music. I recognized the song he played, an old, old ballad of a country lass loved by an elven knight, a Cymraen ballad originally. Softly I sang the words as they should be sung: in Cymraeth. Estmere didn't look up, but a small smile formed on his lips. We finished that ballad, went on to others, not wanting to shatter the spell the music was casting, but at last Estmere laid down his harp, wriggling stiff fingers.

"How did you elude the servants?"

I waved that aside impatiently. "I did."

He raised a bemused brow, but added only, "You have a passing fine voice, Aidan."

It was said so lightly I knew he must be embarrassed at having been caught revealing so much of his inner self. I wasn't. I couldn't joke about the beauty we had just created. "Estmere, your music is *fflam a golau—och*, no, I mean flame and moonlight, near as fine as Faerie harpings."

"Come now."

"Yes! Why, some nights I've heard ..."

But here I stopped. Tairyn had made it quite clear

that his Folk didn't care to be discussed by humans, even by such humans as I.

"You've heard what?" Estmere prompted, amused, plainly determined to keep the tone light. "The Fair Folk singing, perhaps?"

"I have." The words slipped out before I could stop them, and my brother grinned.

"Why, Aidan. I thought you never lied."

"I don't."

His grin broadened. "The start of a jest, then, and here I've spoiled it for you. You might actually have had me believing that ... that.... You weren't jesting, were you?"

"No."

"But ..." He shook his head, eyes soft with wonder. "Tales do say the Folk linger in Cymra. And ... is their music as fair as those tales would have it?"

I floundered for words, and Estmere gave a small, almost wistful laugh. "As fair as that, eh? I think I should dearly love to hear it." But then, just like that, the wistfulness was hidden, and he added shortly, "I doubt I ever shall. Is it a Faerie sword, that strange, crescent-hilted blade of yours?"

"Ah ... yes. It is."

He was too well-schooled in regal tact to ask the obvious—how comes a human by such a blade?—contenting himself with, "Tell me, are all your Cymraen folk so unusual?"

I had to laugh. "No—yes—I don't know! How can I speak for anyone but myself?"

"How, indeed?" But Estmere wasn't smiling. After a moment he said, "I've been avoiding you. Were you aware of that?"

"How could I not be aware?"

"Do you know why?"

"I ... well, I thought you might be ashamed of me, your ... uncouth and illegitimate kin."

"Oh no, never that! Do you really think me so shallow-minded?"

"I hardly know what to think of you," I reminded him, and he acknowledged the point with a wave of his hand.

"Let me be frank, Aidan. I was afraid of you."

"Afraid!"

"Not for myself. For my country."

"I don't understand."

"My—our—father was a very able ruler, as you must have learned by now, and the land prospered under his reign." He stopped at my blank look, and frowned. "You know nothing of the kingdom's history, do you?"

"Nothing, I admit it."

"So. Our great-grandfather had two sons. Only one of them was legitimate. But the other son was an ambitious man. Very ambitious. You must surely be aware that there are always noble factions, sometimes powerful ones, discontent with the policies of any king. The ambitious brother wooed these factions to him. And that, of course, could only lead to one thing: a brief but violent civil *war*."

War? The Anglic word had no parallel in Cymraeth. I guessed from the context that Estmere meant combat, but combat on a far larger scale than the raids and counterraids we knew in Cymra. Odd. Why would princes want to involve so many outside folk in their personal conflict? Where was the honor in that?

Estmere was studying me warily. "You *do* understand what I'm saying, don't you?"

"I'm not sure what you mean by *war*, but pray go on."

He probably took it only as a linguistic lapse on my part. Estmere's gaze never left my face as he continued, "When the fighting was done, the would-be usurper was dead. But so were scores of innocent folk caught up in the struggle. The land was nearly laid to waste, and almost destroyed by those . . . allies on our borders who saw a good chance to increase their holdings in that time of their strength and our weakness."

Kill scores of innocent folk? Lay the land to waste? Suddenly very much aware of how foreign a realm this was, I grabbed at the only sense I could make out of all this: "Obviously they didn't succeed."

"No. But hatred takes a long time to die. And prosperity and peace returned only very slowly to this kingdom."

"I think I'm getting the point of your story. Our father kept the nation happy and secure. And now you are king."

"I am king. And I will defend my people no matter what the cost."

"Hey now, you don't have to sound so pompous with me!"

Unexpectedly, he laughed. "No. From what I've heard, you are the least pompous person at court."

"And did you really think history was about to repeat itself?"

"Why not?" There was a sudden chilling hint of iron in his voice. "Stranger things have happened." But after the briefest pause, Estmere sighed. "What would you? I find it very difficult to believe that your—what shall I call it?—your unique honesty is genuine."

"*Och*, but—"

"Wait. From the first moment I saw you, I couldn't believe you didn't want something from me." He eyed me speculatively. "My throne, perhaps."

"*Gallu*, no! You can't think that."

"I don't know what to think. You seem likeable. And the good Lord knows I wouldn't object to having a brother I can trust at my right hand— No. Don't interrupt." It was a suddenly regal tone. "You may stay here at court if that's your wish. I'll not show less courtesy to kin than I would to some foreign ambassador. But . . . what more do you want? We created some lovely music just now, and for that interval, I thank you. But don't expect me to rush blithely into your brotherly embrace. I can't be that trusting. I can't afford to be."

His eyes were bleak.

"Estmere . . ." What could I say? That I pitied him? More, that somewhere along the way I was finding myself genuinely wanting to befriend him? *Ailanna, you were right. Forgive me, my love, my vow does bind me after all.* "Very well. I'll stay, for a while longer at any rate."

He smiled. But it was a formal thing, king to prince. And when my brother said, "I'm glad of that," neither of us was sure he meant it.

CHAPTER VII

THE BOAR

It was a fine, bright day, and we had gone hunting, Estmere and I and the obligatory courtiers. And a fine, bright sight we made, too, all of us in the royal red and gold, banners flying, horses prancing, and horns and hounds trumpeting bravely into the clear, crisp early morning air.

Though of course one of the natural laws is that some must die that others be fed, I'm not much for the idea of killing as sport, not after a boyhood spent among deer and fox. But I must confess it was good to get away from the closeness of court for a while—*Duwies*, yes!—to be surrounded by clean air and the healthy green life of the forest.

Estmere was clearly enjoying himself, too, with the enthusiasm of someone who has little enough time to be lighthearted.

My poor brother. I only wish I could convince him I'm no threat to him.

But when it came to that, had I been so completely honest with him? No. I was still hiding the fact of my magic from all. It wasn't that I feared for my life. A true magician isn't easy to hold, as I'd proved to those silly

54

villagers who had tried to burn me on my way to Lundinia. But getting myself branded as demon-spawn certainly wasn't the way to win anyone's trust, let alone that of a king!

Of course that's not to say I wasn't making use of the smaller, less detectable wisdoms. How else would I have known that the horse Estmere was riding was both very young and very foolish? I had caught the *feel* of the animal's mind when no human was around, and found not a brain in its finely shaped head.

Sure enough, the silly beast decided to outrace all the rest of us. Estmere, laughing, didn't even try to check its gallop. Terrified that the horse was going to do something truly stupid, I urged my own mount forward and gave chase.

We caught up with them just as a boar erupted out of a thicket. Estmere's horse screamed like a frightened child and leaped sideways so sharply my startled brother was thrown. He fell with stunning force—and the boar turned in its piggish fury and charged him. I saw its eyes glint red, felt the murderous thoughts of its brain, knew Estmere was about to die—

"Duwies, no!"

And the full force of the Power I had denied these past weeks surged up within me with such fury I nearly staggered. Magic blazing like wildfire through every vein, I flung out my hand as though casting a spear and shouted a word of Command. The boar stopped dead in its tracks, confused. The small, fierce eyes looked up at me, their gaze trapped, and I caught the animal mind with mine.

"Fear me," I commanded quietly.

And the boar shrank away. I could *feel* the panic growing and growing in that savage brain, overcoming all urges to rend and slay, I could *feel* its knowledge that, half drunk with Power as I was, there really *was* cause for it to fear me. And all at once the boar yielded. Squealing its terror, it whirled and charged away into the forest, crashing frantically through the bushes.

Silence fell. I slumped in the saddle, the wildfire dying down within me, breathless as though I had fought the boar hand to hand.

Panic sent new energy racing through me and I sprang from my horse to see if Estmere had been hurt.

He was conscious. Staring at me.

"Are you injured?" I asked quickly.

"No." He got to his feet, ignoring my offer of aid. "That beast was scared of you, Aidan. A wild boar is afraid of nothing on Earth. Yet it feared you as though you were the very devil. *What are you, Aidan?*"

"*Fy brawd*, your brother," I said lightly, stalling.

"Half-brother only. Why did that boar fear you? Are you a sorcerer, Aidan?"

There was an iron-cold light in his eyes, and I sighed. "If you mean by 'sorcerer' one who walks the Lefthand Path, who has sworn pacts with Evil—no, I am never such a one."

"What, then?"

"You know my mother was of Cymra. That land is . . . different. Older. Stranger, you would find it." I took a deep breath. "My mother was a wielder of magic, Estmere, and I am truly her son."

"I don't understand. First you say you are no sorcerer, and then—"

"*Uffern!*" I snapped. "Have they taught you nothing of the Old Ways? Well then, listen: there is magic—*Gallu*, Power—and that is a force, a tool neither good nor evil. And there are folk who have been granted that Power, and trained in its use. Agreed? I won't deny that some of those folk abuse their training, deliberately use it for harm. They are the ones you call sorcerers."

"Go on."

Feeling my mother's presence very much with me, I continued, "But there is still the Threefold Law that binds all who work with magic, the law no one can change or evade. And it states simply that each magician bears the threefold return of whatever force has been sent out. If that force is for good, well now, that's a fine thing to have triply repaid. But if that force is for evil . . ." I hesitated, suddenly remembering the one time I had misused my Power . . . the stag I had tried to destroy . . . the sickening horror of its terror surging over me till I thought I would never be free of it . . . I shuddered. "Ethics aside, Estmere, it is slow and torturous suicide, it is condemning yourself to torment or, if the wise folk are right, to eternal death and never rebirth. Can't you see I would never, ever, so endanger my soul?"

Estmere hesitated a long while, toying absently with the hilt of his sword, and I thought, *There goes friendship*, though there wasn't a word I would have taken back if I could.

"Come now, Estmere! If I had wanted you dead, all I had to do was wait just a few short moments for the boar to do the job for me."

"True," he admitted wryly. "It would have made a very convenient hunting accident. And your hands would have been quite unstained by fratricide." The faintest of shudders ran through him, but his voice remained level. "I do thank you for my life. But . . . this . . . magic: why didn't you speak of it before?"

"When we first met? Would you ever have accepted me if I had?"

"No," he conceded.

"Look you, what do you want me to do to prove I mean no harm?" But then a thought came to me. "In Cymra sworn vows are sacred, unbreakable. Is it the same in these lands?"

"After a fashion." Estmere's voice was dry. "But I do know you West Country folk hold vows inviolate."

"Good. Then shall I swear my honesty to you?"

"Yes!" Almost savagely, my brother whipped out his sword, holding it up so that hilt and guard formed a cross. "Swear by this sword."

Och fi. "I could," I said miserably, bound by truthfulness. "But such an oath would mean nothing."

"Nothing!"

I paused, uneasy, uncomfortably aware after my experiences in Estmere's lands that some people feel very strongly about the subject of religion. Sometimes dangerously so.

"Aidan?"

"I . . . many Cymraen folk follow the old ways."

"What are you trying to say?"

All right, be bold now! "I am not of your faith, Estmere, but of one that is very ancient."

"A pagan?" he exclaimed, blunt in disbelief.

"You sophisticated folk are free with labels, aren't you?"

"But—"

"Estmere, I assure you, I do not steal about in the dead of night wearing feathers and paint and offering bloody sacrifices to crude stone idols."

He couldn't help but grin at the outlandish image. "No. I hardly thought you did."

"So. We both worship the Creator. But to me That One is *y Duwies*, the Goddess, Mother of us all. It's as simple as that." Not quite *that* simple, perhaps, but this was hardly the time for a lecture on theology. "Does that disturb you?"

"Of course it does!" Estmere stirred impatiently. "Oh, not like that; no matter what the priests insist, I know there's nothing demonic about the old beliefs. But to confess that you . . . men have died for such confessions."

"I know."

He stared. "And yet you would put your life in my hands. Curse you, Aidan, why are you so very trusting?" But I felt the bewilderment behind the anger, and I waited. At last Estmere said in a softer voice, "I never could be a . . . burner of heretics. And, as I say, sinful or not, I do know a little about your religion. If that's sincerely your belief. . . ."

"It is."

He held up his hands in resignation. I said quietly, "I promised you a vow:

"If I have lied to you in either word or deed, if I have ever walked the Lefthand Path or used my Power for harm against man, woman or child, then may *y Duwies* grant me neither rest in this life nor rebirth into the next."

It was about as serious a vow as one could swear. But I meant what I said. Estmere could only have realized that, because after a moment of the two of us staring at each other as solemnly as a pair of owls, he gave a shaky little laugh and sheathed his sword.

"I said once you were unusual, but I never guessed just how unusual!" He hesitated, head to one side. "It's true, isn't it? You really don't want anything from me, do you?"

"Your friendship."

"Why?"

"I have no human friends. The human side of me was lonely." Much to my surprise, I realized as I said it that it was quite true.

"No human ... you were lonely." He shook his head, but for all my brother's bewilderment, I surprised a certain hint of sympathy in his eyes. "There's never been an enchanter in the family," Estmere commented. "Ah ... 'enchanter,' 'wizard'—what *do* I call you?"

"*Brawd?*" I asked tentatively, and he laughed.

"Yes, brother, of course, but—"

"If you must have a professional term, *swynwr*, magician, is as good as any." I paused uneasily. "Am I still welcome at court?"

"Of course. A magician is a useful friend for a king." His smile took the coldness from the words. But it wouldn't have taken magic to read the amazement still on my brother's face, and I chuckled.

"Wondering what marvels I can perform?"

He didn't quite draw back in alarm, but it was a near thing. "You can read minds?"

"No, nothing quite like that!" I grinned. "Nor can I tell the future, nor 'tear the stars from their courses,' nor 'call up demons from the briny deep.' We-ell, I suppose I *could* do the last. But I wouldn't."

"God's blood, I should hope not!"

"Estmere, 'useful' I may be, but are your people going to accept me for what I am?"

"Those at court, you mean?" Estmere's eyes had lost their dawning humor. "You must keep your faith a secret. Worship as you please in private. But I will not have you used by my foes as an excuse for religious war."

Chilled, I nodded agreement.

"And as for anything else," he continued, "of course there will always be . . . conservative folk who disapprove. But you are my brother and I am the king. If I choose to set you at my right hand, no one will dare question my will."

I gave him the formal little bow the situation seemed to demand. But I straightened abruptly, listening. . . .

"Aidan? What is it?"

"I thought . . . for a moment I *felt* something . . . no. It's gone now."

"*What's* gone now?"

"For a moment someone was eavesdropping. Psychically."

"*What!*"

I shrugged. "When I chased away the boar, I announced to the entire arcane community that a magician was in this region."

"I . . . see." There was much to be said for regal self-control. Estmere must have been shaken at the thought of magic being alive in his lands, but he didn't show it. "Someone was curious."

"Yes. Nothing more."

He was still putting up an admirably calm front. "You would know about such things better than I. And if you're not worried . . ."

"I'm not." Not unless there was to be an open threat. No. Not yet. But Estmere had been asked to accept so much that was fantastic, I couldn't push him any further. "There's only one thing left to do," I said, and watched his hand tighten involuntarily on the hilt of his sword.

"What's that?"

I grinned. "Why, catch your horse, of course, before the fool beast runs all the way back to Lundinia!"

CHAPTER VIII

THE ACCIDENT

The sound of swordplay in the early morning air drew me to the balcony rimming the small courtyard. I looked down at a small swarm of courtiers and their servants, bright as so many spring butterflies, cloaks and tunics rich reds or blues or yellows, gems gleaming. To one side of the smoothly paved yard clustered some of the little royal pages, colorful enough themselves in their red and gold livery. They were fosterlings of noble blood, of course, learning the proper ways of the court, but those here now didn't look like anything but the children they were, all wide-eyed and chattering with excitement.

Understandably. In the middle of that courtyard, laughing, their king duelled with one of his men. Most simply clad was Estmere in white tunic and dark hose in the warm air of late spring, and his hair blazed splendidly in the morning sunlight.

I leaned on the stone balustrade, more interested in swordsmanship than fashion. The shieldless form of duelling my brother was practicing was all the rage in the land. It had only recently reached this kingdom, I'd been told, brought here across the Eastern Sea from the lands to the southeast, but it looked remarkably familiar to me, requiring as it did a much slimmer sword than the old cut-and-slash blades, one with a true point to it, and a different stance and quicker footwork. In short, it reminded me very much of what I had learned from Tairyn.

Estmere was quick on his feet, supple and graceful and clever, a credit to what had been the finest course in weaponry in the kingdom.

I rather pitied his opponent. The guard was no mean swordsman himself (presumably why Estmere was duelling with him, rather than with the Weapons Master; if you're to be any good with the sword, you must practice against as varied a group of opponents as possible), but the combination of worries—that he might accidentally hurt his king or (horrors!) defeat him—was working against him. Now Estmere was forcing him back, back . . . and suddenly the duel was over as my brother lunged in what would have been a killing thrust had they been fighting in earnest. The nobles instantly broke into polite applause, and I saw a quick spasm of annoyance cross Estmere's face: he knew his opponent had been duelling under a handicap. But my brother saluted the man in good-natured jest, and the guard, grinning in relief, bowed low and hurried off as soon as everyone's attention was away from him.

Estmere must have felt my gaze on him. As a courtier solicitously draped a cloak over his shoulders, he looked up, brushing back damp strands of golden hair from his face, and saw me leaning on the balustrade. He gave me the same joking salute he'd given the guard.

"Good morning, brother! Come and join us."

Well? I thought. *Why not?*

Maybe we hadn't yet been able to find a nonalarming way to show the court my magic; it wasn't the easiest of subjects after all. I could at least prove to these pretty butterflies this uncouth Cymraen knew which end of a sword was which. Estmere was waiting, smiling, as I hurried down the stairway to the courtyard, his sword still in hand. Handing the cloak back to the courtier, he asked me, "Care to try?"

"Do you expect me to let you win? I shan't, you know."

His smile broadened. "I know. And it will be a welcome change. Raulf is a fine swordsman, but he just will not believe I won't have him executed if he defeats me! Come now, let's see how they duel in Cymra." His eyes glinted with mischief. "No magic, though!"

"No magic," I agreed, taking a sword from a respectful servant, testing the weight and feel of the blade, adding in surprise, "No edge!"

"God's blood, I should think not! Don't worry, Aidan, these blunted swords can still deliver some painful bruises if you're careless." He stared at me. "Where did you get the idea we would use edged blades."

I shrugged, embarrassed. "From the Folk who taught me."

"The—oh. That Folk. They really don't use practice swords? Not even for training? You must have been a remarkably quick learner, brother!"

I grinned ruefully. "Believe me, if you don't soon . . . ah . . . get the point, you get the point."

Estmere raised a brow. "A sharp remark," he countered, "and a keen and cutting wit." As I winced, he added, "Come, let's to it."

And—that duel was fun. Does the word sound too frivolous? It *was* fun, the two of us moving up and down that small yard like a pair of well-rehearsed dancers, so evenly matched for strength and speed and size that we couldn't so much as touch each other, our two styles of swordsmanship matching remarkably well. At last Estmere, laughing and panting, called a halt, lowering his sword.

"Else we'll be at this all day, and—"

A shrill scream cut into his words. We both whirled, he with a startled, "What in God's name . . ."

It was the pages, the children, and when I saw what had happened, I threw down my sword and raced to them, a trail of excited courtiers in my wake.

The pages were armed after a fashion, of course, everybody wears a dagger for this chore or that. I imagine the children had been imitating us, scuffling as youngsters do—

And one little boy had stumbled and fallen on his knife.

He was still alive, *y Duwies* be praised, and mercifully too stunned to feel pain yet; pain would be slow in coming to such a wound. But his eyes were wide and wild with terror, and his bewildered thoughts twisted and curled away from my touch like smoke. For a moment I longed for night, so that I might use the Faerie sleep charm on him. But as soon wish for the moon in my hand, so instead I set my will on the boy, overcoming the untrained resistance of the child mind, catching it with mine, soothing, soothing, till suddenly he was limp and unconscious in my arms.

The knife was still in the wound. Good. If the boys had pulled it free in their panic, he might already have bled to death. Now I could at least staunch the steady ooze of blood by delicately expanding the focus of my will, but what internal damage the boy might have suffered, I couldn't tell, not here.

The courtiers were all gathered round, fascinated as people seem to be by disaster. As I bent over the child, I could sense them all about me, too close, I could feel their curious minds beating against mine, eating away at the concentration I must keep whole for the boy's sake. And my angry Power responded, raw, unshaped, sweeping them back from me. I didn't dare turn from the child to see what I had done, but I heard the excited clamor of their voices rising to fever pitch till Estmere sharply commanded:

"Silence!"

It must have been he in the sudden stunned quiet who helped me to my feet, the boy gathered in my arms. I don't know for sure; I was too absorbed by then in keeping the young heart beating.

There was a room, a bed: not the boy's own room, of

course; the pages were lodged in a communal hall. But I couldn't have cared where we were. I sent a respectful manservant for clean water, then bent over the boy, thinking, *Duwies glân be with us now.*

Closing my eyes, I willed away all the outside world, dismissing sight, sound, scent, bringing my mind as quickly as I could to the most intense focus of concentration. . . .

No vital organs pierced, praise be, but it was a nasty wound. Abdominal wounds are always nasty, too easily poisoned, too often leading to painful death. There had been one horrid accident back in Cymra when I was still a child, when a woodsman had fallen on his axe and his family had waited too long to call my mother. The only mercy left had been to grant him a swift, quiet passing.

But that wouldn't happen here if I could help it.

I dared not leave the boy to a surgeon's care if I really did mean him to live; I'd seen too much already of barbaric ways such as leeches and filthy knives. But as I studied the wound again, a sly whisper of doubt made my concentration slip a moment. Yes, I had healed injuries before, but never one as bad as this. Could I?

I must.

What I did can't be so easily put into words. I was no longer the green boy who had nearly killed himself healing Elin-the-baker's burn, but as it had then, my Power stirred within me, rising up in thrilling waves, tingling through my fingertips to the boy's skin. Once again I felt that near-anguish, near-ecstasy as I attuned myself to him and began delicately closing layer after slow layer of nerve and muscle, mending that ugly wound with all the careful magic at my will. I could dimly feel my body reaching the limits of its strength, but now there was the wonder of new, healthy flesh weaving together, and I could dare push myself a little further . . . just a little further . . .

I have no idea how long it took. But at last I forced myself back into myself and straightened, letting the servant clean boy and bedding. I was done. In more ways than one.

I gave the awed man instructions, telling him to call me at once if there were any changes in the now peacefully slumbering boy's condition. *Please, please, let there not be any changes!* And then I staggered out of there. A bench was in the hall outside, fortunately, or I would have ended up on the floor. As it was, I landed on that bench so hard my spine quivered, and simply slumped, head down, drained.

But there was someone . . . Estmere. I knew that without having to look up. Estmere, and the inevitable crowd of courtiers, all of whom he was sending away with an imperious wave. Good. I didn't want to be ogled.

"Aidan? God, you look on the verge of death."

"No. *Unig blin.*" That didn't sound quite right. Prodding my foggy brain, I tried again in Anglic: "Only tired."

I felt Estmere sit beside me. "The boy . . . died, then?"

"What? Ah. No." I hesitated, my mind insisting only on Cymraeth. "The wound is *cau—och*, closed, as far along to complete healing as I could manage. *Bachgen's* asleep. He didn't . . . lose more blood . . . than a healthy child should be able to . . . replace." I stopped to catch my breath. "With the will of *y Duwies* . . . and the . . . *cryfder* . . . ? *Grym* . . . ?"

"Resiliency?" Estmere suggested, and I nodded.

"The resiliency of youth, he . . . should be all right."

"Amen," my brother added sincerely, and I looked at him in surprise.

"You really care, don't you? Is the *bachgennyn*, the little lad, some special favorite?"

"No." Estmere smiled sheepishly. "I'm ashamed to admit I didn't even remember till this moment that his name is Arn. I . . . let's just say I hate waste."

"Mm." Kings don't like to be caught showing softness. I frowned as a sudden fact penetrated my haze of exhaustion. "That's not what you were wearing before. . . . What part of the day is it?"

"Early afternoon."

The accident had happened in the early morning. "*Och fi!* No wonder I'm weary!" I sagged against the wall, head back. "Don't ever let anyone tell you magic is easy."

"I didn't think it was."

"No matter what *barddi* say ... can't just wave my hands and mutter a few words. *Gallu*, Power, magical energy has to come from somewhere ... usually from a magician's own life-force ..."

There was a long silence, during which I nearly drifted off to sleep. "You could have killed yourself," Estmere murmured, and I started. "Saving that boy, you could have exhausted yourself right into death."

"There is always that danger, yes. Using Power for healing is ... intoxicating. It's all too easy to squander strength."

There was another pause. Then Estmere said hesitantly, "Take some of mine."

"What?"

"I didn't spend all morning saving a boy's life. I have plenty of strength. Take some of mine."

That brought me sharply back to myself. "You don't know what you're saying. If I wanted to, I could ... kill you like that, drain you dry."

Sheer horror flashed in my brother's eyes, but all he said was a quiet, "You wouldn't."

For a moment I couldn't find anything to say. "Thank you."

"Oh, Aidan! I'm not being a trusting fool. If you wanted to harm me, you would hardly warn me, now, would you?"

I blinked groggily. "I suppose not. *Och*, don't worry about me, *brawd*. I'll be all right. Really. All I need is rest."

He got to his feet, looking me up and down. "And a bath. And a complete change of clothes. Can you stand?"

I could, albeit unsteadily. Estmere chuckled.

"At least now we don't have to worry about introducing your magic to the court. My, but that was spectacular: a great flash of light, and all of us blown back like so many leaves before the wind. The stories are already starting to circulate. Don't worry," he added, grinning at my dismay. "I'll see that the more . . . ah . . . diabolical aspects are quenched."

"I didn't stop to think— I didn't hurt anybody, did I?"

"No." The grin was still there. "Though you did dump some of the more pompous souls right on their dignities." Estmere linked arms with me as I swayed. "Come, brother, let's get you to bed." His chuckle this time sounded very much like Tairyn's speculative what-can-we-do-with-you laugh, but I was too weary to worry about it. "I do think life is going to be a good deal more interesting with you around!"

CHAPTER IX

NEWCOMER

I slept the rest of that day and all the following day and night, and woke to find myself notable once again: word of the king's brother being a magician had already spread throughout the palace and Lundinia as well.

More important to me at the moment, and not surprisingly after all the energy I had expended, I also woke ravenously hungry. I'd intended to look in on little Arn, but if I didn't get some food quickly, I wasn't going to be of much use to anyone. Shooing away the covey of nervous, curious servants who had been watching over my sleep at Estmere's command, I threw on the first clothes that came to hand and, too famished to stand on ceremony, went down from my tower to raid the royal larder.

One of the first to challenge my new status as princely magician was, predictably enough, Father Ansel, Estmere's personal priest. He cornered me, fed but irritable, on my way back from the kitchen through the little palace cloister where once my brother had harped.

Father Ansel is tall and lean, somewhat past middle years, a quiet, gray-eyed man in quiet gray robes. I wasn't used to the company of priests, particularly not one of a faith which has declared itself enemy to my own, but there was nothing of the witch burner in those shrewd, tranquil eyes. Besides, even though I was very much not in the mood for a confrontation, I could hardly be rude to a man who had given me no insult, so I offered him a seat and asked him what he wanted of me.

"Prince Aidan—" He broke off with a chuckle at my involuntary little start. "You're not yet used to the title, are you?"

"I don't think I ever shall be. It gets in the way."

"Now that's a complaint I've never heard before."

"I mean it, it does!" Impatiently, I added, "Listen: I've just come from the kitchen. There I found that one of the little pot boys had scalded his arm rather painfully. Granted, he was an ugly little thing who probably never had an overall bath in his life. But, *och fi,* he was still a child! Yet no one was even trying to help him! So I did my best to comfort him and heal the scald. It was a nasty wound, nasty enough to warrant the use of magic. But fortunately, the spell I needed wasn't a difficult one to work." Graying eyebrows shot up at that perilous thought, *magic,* but I ignored his start, continuing hotly, "Or it shouldn't have been difficult! But every time I tried to ask the boy if *this* hurt, or *that,* all I would get in reply was a scared, 'It don't hurt, Highness, honest.' I'd swear he wasn't afraid of the magic; peasant folk have usually seen some healing charm or other. It was the *title* that terrified him!"

"He *was* only a pot boy."

"*Och,* not you, too!"

"I . . . beg your pardon?"

"Gossip seems to spread like wildfire in this castle. Every noble I've met so far this morning has told me I'm mad for wasting my Power tending the lowborn. As though Power cares about social standing!"

"We are all God's children," the priest murmured; I think he meant it. "Prince Aidan, I must say you are not quite what I expected."

I shifted restlessly. "No bat wings or sulphur, you mean?"

"Please. To be quite blunt, I cannot approve of what you are."

"I assume you don't mean my parentage, but my magic."

"Of course." He fairly radiated discomfort; I must have seemed the very essence of everything he'd been trained against. Yet the gray gaze was steady. "If you were anyone other than the king's brother, I would have urged that you be—"

"Eliminated?"

"Sent back to your wild homeland. The Black Arts—"

"Black Arts!" I exploded.

He blinked, startled. "A poor choice of words, perhaps. Forgive me."

But I was in no mood for forgiveness. Still fuming over the incident in the kitchen, I snapped, "I lose a day and a half of my life saving a child—*och*, not that I regret it. I spend my morning helping another because not one of your good, pure, magickless souls was willing to lift a finger! *Dyri Uffern*, what do you think I am, some hypocritical idiot who heals on one day and conjures Evil on the next?"

He crossed himself at that. "I never meant—"

"Look you, what abilities I possess are mine by the grace of—of Heaven!" I'd almost said, of the Goddess. "They're born in me, part of me, no more unnatural than ... than having black hair instead of blond!"

With that, I clamped my mouth shut before I said something I would really regret, sure that Father Ansel was going to storm out of there to have me banished. But to my astonishment, I caught a hint of relief in the gray eyes, almost as though I'd just passed some arcane test. Just as I was feeling the slightest bit complacent, deciding that maybe he really *had* been listening to what I was trying to tell him, maybe he really wasn't such a bad fellow after all, Father Ansel got to his feet.

"The question's academic, at any rate," he said as

coolly as the politician a royal priest needs must be. "You *are* the king's brother. Good day to you, my son."

No you don't, you fox! You're not leaving me *the one off balance!* "A draw," I called after him, and he turned, puzzled. I grinned. "I declare our duel a draw."

For all his unease, that forced a genuine smile from him. "A draw," he agreed.

He went his way, and I continued on mine to pay a visit to little Arn. The boy was sound asleep, curled up like a puppy and, judging from the coolness of his brow and the *feel* of his injury, healing nicely. A relief, to be sure.

But I was too restless after my meeting with Father Ansel to wait till the boy awoke. I doubted he'd need me, at any rate. So instead, I went down into the city to let off my excess energy, carrying my pouch of healing herbs just in case and shrouded in a hooded cloak to disguise my too-similar-to-royal features.

And there I came upon Stephen, the silversmith, and his wife, Janet, the baker, who pressed a sweetcake into my hand as though I were a child after I helped her move a heavy tray of bread. Munching peacefully as I wandered on, good spirits returning, I found myself tending an unexpected patient, a stocky, embarrassed glassblower who had burned his leg "like a fool apprentice." (This seemed to be my day for burns.) To my delight, he turned out to be originally from just this side of the Cymraen border, accepting things magical without a qualm and not at all impressed by titles. Once I had taken away the pain and danger of infection, we chatted happily together in Cymraeth for a time, and I left feeling much more cheerful.

A cheerfulness that lasted only until I ran into the guards who'd come down from the palace to find me. They were a solid, competent lot, mail shirts under red and gold royal livery, open helms squarely on their sweaty heads. They also blatantly weren't comfortable with the idea of being ordered to find a magician, but there was such an air of grim determination to the lot of them that I asked wryly:

"What's this? Am I under arrest?"

That sent ripples of shock among them. "No, my lord!" one guard assured me hastily. "It's just that your royal brother ... uh ... wished to speak with you. Besides, he ... uh ... feared you might come to some manner of harm down here."

Can't you find a better excuse than that, Estmere? And don't you trust me yet?

The guards eyed me warily as I fumed. "You ... will come with us now, my lord? If it ... uh ... pleases you?"

Well now, it didn't. The idea of being brought back like an erring child didn't please me at all. But I'd be a small sort to take out my anger on innocent men, so I nodded brusquely and obeyed.

I was still fuming when I was ushered into Estmere's presence. He was sitting in one of the smaller audience chambers, a white walled room barely large enough to hold twenty folk and hung round with hangings of sunny forest scenes, his hair glinting dramatically in the rays of sun slipping through the arrow-slit of a window. Before him was a table piled with scrolls, and around him crowded a swarm of advisors, all of whom stared at my approach like so many startled geese.

Estmere raised a brow at my curt little dip of head. "You sent for me?" I asked, biting off each word.

"I did."

With a wave of his hand, my brother dismissed the advisors and the overzealous servants who would have stayed to listen. "Sit," he told me once we were alone. "First, I assume you're quite recovered from healing little Arn?"

"Yes."

"And the boy is recovering nicely. Yes, I've already been informed of that. And of your conversation with Father Ansel, for that matter."

"*Gallu!* Is nothing secret in this place?"

"No. I thought you'd already realized that. Now, why are you glaring at me like that?"

"Am I your *prisoner, brawd?*"

"I ... beg your pardon?"

"That armed escort back to the palace. Am I not free to come and go as I please?"

"Ah. That. No, Aidan. Not really."

"What—"

"Before you erupt, think." Estmere leaned forward in his chair, eyes all at once too weary for someone only a year or so my senior. "You are my brother. Despite our different coloring, the resemblance between us is just too strong for any to miss, even if I hadn't already openly claimed you as kin. And that kinship makes you almost as much a target as I."

I opened my mouth, shut it, opened it again. "Estmere," I began at last, "by now everyone knows what I am. Do you really think anyone is fool enough to attack a magician?"

"Are you proof against arrows?"

"No, but—" *Och*, I'd never thought of it: any malcontent might try to kill me to hurt my brother. "But I will be brushing up on defensive spells," I finished grimly. "Do you really live in such perpetual danger?"

The grin I received was downright sardonic. "Not as much as I might be in if I didn't look the way I do. Oh yes, I'm very well aware of being the golden young king, everybody's dear. Their dear until I start making some edicts folks don't like. Or some of the nobles decide they'd like someone a little more manipulable on the throne."

"Some noble like that sly-eyed Baron Aldingar."

Estmere's grin turned downright predatory. "Ah, Aldingar! You're sure you can't read minds?"

"Quite sure."

"A pity. I'd so like to find out just what's going on in his head. But why do you think Aldingar and others of his ilk are at court?"

"So you can keep an eye on them?" I hazarded. "So

they can't start plotting something because they know they're being watched?"

"Aha! You *do* know something about guile!"

"Something about logic," I corrected. "Look you, I understand the need for caution. But I'm used to the freedom of the forest. I can't live under perpetual guard. My word as a magician, I won't let myself be used against you. Is that good enough?"

Estmere hesitated, then sighed and held up a hand in resignation. "So be it. Besides," he added, "I suspect that if you're allowed to roam as you will, you'll prove a nice source of information as to what the commons are thinking. You seemed to get along well with them today."

"Your spies are amazing!"

"They are, aren't they?" he agreed blandly. "Aidan, now that you're here, what exactly do you plan to do? You don't strike me as the sort to be happy simply bickering over the cut of a tunic or hang of a cloak."

"*Duwies*, no! I'm perfectly willing to start earning my keep, *brawd*."

Estmere gave a startled laugh. "I didn't mean you'll have to labor like a peasant!"

"What, then? I'm willing to do my share of healing, but most healing doesn't really need magic. And— Estmere, what *are* you doing to that scroll?"

He'd been fidgeting nervously with the edge of it. Estmere glanced down as though he'd never seen the thing before and let it go, sitting with primly folded hands. "I'll be frank. For the last day and a half I have been plotting ways to use you, use your Art."

"What—"

"Wait, hear me out! I'm not proud of it. And now none of it seems right or just."

With a sudden burst of that same nervous energy, he got to his feet, staring as well as he could out that ridiculously narrow window. "I have honorable ministers at court," Estmere murmured, "men I trust. And my guard is loyal to me, I know that. But still . . ."

"But still you want the security magic can give you."

He whirled to face me. "Exactly. I don't want anything dramatic from you; I can't risk having the court think I'm holding the throne through magic. What I ask from you, as my brother, is simply that you attend certain of my royal audiences at my side. You told me you can't read others' thoughts, but I imagine you do have . . . well, abilities to tell you when something isn't quite right?"

"To winnow out would-be traitors and assassins, you mean. Yes, *brawd*, that I will do, as best I can." A flash of memory: that day back when I'd frightened away the boar, when I'd felt another magical self brush my own . . . If there was any real peril there, it was something I'd roused. And something I must, of honor, guard against as well.

"Thank you, uh, *brawd*." Estmere grinned in relief. "Oh, and I also think it might be a wise idea for you to accompany me on my spring progression."

Progression? Didn't that Anglic word merely mean a movement from one thing to another? "Your *what*?"

"You'll find out." Mischief glinted in the bright blue eyes. "I trust you have a taste for travel?"

"I came here, didn't I? Besides," I added with a grin of my own, "whatever this progression of yours turns out to be, it *has* to be better than staying stuck in the palace and bickering over fashion!"

CHAPTER X

OF FRIENDSHIP AND SPIES

Every castle, the royal palace included, has an herb garden somewhere within it, to provide for both healing and food seasoning. I'd already had a hand in expanding the royal garden. And now, while I waited to learn what a "progression" might be, I was out prowling amid the neat green rows, checking this plant and that, my cloak wrapped tightly about myself in the early morning chill. The palace walls towered like great gray cliffs all around me, but blessedly not a soul was out here with me. The air smelled sharply of mint and valerian, and I bent to pluck and savor a mint leaf.

"Now God give you a good morning, Prince Aidan," said a sudden cheerful voice.

I nearly shot into the air like a startled cat, springing to my feet and whirling in one move. But then:

"Baron Aldingar." Catching my breath, embarrassed at having been caught off-guard like any magickless man, I added formally, "A good morning to you, as well."

He was elegant from the cut of his sleek brown hair

to the line of his dark blue cloak; his bow was the very essence of courtliness. "Pray forgive me for having startled you."

Och, no politics, Aldingar, not on such a nice, sunny day! But I dipped my head in polite acknowledgement. When he didn't seem about to say anything further, I bent to my work again, nipping off sickly sprigs, checking for signs of frost or insect damage. For a time, the man contented himself with merely strolling up and down the rows of herbs, his fashionable, fur-trimmed cloak swirling slowly about, as though he really had come out here only to catch a breath of fresh morning air.

"A pleasant place," Aldingar said at last.

"Mm."

"Quiet, too. Private."

Private. I straightened. "Come to the point, my lord baron. What do you want of me?"

"Why, nothing, Prince Aidan!" He was the very soul of innocent indignation.

"Come, man, you forget what I am! You did *not* come out here by accident!"

He shot me a quick sideways glance, like a startled horse, presumably wondering just how much I knew about him, then gave me the most urbane of smiles. "I wouldn't dream of trying to hide anything from a magician. Prince Aidan, I have always been loyal to the crown."

"Wise."

"Now, some would have it otherwise. There have been foul rumors spread about me in the past, rumors linking me with . . . well, with those who some might name as less than friendly to the crown, indeed, who might even be—"

"*Och*, enough!" I studied him, physically and magically, seeing ambition, envy, weakness . . . weakness, yes. For all his sleek words and pretty ways, he would never have the will to be a true threat to my brother. "You made some unwise alliances in the past," I summarized, "nothing that could be proven, nothing dark enough to lose you your head."

Of course I wasn't reading his mind, merely combining what I could *feel* of his unease with what I'd heard here and there. But Aldingar's stare was nothing short of terrified.

"That is truly amazing, Prince Aidan." It was probably the first honest sentence he'd spoken so far. "But let me assure you, none of those rumors were true! All were disproved by combat."

Which simply meant his champion had proven a better fighter than whomever had brought the charges against him. "But my brother has yet to quite trust you, is that your problem?" I asked. "You wish me to speak with him? See you back into his good graces?"

He sighed in relief. "Exactly!" As though beginning a totally unrelated conversation, Aldingar said, "One of my servants brought me a *most* intriguing scroll. Of course I cannot read it. But it would seem to be a scroll of the most potent of eastern magics. Surely something of immense value to a magician such as yourself."

"I don't take bribes."

"I beg your pardon?"

"You heard me. *I do not take bribes!*"

He actually blanched. "I didn't mean—"

"Go away, Baron Aldingar."

"You will not—"

"Tell my brother?" Tell him what? That Aldingar was ambitious and a fool? Estmere already knew both. "No," I decided. "Not unless you actually act against the king. And you wouldn't do something so stupid, now, would you, my lord baron?" I fixed him with my darkest, most sorcerous stare, and he took a nervous step backwards, nearly crushing a row of hyssop.

"Be careful where you tread, my lord baron," I told him sweetly, and smiled to myself as Aldingar hastily bowed and all but fled.

Congratulations, Baron Aldingar. You're the first to try to buy me. But I suspect you won't be the last!

* * *

The mysterious progression turned out to be something an Anglic king undertook at regular intervals: a royal tour (in this case, a small army of glittering courtiers and guards and a whole pack train of belongings) through several of the baronies that owed said king fealty.

"A wise ruler spends a fair amount of time on visits of state like these," Estmere murmured to me as we rode along, he waving at the folks lining both sides of the road and flattering them with his smile.

"Why?"

"One reason should be obvious."

I glanced at the wide-eyed watchers, all of them good, down-to-earth people who'd probably never left their farms or villages in their lives. "You mean, since most of these folk—" I stopped to wriggle friendly fingers at a grinning, toothless baby held up by a beaming young matron—"since most of these folk will never have the time or funding to get to Lundinia, this gives them a chance to actually see their ruler."

Estmere nodded. A girl, all youth and coltish grace, thought that nod was *just for her* and burst into a fit of embarrassed giggles that made my brother grin. "That's one reason," he told me, "to give young girls a thrill," and I laughed. "But the other reason," he added, "you'll puzzle out for yourself as we go along."

And so I did. The various nobles Estmere visited might be honored by the royal visit—but it was they who had to provide food and lodging for king and entourage, no small expense. They'd have no funds free for mercenaries or for buying too much power.

Not that there seemed to be much danger in the latter. Most of those people I saw, commons and noble alike—saw with magician's sight, that is—appeared genuinely fond of their young king.

"Just what I told you," Estmere murmured. "They like my pretty golden looks. For the moment. Till I have to raise their taxes or pass some unpopular law."

"Cynic."

"Realist. God, I'm glad you're here, Aidan!" he burst out suddenly. "It's a joy speaking to someone I don't have to tax or legislate!"

And how did I feel about Estmere? I wasn't quite sure. We had so very little in common! And yet, we returned from that procession chattering together as though we'd known each other all our lives. And later, when I watched him at court welcome ambassadors or meet with his ministers, I was impressed by his tact (more than I would have shown to those stubborn folk) and sense of justice. He taught me something of the intricate game of politics in the days that followed. In exchange, I took him down into the city, the two of us disguised in laborers' cloaks, showing him odd little corners of Lundinia I don't think he'd even known were there.

The slow seasons swung their way about from summer through autumn through winter. There's little to be done in a palace during those long, dull, dark weeks, particularly once the bright, cheerful days of Yuletide feasting are past. The roads become too treacherous to allow much work or travel, and everyone stays close to home and hearth. Estmere and I spent much of those chill, dark winter days sitting before the fireplace in his chambers, simply talking. I told him something of what it meant to grow up a Cymraen witch-boy. He in turn, envying me my childhood freedom, I think, told me something of being a king's son, heir to a throne, with all the endless lessons (and, though he didn't actually say it, the loneliness) that entailed. Proud of his skills, since most kings, like most of their subjects, couldn't read, Estmere taught me to be literate in his tongue, and I taught him the rudiments of Cymraeth.

I also discovered an unexpected talent in my royal brother that winter: he threw a wickedly accurate snowball.

The night after the Great and Regal Snowball Fight, I slipped into trance for my usual visit with Ailanna, only to find myself face-to-mental-face with an unexpected interloper: Tairyn.

"My lord Tairyn," I said warily. "You honor me."

The touch of his mind was as cool as ever his voice had been. "You learn the ways of human nobility. Do not forget your former training."

"My Faerie training? Not a chance of that!"

"Indeed." Tairyn's disapproval was subtle but very real.

"Look you, much as you hate the thought, I *am* human! And I'm enjoying my first human friendship, thank you."

The sense of cold disapproval grew stronger. "And is human friendship such an illogical thing? Can it really be based on something as simple as the sharing of scholarship or winter sport or childhood memories?"

I'd been wondering the same thing. After all, Estmere and I didn't even laugh at the same jests! But I was hardly about to admit any doubts to Tairyn. "Estmere is my brother, my closest kin. And I enjoy being in his company. Is that wrong?"

"Humans do need their clan ties."

"And the Faerie Folk don't?" I snapped. "I've seen this proud lord refuse to speak to that proud lord, even though neither one of them had any 'degrading' human blood, just because he happened to be of the wrong clan!"

There was a moment's quiet. Then Tairyn said as coolly as though I'd never spoken, "Be wary, human. Be ready. The time may well come when we shall summon you. And then, remember your vow to me."

With that, he was gone, and I was waking, dazed and shuddering, from my trance. Vows within vows. What *had* I sworn to Tairyn, not in easy words, but in meaning?

Leave me alone, Tairyn, I pleaded silently, even though he couldn't hear me. *I've barely had the chance to enjoy being a brother. Grant me that pleasure, just for a while.*

But I knew that Faerie would come for me when and where it would.

The days passed without another interruption by Tairyn. By the time the spring came round again, I was almost able to put the Faerie Lord's strange message from my mind. He must simply, I decided, have been playing one of his alien little games of Alarm the Human!

As for Estmere, well, I'd finally come to the conclusion that human friendship had little to do with logic. Instead, as a grizzled old palace guard put it, grinning at me paternally (half drunk from the herbs I'd given him so I could tend his broken arm), it was simply a matter of "knowin' there's always someone there to drink with in good times and guard your back in bad."

Well, yes, that was it. To have discovered both blood kin and friend in one when I'd been lacking in both (and hadn't even realized the lack) was a wonderfully bewildering thing.

But of course things couldn't stay so simple.

Cut off from the refuge of my own tower rooms, I raced up the winding palace stairway as quickly as I could without slipping off the narrow steps. Pausing on a cramped landing to catch my breath, I listened for the sounds of pursuit.

Damnio! There they were, and closer than I liked. And if I kept climbing, sooner or later I was going to run out of tower and be cornered up there on the top with no place to run.

Wait. Craning my neck back and aslant, I could just make out that up one turn of the stair was a second landing, with a doorway watched over by two guards. Behind me, the sound of hurrying footsteps was growing louder, so I took a deep breath and cast over me that simple invisibility illusion learned at my mother's side. Flinging open the door, I rushed inside.

And then I froze, staring. Behind me, I could hear the

startled guards snatching at the door, calling in embarrassed tones into the room:

"Pardon, Majesty. The wind musta caught it."

An equally startled Estmere, seated behind a table piled with documents, nodded impatiently and waved them away. As embarrassed as the guards, I was trying to figure out a way to steal silently out again when he frowned and asked uneasily, "Is someone there?"

"It's only me. Aidan."

I let the invisibility illusion fade. Estmere's brows shot up in astonishment. "Now, *that* is truly amazing."

"*That* is nothing more than an illusion. Estmere, I'm sorry, I didn't mean to come storming in like this. I'll—"

"Hey now, you can't just run off like this. In God's name, what's chasing you? A demon?"

He had the look of a man who's not sure whether he's joking. I froze at a sudden sound outside the chamber door and waved him to silence. From without, a sweet, plaintive voice called:

"Prince Aidan? Oh, Prince Aidan?"

There were faint footsteps, the whisper of a silky gown brushing by, then silence. I sighed in relief and turned to my brother, who by this time was watching me in total fascination.

"No demon," I told him drily. "Only the Lady Elspeth."

He laughed. "Pretty little Elspeth? Why, Aidan! Don't tell me you're afraid of a charming young woman like that."

"She's not a woman, she's a child, a child with a head full of old romances."

"And marriage."

"That, too." I sighed. "I made the mistake of flirting with her. Harmlessly, I thought; a Cymraen woman would have understood it was a joke, no more. Something like this, I mean."

I tossed an illusion-rose to Estmere, who was inured enough to me and my ways by now not to flinch. He had time to give the rose a sniff before it dissolved again into air.

"No scent."

"There *are* limits."

"And our little Elspeth misunderstood your intentions."

"Not just Elspeth. Ever since I stopped hiding my magic, I seem to have become the most intriguing creature ever seen at court. I thought everyone's fascination would wear off over the winter, but . . ."

"Well? You have to admit you *are* unusual."

Unusual. The court physicians already hated me for curing patients more successfully than they, though of course they didn't dare do anything about it. And by now, just as I'd suspected, a good many nobles after Aldingar had tried to buy me, to make me use my magics for their advancement. But none of them had known how to hide their true intentions from a magician's sight. It had been ridiculously easy to frighten them away with dark, mysterious glances and the unspoken threat that I would set a demon or—more terrifying to a courtier—my brother at them.

But I wasn't thinking of ambitious nobles right now. "You don't understand! Yes, I can see that little Arn might be awed by me—"

"He should be. You saved his life."

"That's not what—he's a child, it's natural for him to be full of hero worship, but—Estmere, I—" Exasperated, I stopped short and began anew, "I just don't understand it here! I'll be talking to someone, and we'll be having a perfectly sensible, logical conversation—and without warning, in the same sensible voice, he'll ask me the most incredible questions, whether I've ever spoken to an angel or seen the pits of *Uffern!*"

"Well?" Estmere teased. "Have you?"

"Do you think I'd be alive if I had? *Och*, and the ladies! They follow me around like so many silken kittens, purring, 'Ohh, Prince Aidan, do a bit of magic, just for me, Prince Aidan!'" I broke off again, staring at my brother, who was struggling not to laugh, fair skin

reddening with the effort. "D'you know how close I've
come to getting challenged by jealous husbands?"

That was too much for him. He erupted into laughter,
gasping out, "Aidan, my d-dear rustic brother. Many—
many a man would give a fortune to have your problem."

Beginning to feel foolish, I persisted, "I'm not a pet
conjuror."

"No one ever said you were." Gasping, he stopped to
wipe his eyes, not daring to look at me. "Did you never
think the women might be interested in more than a few
pretty charms?"

"Estmere," I drawled, " 'rustic' I may be, but stupid I
am not."

Now he did glance up, face full of sudden dismay. "I
never thought . . . It isn't that your Art demands celibacy,
is it?"

"No, *Duwies diolch*, Goddess be thanked!" Neither
did Ailanna, bless her, any more than I demanded such
unnatural behavior of her: only Estmere's folk insist a
body be made of stone. "Look you, I confess there are
times when I enjoy the smiles and flattery and all that.
It's only . . ."

"Yes?"

But the words I wanted to tell Estmere of my lady,
my love, my Ailanna, just wouldn't come. Literally. *Curse
you, Tairyn. When you bespell a soul, he stays bespelled.*
"Never mind, Estmere," I said helplessly. "Pray forgive
me. I didn't mean to disturb your work." I grinned ruefully. "Should have realized the guards meant you were
here, not in the royal study."

"There's better light here. And I think you've infected
me with that bizarre idea of privacy." Estmere glanced
with distaste at the documents before him. "I wasn't
doing anything vital, merely checking some boundary
lines. A landowner's dispute. Very dull. I assure you, I
wouldn't even be wasting my time on it if it didn't happen to involve the son of a chief advisor: Earl Lukyn."

"*Och fi.*" The earl was clever enough, but agonizingly

insistent on the proper handling of even the smallest detail.

Estmere gave me a weary grin. "*Och fi*, indeed. My appreciation for my—sorry, *our* father's ability to keep all the little threads of the kingdom woven together rises every day." He gave me a suddenly appraising glance. "You're of the blood royal. Why shouldn't you suffer a bit, too?"

"How kind," I muttered, moving to peer over his shoulder. "What are those? Maps of the kingdom?"

He turned to look at me, brow raised at my vagueness. "Has no one taught you your geography?"

"I repeat, stupid I am not! I know that that so cunningly named Eastern Sea lies there on the—what else?—eastern boundary, I know those are various more-or-less allies there to the north, and I certainly know my own homeland and *Mawr Cyfanfor*, the Great Sea, there to the west."

"And to the south?"

"Ah . . . you have me there."

"To the south of us lie several small, neutral kingdoms and baronies, and beyond that, the ancient kingdoms of Brecara, Astarrica and Telesse, which are most certainly not our allies, and with whom we often warred in less stable times—Aidan? What *are* you looking at?"

"A bird, headed this way. A . . . dove, is it?"

"A messenger pigeon. You've seen them before."

"Flying straight to our window?"

"Foolish bird has itself a bit turned around, that's all." Impatience edged Estmere's voice. "It will straighten itself out."

"No . . . I don't think so . . ."

And then I knew what I had sensed, and sent out an angry mental shout to what was just then more than a bird:

"Get out of here, spy, or I'll kill the bird—and your mind with it!"

I caught one distant flash of pure psychic rage from someone's sorcerous brain. But, trapped like this, consciousness so far from his rightful body, there wasn't anything for the spy to do but yield. Suddenly the bird was only a bird, flying busily away.

"Aidan?" Estmere was at my side by the window, knife in hand.

"Sheathe your dagger. There's no danger."

"Then what was all that about?"

"A spy."

He had been quick to learn what rules of magic I'd thought it prudent for him to know. "Some other magician, you mean? Controlling the bird?"

"Exactly."

Estmere stiffened. "From my court?"

"No. There are no magicians here save me." When I'd investigated Aldingar's "magic scroll," I'd found it to be a sham, and of course I would have sensed if anyone had been working genuine spells. "Whoever that was, was working his spell from a great distance. The *feel* of him was foreign, too. And," I added thoughtfully, "familiar as well."

He tensed anew. "That day when you saved me from the boar—is this the same eavesdropper?"

"Yes. I recognized the touch. But I still can't put a face to him, or a name."

"Could he simply be keeping an eye on the ... ah ... royal magician?" Estmere didn't sound as though he believed it. I didn't believe it, either. "Perhaps," I said noncommittally. "Are you still planning a visit to— what's his name?"

"Lord Osmarc. Yes." A sudden gentleness warmed the blue eyes. "Osmarc has been a good friend of the royal family for years. He and his lady have been praying for a child nigh five years now. How could I not promise to attend that longed-for baby's christening?"

"Am I invited?"

That earned me a startled glance. "Do you want to be? I mean, a christening ... different faiths and all that ..."

"It wouldn't embarrass me," I assured him drily. "And

I wouldn't embarrass you, either. But would it look odd if I suddenly showed up?"

"Why no, not at all. Osmarc would probably be flattered." But Estmere's hand was toying with the hilt of his dagger. "Enough light words. What are you trying to say? If there's danger ahead, for God's sake be honest with me."

"I really don't know what's ahead. But after that winged intruder, let's just say I think it best that I go with you."

CHAPTER XI

ANFONIAD

There we were, Estmere and I, returning to Lundinia, riding along the forest road surrounded by walls of trees, rustlings of leaves and rich green scents, followed by a procession of guards and courtiers, of their bright clothing and banners dulled somewhat by the dim gray light of the overcast day.

Dull sky or not, I was humming cheerfully to myself. Estmere flashed me a quick grin. "You're in good humor, brother."

"I rejoice whenever I have forest around me." Seeing his skeptical glance, I shrugged. "Blame it on my childhood. Still, you have to admit that being surrounded by all this green life is better than being trapped behind even the most finely carved of your dead stone walls."

"Each to his own," he said diplomatically. "But you seemed to enjoy being within Osmarc's keep well enough."

"I did. It fairly radiated joy."

"And it would seem your suspicions were unfounded. Not that I'm sorry."

"Nor I."

"Osmarc liked you."

"And I liked him. And his sweet-faced wife. And even that very vocal little offspring of theirs."

"Ah yes, they're so very happy a family."

I detected the faintest of wistful notes in his voice and thought in surprise, *Why, Estmere, you secret romantic, you envy Osmarc!*

A cold, damp wind swept down on us before I could say anything, and we both caught quickly at our cloaks. Estmere shivered, wrapping the warm wool tightly about himself. "Wonderful forest, eh? Maybe you enjoy this, but I'll be glad to get home again. Especially with the weather turning foul."

I glanced up at what patches of cloud-heavy sky could be seen through the shifting branches and listened to what the wind was telling me. "It's going to get worse. We'll be lucky to escape a wetting; the rain's very near."

As though I had given a signal, the heavens opened. *Och fi*, that was a rainstorm! Instantly soaked as wet as though I'd gone swimming fully clad, I lost all sight of the others in those sheer walls of water, wondering if it was possible to drown on horseback.

There was a dim shape moving just ahead of me. "Aidan? Is that you?"

"Estmere. Do you see the others?"

"No." He forced his unhappy horse to my side. "They must have turned aside to find shelter."

"Wise idea."

We managed to squeeze our horses and ourselves under the broad branches of an oak. I glanced at Estmere. Even though he had gotten the hood of his cloak up in time, he still looked as miserably wet as I felt.

"Wonderful forest," he repeated under his breath. "Can't you do something about this?"

"Stop the rain, you mean?"

"Well?"

"You've been listening to too many ballads. I could probably call up a storm, given enough time and effort and the goodwill of *y Duwies*. But stop the rain?" I shook my head, showering myself anew. "It's like reversing a spell: it can't be done. All you can do is add a counterspell to balance it."

"And by that time, the rain would be over anyway. Ah well, I don't suppose I can get any wetter."

"At least storms this strong don't last very long. See, the rain's already slackening."

"Doesn't look as though it's going to stop altogether," Estmere muttered. "Still glad you don't have a castle roof over your head?"

"Roofs," I said shortly, "leak."

My brother sighed. "I'm not going to argue with you. Come, let's see about gathering up the rest of our party. It's going to be a soggy road home."

But with our horses' first steps forward, I gasped, a cold shock racing through me, and turned my head sharply, questing . . .

There.

Silently I handed the reins of my horse to Estmere and slipped from the saddle.

"What is it? Where are you going?"

I didn't answer, too busy studying that which I had just seen through the rain.

"Aidan? What is it, man? Do you see our courtiers?"

"No. Nor are we likely to see them." I glanced up, seeing the bewilderment plain on my brother's face. "You have my full permission to call me a fool."

"What do you mean?" And then, sharply, "What's carved on that rock?"

"*Sbel Drysu*. In Anglic a . . . Rune of Entanglement." I paused, magician's curiosity stirring despite the peril. "It does have certain odd modifications to it. . . . Still, I should have sensed its presence."

Estmere couldn't have understood too much of that, but he defended me bravely: "What, in all this rain?"

"You don't understand. If I read it correctly, the rune wasn't drawn for us, but for the rest of our party."

"To get them away from us?"

"Exactly." I was studying the curving pattern carefully.

It wasn't as elegantly drawn as some—I could have done better as a boy—but it was effective enough. "Our men are in no danger. But these modifications see to it that they wander helplessly, no doubt fully convinced they're following us." I drew my dagger, scratching careful, defacing lines across the rune. "The further they get from this thing, particularly since I'm letting its Power drain, the weaker its influence will become. But by the time they come to their senses, our party is going to be too far away to come to our aid."

"Do you think we'll *need* aid?"

"Estmere, I strongly doubt this is someone's idea of a joke."

"Think it's our bird-controlling spy again?"

"Probably." I sighed and straightened, flinging back my wet hair from my face. "I know he didn't cause this storm. That much magic I definitely would have sensed from the first." Sheathing my dagger, I took the reins back from my brother and remounted, murmuring soothing phrases to my horse when it danced uneasily. "But how he must have welcomed it! He would surely have known how so much rain would dull my senses."

"Forget that. What are we to do now?"

"Go on. Till I figure out what he's trying to do, that's all we can do."

Silent and wary, we rode on through the wet forest. But things do, eventually, tend to get better, and at last it stopped raining. I glanced up, taking a deep breath of the clean, wet air, and saw leaves stirring in a freshening wind.

"Should be blue sky soon. Eh, and here's the sun. But what's that glinting ahead of us? Water?"

"It looks like . . . yes. Lake Cala."

We rode out of the forest into full sunshine, the lake a clear, deep, wondrous blue on our left, the wet leaves and grass twinkling in the sunlight. It was a beautiful, heart-lifting scene.

And that, of course, was where the trap had been set for us.

I had been expecting it. This time I wasn't going to be caught off guard. Even as my startled horse reared in terror, I was off his back, letting him race away, not wanting him getting in the way of my magic—

But with sudden cold certainty I knew I dared not use magic.

"Estmere! Get out of here!"

Too late. He had already thrown himself from his frantic horse and now stood at my side, sword in hand. "God help us, what is that thing?"

"*Anfoniad*. A Sending."

It was ugly, roughly man-shaped though taller than any man, featureless and sexless, mud-colored and smelling of the earth from which it had been shaped by the sorcerer who'd sent it to meet us. Though the *anfoniad* had no life of its own, it was animated quite effectively by the sorcerer's will.

And it was very, very deadly.

As I'd expected, the Sending came at me first, moving with disconcerting speed. I whipped out my sword, the Faerie runes on the blade blazing up as such do in the presence of sorcery, and slashed at the thing. You can't truly kill what isn't truly alive. All I hoped to do—all I could do—was whittle away so much of the *anfoniad* that the sorcerer's spell would snap and the Sending dissolve back into the earth.

That was what it wanted, as far as it could want anything. I could vaguely sense the dim, cold, alien longing to return to nonthinking mineral quiet, and for one foolish moment I wondered if I could communicate with it.

Foolish, indeed. The will binding it was too strong. And so it could do nothing but kill.

My first slash missed. I tried again, but one great arm lashed out even as I struck at it. The Faerie blade bit deeply—and stuck fast! Before I could free it, the sword was torn from my hand.

Och, that earth thing was fast! The *anfoniad* shook itself, sending my sword flying. I made a frantic dive for the weapon, but a blow with what seemed like the weight of the Earth behind it sent me hurtling. Had I struck rock instead of mud, I don't doubt I would have died. As it was, I lay stunned, gasping for air, helplessly aware of the massive Sending looming over me.

Estmere saved me. I don't know what he was yelling—some family war cry—but his sword cut across one earthy arm and sent a muddy slab tumbling to the ground. My brother saw that slab melt right back into the parent form, and his eyes widened in horror, but he recovered quickly, neatly ducking one frighteningly fast blow then darting aside like a cat, leading the *anfoniad* away from me.

But what good was that going to do? Right now I still felt as though every nerve in my body had been cut, and by the time I managed to get my shocked system under control enough to just let me stand, Estmere's merely mortal strength would run out, and he would die, and so would I—

Not like this! We will not die like this!

Splendid. But how was I to prevent it?

Years back, my mother had introduced me to the four Elements—Air, Fire, Water, Earth—and in the process scared me into several nights of sleeplessness at the thought of those basic, utterly alien, utterly *uncaring* forces. Even now I wanted nothing to do with the wild Power that is the Earth-force, even now I tried desperately to find another way out. But when I tried to stand, my wobbly legs gave way beneath me. Estmere, distracted, gave me a quick glance, and in that moment's hesitation nearly had his head bashed in by the *anfoniad*.

The danger of Might Be paled beside that of Here and Now.

Face down in the mud, allowing myself only enough space to breathe, I stared right into the earth, focusing my will as best I could, silently reciting every calming discipline I knew. And gradually I won control . . . forcing my mind empty of the desperate struggle going on near me . . . forcing away the merely mortal world of sight and sound . . . forcing myself to quiet, cool, inhuman quiet ... I felt the Earth-force through me, the inner Earth, the rich, strong, endless dark ...

Suddenly my mind recoiled as psychic flame engulfed it. I had made contact with the spirits of the Earth, the Elementals, I *felt* them—as much as any mortal could and live—as liquid fire racing incandescent through the veins of the world. Loathe are those Others to speak with mortals, so alien are they that the magician who claims to understand them lies. But I did have this one chance for bargaining:

"It is part of your being that is held from you, part of your being forced into mortal action."

There were no words in return, of course, they have nothing so common as mouths. But I felt their reply rumble through my body like a tremor of the Earth:

We would be at one again. That cannot be.

"It can—if you help us." Struggling to hold contact without their fire searing my mind, I made my request. *"Is it agreed?"*

I waited, conscious on one level of the pain in my head, the pounding of my heart, well aware of my peril. For all I knew I had somehow angered the beings by one misplaced word. They might not even have understood me. Worse, they might simply decide to end their troubles in one vast shaking of the Earth. I would as lief be torn apart by the *anfoniad* as buried alive!

But then I felt a murmur of reply through the whole of my being, and almost laughed in relief.

It is agreed.

They told me what to do. Then the contact was broken, leaving me shaken and dizzy with relief at the sudden return to simple mortality. Doggedly I got to my knees, fighting body and mind for control.

Estmere was still holding his own, thrusting at the *anfoniad* when he could, dodging its attempts to crush him, but he was panting, and there was desperation in his eyes. I caught a flash of bright metal not too far from where I knelt—my sword! Forgetting dizziness, I snatched it up, closing my hand firmly about the silver-wound hilt.

"Estmere! Do as I do!"

Thrice I whirled the bright blade about my head, then plunged it into the ground. Raw strength came surging up that sword into my body, blazing through nerve and muscle, the strength of the Earth itself, and for one panicked moment I thought it would be more than I could hold. But then, drunk with borrowed Power, I no longer cared. As the *anfoniad* turned towards me, I laughed in sheer, wild exuberance and swung my sword with a speed I had never known before. I felt the blade strike home, saw it slice an earthen arm clean off. Of course the *anfoniad* showed no reaction, of course it could feel no pain. But this time the severed earth faded harmlessly into the ground.

"Strike, Estmere! We have it now!"

He was more daring than I. Eyes bright as blue fire in his new strength, my brother dodged in past the remaining arm, swung his sword with barbaric force, and cut the legs right out from under the *anfoniad*. As the thing fell, trying to catch us beneath it, we harried it as dogs do a bear, springing in and out, cutting at it. And each time a lump of earth fell away, it melted neatly down into the ground.

But the Sending refused to surrender. That was the worst of it, that the *anfoniad* made no attempt to protect itself. Even as we hacked at it, it continued its mindless efforts to kill us. And I felt the first prickles of unease. At the back of my mind had been the fear that the Earth-strength would burn at us till we died of it. Now I realized that our merely mortal bodies simply couldn't hold it; the wild Power was rapidly draining away. And as soon as it was gone, the sorcerer would rebuild his Sending—

The sorcerer! *Duwies glân*, I was missing the real target! Though his body might have been who knew how far away, the sorcerer still had to have his mind, his essence, focused here in his muddy creation.

Gathering the last of the Earth-force within me, I *felt* the center of that focus, and knew exactly what to do.

Estmere glanced at me aghast as I gave what must have been a truly savage smile and lunged at the *anfoniad* with all the strength within me. My sword pierced right through the Sending's chest—and the sorcerer had no chance to pull his mind free.

The impact of such a blow, Faerie metal stabbing human essence, must have been agonizing. I caught one distant psychic scream of pure anguish—

Then the *anfoniad* sank in on itself into a formless mound of mud. In less time than it takes to tell this, it was gone, dissolved back into the ground. And only the earth torn by our feet proved that there had been a battle at all.

For a long while Estmere and I just stood, swaying with exhaustion and struggling to breathe regularly as the last of the Earth-strength drained from our bodies. But as soon as he had managed to draw in sufficient air, my brother, not surprisingly, began stammering questions.

"What—who—"

I told him what I could. He stared.

"Estmere?"

"I'm all right. I only—do you really live like this, Aidan?"

I laughed weakly. "Hardly. This is a little out of the ordinary even for a magician."

"But that ... *anfoniad* ..." He pronounced the word gingerly. "Our bird-spy sorcerer sent it? Why? It seems an overelaborate attempt at assassination."

"It wasn't meant as one."

"What then? A test? Was he testing your powers?"

I nodded, and my brother blinked in confusion.

"But you didn't use—I mean—surely you could have cast a spell to melt the thing."

"No. *That* was the true test. The *anfoniad* was built to be impervious to magic. Had I tried like some frightened novice to use Power against it, that Power would have recoiled on us both: fatally."

For a moment Estmere continued to stare. Then, quite reverently, he crossed himself. Still, kings are made of stern stuff. His next question was a controlled, "Was the sorcerer working on his own?"

"Out of simple professional jealousy, you mean? Not likely! Between the drawing of the Rune," which, I was beginning to realize, could only have been done from afar, a miserably difficult task which explained the Rune's sloppy design, "and the summoning of the *anfoniad*, our sorcerous friend used up a dangerous amount of inner energy. You don't risk your mind and body out of casual dislike for a stranger!"

"Then you're saying he was in someone else's employ. Can't you tell who that someone else might be?"

I mentally reviewed the list of all those nobles who had tried to use me. Aldingar? No. And no for any of the others, too. None of them would ever have dared (or, for that matter, have known how) to hire a foreign sorcerer. "I was rather hoping *you* could tell *me*."

Estmere sighed. "I have a good many foes. Not all of them open about it." He raised a quizzical brow. "You *are* sure he wasn't after you?"

"Sorry. I'm not involved in any arcane feuds." I grinned fiercely. "At least we won't have to worry about any new sorceries from him for a long time. If he even survived." Quickly I explained to Estmere what I had done, stabbing the sorcerer's essence through with the innately magical Faerie blade. He thought about it, winced, then echoed my grin.

"My, you magicians do play nasty games! I fear I can't pity him, though." He bit back a sudden yawn. "Dear Lord, but I'm weary."

"What would you expect? We'll both sleep like the dead tonight, which is a hundred times better than *with* the dead, and—now what?"

Estmere, red-faced, was biting his lip, quivering.

"All right, *fy brawd*, what's so funny?"

He exploded into laughter. "Y-you!"

"Estmere?"

"I—I didn't have a chance—didn't truly look at you! You—you look like you've been wallowing in mud!"

Which was, after all, pretty much what I'd been doing. "Now, really. A little mud—"

That started him off anew. "A *little* mud!"

It was a delayed reaction, of course, from our ordeal. I knew that. I tried to control myself, really I did. But he *would* go on laughing.

I don't even think he knew that little burst of will (and "little" was all I could have managed just then) came from me.

But that is why, when our party finally located us, they found His Most Gracious Majesty, King Estmere II, still laughing his royal head off. And sitting, most satisfactorily, in a nice, thick puddle of mud.

CHAPTER XII

HIRAETH

I slouched in a chair in my tower rooms, head in hands, struggling with the magical backlash of a failed spell: Power unspent recoils upon the sender. Fortunately for me, I had cast only a relatively mild Spell of Searching, nothing to endanger life or mind, but the headache its failure left behind was real enough.

Just when I'd managed to work enough restorative magic on myself to reduce the pain to a dull ache, there came a timid rapping on my chamber door.

"Go away," I muttered, but whoever was out there either didn't hear me or was under stronger orders than mine, because the tapping came again, a little more insistent this time. "Enough," I yelled (and, wincing, wished I hadn't), "I hear you," and released the Signs that had been guarding the door. "Enter."

It was Arn, the little page whose life I had saved, now totally restored to bright young health and still ablaze with hero worship, bearing a message from Estmere:

"His Majesty, your royal brother, fain would speak with you in his chambers."

A royal summons was the last thing I wanted to deal

with right now, but, "So be it," I said, and went to splash
cold water on my face and hopefully make myself look
halfway human again.

A stray ray of sunlight had found its way through the
narrow windows into the royal chambers, sparking tapestries into jewel-bright life, glinting dazzlingly off the intricate pattern of the tiled floor, brightening my brother's
hair to brilliant gold. A pretty sight, but after the trip I'd
made down from my tower, across the breadth of the
palace—having to stop and acknowledge various polite
and politic salutations along the way—and up again to
this elegant maze of rooms, my headache had returned
and I was totally out of breath.

Whatever Estmere had been going to say went unsaid
as he stared me.

"God's blood, man, you look dreadful!"

So much for trying to look presentable. I shrugged,
but Estmere persisted, "Are you ill?"

"Just tired."

"Come, sit."

As I gratefully obeyed, sinking to the high-backed,
square-sided chair that was a twin to his own and once
again willing my headache away, Estmere signalled to
one of the omnipresent servants, who shyly presented
me with a hastily filled goblet. When I hesitated,
expecting the abysmal court wine (which, I was convinced, was in fashion more for its imported expense
than its sediment-ridden flavor), my brother grinned.

"Mead, Aidan. You've corrupted my taste."

As I sipped appreciatively, feeling the golden warmth
steal soothingly through me, I felt Estmere studying me.

"You're not still trying to learn who sent the
anfoniad?"

"I am. With crystal and mirror and smoke—"

"You had half the court convinced your tower was on
fire with that last one. Give it up."

"No."

"Yes. Aidan, it's been nearly three months! I've had

my spies out, too, and no one has found anything more than petty feuds and quarrels—the usual things, with not a trace of magic to them."

When I stared down into my goblet and said nothing, Estmere continued cajolingly, "Come now, brother. The sorcerer probably did die with his sorcery."

"Perhaps."

Suddenly I couldn't bear to sit still any longer. Putting my goblet down on the small table between our chairs, I got to my feet and moved to a window, courtiers and servants hurrying out of my way, and stood looking restlessly down through the narrow slit to where the broad Taemese gleamed like polished silver below the castle walls, thinking absently that though it was full summer down there, up here behind this heavy stone it was eternally dim, cool, timeless. After a moment I heard a flurry of motion—Estmere dismissing everyone—and the click of a door being quietly shut. Then my brother was at my side.

"What *is* the matter with you?"

I sighed. "Nothing. Nothing you can mend."

I wasn't about to tell him I was aching with *hiraeth*, that soft, sad homesick longing. I *couldn't* tell him about Ailanna.

Ailanna. *Duwies glân*, I was sick of dreams and visions! I ached to hold a warm, tangible, living Ailanna in my arms, to make a home for us amid the forest of my own land. . . .

My own land. What a sweet phrase that was, enough to fill me with bittersweet pain, with unease—

Unease?

There was an almost visible aura of nervousness in the air about us, and it certainly wasn't from me. I banished my brooding, all at once remembering that my brother must have had a good reason for summoning me. Estmere was usually quite respectful of my privacy, even though (since he accepted rooms crowded with courtiers as the norm) he still didn't quite understand it.

"What is it, Estmere? What's wrong?"

His fair skin flushed with embarrassment. "I . . . you've been here a year now."

"Yes." Suddenly I was wary, wondering.

"I think the people have accepted you."

What was he trying to tell me? I shrugged. "Up to a point. Despite the occasional uneasy soul who makes signs against magic when he thinks I'm not looking. And of course people come to me for healing. Even if they sometimes expect miracles: love potions, elixirs of immortality— Estmere what *is* the matter?" Had some of those nobles I'd rejected been speaking out against me? Or, instead of nobles, had it been priests? I'd thought Father Ansel and I had come to an understanding, but . . . "Planning to get rid of me?"

"Good Lord, no! Did you think? No. I . . ." He muttered something unregal under his breath, reddening even more. "I admit this sounds foolish, but, do you think I'm doing a proper job?"

"As king?"

He snorted. "Of course as king!"

"Mm. You've kept the markets open, the borders peaceful, and the nobles from each others' throats. I'm not an expert at politics, *y Duwies* be praised, but that sounds successful enough to me. Why the self-doubts?"

"I . . . oh, dammit all! You know that I'm betrothed."

"To be married?" I squawked like an idiot. "No, I didn't know, you never mentioned—who is she? Where did you meet her?"

"Aidan, you romantic, I've never met her. I've been betrothed since I was a babe in the cradle. It's standard royal practice; surely you knew that." He paused. "No. I can see you didn't. My dear, innocent brother, all kings must marry and produce heirs as quickly as possible. So, the sooner the problem of finding a suitable wife can be concluded, the happier everyone is."

"And of course romance doesn't enter into it."

"How could it?" He wouldn't meet my glance. "This is strictly a business proposition."

"Indeed. Then why are you so nervous?"

Estmere forced a laugh. "Not nervous: terrified. All these years I put the thought of my betrothal out of my mind, so successfully I frankly never realized you didn't know about it."

"But now the date for concluding this 'business proposition' is suddenly closer than you'd expected."

"The years *do* have a way of passing, don't they?" Estmere let out his breath in a long sigh. "I know I'm a decent ruler. I should be: I've been in training for the job all my life! But now this ... I ..."

He stopped awkwardly, that embarrassed and embarrassing flush returning, and I remembered how uncomfortable these more ... modern folk were with thoughts of mating. Fighting down the bawdy, honest Cymraen jests that sprang to mind, I asked delicately, "But now you're worried about being a good husband as well? Estmere, you will be! I saw the envy on your face when we visited Lord Osmarc and his wife."

Something wistful flickered in Estmere's eyes. "Yes, but theirs was that rare thing, a true love match, not something arranged to seal a treaty or consolidate a royal— Ah, Aidan. I shouldn't be bothering you with this. You folk of the older faith probably look on our arranged marriages as immoral. But ... I just can't go to anyone else. If I did, my fears would be all over the court by morning."

Well, I *did* think it immoral. But I wasn't defending it, I argued with myself, I was defending my brother. "Think, *fy brawd*. Your parents' marriage was an arranged one, wasn't it?"

"Of course."

"But you just told me there was more than mere royal duty between them. Despite all burdens, they truly loved each other, didn't they?"

"Oh, yes."

"Well? If such a wonder can happen once, who is there to say it can't happen again?"

He stared, laughed, stared again. In a voice quivering with the beginning of hope, my brother said hesitantly,

"It could . . . she's kin, after all, not a total stranger . . . if I work at . . ." He stopped, then began again, almost defiantly, "Yes, of course it could happen. And it shall, God willing."

I smiled, and Estmere grinned in return. "Thank you for your counsel, brother," he began formally, then exploded, "By my faith, you make me look a fool!"

"No. Merely human."

"Don't belittle yourself. Look you, if I had been naive enough to go to anyone else, what do you think I'd have heard? Nothing but cold lectures on duty and obligation to my face, and mockery behind my back. But in a few simple words you set my mind at ease!" His grin widened. "Were I some tyrant of old, I swear I would keep you in a gilded prison as my most precious counselor—oh, don't give me that terrified glance! I'm only joking." Estmere threw a companionable arm across my shoulders. "You didn't think I'd ever do anything to hurt you, did you? Still, I do need you at my side, brother, surely you know that. There are times when I wonder how I ever managed without your good, plain common sense."

I pulled away before he could feel me wince.

Why had he said that? Why, when my heart ached with longing for my lady, my home, had he reminded me of my vow? It had been meant so kindly. But I felt the bonds of friendship, of my vow, come tightly about me like the strands of some gentle, unbreakable web. And for a moment I just couldn't bear to meet his hopeful gaze.

Eh, wait . . . a wife. What if she proved to be a true partner and friend to Estmere? It could happen. It happened all the time in Cymra. (My mind raced blithely over the fact that those were never arranged marriages.) And if Estmere had such a lady at his side, why then, surely my vow would be fulfilled!

My mind all at once was full of such happy pictures of Estmere and his love, of me and mine, that I nearly laughed aloud.

"Aidan? What's so amusing?"

"Never mind, never mind. Do I have to bespell you, *brawd*, or are you going to satisfy my curiosity on your own?"

"About?"

"Come now, Estmere! I think I'm entitled to know the name of my sister-in-law-to-be!"

He laughed. "Of course. After all, she's your kin, too, our . . . let me see . . . third cousin on our father's side, the last eligible female left in the direct royal line: the Duchess Clarissa."

The Duchess Clarissa, I echoed in silent dismay. The name and title together put me in mind of some sour-faced old dowager.

I couldn't have been more mistaken.

CHAPTER XIII

ROYAL WEDDING

Och, the excitement that gripped the royal court as the wedding grew nigh! Each day the courtyard was crowded all over again with arriving guests, both Estmere's vassals and emissaries from other kingdoms. In one morning alone I counted nearly twenty nobles alighting from sleek, fidgeting horses or elegant carriages gleaming with fresh paint (elegant to the eye, that is, rough, jouncing torment to spine and seat), ten minstrels, two whole troops of acrobats, thirty musicians and their lutes, horns and tabors, and even one man with a dancing bear. All of them seemed determined to occupy that rapidly diminishing courtyard space at the same time, and all of them seemed equally determined to be the only ones seen and heard, crowding the air as they crowded the courtyard with a jangle of human noise and animal noise, pomander scent and sweat.

Nor was it any calmer within the palace. Everywhere I went, I found new and increasingly frantic activity. The guards were rapidly going gray with worry over checking everyone's credentials, while the courtiers were in their glory, making lists and gossiping over who outranked whom, who should sit above the salt at the wedding feast, in those more honorable places nearer the king, and who weren't so important and must sit below.

As if this wasn't confusing enough, both guards and courtiers were constantly being tripped up by the royal milliners, who were working apace to fill every available space with bright new banners showing the golden eagle of the royal household clasping the three white roses of Clarissa's family device. Where banners wouldn't fit, they crammed in smaller, eye-dazzlingly bright hangings and draperies and what seemed like acres of ribbons.

Meanwhile, the kitchen (where my little pot boy had been promoted to second cook's apprentice and bathed at least once a month) was like a vision out of Father Ansel's description of Hell, full of smoke and flame and bustling devils waving knives and spoons, the air so thick with the mingled smells of grease and roasting meat and marzipan it was nearly strong enough to stand by itself.

And as for me, the hysteria around me wasn't merely incredible, it was downright dizzying. Even with all my psychic defenses in place, the flood of emotions managed to spill through the cracks, as it were. By the day Estmere's bride was due to arrive, I simply couldn't carry the weight of everyone else's nervous excitement on top of my own. For the sake of my mental well-being, I up and fled to the peace of my tower rooms where, for a time, I was bothered only by the chirpings of two nesting sparrows outside a window.

But of course even that sanctuary was invaded. The servants were uneasy about intruding in what I knew they'd dubbed "the magician's roost," but they were also determined to see that Prince Aidan was suitably garbed. They were so quickly efficient about it that before I could protest—before I even realized what was happening!—they had clad me in russet and blue velvet (which looked handsome enough, I had to admit), including a hot and heavy cloak, ridiculous in this warm weather. They placed on my newly combed hair the thin but amazingly heavy gold circlet I usually refused to wear, and hurried me almost by force back down through the torrents of excitement to my brother's side at the head of the castle steps.

"Where were you?" he hissed.

"Hiding!" I whispered back.

"This isn't any time for jokes!"

"Who's joking?"

"Shh!"

I glanced at him. *Och*, but Estmere was splendid! Carrying the weight of the ceremonial crown—that gem-encrusted monster—and of his richly embroidered white and gold robes of state with apparent ease, he looked the very image of royalty and romance. I wondered wryly how he managed not to perspire under all that, and thought with a surge of affection that no one who saw him could have guessed at his nervousness. And nervous he most certainly was.

He wasn't the only one. It was just now striking home to me that this was it, this was the moment when I would learn if Estmere would be happy and, indirectly, I with him. My heart was pounding almost as though *I* was the one to be wed!

Clarissa's pretty green and yellow coach, the three white roses painted on its door, entered the courtyard with a rattling of wheels and stopped at the foot of the stairway. Elegant footmen in green and yellow livery opened the coach door and respectfully handed out a small figure wrapped in a glamorous white cloak. Estmere, too courteous to let her make that long climb alone (or too tense to wait a moment more) disregarded tradition and went down to meet her, courtiers scurrying in his wake. Formal introductions were made, a formal kiss was exchanged. Then, together, they started back up the stairway to where I waited, rigid with suspense.

And so I came face to face with Estmere's bride. The Duchess Clarissa was young, very young, with thick, ashy blond plaits and great blue eyes in a fine-boned face almost as pale as her cloak: a small, lovely, fragile lady delicate as an aristocratic flower.

I wish I could say I was instantly charmed by her. But

as our gazes met as we were introduced, I was horrified to feel a little prickle of distaste steal through me, the sort of quick, irrational reaction sages say means you had a reason in some former life to hate the person you only think you're meeting for the first time.

Who knows?

At any rate, the distaste was clearly shared by Clarissa. The warmth faded from those soft blue eyes, leaving them pale and gray as ice.

"Prince Aidan." She inclined her head a formal fraction.

"Duchess Clarissa." My bow was just as formal. "May I add my welcome to those you have already received?"

She acknowledged that coolly, then added, "I have heard strange rumors about you, Prince Aidan."

"Rumors?"

"I've been told you are . . . somewhat of a magician." She made it sound as unsuitable for one of even my diluted royal blood as pig farming.

"Somewhat," I agreed drily.

"Indeed. How interesting."

With that, she . . . simply dismissed me, leaving me to sternly curb my rising anger.

She's young, I reminded myself. She's only very young, and weary, and a stranger here, come to marry a stranger.

Besides, for all I knew, her women had been terrifying her with tales of the king's sorcerous brother. Maybe rudeness was hiding fear.

Estmere hadn't noticed any rudeness. Estmere wouldn't have noticed if she'd slapped me. All but radiating his delight and relief, he was blatantly smitten by our pretty cousin.

Now that I thought of it, Clarissa hadn't seemed at all displeased by her first sight of Estmere, either. Maybe things wouldn't work out so badly at that. It didn't matter how I felt about it, as long as they were happy together.

After all, *I* didn't have to marry her!

* * *

How did I manage in the royal chapel? This wasn't my faith, after all; I could hardly actively participate. But since no one save Estmere knew my true religion, I could hardly *not* be there, either.

The answer is a simple one: soon after my acceptance at Estmere's court, when I realized that as the king's brother I would be expected to attend chapel at least once a week, if not once a day like many folk, I had worked out a milder variation on my invisibility illusion—a clever thing, too, if I may praise myself. It simply confused people's minds to the point where they knew they had seen me there, but couldn't quite remember what I had actually been doing—or not doing.

Tactful, Estmere and I agreed, and useful. Particularly now, when I had no intention of missing my brother's wedding!

That wedding was a lovely thing, what with the bride and groom looking so young, so beautiful, as they knelt at the altar side by side, the massed candles casting a soft golden glow over their golden hair and shining faces. Even their splendid white wedding robes and long cloaks of crimson velvet and snowy ermine gleamed with gold.

Estmere had arranged for Father Ansel to marry them, which, I thought, was kind of my brother; as king, he could have, after all, called on some high officer of their church to do the honors. The priest's face was radiant with joy as he blessed the new union, and I almost wept when a choir of boys raised their sweet, clear, almost inhumanly pure young voices in songs of rejoicing.

Her heavy wedding robe, stiff as it was with metallic embroidery and glittering gems, almost undid the bride; delicate Clarissa needed her ladies' help and her new husband's arm to get her to her feet once more. It was close within the royal chapel, crowded with everyone with any pretension to nobility, and the air hung heavy with the smell of incense and candle wax and too many people in too small a space. I wasn't at all surprised to see Clarissa falter, her face gone deathly pale. I started forward in alarm, healer's instincts aroused, but of course

Estmere was there at her side, supporting her. In the next moment she had recovered, and was smiling up at her husband, assuring him it was nothing. Even so, Estmere hurried her out into the open air as soon as it was politely possible.

There, of course, amid a wild, joyous pealing of bells, they faced a new ordeal, that of greeting the solid mass of humanity that was the commons, who had been allowed to crowd onto the palace grounds this once to help celebrate the occasion.

Nor did the new couple escape once they were back within the palace. No, now came the seemingly interminable wedding feast, with its dizzying procession of course after course, red meat and fowl and fish of every sort, pastries and pies and those bizarre desserts known as subtleties (why, I have no idea, since there's nothing subtle about them) without which no feast in Estmere's lands is considered complete. Some of those subtleties were spectacular enough to seem almost magical: a golden swan swimming upon a sea of blue-green marzipan; a hound-sized, red-scaled dragon that breathed steam from his gaping mouth; a marzipan replica of the royal palace in perfect miniature. Laughing, I ate a piece of "my" tower, and told myself that now it truly belonged to me!

All about me, the great hall rang with music and song and a confusing babble of voices. The babble grew more confusing with each sip of the mead that Estmere (kindly remembering my preference) had ordered I be served in place of that detestable wine.

But of course no magician dares drink enough to lose control. When I realized I was starting to let an illusion of green vines twine about the arms of my chair and start up onto the table, I put the goblet firmly aside, and let the happy confusion sweep on without me.

As the day wore on and night closed in, the joviality began to take a ribald turn, nothing to embarrass anyone from Cymra, used as we are to frank speaking, but certain to redden the cheeks of more delicate folk.

Such as the fair Clarissa. She had managed to ignore me throughout the whole affair (no easy thing, since we were sitting side by side), which bothered me a little but surprised me not at all. I watched her out of the corner of my eye, a bit concerned about the state of her health after that moment when she'd nearly fainted in the chapel. How could such a fragile lady be enduring this endless day so well? *Y Duwies* knew *I* was growing weary.

But through all the pomp and glory and loud rejoicing, the king and his new queen did seem to be holding up amazingly well, regal and apparently quite at ease. Training, of course. But I saw the glances they stole at each other, shy, appraising, very human glances, and I thought in a sudden fierce surge of renewed hope, *It may be well between them. Please, please let all be well between them!*

CHAPTER XIV

CLARISSA

At first all did seem to be well. Clarissa settled into palace life with remarkable ease. Of course, as a high-born orphan (yes, her parents were dead; how else could she, so young, have inherited her title?) she already had a good deal of experience in handling a regal household. But even so, she seemed to be taking to her new status with both dignity and delight.

It wasn't mere self-interest, either. I had no doubt that Clarissa cared for Estmere and loved the very idea of being in love. Given time and any chance at all, I thought, that idea might become reality. And Estmere was as enchanted as ever a young man was with a pretty bride. Watching them together in those early days was a bit like eating a surfeit of sweets.

"I'll be home soon," I told Ailanna during one of our meetings-by-trance. "*Y Duwies* willing, love, I'll be home soon!"

But she, more skeptical of humanity than I, refused to say more than, "Wait. Aidan, wait."

"Wait for *what*?" I forced a laugh. "Look you, I agree this is hardly the sort of thing I imagined when I first set out to meet Estmere; I don't exactly have a heroic role to play. But that doesn't matter! What does is that they love each other, all will be well, and I'll come home to—"

"No!" The mind that brushed mine blazed with a sudden frustrated rage.

"What's this?" I tried to tease. "Don't you *want* to see me again?"

"Curse you, Aidan, don't mock me!"

"I didn't mean—"

"Don't you think I ache to hold you in my arms? Don't you think I hate the vow that keeps you from me? But this *isn't* the end of it! I know it, I *feel* it in my heart though the thought sickens me!"

With that, she pulled free of the trance and left me dazed and alone.

And alas, she was right. Ailanna's skepticism proved more honest than all my foolish, wild hopings. Too soon, I saw the bright edge leave the new couple's happiness. It wasn't all that noticeable, certainly not for anyone without the Power to see clearly, nothing more than the slightest of hesitations before a smile, the nearly imperceptible shadow in a glance or hint of gray uncertainty in an aura. But it was there. It was real.

It's the season, I tried to tell myself. They had been wed in the blind optimism of late summer, when no one will admit the warm, green time is nearly past. They were still joyous together in those wild, crisp days of autumn, with the air like wine and the spirits of human and beast alike full of cheer. But now it was full winter. And didn't nearly all of humankind feel moody and unhappy when the darkness reigned and daylight came so briefly? *That's all that's wrong, surely.*

Yet the year swung about past the Midwinter Solstice towards the spring again, and the shadow between Estmere and Clarissa failed to lift. Indeed, with every day, it deepened. I ached for them, thinking of Ailanna, of the sure, bright knowledge we had of *belonging,* one to

the other. We loved each other, of course, but we liked
and trusted each other as well.

Trust. There it was. Clarissa might love her husband,
but she still didn't quite trust him, or his court—

Or me.

The little palace cloister was rich with birdsong and
new spring flowers. I'd been soaking up the sunlight out
here, idly amusing myself with luring a pert little sparrow
to my hand, when suddenly the bird gave a sharp chirp
of alarm and took wing.

"Hello, Estmere," I said without turning.

There was a moment's silence. Then, "How *do* you
do that?"

"Now, what manner of magician would I be if I
couldn't recognize my brother's aura?" But when I
turned to see the discomfort in his eyes, I couldn't continue the pretense of light good humor. "Estmere?
What's wrong?"

"Do I need an excuse to see you?"

"Hardly."

But I was disconcerted to see him hastily drop his gaze
in the way I'd taught him were he ever in need of hiding
his thoughts from a magician.

From me? "Come, Estmere, what would you?"

"I . . . we've seen very little of you lately."

"Deliberately. *Och*, don't frown! I haven't been off
sulking in some corner. I'm not a little boy jealous of his
brother's wife."

Actually, even if I had been foolish enough to sulk,
there hadn't been the time. Predictably, the winter ice
and snow had brought about a fair number of wrenched
limbs and broken bones for courtier, commoner and
beast alike. Those increasingly hostile court physicians
notwithstanding, the magician-prince had usually been
the healer of choice, even when I hadn't needed to use
the smallest of spells. When I'd had a chance to catch
my breath, I had welcomed the chance to be alone, to
study and experiment up in my tower and, when the

weather permitted it, out in the fields outside Lundinia: magic, like any other craft, demands practice.

Estmere couldn't know that. "Then why—"

"*Brawd*, please. You two have small enough privacy at court as it is. I hardly thought it would help a young marriage to have me hanging about your necks as well." I paused. "And now that we have that out of the way, maybe you can tell me what's wrong."

"Nothing."

"Of course. You merely abandoned your royal duties because you felt like watching me tame sparrows."

"Pray don't push me, Aidan."

"*Fy brawd, annwyl brawd,* my dear, touchy brother, you seek me out, you stand there radiating confusion and despair, you refuse to look me squarely in the eye—and then you pretend that nothing bothers you."

He stirred restlessly. "I don't know how to word this."

"It's about Clarissa, isn't it?"

"I . . . yes," he began awkwardly, and got no further.

I sighed. "You don't have to worry about sparing my feelings. I know how she feels about me."

"What do you mean?"

"*Och fi,* I'm not blind! Even without magic, I'd see how uncomfortable you've become in my presence. And I certainly can't *not* be aware of your wife's hostility."

"You're exaggerating."

"Am I? Look you, I don't know if the woman is trying to exorcise me or just embarrass me, but you can't tell me you haven't noticed she's had more holy signs and symbols placed about the royal chambers—about the whole palace—than I've seen in the hut of the most superstitious—"

"Enough!" The word was sharp as the crack of a whip. "Remember of whom you speak."

"The queen. Your wife." I shook my head impatiently. "You know I mean no insult. I've been trying my fiercest to stay out of the way. But—why does she hate me?"

"She doesn't hate you."

"You lie badly, *brawd.*"

"She doesn't hate you! She . . . simply isn't used to the world you inhabit."

"You managed to accept it easily enough."

"But she's not me. She's . . . delicate."

Och, I was weary of that word! "As she never fails to remind you!" I snapped. "Yes, Clarissa *is* delicate, and I wish she'd let me concoct some strengthening potions for her. But she won't let me near her! And I swear she uses that delicacy as a weapon against me! *Gallu!*" I exploded. "What does she want of me? That I give up my *Duwies*-given Power and—"

"Aidan. Please."

Estmere's eyes met mine. And they were radiating an anguished pleading no king could ever have voiced aloud:

Please, please, have patience. She'll come to trust you, to love you as I do. Oh please, I would not see either of you hurt!

Well. That took the sting out of my anger, as you can imagine. I watched Estmere leave, his face a mask, and sighed, ruefully admitting to myself I was too proud to tell Ailanna she was right and I'd been wrong. The only solution I could see to this mess was to ignore my own feelings on the matter and try to win Clarissa's trust—or at least to convince the silly woman I meant her no harm.

Easily decided. Not so easily carried out.

I first tried to meet with her and Estmere. But Estmere never did seem to have a moment free. It was perpetually a case of: "Sorry, Aidan, I can't talk now" and "Later, Aidan, please." He wasn't making false excuses, either; even a newly married king can't escape affairs of state forever.

So be it, I told myself. It probably hadn't been a good idea to get him involved in this at any rate. I would meet with Clarissa and her ladies instead.

Clarissa had other ideas. Each time I tried to speak with her, I was met by an apologetic servant telling me the queen was otherwise occupied with this task or that. Some of those excuses were fairly transparent. But what could I do? Call the queen a liar? Use magic to barge boldly in, terrifying her and ruining any hope of peace between us?

Clarissa, I don't doubt, was enjoying the whole thing, happy to make the magician-prince look like a fool in front of the court; said court was beginning to buzz delightedly (and carefully, of course, out of Estmere's hearing) about the hostilities between the king's wife and the king's brother. And of course, foremost in their buzzing ranks were Baron Aldingar and his cronies, taking malicious delight in gossiping against me, never *quite* saying anything libelous, he and I both knowing that if I retaliated without proven cause, I'd look like a tyrant.

And how *that* would have thrilled Clarissa! *Och*, how I ached to put that ... spoiled child in her place!

But losing control certainly wouldn't help matters. Instead, I decided to make one last stab at diplomacy. So I sat down in my tower study and wrote the queen a letter.

It wasn't easy. Even though, thanks to Estmere, I could now write in a reasonably fair hand, the proper flowery language of court etiquette has always eluded me. And what finally went down on the parchment after much agonizing was a blunt and simple:

> "To Clarissa, queen and sister:
> If life is to run smoothly and peacefully for
> Estmere and you and me, we two needs must
> speak honestly.
> I pray you, grant me an audience, either alone
> or with your ladies in attendance.
> Your husband's brother, and so, your own,
> Aidan ap Nia."

I studied my handiwork with a critical eye. Not a masterpiece of subtlety or charm, but as good as it was likely to get.

Rolling up the parchment and sealing it with a drop of candle wax, I called for a page (no easy thing from my isolated tower; it meant leaning perilously out a window and shouting my request down to a passing guard). The boy I received at last was the one I'd healed of the knife wound: little Arn.

Or rather, not quite so little Arn. I smiled to myself at the bow he made me, a reasonably graceful thing despite his coltish new gawkiness of limb; a boy grows in quick spurts, and the child I had rescued was showing more than a few hints of the tall nobleman he would become.

"Take this message to the queen, lad."

He bowed even more deeply over the sealed parchment, his pride at being trusted with a royal errand spoiled only by the lock of yellow hair that promptly fell into his eyes. I bit back my amusement as the boy surreptitiously brushed back the unruly strand, started to bow again, thought better of it, and vanished with a determined:

"At once, Your Highness!"

But he was back in very short order, looking very young and very, very crestfallen. I saw the parchment still in his hand, and frowned. "That never saw the queen."

"No, Your Highness," he admitted in a subdued voice. "I ..." He shook his head miserably, and I prodded gently:

"Go on. You know I won't hurt you."

Arn swallowed. "I d-did give your message to one of the queen's ladies, and she really did take it to the queen, I saw it. But when Her Majesty learned who had written the letter, she ..." The boy paused as though desperately hunting a way out of a trap, then continued hopefully, "She said that her head ached so foully she would not even let one of her women read to her."

"Arn *bachgen*, we both know that's not what she really said."

"N-no ..." He sounded on the verge of tears, but he continued bravely, "She said she would not touch a parchment written by a sorcerer, nor listen to a word of his—his dark spells— Your Highness, please, those were her words, not mine!"

Dark spells! Curse her, if she wanted dark spells— I spat out certain Words, and the parchment blazed up into flame in my hand.

I had forgotten about Arn. With a gasp of horror, he tore the fiery thing from me and hurled it into the fireplace, then whirled to me, white-faced.

"Are you hurt? Oh, are you hurt, my prince?"

My prince. "No, Arn."

"Oh. I . . ." He blushed. "Of course. It was enchanter's fire, wasn't it? I mean, it wouldn't really have burned you, would it?"

"It might have. You acted rightly, Arn." But he was trying to hide one hand behind his back, and with a sudden sharp pang of remorse I realized, "You're hurt!"

Predictably, the young hero said, "It's nothing."

"Come, let me see."

Fortunately it wasn't much of a burn; Arn had moved too quickly for serious injury. But that didn't stop me from a stab of guilt. Losing one's temper is one thing; losing magical control, another. I hastily took the smart from the reddened skin with a murmured spell, then added an herbal salve, very much aware of the boy's worshipful eyes as I worked.

"Don't look at me like that, Arn. I'm just a man, truly. And it's my fault you were burned."

He shook his head dramatically. "No matter. You are my prince. I owe you my life, and I shall not forget."

"Good. Now, how does that feel?"

He moved his hand experimentally, then gazed at me with new wonder. "It's completely healed, my prince!"

"Not completely. Keep it covered and—hey now, what are you doing?"

The boy had gone down on one knee, and I knew that if he'd been wearing a sword, it would have been sworn to my service then and there.

"*Och*, Arn, get up. I'm not belittling you or your bravery. But I . . . have other things on my mind."

"The queen," he said, greatly daring, then, with the desperate air of someone who knows he's speaking treason, burst out: "I think Her Majesty treats you shamefully! As though you were a s-servant, not a prince! She doesn't seem to realize what you could do with your powers to—"

"Enough." I stared severely at him, and he winced but bravely didn't look away. "I do *not* use my magic for harm. Is that understood?"

"I—I didn't mean—"

"And I trust you haven't been talking like this to anyone else?"

"No, my prince! Never!"

Unspoken was, *I'd never be such a fool!* A true courtier already, I mused, even if he was only . . . "What age are you now? Ten? Eleven?"

He straightened indignantly. "Nearly twelve, Your Highness."

"Ah. Pardon me, Master Arn." I fought not to smile. "I'm not mocking you, lad, really I'm not. And I do thank you for your concern. But now, I would be alone."

"As you will, my prince."

And even the hair falling once more into his eyes didn't spoil the dignity of his bow.

Once the boy was gone, I glanced at the fireplace. The magic-consumed parchment was nothing more than ash by then, but it began to glow a sullen orange as I murmured:

"Enough games, Clarissa. I must speak with you, and by *y Duwis glân*, I will."

And so it was that I set a summoning spell upon my brother's wife.

CHAPTER XV

BATTLE ROYAL

Now, I had carefully chosen both the time and the place of our meeting. *Och*, yes! Since castle folk were already gossiping about us, I certainly didn't want anyone thinking I was after the queen's honor or soul!

So it was innocent afternoon when a bemused Clarissa, her pale face softly flushed, her blue eyes dreamy, wandered gently towards me. The room into which she wandered was one of the smaller audience chambers, the same that Estmere often used for meeting with his advisors, private enough for a conversation but near enough to guards so that she wouldn't feel threatened.

I had learned at least some caution at court.

Which didn't reassure Clarissa in the least when I broke the thread of the summoning spell (which had been slight enough, no more than a focusing of will on a piece of fabric torn from one of her gowns), and she blinked and stared and slowly came to realize what had happened.

"Oh . . . oh my God, you've bewitched me!"

"Nothing more than a harmless—"

"How dare you!" The sudden ferocity took me aback.

I stared foolishly at the bright spots of color on the pale cheeks, at the brilliant, blazing eyes as she cried, "How dare you try your foul sorcery—"

"Clarissa, please. Listen to me."

"And if I don't? What loathsome spell will you work this time? Well? Tell me!"

"No spell." I paused, searching for the right words—hastily, before she could open her mouth again. "Look you, I admit I was a bit dramatic. And if I've offended you, pray forgive me. But I just couldn't think of any other way to speak with you. And speak we must."

"I think not! I—"

"Why do you hate me so much?"

That took her by surprise. She glared at me with eyes like bright blue ice. But there was more than a hint of fear beneath the ice, and I sighed and said, "No more enchantments. I promise."

"The word of a sorcerer!"

"The word of your husband's brother. Estmere is my closest kin. I love him. I want to see him happy. And I certainly don't want his wife as my enemy!"

Her eyes narrowed warily. "Oh, no. Such naivete may work on Estmere, not on me."

Naivete. I studied the woman, *feeling* in her such a turbulent mixture of emotions it fairly staggered me: the anger and confusion and insecurity of a pampered young woman thrown into a situation beyond her training. She fairly seethed with fury and fear and—

"Jealousy!" I said aloud, and Clarissa looked at me as though I'd gone mad. "I should have realized— You don't have to be jealous of me."

"Don't I? When all I hear from Estmere is 'Aidan this' and 'Aidan that'—"

She broke off abruptly, having plainly said more than she had intended, and I murmured, "It's more than simple jealousy, isn't it?"

"Oh most clever sorcerer! What, can't you read minds?"

Why *do* the magickless always focus on that? "No," I

told her wearily. "Only emotions and the like. What would you tell me?"

"Nothing."

"Come, Clarissa, what would you tell me?"

For a stubborn moment more she was silent. Then all at once she burst out with, "Very well, there's this: the good Lord willing, I shall bear Estmere a son some day, a fine, strong son to be king after him. And, the good Lord willing, all our futures shall be bright. But—they can't be bright, not while your dark menace looms over us!"

"Menace!" I echoed, astonished. "*Me?* That's the most ridiculous—look you, I do have some royal blood in my veins. But—*Gallu!* The last thing I want is the burden of a crown!"

"I find that very difficult to believe."

"It's the truth. I would no more think of hurting Estmere or you or any child you might bear than I would—"

"Then why come all the way to court?"

I grit my teeth. "I went through all this with Estmere over a year ago. Ask him."

"I did. He evaded me with smooth words! If your motives are so pure, tell me why you came here."

"I came to be my brother's friend."

"A sorcerer? A sorcerer who—"

"*Damnio chwi, will* you listen to me?" I stopped short. "Forgive me. I didn't mean to say that."

"Didn't you?" Genuine terror blazed up in her eyes, terror of me, of my magic, of everything that didn't fit into her neat, predictable, civilized world, and I watched her cover it as best she could with rage. "*Damnio* means 'damn' in Anglic, doesn't it? The sound is close enough. You really would like to see me damned, wouldn't you? Damned and dead and out of your way!"

"No! Hush now, *chwaer*, sister, people will hear—"

"All they'll hear is the truth! You want me dead!"

"Stop that!" I snapped. "You're a queen. Stop acting like a child."

That got to her. With a stifled sob she fell silent. For

some time we stood staring at each other. And a fire would have frozen beneath the chill hatred in her eyes. Then suddenly Clarissa gave a long, shuddering sigh.

"All right. No more shouting. Just this, sorcerer: I will not let you interfere with my life. I will not let you interfere with my marriage. Do you understand me? There is no place for you here, sorcerer, king's bastard though you be. *I will not have you here!*"

"Why, you ignorant, close-minded little—"

No!

Horrified, I *felt* wildfire blazing up within me and remembered the parchment bursting into flame. The first thing any wielder of Power must learn is that he must never, never lose control over himself, yet I had already hurt Arn, and now I was all aching to strike—

Duwies, no!

Furious and very much afraid of my fury, I turned and fled, leaving Clarissa to think what she would. Taking the first refuge I could find, I dove into the opening of a stairway (servants scuttling out of my way, aghast), and burned out my anger in climbing up and up the spiral till it ended at the small, flat, crenelated top of one of the taller palace towers. No one else was up on this high, windy space, and I let myself pant freely, leaning on the crenelations, a little dizzy from the height and my narrow perch, and by that point as angry with myself as with Clarissa.

You hurtyn*! You idiot who call yourself a magician, yet can't even deal with a silly little girl who—*

But thoughts of Clarissa were still too dangerous. Not wanting at all to be surprised by some patrolling guard, not while I was in such a foul mood, I set an Avoidance on the tower top, the simplest of things, barely a spell at all, akin to the way a deer misdirects attention from itself by just being part of its surroundings.

At least you're good for that*!* I snapped at myself, staring broodingly out over the city and the fertile fields beyond.

Was *this* what my mother had meant when she'd seen

a strange and wondrous destiny for me? Was I to end
up wasting my magic on spoiled little girls and small-
minded courtiers? Was this—this *pettiness* all I was ever
going to achieve?

Och, well, the slow afternoon passed in such bitter
nonsense. As the day faded slowly into twilight, the sunset blazed up all around me, so mightily red and golden,
so much bigger than anything merely human, that it
jarred me back to myself. All at once I was thoroughly
sick of anger and self-pity both. I would go back down
and see if there wasn't some way I could weave things
back together with Clarissa. Much as I didn't want it.

But without warning the *feel* of magic, sharp, fierce,
alien magic, was enfolding me: Tairyn! His image was
wavering and unsure there in the air before me, but that
he could manage any sending at all, with me not in
receptive trance and the sun not yet below the horizon,
hinted at such incredible Power that a chill little shiver
prickled up my spine.

"Not now," I groaned before I could stop myself. "I
haven't time for Faerie right now."

"Unfortunate." It could not have been said with more
scorn. "Remember your vow."

It took me a startled moment to realize Tairyn had to
mean the one I'd sworn to him so long ago. What, exactly,
had I said? *To come when they have need of me*— "No,"
I said, "*och*, no. I can't. Tairyn, I'm sorry, but this really
isn't a very good time to—"

"A child has died." For the first time since I'd met
him, emotion echoed in Tairyn's voice: clear, sharp pain.
"One of my subjects has been slain, yet I could do nothing." The slanted green eyes, the clearest part of the
image, stared at me with such bitter anguish I couldn't
meet their gaze. "Do you think I would come to you, to
a human, for aid if I had any choice?"

What would I say? A child slain ... Sorrow enough
for humans, but I knew how fiercely the children of
mostly infertile Faerie were loved. The anguish blazing
from the Faerie Lord's eyes burned at me.

Vows within vows ... I thought uneasily, and asked, as politely as I could, "You will return me to this place and time when we are done?"

He dipped his head in the curtest nod. "My word on it."

Bound by my vow to him, I could do nothing else after that but say, "I will come. But how—"

"Call." With that, Tairyn's image flickered and was gone. *"Call,"* one last mind whisper told me.

Call. Call for what? Couldn't Tairyn do *anything* without mystery? What manner of ride had he arranged for me?

But before I did any riding at all, I detoured hastily down to the kitchen for a flask of water and a rider's carrying bag of food—dried meat, dried fruit, lightweight, nourishing and durable. Tairyn might need me right now, but that didn't mean I could trust him; I was *not* going to risk being ensorcelled by Faerie food or drink. Just in case, I also stopped in my chambers long enough to snatch up my Faerie sword and belt it about my waist. But you didn't keep an Otherly being waiting, so I raced down from my tower and back up the winding stairs to the other tower's flat roof, where I stood panting and wondering.

Call, Tairyn had said, and call, once I had the breath, I did, trying not to mind that I had no idea what I might be summoning.

And something came, great-winged and huge against the fading sunset.

"Gallu ..."

Tairyn had sent me a griffin. *Och,* yes, most folks think such creatures only fable. But there wasn't any doubt that the beast coming to a nervous, beak-clashing landing was real. I could see it, hear it, smell it as it perched with delicate unease on the tower's narrow crenelation, all four feet together like a cat.

For a time I did nothing sensible at all, staring like any magickless boy in open-mouthed wonder. Childhood memory awoke, reminding me that for all their fantastic appearance, griffins are perfectly real, if exquisitely rare, animals. They're found more often in Faerie than in our mundane realm, but they can cross over easily enough if permitted; being true beasts, they're not bothered by mortal air or sunlight.

Which was presumably why Tairyn had sent this one. Of course, being Tairyn, he'd never deigned to see if the beast was tame; that, I could almost hear his cold voice say, was my problem.

A problem I'd better start solving. The griffin, a young male in the first flush of adult strength, was showing every sign of wanting to be up and away from this place that reeked of humanity.

"Gently, my lovely one," I crooned to him in the Faerie tongue. "I mean you no harm. Come, sniff my hand."

I was prepared to snatch it back to safely if the griffin showed any hunger for human fingers. But the beast must have scented the magic within me, for in the next moment he stepped with elegant care off the crenelation to stand beside me, just barely fitting in that narrow space. Crowded up against me, the warm, furry, not-quite-cat, not-quite-bird smell of him all around me, he let me scratch behind his tufted ears while he kept up a rumbling purr, and I smiled.

"You're a fine, handsome fellow," I told him, while the griffin returned the favor by nibbling gently up and down my arm. He *was* handsome, not that awkward merging of eagle and lion so fancied by artists, but a beautifully designed creature in and of himself, sleek and lean, yellow eyes fierce, the smooth, dusty-smelling feathers and short, rough fur a tawny gold, the beautiful wings wide and strongly muscled.

Strong enough to bear us both with ease.

I slipped warily up onto the warm, tawny back, locking my legs around the base of his wings, trying not to think about the deadly power of that hooked, predatory beak. The griffin gave a little murmur of unease, sidling like a nervous horse. I felt his muscles tense beneath me, and held my breath, because there wasn't any room for me to throw myself aside.

But after that first, nervous move, the griffin made no attempt to toss me off, and as I stroked the sleek neck and crooned to him, he gradually relaxed, accepting my weight.

"So now. Come, my friend, Tairyn awaits us."

I felt the powerful hindquarters bunch as the griffin pushed off against the crenelation. And then we were airborne, the griffin spiraling up and up into the clear evening air. He was clumsy at first, adjusting to my unfamiliar weight, then graceful as any eagle as he caught the wind, sporting and playing in the sky, responding to my delight, glorying in his young pride and strength. I watched the great royal castle dwindle beneath me into a gray-walled, lead-roofed toy left out in the night, set by a river no wider than a dark, glinting ribbon. Lundinia was spread out before me, what I could see of houses and streets and bridges in the darkness looking like some perfect miniatures from a craftsman's fancy.

Can they see us down there? There might be just enough light left in the sky. What must they be thinking?

I already knew what the guards on the palace ramparts were thinking: they *had* seen us, and we'd left them all busily crossing themselves. What of it? They knew what I was.

I hoped the griffin knew where he was going; I certainly didn't. We swept out over the city walls, riding the wind, over a rich blackness that I knew hid fields and hills. I crouched low over the tawny neck, wind whipping at hair and clothes, the first stars above us, hearing the steady beat of yellow wings as the griffin caught and discarded this current and that, then feeling those wings straighten as he found a wind to his liking, soaring down the sky in a long, silent, glorious glide.

And without warning, we flew right through a suddenly glittering Gateway, a shimmering blaze of magic, and left the human world behind.

CHAPTER XVI

THE OUTSIDER

We came out through that magical Gateway into glory.

How to describe Faerie to those who will almost surely never see it? It was true, just as stories claimed, that no sun shone in the deep blue sky. But I barely noticed the lack, for all around us was color, as though all the realm had been painted in the very first, the Primal, colors, yet untouched by time, glowing with their own wild sense of being. The sky, the ground, the very air blazed with magic, more than my merely human self could ever hope to control, and it was a fortunate thing the griffin took that moment to land lightly in a tiny, forest-girded meadow because otherwise I think I would have fallen dizzily from his back. As it was, my dismount could hardly have been called graceful, and I clung frantically to his warm golden side as though I was drunk.

And still the magic that was Faerie beat at me, demanding to be drawn into my being, to be used, to overwhelm and kill my human mind. . . .

Hastily I slammed shut every mental barrier I knew, silently reciting Discipline after calming Discipline until, with a strange, almost physical *snap*, the pressure on me was gone.

The land had accepted me. At least as much as it would accept any human magician.

Well, thank you, I thought wryly.

At any other time I would have loved to explore the glowingly green forest around me (yes and, very gingerly, the magic it held, too). The trees were sturdy, graceful things, intriguingly not quite those I knew, and their leaves were starred with flowers like bright, living gems. The underbrush seemed to consist mostly of sleek, dark green ivy, again not quite like any plant I could name, each leaf outlined in palest silver. The whole smelled like a good, healthy forest, though there were strange, sweet or spicy undertones I couldn't place. Nor could I put a name to the birds that were singing so lustily all about me, their voices like so many silver flutes.

Lovely, yes. But none of this is telling me why it was so urgent I come here.

"Where *is* everybody?" I asked the griffin, in my heart meaning Ailanna, only she, because surely my love belonged in so enchanted a spot. "Where—"

"Here," a voice said suddenly.

I nearly knocked myself over spinning around to face: "Tairyn! *Gallu*, man, did you have to . . ."

But one didn't take that tone of voice to a Faerie Lord, most certainly not in his own realm, so I started again, more carefully, "What now? Where are we? And where, for that matter, are your people?"

Tairyn was clad in a silky tunic and hose, simple and elegant of cut, of so many subtle shades of green the eye couldn't trace them all; standing against a background of forest as he was, he was nigh invisible, save for the long, straight silvery hair and the fairness of his sharp, fierce, beautiful, face.

That face right now was unreadable as stone. "I shall not involve them. There is too great a peril."

Wonderful. Too great a peril for Faerie Folk, yet here he was summoning a human—

Wait, now. Tairyn was hardly the sort to do anything at random. What could possibly imperil someone of Faerie yet not harm a human? No danger from sunlight, not in this sunless place . . . but there was still . . .

"Iron," I said very softly, and saw the faintest of flickers in the cool green eyes. "That's it, isn't it? Someone has brought iron into your realm."

Tairyn remained still as stone, plainly waiting for me to puzzle things out for myself.

"But *how*?" I exploded. "This doesn't make sense! Only humans can safely make use of iron, yet no human could find a way here, let alone survive in this realm without your permission. And no one of Faerie would be crazed enough to try handling something that could slay with the merest scratch—" I stopped short, staring at Tairyn, my mind racing.

"Crazed . . ." I murmured. "Of course. Whoever is trying to work with iron in this realm is no longer sane."

The Faerie Lord stirred at last. "No."

"Ha, you didn't want to admit it, did you? It hurts to realize one of your superior race can go just as mad as one of my poor little mortal kind!"

"It hurts," Tairyn corrected coldly, "to realize a child has died."

I winced. "It does, indeed. So be it, Tairyn. Which way?"

"I cannot tell you."

"What?"

"I am not being petty, human! If I use the smallest bit of my Powers to trace the *shataliach*, the . . . mad one, that one will know I am on the hunt."

So there's a Faerie word for madness, eh? Means such isn't as rare as you'd like, my haughty Tairyn! Of course I didn't say any of that aloud, only mused, "But he, she, whatever, would neither expect nor have a way of picking up my alien aura?"

"Exactly."

Suddenly I ached to shake that icy calm of his. "*Och*, Tairyn, you expect wonders from me! Look you, I'm truly sorry for the poor child and its parents. But just a short time I was thick in the middle of human affairs, and suddenly, *wham*, here I am in your realm instead, expected to turn from courtier to hunting hound without the slightest hint of a track."

That didn't move him? Of course not. Tairyn hadn't any comprehension of human pity or human confusion. I sighed at the sight of that fair, cold, impassive face and asked in surrender, "Can you at least show me where the poor little one died?"

Tairyn dipped his head. "Follow."

He dismissed the griffin with an absent wave of his hand. I'll admit it wasn't without a qualm that I watched the beast obediently soar away. Now I was completely dependent on Tairyn if ever I wished to find the way home again.

If the thought had occurred to him as well, he didn't show it.

Far to my left I could see an intriguing hint of soaring towers looking for all the world as though they had been carved from ice or crystal. Tairyn's palace? I started to ask, but he never even glanced that way. Moving with a wild animal grace that barely stirred a leaf (and yes, roused my envy), he led me straight ahead into a small, pretty grove. Seeing the bright, luscious-looking red berries clustered on every bush, I could understand what might have lured a child so far from everyone else.

Ahh, but there, there was the spot where the child— the boy, I sensed that now—had been struck down. The grass was burned black from the touch of iron, and my heart began racing in sympathetic panic as I *felt* the echoes of fear and pain still shivering in the air. Although I wanted nothing to do with the place, I forced myself to kneel and touch the ground where the small body must have lain—

And shot back to my feet. "He's not dead!"

"Impossible."

"I'm telling you, Tairyn, the boy is not dead!"

"But—that—this is ridiculous. I saw the body myself."

"Look for yourself!"

I gestured to the small, charred spot. Tairyn took one small step forward, then stopped, fair skin gone even paler. "I . . . cannot," he murmured through clenched teeth, and I realized that even the residue of iron was strong enough to sicken one of Faerie-kind. And an idea struck me.

"I wonder, now," I began carefully, *"did* you see the body?"

"What are you—"

"Look you, the death was supposed to be from iron, yes?"

"Yes," Tairyn repeated flatly.

"And the very thought of such a death horrifies you."

"Of course it does, human!" For an instant, his Faerie calm was shattered, for an instant I saw true terror blaze from him. Then Tairyn slid quickly back into his imitation of stone. But I could still sense the fear hiding behind that smooth surface.

"I don't blame you for your terror," I murmured. "Ailanna's told me what an agonizing death iron-poisoning is: cruelest, perhaps, in that there's no hope, no way to cure it."

Too late, I remembered how dangerous it is to speak too knowledgeably of Faerie ways. Very much aware of Tairyn's sudden predatory tenseness, I knew I didn't dare show my sudden alarm. So instead I snapped as sternly as I could, *"Och,* don't give me that menacing stare! I'm not your enemy, man! I won't go spreading word throughout the human realms!"

"No."

That could have meant a world of things, but I took it as acceptance and hurried on, "Those of your people who handled the corpse would have needed to be very wary, lest the smallest shard of iron be on the body to scratch them as well. They would have been too fearful to look too closely. *Will* you stop staring at me? I am *not* insulting your people's courage!"

"But you are saying we were fooled."

"Well? Isn't it possible?"

A human might have hesitated, quibbling over this or that. The Faerie Lord, incapable of falsehood, said only, "Yes. The body might have been nothing more than a seeming."

"And of course not even the boy's mother would have known the truth. I'm sure that for safety's sake she would have been kept from even touching her iron-slain son, no matter how great her grief."

"Yes," Tairyn repeated, and to my immense relief, I saw that he was suddenly accepting what I was trying to tell him. His eyes kindled into cold green flame, so cruelly alien in that moment I didn't dare meet their gaze. "Come," he said shortly. "Let us find this iron-wielding *shataliach*, this stealer away of children."

Of course. Easily said. I'd just put my nose to the ground like the hound he seemed to think me and scent out the track.

But my sarcasm, fortunately, was silent. Because as it turned out there really *was* a track: iron is so very alien to Faerie that its use had disturbed the very essence of the land, leaving a trail like the faintest line of heat that cut through the forest and air alike. I set out in wary pursuit, Tairyn silent at my side; if the echo of iron bothered him, he showed not the slightest sign. Neither of us dared use any spells by this point, lest even my "alien" human magics alert whoever was holding the child captive, but I kept my hand curved about the hilt of my sword, wondering if this would be the first time I'd use it in combat, not sure if that idea thrilled or alarmed me.

If I'd had any doubt the one we sought was crazed, I lost that doubt when we came upon the cave. Or rather, when we came upon where the cave had been. Right now, it was hidden beneath such an insane tangle of clashing concealment spells—each one threatening to cancel the next—that only the truly magic blind could have missed it.

"Crazed, indeed," I murmured.

Tairyn nodded curtly, hunter tense. "But how do we

get past all ... that without alerting the *shataliach* of our presence?"

How, indeed? I took a wary step forward—

And the small, furry brown earth sprite that had been huddling, unnoticed amid all the chaotic magic, right by my feet, took fright. Leaping up with a shrill little shriek I nearly echoed, it darted off like a terrified cat, knocking my sword askew, tripping me. I fell headlong, crashing through the concealment spells like any clumsy lout.

Time seemed to stretch. As I lay sprawled on the floor of the cave, I saw that there before me was the one we sought—*och*, no doubt about that! If the concealment spells had been bizarre, the aura of distorted, crazed magic swirling here was a hundredfold stronger, jarring as a flood of garish hues and discordant sound, a stunning impact on every psychic nerve. And through it all, sharp, ugly, *wrong*, was the cold chill that was iron.

The *shataliach* was a woman, kneeling on the cold earthen floor as though feeling nothing of its chill. She was wildly disheveled, her soft blue gown soiled and torn, her silvery hair a tangled cloud, but the ghost of her Faerie beauty still clung forlornly to her.

Ghost, indeed. To my horror, I realized that what glittered in her green, mad eyes and shimmered on her fair, empty face was something alien to humanity and Faerie-kind alike.

Cythraul. In the Anglic tongue: demon.

No, not the banal, forked tail figure out of Anglic tales. *Cythrauliad*, demons, are real enough, entities of a very different realm, whether *Uffern* or some other place of endless evil I cannot say. *Cythrauliad* are cruel, empty creatures full of empty, empty hate for anything that lives, anything that knows love or joy, the things no demon ever can know.

This was, mercifully, but a smaller demon, its powers chaotic and confused: where a greater Evil would have instantly reacted in enmity to my magic of the Righthand Path, the thing was barely even aware of me. How the woman had ever summoned it, I have no way of knowing. But *why* she summoned it, let it possess her—

"Lalathanai." From the way Tairyn said it, I knew it to be the woman's name. "Her own son died."

There was no pity in his voice, of course; being of Faerie, he could know none. But there was a hint of regret for a young life lost.

Yes, and now crazed Lalathanai was very plainly trying anything she might to bring her son back to her. Even if it meant slipping into human realms to steal away an iron knife, so cold and deadly to her kind it, in turn, stole away the last of her sanity.

Even if it meant risking demonic possession.

Even if it meant murdering another child.

Lalathanai, or what was left of her, didn't seem to notice us. She continued to croon softly to the knife, to the child who lay drugged or entranced on the floor before her. With that insane swirl of magic filling the cave I had no way of telling if she really was working an incantation, but when she raised the knife for a killing blow it didn't really matter. No time to draw my sword: I hurled myself forward from my knees with all my might. We crashed to the cave floor together, Lalathanai beneath me—

For the moment. Wild with demonic strength and her own madness, she wrenched herself free, hissing, the sound somehow more terrible than any honest scream, stabbing at me with the knife. Struggling to my knees again, I caught her wrist in both hands just in time, trying to make her drop the thing, and she bit me, hard enough to make me gasp. Her terrible, demon-haunted eyes blazed into my own, and for one dizzying moment my arms lost their strength. . . .

Lalathanai twisted free again, leaping to her feet, lunging—

Tairyn's coolly thrown rock hit her cleanly on the side of the head. The iron knife went flying from her hand, but to my horror, Lalathanai never even staggered. Even though her face was now awash with blood, she raced silently for the weapon.

I got there first. As my hand closed about the hilt, Lalathanai threw herself at me. And I—I gave her the only mercy I could.

As the iron knife pierced her heart, I heard the *cythraul* flee, silently wailing its psychic pain. The madness fled with it. Lalathanai, or what was left of her essence, smiled at me, silently blessing me with peaceful, grateful eyes even as the life faded from her. I lowered her lifeless body to the cave floor, wondering numbly if I should say some manner of prayer.

As I hesitated, aching with pity, wishing her healing in whatever afterlife her spirit might find, Tairyn was waking the ensorcelled child. "Take the knife," he told me, but the coldness in his voice was countered by the gentle curve of his arm and hand around the whimpering boy who clung to him. "It cannot remain in this realm."

No, it couldn't. Healer that I am, I'm hardly squeamish at the sight of blood. But this ... I couldn't look at the knife. Instead, I wrapped it hastily in a scrap torn from my tunic and stuck it into my belt.

Tairyn was staring at me. If I'd expected some miraculous thawing of how he felt towards me, I'd been mistaken. Helpful or not, his glance told me, I was still human. Alien. Inferior.

Why, you cold-blooded, unpleasant—

"You rescued a child," the Faerie Lord said, stopping my almost certainly suicidal words just in time. "A child shall rescue you."

"Now what might *that* mean?"

"Exactly what I said." Tairyn's eyes glittered. "You are a hero. You rescued a child and freed a haunted spirit. Name your reward."

"I didn't do this for reward!"

"I am not accusing you. Name your reward."

"Ailanna—"

"Is not here. She chose to remain in your mortal realm

and wait for your return." Tairyn didn't even try to hide his disapproval. "Name your reward."

"All right, then, lift that *damniol* secrecy spell from me so I can tell my brother about her."

"No. My people and I are not for humans to discuss. Come, I am lord of my lands, and my lands are hardly poor. Name what of my riches you would have."

I grinned in sudden fierce suspicion. "And have you bind me to you forever as your slave through whatever I took from you? No, my lord, I think not."

He gave not the slightest sign, but I knew I'd guessed aright: it really *had* been a trap. "So be it," Tairyn said shortly. "The griffin waits without. Mount and return to your realm."

"To my proper place in it? And my proper time?"

That stung him. "So I have already promised. I am not human, to renege my sworn word. Go."

Fuming at his arrogance, I went, knowing even as I did that anger was useless: he was as he was, truly of Faerie as I was not.

Ailanna, Ailanna, thankful I am of your human blood!

My one regret as I flung myself astride the griffin was that I wasn't going to get a clear look at that mysterious, exquisite palace or see the boy's parents' joy when he was returned to them. But then, as the griffin launched himself back through the glittering, magical Gateway, I had to laugh at my foolishness. To enter Tairyn's palace—after he'd already tried to snare me—would be walking all wide-eyed and innocent into bondage. Did I really want to risk the very freedom I'd just saved?

"No, indeed no!" I told the griffin, who cocked a furry ear back to catch my voice. "Being free, my friend, is worth more than all the palaces that were ever built! Now come, let us fly!"

CHAPTER XVII

STORM WINDS

We emerged from the Gateway into a blaze of early morning sunshine. It had been night, of course, when we'd left, and for one terrified moment, surrounded by this unexpected light, I thought sure we were lost in time and space.

But no. My magician's senses told me without a doubt this was indeed my own true realm. Regardless of what the Faerie lord had so haughtily assured me, some time *had* passed in mortal lands—but those senses also told me it had been less than a half day, hardly worth worrying over. Besides, it was wonderfully satisfying to realize Tairyn wasn't perfect, after all!

My mind was still half-stunned by the change from realm to realm, half tangled in thoughts of Faerie, and of what I had done. In a sudden surge of disgust, I pulled the deadly knife from my belt and let it fall down and down to land harmlessly in forest. There let it stay, and there let it rust!

Where now? My brother's palace? After all that wild, eerie, wonderful magic, I couldn't bear returning to the world of walls and politics, not yet! Besides, the day looked to be so fine and clear, a perfect day for flight. Ha, yes, this time I could actually see the rich green tapestry of forest and fields so far below us!

I could, indeed. For a sickening moment my head swam at being up so high and my stomach lurched at the thought that nothing stood between me and down there but the whim of a hardly predictable animal.

But the griffin seemed to be bearing my weight with ease and enjoying himself as he did. In the next moment I caught my bearings and balance, and began enjoying myself as well, laughing with delight at the sight of farmhouses and villages reduced to the size of perfect toys. Crouching low over the griffin's tawny neck, I felt the wind whip coldly at hair and clothes, heard it whistle in my ears, nearly drowning out the sound of steadily beating wings. Then once again the griffin found a wind he liked and soared smoothly, gloriously down the sky, faster and faster yet. *Och*, wonderful! Wind-drunk, flight-drunk, freedom-drunk, I know I laughed, and I think I sang.

"Ah, Ailanna! If only you were here to share this with me! If only I was with you!"

Why not? Why not fly straight and straight for the West Country?

Alas, no. If I disappeared from Estmere's court, he would certainly worry (even if his wife exulted) and waste precious hours hunting me. Besides, the griffin might be as incredibly strong as all his breed, but he was still only mortal flesh and blood. He would need to rest, to feed. He would never be able to fly so far and back in only a single day.

But this was too glorious a morning for regret. "Where shall we go, my friend?" I asked, and saw the tufted ears tilt back again to catch my voice. "East? I've never seen the Eastern Sea, and we're not all that far from it now. Come, friend griffin, eastward, and let nothing stop us!"

I really must have been flight-drunk to tempt Fate like that. We hadn't flown very far before dark clouds came boiling up on the southern horizon. A fierce, cold wind came with them, making the griffin struggle in the air.

"But there wasn't the slightest hint of a storm brewing!" I protested to him. "It's as though it were . . ." My voice trailed into silence. There was a *feel* to that growing wind, a certain familiar sharpness— "Aie, yes! As though it were conjured!"

Conjured, indeed. That wild plunge through the Gateway into Faerie would have been a blaze of magic to anyone with *sight*—and *sight* a certain foe most certainly possessed: the sorcerer of the *anfoniad* wasn't dead after all. He obviously hadn't forgotten me, and the hours from my disappearance to my return would have given him time enough to prepare.

And here we were, offering him a perfect target!

"Down, friend griffin, down! Hurry, *down!*"

I said that in Cymraeth, Anglic, Faerie. I said it with increasing frenzy, but the griffin didn't heed me. Ears flat with terror, he seemed determined to outrace the storm.

Impossible. A great wall of cloud boiled up with horrifying speed. As it loomed over us like some demonic thing savoring its prey, I frantically searched my brain for a spell, any spell, to dissolve it. But it was all happening too swiftly, I was still too dizzy from the effects of Faerie!

And then it was too late. We were engulfed in chill, eerie darkness and wind struck us such a blow the griffin was thrown sideways in the air, wings beating frantically. I clung to him with all my might, blinded by the darkness, buffeted again and again by wind that hit with force enough to tear the very air from my lungs. Helpless, gasping, shivering convulsively beneath the waves of cold and wet, I could do nothing *but* cling to the griffin and pray he could keep himself aloft.

We were driven far that day, though, trapped as we were in that savage, roiling gray-blackness, with never a glimpse of land, I had no way of knowing just how far. I was rapidly passing the point of caring. Dimly I wondered how I could be growing numb and yet ache in every muscle at the same time. It would be so wonderful just to let go. . . .

No! That would mean my death!

In the next moment it didn't matter. The poor, weary griffin gave one fierce, despairing cry, twisting wildly in the air. I felt myself slipping from the rain-slick back, numbed fingers grabbing frantically at a non-existent mane—

And then I was falling.

As I plummeted down through fierce, swirling layers of storm, wind roaring in my ears, sheer panic blazed through me, the mindless panic that is a primal shout: *I will not die!* Without time to think, *This won't work*, I cast that one spell I'd never been able to master—

And I shape-changed.

It wasn't easy. *Och fi*, it hurt almost worse than the death I was trying to escape! But, transformed to a great winged bird-thing, I managed to slow the swiftness of my fall, and struggled safely down to earth, landing with a thump.

There I let the bird form fade, convulsing in anguish as I regained my rightful shape. The pain fled as swiftly as it had come, and I collapsed on the nice, wet, solid earth. All about me the storm raged on for a time, until the magic binding it dispelled and let it fade.

I faded for a time, too.

Silence roused me. Silence, and cold. Shivering, I got to my unsteady feet, aching in every joint and brushing off mud as best I could, to find that the fickle lady Estmere calls Dame Fortune had dropped my clothing and sword, discarded in the frantic shape-change, almost at my feet. Gratefully I dressed, wondering where in the name of all the Powers I had been dropped. There was little enough light to see by: though the storm clouds had all but completely dispersed with the swiftness of completed sorcery, it was late twilight by this point, with a rather unpleasant blue-grey glow to everything.

Not that there was much to see: a straggly forest, some fiercely thorned bushes of a kind unknown to me, and a good deal of bare, reddish earth. These were never Estmere's lands. During all the excitement, I had thought I'd felt the storm winds slue about from south to north. Could they have brought me all the way into one of the harsh southern kingdoms?

That wasn't a comforting thought. I could remember with painful clarity my brother saying:

"... *the ancient kingdoms of Brecara, Astarrica and Telesse, which are not our allies.*"

Wonderful. While at Estmere's court, I had amused myself with learning the language held in common by those three lands, finding it a relatively simple thing after the convoluted Faerie tongue, but I wasn't exactly eager to test that learning. And wouldn't one of the lands' rulers love to get his hands on King Estmere's brother? What a wonderful bargaining tool I would make—assuming he even let me live.

And what of the sorcerer? Apparently I'd eluded him by escaping his storm in bird form, but I didn't doubt he would be searching for me.

Ah, and where was the griffin? I hoped the poor beast had survived the storm, but he was nowhere to be seen, and I dared not reveal my presence by attempting to call him.

There was still another problem: no one at Estmere's court knew where I'd gone. That meant, of course, no one would know where to search for me.

So be it, I thought wryly. *It's up to me to rescue myself. Just a few small problems, nothing to worry me. Ha.*

Damp clothes clinging to me, I climbed the tallest of the crooked trees, overtaxed muscles complaining all the way up, to see what I could find. There on the horizon was a city. I could just make out its high surrounding wall and some red-tiled rooftops from here, and glowering over the whole thing a castle grim as any war fortress. It all looked picturesque in the fading light, peaceful as a city in a tapestry, and perfectly normal.

And, with some unnamed psychic sense, I feared it.

If that isn't the sorcerer's home, I'll be very surprised.

But there was something else about the castle . . . For a time I let my mind search after that disturbing trace of . . . of what? I was still weary and sore, and at last I had to give up, unsure of what was bothering me, knowing only that I should get as far away from that castle as possible.

So I scrambled down from my prickly perch and set out into the forest. That wasn't such a pleasant choice, either. The air was warm enough; there was no danger of catching a chill from my rapidly drying clothes and hair. But . . .

It was a forest hushed as though turned to stone, with never the twittering of a bird or the rustling of a leaf to give relief from the ear-hurting silence. The trees were still alive, yes, but all the energies of life seemed to have been sapped from them. There was none of the familiar crackling of last year's leaves beneath my boots, only a soft, soft whisper, as though I walked on the powder of long dead vegetation. It all smelled not of normal decay, but like the heavy air of a room kept shut up too long.

And when I came to a pool, I shuddered because it, too, lay motionless, silent as water in a painting. Dead water.

Only one thing could have so destroyed the soul of a forest, and that was sorcery, and the worship of . . . that which I really wouldn't want to meet. A shiver raced through me as I remembered poor, demon-haunted Lalathanai. That had been such a small Evil, but it had still been strong enough to nearly slay me with that cursed knife. Despite my magic, I was still only human. Were I to run afoul of anything stronger—

No. I wasn't about to let myself think such self-destructive thoughts, not in this place. But there didn't seem to be much doubt that my sorcerer foe had been here, and that he came from that strangely sinister castle.

The last of the twilight had faded so gradually I hadn't been aware of it till all at once I realized I couldn't see where I was going, save by the use of Power. But using Power would be like lighting yet another magical beacon, letting all trained eyes know exactly where I was. Better to meekly and unmagically wait out the night right here. A little silence wasn't going to hurt me.

Bravado. As I sat on a half-rotted log, wondering if it would hold my weight, I could feel myself starting to shiver, and recognized that with a healer's knowledge as the edge of shock: too much had happened too swiftly. I opened my carrying bag and forced down a sliver or two of dried meat, though I wasn't really hungry (even though only *y Duwies* knew when I'd eaten last), savoring the salty taste of it, then drank a bit from my water flask. *Och*, but I was glad I'd had the foresight to take food and water with me! Particularly the water. Nothing on Earth was going to make me drink from that dead pool!

Time passed. The night deepened. I had begun to make myself as comfortable as possible amid all that unfriendly silence, my ears aching from the pressure of heavy stillness, when without warning the silence was broken.

Sobbing? I wondered uneasily. Was someone else in trouble in this desolate place? Or . . . was that the sound of a trap?

That last seemed all too likely. So I waited, trying to ignore the soft, unhappy sound, hoping it would stop. But it didn't stop, and of course it couldn't really be ignored. At last I got to my feet, knowing I had to find out who or what was weeping—or at least seeming to weep.

What I found, to my astonishment, was the last person anyone would sensibly expect in such a place: a boy out of Faerie. He was very young, even by human standards (though not as near to babe as the child Tairyn and I had saved), but there was no mistaking the grace of that small, slender form, or the long, silky flow of silvery hair.

"Boy," I said gently in the Faerie tongue, "what troubles you?"

He looked up with a startled gasp, brushing the tears from clear green eyes with a long-fingered hand, meeting my gaze with a glance all at once as cool and controlled as that of any adult of that self-possessed race. "It was only a moment's despair." His dialect was musical but odd to my ear; it hadn't occurred to me till that moment that there might *be* different Faerie dialects. "But why is a human who somewhat speaks our language wandering in these lands?"

The contempt behind that "somewhat" amused me. "You wouldn't happen to know someone named Tairyn, would you?" I asked drily. That earned me only a blank stare, so I continued, "I'm here through misfortune. And why were you in despair?"

For a moment I thought he was going to tell me to mind my own affairs. But then the cold green gaze wavered. Suddenly he was no more than a small, frightened boy. "This used to be a fair and pleasant place," he began, voice not quite steady. "So my mother and kinfolk told me. But . . ." He made a helpless little gesture. "Mortal time means nothing to us. We had no way of knowing what had happened here." The boy swallowed drily. "Human sorcery, human i-iron has taken the soul from these lands."

"I know."

"We cannot stand such places. We fled, back to Faerie. Or—or at least most of us did. My mother and I were confused by the Darkness here, and the echoes of iron. We lingered a bit too long. S-she was overcome by the deadness here. I was seeking water for her, because the Power in good, fresh water will revive her. But all the water here is dead, too!"

That last was a purely childish wail.

"Not all," I said, and showed him my flask. "Admittedly the water in here is warm by now, and tastes somewhat like leather, but it was gathered in cleaner places." I hesitated. "You're sure that all your mother needs to help her is water?"

The boy nodded, wide-eyed.

"Then give this to her with my goodwill."

He took the flask with almost reverent care, thanking me with radiant eyes. Then, before I could say aught else, he was gone more swiftly and silently than a fawn into the forest.

For some time I stood staring after the boy, feeling now painfully alone, wishing he had given me the chance to follow him. But of course the Faerie Folk don't think like humans; it hadn't even occurred to the boy that I might be in trouble, too.

So much, I thought cynically, for Tairyn's promise that as I rescued a child, a child would rescue me! Ah well, at least *someone* was going to benefit from all this.

Nothing to do now but wait till morning. Lapped round once more by silence like a thick, suffocating blanket, I summoned up calming Disciplines for mind and body. And I managed so nicely that I was soon asleep.

I awoke in wild panic, the stench of sorcery heavy in the air—and found myself ringed in by a circle of spears held by grim-faced warriors.

"Lay down your sword," one said in the language of the southern kingdoms, and only then did I realize I had drawn the blade, its runes blazing. "Lay down your sword," he repeated carefully, as though speaking to an idiot, "and come with us."

What good is a sword against spears? "Of course," I replied meekly, but my mind was racing, finding and rejecting spell after spell. Surely there must be something I could use to defend myself—ah.

As I bent as though to obey, I caught up a handful of earth, then hurled it aloft with a shouted Word: a simple charm, a child's toy. The earth whirled out and out in a net of air, and the warriors cried out as the dark, dusty cloud enveloped them. They struck about in their vain attempts to find me, and I dodged their wild flailings, snatched up my sword, and ran. That little trick, one of the first I had learned, had a duration of only a few moments, and even a Faerie sword wouldn't be of much use against thrown spears.

Suddenly the blade's runes blazed up with new brilliance. I skidded to a halt before a hooded figure. Too breathless for magic, I lunged, but the figure faded like smoke—my own invisibility illusion used against me—then reappeared at my side and struck me lightly on the head with a dark staff. A wild, wild dizziness surged through me. I know I cried out, furious at myself for having been snared so easily. . . .

But I remember no more.

CHAPTER XVIII

A ROYAL GUEST

It was a fine hall, the smooth stone walls all but hidden by rich rows of tapestries in muted reds, brightly lit by scores of candles in black iron holders. The style of furnishing was foreign to me, but impressive enough: massive chairs and chests carved of some dark, heavy wood. The floor was paved in dark red tile, without so much as a bunching of rushes to mar its expensive solemnity. A fine hall.

And it stank.

I don't mean literally. There was nothing offensive in the mingled scents of stone and candle wax and smoke. But the aura of that place, the soul of it if you will, was most oppressively stale and heavy. Sorcerous.

I most certainly did not want to be in that hall. But there wasn't much I could do about it, not with my arms bound behind me by chains enhanced with dark spells for which I knew no counterspell, not with those grim-eyed warriors on either side.

I tensed. There ahead of me was the one who could only be my sorcerous acquaintance, the man who'd spied on me in bird form, the man who'd sent that foul *anfoniad* to test or kill me. The man who, curse his soul, had captured me with one blow from his staff.

And . . . do you know, I almost laughed at the sight of him? Without the mystery of his hooded cloak, the sorcerer looked like nothing more impressive than some bone-weary, nervous, middle-aged merchant.

That's it! I realized. *He is a merchant!*

Sorcerer he was, yes, follower of the Lefthand Path without a doubt (which, of course, made us natural enemies), but he hadn't a shred of innate Power. He was, as my mother would have said, *llyfr-dwin*, only a book-sorcerer, limited to what he could cull from scrolls and grimoires. And even under the circumstances I couldn't help but feel a twinge of contempt. Granted, he had a fair amount of skill, summoning a storm and an *anfoniad*—but only someone without a true feeling for his craft would ever have made such dangerous mistakes as letting his mind be trapped within that *anfoniad*.

With a little jolt of surprise, I realized that the Sending hadn't been created from hatred or jealousy or anything else so dramatic. The man had merely been trying, like any good merchant, to sell his wares and please his patron—a patron he feared, judging by that harried face and those haunted, nervous eyes.

Now, who was his patron? Ah, of course. The merchant-like sorcerer stood beside a great throne carved of that somber black wood. And there, without a doubt, sat his lord and master, the king of these lands: a tall, lean young man, not at all unhandsome, with strong, clean features and glossy blue-black hair and beard. He was clad in rich royal robes of dull purple, a crown of iron set with purple stones on his brow.

And his dark eyes were those of a predator.

More about him I couldn't say just then; this king was certainly no sorcerer but, like Estmere, had learned enough to guard his inner self from a magician.

"Who is this you've brought before me?" he asked.

The sorcerer looked at his master in surprise. "Why, sire, this is King Estmere's own magician. Surely you—"

"Estmere's brother? The prince called Aidan ap Nia?"

"Why, yes—"

"And you dare treat royalty in so shameless a fashion? Bringing a prince before me bound like a common criminal— Release him at once!"

The uneasy sorcerer hurried to obey. As the magic-enhanced chains fell away from me (I refused to give the man the satisfaction of rubbing my sore arms), I heard the king say to me, "You must forgive my servant's boorishness, Prince Aidan."

"Of course." I wasn't quite as at home with the language as I had fancied back in Estmere's court, but at least I could understand it. "But I fear you have the advantage over me. You would seem to know my name, my title, but I have not . . . *do* not know yours."

"I am Bremor, King of Telesse, ruler of these lands onto which you have strayed."

"Believe me, King Bremor, it was never my . . ." Intent? No. Ah, I had it! "My intention to trespass. I—"

"No, no, Prince Aidan. No need for apologies." Was that mockery glinting in the hard eyes? As I wondered, he continued blandly, "In the past, our two kingdoms were often . . . less than friendly. But these are days of peace. Pray accept my hospitality."

It was not a request. I dipped my head in wary acknowledgement, but said nothing.

"But now, Prince Aidan, you must be weary from your unfortunately rough handling."

That was true enough, but I was hardly about to admit any weaknesses to him. He signalled to a servant, who took me from that hall. I glanced back just in time to see Bremor give a slow, secret, cruel smile.

The rooms I was assigned were spacious, almost elegant, though I was growing heartily sick of those depressing, seemingly inevitable dark wood furnishings. The clothing I was given was of fine quality, well befitting royalty. The servants were all efficient and quietly polite.

And, Bremor's fair words to the contrary, I didn't

doubt for a moment that I was meant to be a prisoner. That wasn't quite an alarming thought; a magician, as I've said before, is a difficult captive to keep, enemy magics or no. It was the sorcerous reek of the place that truly disturbed me, weighing down my mind.

There came a discreet cough. I turned a bit too sharply and found myself face to face with one of the servants, a dark-faced, aging man. We both recoiled, he startled, I in shock.

For ah, the dull despair I read in his eyes! Not even the lowliest of kitchen drudges in Estmere's castle, not even my little unwashed pot boy, bore such hopelessness as was in that man's heart. I turned to the other servants, magically alert now, and was sickened to *feel* the same death-in-life in them, as well.

Sorcery.

Not directly worked against common servants, of course not. But the residue, the unavoidable psychic miasma of Power misused, has a way of stealing into magickless, defenseless folk such as these, chilling their souls as surely as ever the mists from the fen chill men's bones.

But this was impossible! That merchant of a sorcerer could never have created such a backwash of Power.

"Your Highness?" one of the servants asked me uneasily.

"Your master," I said sharply. "Take me to him."

Enough was enough. One way or another, I meant to find out what King Bremor of Telesse was hiding behind his smiles.

King Bremor, sleek and elegant in his regal purple, was relaxing in a small, roofed courtyard, a pleasant place of bright mosaics and the splashing of fountains. But to my eyes, the sunlight flooding down from the high, narrow windows was dull and muted, almost like light seen through mist, and I wondered at it, uneasy.

Bremor glanced up as I entered and gave me a charming smile that might or might not have been genuine. At this close range I could see he was even younger than I had first thought, perhaps Estmere's age or my own. His eyes, as I had noted, were the hard eyes of the naturally cruel, but there was as well an ... oldness to them that had nothing to do with mere physical dissipation.

"Ah, Prince Aidan. Have you recovered from your ordeal?"

"*Och*, quite. King Bremor, am I your prisoner?"

He did a very pretty imitation of surprise. "Now why should you think that? You are said to be a magician. Surely no one can hold a magician prisoner."

"You evade my question very nicely."

"Come, have I offered you any threat? Done you any harm? No! I have offered you nothing but hospitality." He smiled blandly. "It is true, then, that you are a magician?"

I was trying my best to read the truth behind those odd, cold, weary eyes. But he, as though guessing my purpose, just would not meet my gaze squarely. So I answered flatly, "I have never denied it."

"Ah. Like Ybarre."

"Your sorcerer?" Did he mean it for the insult it was? "No. Not exactly."

"No," he agreed with smooth, subtle mockery. "So Ybarre has advised me."

I sighed. "King Bremor, I am no skilled fencer with words. Why was I brought here?"

Bremor smiled. *Curse him,* I thought, *he's playing a game with me. There's something about him he wants me to discover. But what?*

Then my eye was caught by the pendant he wore, a flat golden medallion on a thin golden chain. And as suddenly as that, I knew the truth.

"*Gallu nef.*" There was no way to hide the disgust in my voice. "And I thought that Ybarre was the only worshiper."

"Ah?"

"I should have realized. The darkness that ..." I was

frantically hunting for words, "that smothers this castle could only be caused by the corruption of its king."

"So-o!" Bremor raised an eyebrow. "I can see tact isn't one of your weaknesses."

As he spoke, his hand caressed the medallion, turning it to reveal the reverse. He could have spared himself the trouble: I already knew what must be there. Roughly engraved on the soft gold by Bremor's own hand, was a pentagram, that Powerful five-pointed star. But this wasn't the ancient symbol of Light, which is always drawn with point upward. This was that debased variant, point downward, which was so often flaunted by those who, for whatever obscene reason, worship Evil.

"But why?" I asked. "I can see Ybarre, that fool of a *llyfr-dewin*, being so desperate for *Gallu*, for Power, he might be snared. But you're a king! Why should you need such"—there was no way around the word—"Evil?"

Bremor looked at me as though I were mad. "For power, of course."

It took me a moment to realize he meant politics, not magic; in this language the word had no arcane connotation.

"Power," I repeated, and Bremor gave a short, humorless laugh.

"You don't understand, do you? Telesse is at the heart of it." He paused. "What, still no comprehension?" A hint of iron edged the suave, smooth voice. "You see, Telesse was once a mighty land, ruling over a true golden age—but you would surely know that."

I didn't, but I wasn't about to display my ignorance. Bremor must have taken my silence for passive agreement, rather than the battle to follow the language it really was, for he smiled thinly and continued, "Unfortunately, years of peace and plenty soften a people, bring stagnation to a land."

"Meaning?"

His eyes blazed. "Meaning I will not see this, my Telesse, decline into a land of peasants drowsing in the sun!"

How theatrical, I thought drily. *Is this your personal*

style, or are all your people so florid? But that was hardly the sort of thing I could ask him. When I didn't respond, Bremor continued, urbane once more:

"Unfortunately, no king can act without his people's support."

"Neither well nor for very long," I agreed, a little pleased at myself for managing even a slight quip in a foreign tongue, and received a sharp flash of those hard eyes.

"Clever. But alas, Prince Aidan, my people do tend to be"—he shrugged at the cliche—"sheep. Sheep content with their own little lots, unwilling to see the need to rouse themselves for their country. To die if need be."

He was throwing words at me too quickly for a mind still attuned to Anglic. And that overblown style wasn't helping. Not quite sure what Bremor actually meant, I asked carefully, "Are your borders so insecure?"

Is that it? I wondered. *If a king loved his land enough, if that land lay in too much peril, he might grab whatever strength he could to guard it, just as Lalathanai did for grief of her son. . . .*

"My *neighbors'* borders are insecure!" Bremor snapped, putting a sharp end to my theory. "Or they will be when I force my people to see the truth: Telesse *must* regain its greatness. And the only way it can do so is by force of arms!"

Patriotism, I thought. Warped, perverted and cruel, but patriotism just the same. But *och*, I was growing weary of his melodrama! "Why tell such things to the *brawd*—the brother of a rival king?"

"Don't look so worried! I'm not about to threaten your brother's peace."

Yet, I thought.

"No," he continued blithely, "there are far more promising lands to the south."

Which, of course, translated into: there are less well-guarded lands to the south. I wasn't all *that* confused by the language.

"Prince Aidan, if Telesse is ever to be restored, I must

shake my people from their complacency. You don't
know these folk; I do. They are the sort who can only
be impressed by a display of strength. Strength beyond
the merely human. My father was a strong enough ruler,
but *he* couldn't rouse them, not even with that *guerra*
against Lorcana."

Guerra? The word meant nothing to me. I had no
idea what Bremor's father had brought against Lorcana,
or who or what Lorcana was, but as I struggled to keep
up, I thought that maybe the man hadn't *wanted* to rouse
his people. Not everyone sees peace as stagnation. Or
conquest as patriotism. "So you turned to Evil for that
strength."

Bremor frowned impatiently. " 'Evil' is a relative word.
Let us merely say I've found the Patrons I need, who
will more than grant me the strength I must have."

Patrons? Now *that* I understood only too well. He
meant *cythrauliad*, of course, demons. And most surely
stronger entities than that which had destroyed Lalathanai. Of course. Such impossibly alien, impossibly cruel
beings would have delighted in answering Bremor's call.
How much more satisfying for them than the possessing
of one poor madwoman's mind! How satisfying to turn a
king's dreams to waking nightmare!

And he's proud of himself! He doesn't even realize—
"Bremor," I said, knowing even as I spoke that I couldn't
sway him, knowing I still had to try, "Bremor, no. Don't
do this thing." The flash of contempt in his eyes made
me continue impatiently, "I am not talking about politics!
I'm a magician, it is my . . . my profession. I *know* what
your patrons are like, and I know what will happen to
you and your land."

"What, visions of Heaven and Hell?" he cut in. "That's
what the priests foretold. Before I banished them."

Silently cursing the barrier the unfamiliar language
kept throwing in my path, I struggled on: "You see yourself becoming *ysblennydd*—" No, *damnio*, that wasn't
right! "—a figure of . . . of dark splendor, yes? Of course
you do. The old tales all make Evil sound so dramatic,

so romantic. But . . ." *Och,* would it translate? "The Left-hand Path isn't like that. There will not . . . won't be any splendor for you. Not once you are safely snared and your Patrons can drop pretense. They will eat at you, leach all hope, all will, all joy of life right out of you."

"Indeed."

"I've seen it happen!"

"Of course you have."

"Look you, do you want proof? Think of the place where I was caught, that terrible, empty forest." By now I didn't care whether my words or grammar were correct: he *must* hear me out. "You will be that forest, Bremor, alive but empty. You and your land both, for in magic the kingdom and the king are one. Is death-in-life what you truly want for Telesse?"

Cynical amusement had never left Bremor's face. "Finished?" he asked so politely it was an insult. "That 'empty' forest, as you so emotionally call it, was caused by one of Ybarre's experiments, no more than that."

"Is that what he told you? And you believed him?"

His eyes said plainly, *Sooner than I would believe you.*

"If you think I am lying, Bremor, just look at your servants! Look into their eyes and even a . . ." *damnio,* what was the word? " . . . a nonadept like yourself should see what has happened to them—"

"And that is what? Some mystic malady of the soul? Some perversion of spirit?" He smiled. "I would have been disappointed in you, Prince Aidan, if you hadn't tried to sway me with some fantastic tale. After all, I would have tried the same had I been in your place. But tales of doom never did frighten me."

Indeed? I shrugged and continued on a different tack, very coolly, very professionally, "I must admit you have acted with surprising skill. Despite all the silly stories of . . . devil raising, not many people could have called up your Patrons. Even with a sorcerer's help. I am curious, though: what bargain did you strike with them? What will They ask in return? There is always a price—but of course you know all about that by now."

That struck home where my more emotional warnings had not. For all his regal schooling in composure, Bremor still didn't have the control of a trained sorcerer. For a startled moment his mask slipped, just enough for me to glimpse a bewildered and—for all the brave words—frightened man.

"No price I cannot pay," he said, but his eyes said otherwise. "Telesse will be restored, and that is enough."

And in that moment before Bremor could glance away, I had him. How I ached to work a spell strong enough to snare his mind! This was hardly the time to worry about ethics; anything that would get me out of this pretty prison was fine with me!

But I didn't dare rouse Ybarre. So, instead, in this tiny instant of Bremor's lowered guard, I cast the smallest, gentlest "I mean you no harm" spell, not enough to alert his pet sorcerer looking for mightier magics, just enough to let me reach the young Bremor-who-had-been and learn who the Bremor-who-was really was . . .

. . . *the boy, so young, aching for approval from the father looming over his life like a fierce, dark god, fearing to show weakness before this deity, following him to* guerra *against a neighbor's lands* . . .

Guerra. War. I realized the words meant the same in two languages. And *Duwies glân*, what raw red ugliness that meaning held! I saw that *guerra*, that *war* through a boy's eyes, saw and heard and felt the anguish. Mine are not a weak people; when you worship *y Duwies*, the whole fierce, wild, wondrous force that is Creation, you cannot be weak. We defend our own. And in the past, it's true, one chieftain might raid another, stealing goods and the occasional head of someone careless enough to lose it. But we never knew *war*, never had a word for this foulness, this deliberate power lust, this lust for killing, killing, killing. . . .

"Why?" *I asked the boy, and felt his joy and excitement and trust in his father . . . his father willed this thing, and therefore it must be right, this war for honor, for glory—*

Honor? In *that*?

"What's this, Prince Aidan? You've gone so pale!" False sympathy edged Bremor's words. "Have you become ill?"

Yes, I have, with the horror out of your past that you don't even know I've seen, the horror that is no horror to you.

But my spell was still alive, there was still the barest bit of time to learn and see . . .

. . . the young king barely out of boyhood, cast too soon upon the throne, his father slain . . . the assassin's blade . . . the boy standing frozen in horror because the slayer was his uncle, his father's own brother whom he'd loved and trusted . . . the boy deciding wildly as his gods crumbled before his eyes: no, that will not happen to me . . . I shall not dare to love or trust . . . I shall be strong, stronger than any fear.

It's such a small, small step from fear to despair, from refusing to love to refusing to care. If only there'd been honest men about him, someone to comfort him, to love and guard him from his growing inner dark. . . .

My tiny spell had run its tiny course, occupying no more than one heartbeat's time. Dizzy with past and present all tangled in one skein, for one moment I could see only that lost, lonely, bitter boy and heard myself cry out, "What of the lives lost? Do they really mean nothing to you?"

It was a stupid question; I knew it even as the words left my lips. After what I'd just seen, how could I expect any others to matter to him?

Sure enough, Bremor asked coldly in his florid style, "What are common lives to a king? Come, Prince Aidan, don't presume to preach to me."

"I would not dream of it." My mind still ached with pictures of that mindless, mindless *war*. . . . *Och*, no. This was getting me nowhere at all. "These . . ." *Datguddio . . . datguddiad . . .* ah! "These revelations are very interesting. But why am I here? Yes, I already know the storm that caught me was no accident."

He conceded that with a mocking little smile. "The

storm was Ybarre's toy. He did make a mistake, though:
he hadn't thought you adept enough to shape-change."
Just as I hadn't thought him adept enough to summon a
storm. "Had you not struggled," Bremor continued, "you
would have been brought quite comfortably to our doors.
No matter. You are here now."

"Why?"

"Oh, don't be naive! Surely you must see you're far
too valuable a weapon, magician, to be left in the hands
of a king who is ever a potential threat to us."

"No threat," I drawled, "to those who offer *him* no
threat."

Bremor smiled, ignoring me. "As soon as Ybarre recovered from the ... ah ... blow you had dealt him, he
began his work."

"What a pity he recovered."

"Please. Surely you wouldn't want me to lose so useful
a tool."

"Tell me, Bremor, what is it makes a sorcerer so ..."
dychrynu ... brawychu ... "So terrified of not doing
your bidding? You tricked him, didn't you? You tricked
him into a pact of your own."

His grin was a quick, sharp thing. "A learned man isn't
always a clever one. To put it briefly: should Ybarre ever
fail me, my Patrons shall punish him. But now, to return
to the matter at hand, I must confess," Bremor said
lightly, "that we were curious about you, Ybarre and I.
We wished to see you for ourselves, for you are quite
unique. I can name no other prince outside of fable who
is also a magician. Albeit one foolish enough to limit
himself to the ... gentler magic of the Righthand Path."

"Now you have seen me. You will pardon me if I
don't stay."

"You're not going anywhere just yet, Prince Aidan."

"An empty threat, Bremor. Your pet sorcerer isn't here
right now. And despite your Patrons, you have no magic
of your own. Get out of my way, or I'll strike you down
where you stand."

An empty threat on my part, too. Bremor knew I

wasn't going to commit what would amount to murder. He also must have realized that the release of such strong magic would attract Ybarre, and with him the start of a duel that, surrounded by foes as I was, I would never win. "Go ahead, then!" the king taunted. "Strike!"

But I didn't bother with magic. My fist connected squarely with Bremor's jaw and felled him like a tree before an axe. As I stood over his crumpled body, rather astonished at my success and rubbing my sore hand, I told him silently:

You underestimated me. You never dreamed I'd not have been too proud to fight like a peasant. No knowledge is ever wasted: I had learned that skill back in Cymra from a bewildered but agreeable young farmer, neither of us dreaming I might ever use it.

But now, how to find my way out? There were four exits from the courtyard. I chose one at random, cast open the door—and found myself face to face with a very startled guard.

"Ahh, curse the luck!"

I slammed the door shut, but of course it was already too late. My exclamation had unthinkingly been in Cymraeth, and the guard probably thought I'd cast a spell on him, but that didn't stop him from sounding an alarm.

I glanced wildly around, trying to find a way out. Ybarre's magic would certainly negate any chance of using Bremor as a hostage, while even if I managed the shape-shifting charm again, the windows were far too narrow for me to literally fly away. But a balcony ran the length of the courtyard. As guards rushed in from all four doorways, I was up and onto that balcony like a squirrel, blessing a childhood of tree climbing. Áie, but:

More guards up here! I'm trapped!

No help for it. Ybarre or no, I needed my magic. Flinging up my arms, I hastily called up the Power within me. Here there was no convenient earth to create that Fog of Confusion such as I'd cast in the forest, but I called out the Word just the same, twisting it with a slight Faerie intonation. A ridiculous, dangerous time for experiments, but I couldn't, for the life of me, think of anything better.

And, with a nod from Estmere's Dame Fortune, the change was just enough. To my relief, I brought an illusion of darkness tumbling down about the guards (thinking the while, *I've got to remember how I did this!*), leaving them crying out and stumbling in the blackness their minds believed was real. I hadn't the vaguest idea how long this improvised spell would last, so I slipped through their ranks and ran with all my might down the first empty corridor I found, unreeling darkness like a bolt of cloth behind me.

And fickle Dame Fortune turned her back. I nearly ran full-tilt into Ybarre.

For a moment we stared, equally stunned. I had time to note that his eyes were very, very nervous, and couldn't resist a quick jibe:

"Don't worry, I didn't kill him. His Patrons won't be coming after you yet!"

He flinched, but didn't waste time answering. I felt a sudden tingling like the tension in the air before a storm, and knew he was trying to catch me in a psychic web. And *och*, it would have been lovely to rend that net and fight Ybarre spell for spell!

But this was no place for a duel. I had lost my hold on the darkness illusion, which meant that, their minds suddenly unclouded, the guards were running full out after me.

The corridor branched in two. I shoved Ybarre into the lefthand branch (fitting irony), sending him sprawling ignominiously, and ducked into the one on the right.

It was my undoing. That narrow way led only to a small, windowless room: Bremor's "chapel" to his demonic Patrons.

It was no more in seeming than a plain, featureless room, its walls unornamented stone. And yet there was an aura—no, *y Duwies* help me, more than that. There was a true, terrible . . . awareness, as somewhere in a realm very much beyond our mortal comprehension,

Bremor's Patrons, far and far again more powerful than Lalathanai's fragile little demon, sensed my presence in a place where no follower of the Righthand Path should be.

And they struck. Not physically, none of Them can enter our world without the foothold of a sorcerer's summons, but—They struck. Ah, and the unbearable weight of mockery, hatred, contempt! I couldn't fight. There was no mortal defense against that casual cruelty, that joyless, senseless Evil, empty and Powerful beyond comprehension.

It was more than any simply human mind or body could endure. Despairing, I was engulfed, smothered, buried alive beneath that scornful attack, no more in my distress than a helpless child, unable to see, to breathe, to think . . .

And of course King Bremor's guards, protected by their total lack of magic and quite unaware of horror, caught me in that place.

By that point I was past caring.

They brought me, dazed and exhausted, back before King Bremor, my arms bound once more by Ybarre's sorcerous chains, nor were they particularly gentle about it. Bremor was conscious again, apparently calm and unruffled. But I took a savage delight in the bruise blossoming purple on his jaw.

There wasn't a trace of emotion on his well-schooled face. "An interesting attempt at escape." Bremor's speech was careful and precise; for all his control, that bruise was hurting him. "But I have said you are not to leave yet, Prince Aidan."

"Your hospitality becomes . . . oppressive, Bremor." I was struggling to master my dizzy senses, hold fast to the language, and somehow match his coolness. "And may I say, the . . . stealing of a prince is not a . . . a wise political move?"

He merely smiled. "Ybarre assures me that neither

your brother nor anyone else knows you are here. I am under no restraints, Prince Aidan."

"What are you planning to do with me?"

Bremor's smile hardened. "I'm not at all interested in your royal status. King's bastards are common enough. But, as I've said, your magic intrigues me."

"*Damnio chwi,* answer me!"

"Indeed. Ybarre and I plan to study you, Prince Aidan. We shall learn from you all that we can, all that you are and all that you know."

Bremor turned from me to his sorcerer.

"He is yours, Ybarre."

CHAPTER XIX

CAPTIVE

I will not dwell on the time that followed. How long I was in the dark hopelessness of their dungeons, what was done to me. Oh, it was nothing so crude as physical torture, I assure you.

But it took its toll. . . .

There was a time when I was conscious, dimly aware of huddling on a hard stone floor, back to a hard stone wall. The cold, sorcerous chains that blocked my magic and were too short to let me stand were draped over my arms, and I ached in mind and body.

Up to this time I had managed to cling to sanity by taking refuge in memory; often and often I had escaped my tormentors by turning my mind inward with all my magician's will, by walking through the cool green woodlands of my home with sweet Ailanna. And when those tormentors, time and again, had shaken me from my shadowy peace, still I had held fast to sanity, more savagely, picturing Ybarre shriveling in the heat of my magic, screaming as he'd made me scream, seeing my

169

keen Faerie sword piercing an anguished Bremor to the heart—

Oh, I hated well in that time. It was hatred that kept me from starving myself to death, that kept me exercising my body as far as the limits of those cursed chains would permit. Hatred and a grim refusal to let Bremor have the final satisfaction of my death.

But I could no longer keep thoughts of defiance in a brain so fogged with exhaustion and despair. Bremor had my sword and he had me, and I must surrender to the fact that there would be no revenge and no escape. . . .

Suddenly a soft voice asked, "Human? Human, are you still able to hear me?"

I looked up dully, staring for a moment without understanding. But then a wild blaze of hope burned the shadows from my mind. The green-eyed Faerie boy from the forest stood before me, my sword slung over his shoulder.

"How . . . did you get in here?"

"Oh now, surely you know enough to know no mortal bars and locks can keep out the Folk!" The boy studied me with his young-old eyes, head to one side, and the faintest of shudders ran through him. He wrinkled up his nose in distaste. "My mother was right. She told me you were being most foully misused."

It was an odd place for courtesies, but I heard myself asking, "Your lady mother is well?"

"Quite well, thanks to your help, and safe with others of our kin. We are in your debt, human. Would you be free?"

Och, foolish question! "I would!" I tried without thinking to spring to my feet, only to be pulled harshly down again by the too short chains. "Ahh, but how? There are no keys to these chains, and the links are stronger than human strength. I know that only too well." Sick with renewed despair, I looked wearily up at the boy. "Don't you see? Only Ybarre's counterspell can unlock them."

"Indeed?" the boy said, eyes alight. "You shouldn't believe such a foolish thing."

He murmured something softly in the Faerie tongue, and Power surged and gleamed about the words. As the boy fell silent, the chains that had been so very cold and harsh crumbled away from me into dust. Scarcely believing what had happened, I staggered up on legs feeble from disuse, and stared blankly at arms no longer bound. *Duwies glân*, Tairyn's promise . . . *a child shall rescue you.*

"I . . . thought the Folk . . . couldn't touch iron."

The boy grinned. "I didn't touch it, now, did I? All I did was cancel the sorcerer's human charms with a bit of Faerie magic. He'd put so much work into the stupid things that when they fell, they took the metal's strength with them!" His eyes widened. "Aie, don't faint!"

"I have no intention of fainting," I retorted weakly. "But . . . if only Tairyn had taught me that one spell. . . ." Dizzy, I closed my eyes, trying to summon enough will to continue standing. "It seems Faerie magic is even stronger than I dreamed."

"Aye, aye, but Faerie magic won't save us if the sorcerer catches our scent! Come, human, this is no fit place to linger."

So we struggled out of there together, me staggering with the weakness of torment and confinement, he staggering under my weight.

"Where are all the guards, boy?"

"Asleep."

"Your doing?"

"Of course. Come, you great, tall, smelly human, you're not getting any lighter, and the sleep spell won't last forever."

We passed several guards in our travels, but all of them were still snoring peacefully away. No one stopped us as we maneuvered a maze of corridors. Gasping and exhausted already, I looked up at the daunting flight of stairs we faced, and wondered dully if I shouldn't give up right now.

The Faerie boy pulled nervously at my arm. "Hurry, human! I sense life stirring in the castle!"

I took a deep breath and started forward on that night-mare of a climb. After the first few steps, my prison-weakened legs didn't want to support me any further. Stumbling, staggering, barking my shins again and again on the steps, crawling as often as climbing, I fought my frantic way upward, laboring for breath. I could hear the blood roaring in my ears and felt myself trembling so strongly with fatigue that only the boy's desperate grip on my arm kept me from falling helplessly all the way back down.

Duwies glân, I can't go any further, I can't. . . . But if I gave in, there would be a return to chains and dark-ness and pain—no! Better to die of exhaustion than that! But was there no end to this stairway? Had Ybarre some-how cast a spell of timelessness on it? Would he find us climbing helplessly up and up, never reaching the top, like two kitchen dogs on a treadmill?

But there was no spell, and at last we reached the stairway's top and stood, unchallenged and alone, on a tower roof. The moon was large and full, and the sharp silver light hit me like a blow, too strong by far for my darkness-accustomed eyes. I cried out in pain, hands flung over my face, in that moment helpless as one newly blinded. But slowly my vision cleared, and I dared lower my hands to look around.

A coughing roar made me start. And there, to my delight, was my griffin, pacing nervously on the narrow space, now and again snapping his beak or ruffling his yellow wings. He stopped short when he saw me watch-ing him, tufted ears pricking up, then gave a glad little chuckling sound and hurried to my side, nibbling gently up and down my arm, purring like an overgrown cat. I leaned gratefully against the griffin's side, letting the warm, tawny strength steal through me, melting some-thing of the prison chill. But the Faerie boy was watching me intently, and I sighed.

"Yes, lad, I know. This place won't be safe for long."

"I'm glad you have some measure of sense, human. Come, take your sword." His small, deft hands buckled the swordbelt about my waist. "Now mount your griffin and be off!"

"What of you?"

He gave a child's delighted laugh. "I don't need griffin wings to fly! The debt is paid, human, and now I can leave this ugly place and join my kinfolk. Farewell!"

And, just as simply as that, he was gone, vanished in a small swirling of wind.

"Wish I could travel so easily," I muttered to the griffin, then pulled myself slowly onto his back, hearing him chitter softly as though annoyed at my clumsiness. "Sorry, friend. I can't manage grace right now."

He roared. Powerful wings unfolding, he began to race forward, claws biting at stone as he gathered speed. Almost, we were airborne—

Then, with a wild cry of alarm, the griffin shied aside, nearly unseating me.

Ybarre stood before us.

I wish I could tell you how I leaped from the griffin's back to bravely face my foe, how we fought a true sorcerer's duel, calling down the fury of the elements on each other. Instead, too drained to move, I merely sat staring like a fool.

Ybarre never said a word. But panic was so sharp in his eyes that I knew he would dare anything rather than fail Bremor and his Patrons. I could *feel* him hastily gathering his sorcery, knew I wouldn't have a chance in a fight—and the sheer will to survive took over. With a wild shout, I urged the griffin forward, and the startled beast sprang sharply upward, wings beating frantically with the effort to keep aloft, sending Ybarre scuttling for safety.

But then the desperate sorcerer, all finesse forgotten in his haste, hurled a wild, raw, deadly mass of Power at us. No time for conscious thought—I threw up an equally inelegant psychic shield. My mind recoiled from a tremendous blow that felt like the impact of a lightning bolt. Stunned, I was nearly hurled from the griffin's back.

But somehow I clung to consciousness, somehow I didn't fall. And somehow my shield held.

Which meant that the raw, terrible, killing surge of Power could do only one thing: force unspent, it rebounded in all its fury on its creator.

And that was the end of Ybarre.

CHAPTER XX

THE PRODIGAL RETURNS

I don't remember all that much of what followed after Ybarre's death. The only thing certain in my exhausted mind was an ache not to return to the troubles of Estmere's court, but to Cymra, to my homeland and Ailanna—

Och, Ailanna! My poor love wouldn't have known what had happened to me. She wouldn't have known why she couldn't contact me. Did she think me dead? I made a gallant try to reach her with my will. And for one brief, wonderful moment I thought I felt her mind brush mine. . . .

But then my strength gave way. I lost my hold on the contact, and nearly lost my hold on everything else, too. I couldn't have actually fainted, or I would have fallen to my death, but my next clear recollection is of early morning sunlight warming me, and of the griffin, with no clue as to where I wanted him to fly, swooping smoothly down to a landing on a rampart of Estmere's castle.

So be it.

I slid resignedly from the griffin's back—and kept right on sliding, ending up in a crumpled heap at his feet. The griffin shrilled in alarm, his wild animal panic tearing at my nerves, and I struggled up again to stroke his tawny coat, thank him as best I could, then send him on his own free way. I watched his slowly diminishing figure till it was out of sight, then turned slowly away, wondering if I could possibly make it all the way to my tower before I collapsed. Despite the sunlight pouring down on me, burning at my head, the dungeon chill seemed to cling to me till I felt I would never be warm again, and I was so unutterably weary I wanted nothing so much as to lie down right where I was and never move.

"Your Highness!" The voice was high and childishly shrill with alarm. "My prince, what have they done to you?"

It was my young friend, Arn. He hesitated a moment, stunned shock in every line of him, then rushed forward to give me his arm.

"Gently, lad ... or you'll ... knock me over."

"I—they all said—" His voice sharpened with renewed panic. "But you shouldn't be here, you mustn't—"

"Arn, I have no strength for riddles. Either help me ... or go find someone to carry me...."

"Oh, my prince, lean on me, do!"

By that point, there wasn't much choice. But something penetrated my exhaustion haze: why was Arn's bright livery now muted by black?

"Arn, what is it?" Sudden fear gave me a spurt of strength. "My brother—has something happened to my brother?"

"You ... really don't know?"

"Know what?" I would have shaken him if I could. "Tell me!"

"Tell him nothing." The voice came from behind us, and it was terrible in its pain.

"Estmere!" I cried in relief and, "Your Majesty!" gasped Arn.

"Leave us." The words were flat and so very deadly that the half-dozen courtiers behind Estmere promptly scuttled away. Only Arn remained, frightened but gallantly facing his king.

"Sire, please, I—"

"Leave us!"

The boy shot me an anguished glance, saying without words, *Forgive me, I dare not disobey.* I pulled free from his support, nodding to him that it was all right. As the boy hurried unhappily away, I turned to Estmere—and recoiled, shocked at the mingled horror and fury raging in his eyes: fury at me.

"Estmere . . ."

"Are you such a fool? Are you actually such a fool as to return?"

What in the name of all the Powers? In my confusion, I seized on the only thing I could possibly have done wrong: "Granted, I should have done you the courtesy of telling someone where I was going, but things were happening too swiftly and—"

"Enough! Don't try to charm me with your smooth magician's words!"

Gallu. He was coming to sound more and more like Clarissa. And I—I wasn't going to be able to stand much longer. "For the love of *y Duwies*, tell me what I'm supposed to have done."

He stared at me, radiating such anguish he was unable to speak. And what he wore registered for the first time.

"All in black . . . ? First Arn, now you . . . mourning garb? *Och, brawd,* who—"

"And still you pretend! I never thought you, *you*, my brother whom I loved—oh God, I never thought you could be so cruel!" Cold-eyed, trembling, Estmere continued, "Very well. Play your little game. Pretend you know nothing of the fever."

"What fever?"

"Damn you! The fever that took Clarissa!"

An image of Estmere's wife as I'd last seen her, so full

of rage and life, flashed through my mind, and I gasped, "Estmere, no, she's not, she can't be—"

He continued remorselessly, "It was a fever you could have cured. God knows you spend enough time healing peasants. But when I sent everyone in search of you, we found you had oh so mysteriously flown away." His voice faltered. "And . . . with you gone . . . the court physicians did their best, but . . . She was so delicate, it happened so swiftly . . . they could do nothing."

Clarissa, poor, jealous, frightened, helpless little Clarissa. Sick with shock, I stammered, "I—I'm so very sorry."

His face was as hard as a tomb effigy. "She became ill just one week after you left. Isn't that odd? One short week after folk had heard you quarrelling. You threatened her, didn't you?"

For a moment I stared at him without comprehension, struggling desperately to remember what I had said. But my overtaxed mind refused to function, and all I knew was that there had been a meeting, harsh words. . . .

And then I realized what Estmere was trying to say, and cried out in horror, "You can't believe I'd hurt her! Yes, we argued, at l-least I think we argued, but she was your wife! And—and what you're accusing me of is murder!"

I should have said more, should have forced him to listen to me, but I was past the point of coherency. And Estmere quite shut his mind to the stammerings I managed. The raw fire of his anguish and rage burned and burned at me like Bremor's torments till I cried aloud in pain, till I couldn't hope to defend myself, till I couldn't even think. Estmere's fury drowned me in waves of despair till at last my hold on reality was shattered.

And I fainted dead away.

I returned to reality in slow, weary stages. The first waking was a vague thing of sheer, bewildered panic, not knowing where I was, half expecting to be back in the cold hopelessness of my prison cell. The relief of realizing

I lay not on hard stone but in a soft bed was so great I nearly wept. But before tears could fill my eyes, someone was pressing a goblet of wonderfully cool water to my lips. I drank thankfully. Then, too weak to notice aught else, I slipped back into sleep.

The second waking didn't last much longer. But at least this time that mindless panic was gone. I was able to accept the wonderful fact that I was free, to know the bed in which I lay was my own, in my own tower rooms. I was still weak as a sickly fawn, though, with a vague memory of fever and delirium. And ... hadn't Father Ansel been at my bedside at one time or another, murmuring words from his faith? Had I been *that* ill?

Someone was sitting at my bedside. I turned a head that seemed heavier than stone to find Estmere watching me. I tensed, hardly in the condition for a renewed attack, but there was nothing of anger left in my brother. He looked ... *och*, piteously worn, far older than his years, his eyes deeply shadowed.

"Aidan?" he began tentatively. "Do you know where you are?"

I made two attempts, finally got out, "Yes," not sure in which language I'd said it, and promptly slid right back into sleep.

With the third rewakening I finally felt more nearly human. Once again Estmere was there, asking warily, "How do you feel?"

For a frantic moment I couldn't find a word of Anglic. But then I managed to retort, "I've ... heard more ... tactful questions."

My brother laughed with an enthusiasm born, I think, more of relief that I could even try to jest than of humor. "Your voice sounds painfully dry. Wait, now ... I've watched how this is done; I should be able to help you drink without drowning you or soaking the bed."

While he filled a goblet with water for me, I made a quick self-inventory. Some nameless servant (to whom my gratitude went out) had bathed and shaved me, had even untangled and trimmed what must have been a briar bush of hair, and my inward survey found nothing worse than a score of scrapes, bruises and the inevitable prison sores, and two bandaged wrists. No trace of lung sickness, *Duwies diolch*, or any seeds of the bone-and-joint illness.

Estmere supported my head with a surprisingly gentle arm so I could drink. As I lay back again, throat soothed, I added, "I'll live."

It had been meant as another, admittedly feeble jest. But Estmere, though he usually wasn't so dramatic, murmured something reverent and crossed himself. I stared. "Now, was that out of gratitude or regret?"

"How can you ask that?"

"After the welcome I received ..."

"No. Wait. First, do you think you're up to so much talking?"

"If you ... don't expect too much from me."

"I'll try not to weary you. Especially after ... God, when you just collapsed like that, I thought you were dead. For all the sorry state you were in, I just hadn't realized you were so ill."

Neither had I. Most of it had been total exhaustion, of course, and prison fever, and the result of Ybarre's little pleasantries. But I suspected the court physicians had been in on it, too, overly zealous in their attempts to heal the magician-prince and prove themselves a better healer than he; they'd nearly finished me off. "How long was I out of my head?"

Estmere winced. "Three, almost four days." As I stared at him, he burst out, "Where in God's name were you? Vanished for so long—"

"How long?" I had lost all track of time. "A week? Two?"

"Two weeks! Almost two months, Aidan."

"Two ... months ..." Suddenly I saw only a dark, dark cell, suddenly I felt the weight of my chains. "Was I in that foulness for two long months?"

"Aidan? Aidan, what is it?" Estmere's hands fastened on my shoulders, dragging me back from shadow.

"Nothing," I said wearily. "A memory."

"But what happened to you? Gone for two months you're plainly horrified to recall, then reappearing like some poor wretch of a ..." He stopped, touching one of my bandaged wrists with a gentle hand. "There are the marks of chains on you. What happened to you?"

I shook my head. "Some other time, Estmere. Please."

He sighed. "Just remember, you are a prince, brother to a king who—"

"I take my own revenges."

Worn out by that fierce little touch of pride, I had to stop to catch my breath. My brother hesitated, then got to his feet. "You should rest now."

"Wait."

"What would you?"

"What am I to you now? Your prisoner? Your enemy?"

He froze. "Certainly not my prisoner. Never my enemy." Very slowly, Estmere sat down again at my side. "They thought you were going to die. The physicians— no, I won't grace them with that name! Those fools, those frauds thought you were going to die, and so they sent for me." His eyes were suddenly very bright. "Even if you *had* been my enemy, it would have hurt my heart to see you so. I believed them, I believed them— Dear God, I was so sure this was going to be your deathbed, that in less than two little months I was going to lose the second of the two most dear to me."

That fierce, despairing brightness was painful to watch. I let my gaze fall to give him at least a semblance of privacy, waiting for him to regain control. And what I recall most clearly is the sight of Estmere's hands, so neatly folded, so savagely clenched.

But after a time those hands relaxed, lying limply on his knees, and my brother continued wearily, "I stayed by your side as much as my duties permitted. And while I was watching you, and waiting for ... one thing or the other, I had rather more time to think than I wanted."

"Meaning?"

"Meaning that I considered everything I knew about you—and it really is very little, do you realize that? Oh, you've told me charming stories about your Cymra and its people, but only seldom anything about you, the inner Aidan."

I blinked. "I never meant—"

"No. Let me finish. What I came to accept after all that lonely time was what I suppose I knew from the start. No matter what the fools at court were insisting, no matter what cruel, stupid things I said to you up there on the ramparts, I know you never could have used your Art against Clarissa. I know you never could have harmed her. Deliberately harmed her." He added painfully, "No matter how much you two might have hated each other."

That "deliberately" bothered me. "I never hated her."

Estmere got abruptly to his feet. "Enough talk for now. You look most dreadfully weary."

I was. But I called after him, "Please. One thing more."

He sighed. "Do you want the fever to return? You must rest. We can talk later."

"No. Estmere . . ."

"Ay me, very well. What is it?"

"Why did you say I never would have *deliberately* harmed Clarissa? What did you mean?"

He stood for a long moment, back to me, hand on the door. But at last Estmere turned to face me again, his face a mask.

"There were times during your fever when you grew so violent we feared you would hurt yourself. At last I had my harp brought to me, and I played to you. The music did seem to be soothing, for you stopped your struggles and smiled. And you spoke words in . . . another language."

"The nonsense of delirium, surely."

"No. It *was* a language, very beautiful, very strange. And after a time I knew it must be the Faerie tongue." I must have shown some small sign of alarm, for Estmere gave an odd little laugh. "You can't deny it, can you? You spoke it with the ease of long familiarity, almost as though you spoke your native Cymraeth."

In my weakness, that struck me as so wonderfully ironic I burst into laughter. *Tairyn, Tairyn, here you've been so careful to keep me from revealing your secrets— and your own training of me betrays you!*

Estmere was staring at me in alarm. At last he touched a hand to my forehead, but I turned away. "I'm not fevered."

"No." But he was still staring. "Or . . ." he murmured, almost inaudibly, "quite human . . . ?"

"Don't be ridiculous! You know who my father was, and my mother, witch or not, was fully human. As am I!"

"Between the magic and the Faerie Folk, I wonder."

"What are you trying to say?"

"I hadn't realized till that moment when I heard you speak their tongue just how familiar you are with the ways of that Folk." His voice was light, as falsely casual as though he were speaking to some not-quite-to-be-trusted ambassador. "It's hardly surprising that you might see life through their eyes."

"Please. Come to the point. Of what am I accused?"

"Of nothing. Would I accuse a fox of being true to its foxy nature?"

"Estmere . . ."

"Very well." Though his voice was as determinedly light as ever, his eyes had gone dull as winter ice. "The Faerie Folk aren't evil, are they?"

"No! Alien to human ways and thoughts, but never evil."

"But they *are* practical, all the old tales agree on that, very coolly practical." Estmere's voice was slipping with each word into bleakness. "You must have known of Clarissa's illness, as a magician you surely must have known. But . . . the Folk are ever practical. I know you had nothing to do with the cause of her illness; you are no murderer. But what more practical way to be rid of an enemy—too strong a word?—of an encumbrance, then, than to simply step aside, to fly away and let illness do what you would never—"

"Estmere, no!"

"I'm not blaming you. You only acted according to your nature."

"No! Listen to me!" I was frantically trying to scour my memory—but I couldn't remember! I couldn't remember anything!

Wait. That wasn't true. I knew who and what I was, I knew Estmere, and—and . . .

Desperate lest Estmere leave before I could explain, I tried to force memory again, terrified at how many blank spots I found. I thought I remembered that final confrontation with Clarissa, at least I remembered being in the same room with her. Hints of Faerie afterwards, and . . . and . . . and *what*? Everything after that was dark: painful, nightmarish scraps of the recent past that whirled aside like leaves in the wind when I tried to concentrate.

Of course I knew about shock. I knew, as any good healer does, how a mind that's undergone some horror may temporarily lose track of the past. But nothing I had learned had prepared me for the sheer terror of that loss, feeling the solid ground of history turned to mist beneath my feet, or for the anguish that shot through my head when I fought to remember. Yet I must remember! I needed every memory of that last meeting with Clarissa.

But all I could find was a quick flash of those too-bright eyes, the patches of bright color staining her pale cheeks. The result of anger? Or the first warnings of illness—*Duwies, had* I known? Had I, and yet done nothing?

No, I couldn't, I wouldn't . . .

But I couldn't be sure, I just could not *remember!* Nearly sobbing from the pain blazing through my mind, wild with the need to convince myself as well as Estmere, I gasped out, "To have known Clarissa to be so ill, and yet to have abandoned her—that would have been murder as surely as though I'd struck her down myself!"

"You're exhausting yourself," he said flatly, and turned to leave.

"Estmere, wait!"

In my frenzy to stop him, I sprang from my bed—which wasn't the cleverest thing I've done. The blood surged painfully in my already aching head, my legs went right out from under me, and I would have fallen headlong had Estmere not made a catlike leap to catch me. I remember the strength of my brother's arms supporting me, I remember trying and trying to get him to listen, though I couldn't seem to get the words out right, I remember him shouting for servants. . . .

And then it was quite literally as though someone had pulled a black curtain down in front of my eyes.

CHAPTER XXI

WARNINGS

A half week of rest, and I began to feel more nearly human, though my memory remained disturbingly vague, tormenting me with vicious headaches whenever I tried to sharpen it, and my nights were often filled with confused visions of horror.

But then my stunned Power began to revive. Though, maddeningly, I still couldn't focus my will long enough to contact Ailanna (*Duwies diolch*, Goddess be thanked, whatever else I might have forgotten, I remembered *her*!), at least magic could destroy nightmares and speed my healing—particularly, I thought with a touch of vanity, the healing of those ugly chain scars circling my wrists; I most certainly did not like looking like a felon.

A full week of rest, and I was bored to distraction. And worried: I was beginning to wonder uneasily if I ever would regain full use of my magic. The worst of it was that I still couldn't focus properly to reach Ailanna.

Please let her be watching me, somehow. Please let my poor love know I'm still alive!

At least I was on my feet again, albeit over the protests of the very subdued physicians, albeit with an annoying tendency to stagger like a newborn fawn. But if I was to go down into the rest of the castle, I must wear something appropriate to the royal period of mourning. I had no idea what was proper; we didn't wear mourning in Cymra. Besides, the circumstances were a bit ... awkward. The servants I summoned finally dressed me in a tactful compromise of a costume: an ankle-length tunic of deep, dull blue under a long black surcoat cinched in by a black leather belt.

Good enough. Even if it did make me look, what with my black hair and eyes, two months' pallor and gauntness, like one of the less appealing creatures out of the Hollow Hills. There was, after all, a limit to what even magical healing could restore.

As I made my not quite steady way down from my tower into the castle proper, I couldn't help but notice servants and courtiers alike recoiling from me, and not just because I looked so Otherworldly: everyone at court was debating whether or not I was still politically "safe," wondering what the relationship might be now between their sadly bereaved king and the magician-prince.

The magician-prince was wondering the same thing—and half afraid of the answer I might receive.

No matter. There was something I must do, of honor.

The shortest way to the royal chapel took me along the balcony overlooking the small courtyard where—how long ago it seemed!—Estmere and I had once had our friendly duel. The sound of clashing swords caught my attention, and I glanced over the balustrade, my faulty memory giving me flashes of the past so that for one confused moment I expected to find time turned back.

But those weren't grown men duelling down there, only boys. I recognized Arn by his wild yellow hair. The other boy, stocky and brown-haired ... I knew him ... if only I could remember ... Gerin, was it? Yes. I found that little memory with relief. But there was something else about him ... something ...

Ah. He had been one of poor Clarissa's pages.

But what do the young idiots think they're doing?

They know they're not supposed to handle swords without the sergeant-at-arms!

It wasn't any boyish prank. The two of them were fighting in silent earnest, the air about them fairly rippling with anger, making up in ferocity what they lacked in skill. I glanced about, looking for someone to stop the duel before it got too perilous, seeing only servants scurrying on their way, pretending they noticed nothing. Wasn't anyone going to stop the boys? Wasn't anyone of sufficient rank?

No. Of course not. There were always noble folk wandering about, save for this moment; Dame Fortune is a perverse lady.

I don't need this, I really don't need this.

My body was already protesting the exercise. All I wanted was to visit the chapel, then stagger back to my tower and bed. But if I abandoned the boys ... as I might have done to Clarissa ...

No. I wouldn't think of that, I couldn't.

I wasn't Estmere, to regally call out, "Hold!" Nor, frankly, did I have the breath to spare. But a small summoning of will sent a flash of illusionary blue fire crackling down about their blades. Both boys yelped, dropping their weapons and crossing themselves, then whirled to face me. I must have looked singularly sorcerous, because even Arn gasped, and both boys went down on one knee before me in a reverence more suited to a king than a prince.

I swept slowly and grandly down the stairway (the only way to keep both footing and dignity in that ankle-length tunic) and stood for a moment looking down on Arn's yellow head and Gerin's brown one, letting them worry. Then: "Up!" I commanded shortly, and the boys scrambled to their feet, red-faced with exertion and embarrassment, still shooting looks of fury at each other. "Stop that, both of you! Are you fools?"

"My prince," Arn began tentatively, "the swords weren't edged."

"I know that!" I snapped, and he winced. "I also know

that even unedged blades are dangerous weapons in the hands of half-trained, hotheaded boys!"

They stirred resentfully, but of course neither dared retort. After a moment, Arn asked, very warily, "But . . . even if we did get hurt, more than a—a scratch, I mean, couldn't you—"

"Piece the bits of a shattered arm or elbow back together like a potter mending a broken jar? Yes, I can heal wounds," I added sharply to forestall him, "but there *are* limits. Do either one of you would-be heroes really want to end up crippled? Well? Do you?"

"No, Your Highness," murmured two subdued voices.

"Now, what was this foolishness about?"

Arn and Gerin exchanged quick, hot glances, daring each other to be the first to speak. Then Arn said resolutely, a stalwart knight facing a hostile king, "It was . . . only a quarrel, my prince. Pray forgive us for disturbing you."

A quarrel. Gerin, my uncertain memory told me, had adored his queen with the wholeheartedness of a boy in love for the first time. I sighed. Judging from the hating looks he was flashing at me . . .

"Gerin, you blame me for the queen's death, don't you?"

He started. "How could you know?"

"And you, Arn, decided to defend my honor. Whether or not it needed defending."

That was too much for my staunch protector. "He called you a murderer, my prince!"

"Did not!"

"Did too!"

"Enough!" I shouted, and they fell silent, watching me like frightened puppies. "*Och fi*, you two make my head ache. Gerin, no matter what you think, I did *not* murder anyone." At least, I prayed not. "Arn, the next time you decide to defend me, ask my permission first. Now, get out of here, both of you!"

They scurried away. But then Arn stopped and said

shyly, "It's good to see you up and about again, my prince."

Before I could answer, he hurried off. And I—I was suddenly aware of eyes upon me: now, of course, there were courtiers aplenty. They and their servants were pretending to studiously go about their business, but I knew only too well, as I started my slow way off to the chapel once more, that half the court was watching me. And how many of them, as well, thought I was a murderer?

Was I? My memory stubbornly refused to give me an answer.

My footsteps on the chapel's marble floor sounded very loud to me. The last time I could clearly recall being in here was for my brother's wedding (no, I wouldn't think of that), but I was no more at ease now than I ever was, glancing about nervously in the dim blue light as I always did, staring at the glorious stained glass windows, blindingly red and blue in the sunlight, at the tall columns and beautifully arched roof, at the splendor of the altar with its golden screen, at all the very, very alien surroundings.

It was going to get worse. I needed to visit not the chapel itself, but the royal crypt below it. I had been down there once before with Estmere, to pay my formal respects to my father's tomb. At the time, the smell of age and death and the faint whispers of ancient griefs had torn at my nerves till I was thankful for the return to the world of light and life. I doubted it would be any pleasanter for this second visit.

The guard of honor, resplendent in their royal red and gold, looked at me somewhat askance. But I had, after all, every legal right to be there, so one man unlocked the great bronze gate then stood aside so I could descend. I climbed down the chill stairway, very much aware of the guards' wondering stares. For a moment I hesitated on the last few steps, darkness and the smell of cold stone jarring a terrifying flash of memory (*a dark, cold cell, chains* . . .) but then I lit the torches at the bottom with a determined flash of will, and made my wary way past the seemingly endless array of stone monuments to long-dead folk whose names and regal titles meant little to me, even though they were my ancestors. Halfway my ancestors.

Now normally, I have no fear of the dead, no more than does any other Cymraen who knows his body will rest peacefully in earth and his spirit in the arms of *y Duwies* till the time for rebirth. But here the dead were kept from the earth and the proper order of things. The heavy, somber silence and residue of ancient sorrow once more pressed in upon me till I found myself struggling for breath and shivering convulsively, the healer in me wondering at the wisdom of being in this chill place so soon after my illness—

But here was Clarissa's tomb. And *och*, it was a piteous sight! She had died so suddenly, so unexpectedly, the stone carvers must have been impossibly rushed. But there the young queen lay, her marble effigy still shining with the newness of its cutting. I saw the dates of birth and death, and winced.

So very young, indeed. My poor, fearful Clarissa, if only I'd had the sense to realize you were just barely sixteen!

I knelt at the side of her tomb in the fashion of Estmere's folk, intending to say some sort of prayer, wondering vaguely what might be suitable. But instead, to my utter and complete astonishment, I found myself weeping.

From guilt?

I don't know, I don't know, I can't remember!

At last, spent, I dried my eyes as best I could. Too weary to rise, I huddled where I was, struggling once more to remember . . . to remember . . .

A voice behind me said, "Aidan."

I shot to my feet so sharply I nearly cracked my head on the side of the tomb. "Estmere!"

He caught me by the arm as I staggered, steadying me, though to his watching courtiers it must have seemed no more than a brotherly greeting. "All right?" he asked softly.

"Yes. Thank you."

Estmere nodded curtly, releasing my arm so quickly I had to wonder if he really didn't like the idea of touching me. "What are you doing here?"

He plainly hadn't known I'd been weeping. The cold wariness in his voice stung me. "*Gallu nef,* you can't think I was planning to despoil my ancestors' graves! Or cast some foul spell on poor Clarissa's remains."

His courtiers all quickly crossed themselves at that, and Estmere's eyes glinted angrily. "This is no place for such jokes, Aidan."

I sighed, very much aware by this point that it was only my first day back on my feet, wanting nothing so much as to be in bed. "I was paying my last respects. Nothing worse."

He glanced back at the courtiers, who had moved tactfully just out of hearing, giving us as least the illusion of privacy. "I had planned to discuss this with you later. But perhaps now . . ."

His voice trailed off as he studied me, and I surprised an uneasy flickering of sympathy in his eyes. Perversely, it annoyed me.

"I'm not about to collapse. Say what you would."

"Are you aware of the mood at court?"

"About us, you mean?" I thought of Arn and Gerin, and bit back a sharp laugh. "How not? I'd have to be mind dead not to feel the cracklings of emotions. Some folks are with me, some claim I'm demonic, but no one is sure how things stand between us now. I'm not so sure of that myself."

His glance flicked away from mine. "So. I think it time we crush some rumors."

"How?"

Estmere's face was a mask once more. "You will be seen in public in my company, my very obviously friendly and unsuspicious company, for the next few days. That should keep any hotheads from using you as an excuse for plots."

So instead you *would use me, eh, brother?* Bitterly I asked, "Are you that good an actor?"

He shot me a knife-sharp glance. "What does that mean?"

"What do you think?"

"Don't play games with me. Most certainly not here. Either obey me or leave me."

I was past the point of caring much what I said. With a sweeping, unsteady bow, I told my brother, "Yes, your majesty. Of course, your majesty. At once, your majesty."

Estmere stared at me, furious. But after a moment's keen tension, he said only, "You've been ill. I won't blame you for this unseemly mockery."

With that, he gave me leave, for all the world as though nothing unusual had passed between us. And I went.

It was only afterwards, alone in my tower rooms, slouched moodily in a tall-backed chair, that I could acknowledge the pain that had flashed in Estmere's eyes at my words. And even through my anger, my conscience smote me.

How could I have forgotten? He was the king, he just could not be as familiar as other men, not in public. *Duwies glân,* I'd heard him use that regal tone on me before; it didn't mean anything more than that his courtiers were listening.

Ah? Then why had his eyes been so cold?

From grief, surely. He hadn't yet been able to come to grips with the tragedy. And because the affairs of state were always staring him in the face, Estmere couldn't afford a common man's luxury of simply breaking down and—

"Dyri Uffern!" I snapped. This was ridiculous! I couldn't even stay angry with Estmere without starting to feel sorry for him.

Enough. Forget him for now. I rose, stretching weary

muscles with a groan. No one was likely to enter "the magician's roost" without the magician's permission, but just the same I took the precaution of tracing my usual guarding Signs at door and windows, then returned to my chair and closed my eyes. I would test my will one more time. . . .

It was quite a struggle at first to keep from simply drifting off to sleep. But all at once, to my immense relief, I felt my Power doing what I wanted it to do, and sent my consciousness soaring out from that tower, out and out till it finally touched another, most familiar, most wonderfully welcome mind.

"*Aidan!*" It was a psychic scream. "Are you all right? Where are you? Where were you? What happened to—"

"Gently, love, gently! Yes, I'm fine."

"You don't *feel* fine! What's wrong? Are you still ill?"

" 'Still?' You *have* been watching me, then?"

"As best I could. At—at least when I could find you. . . ." She murmured a word in the Faerie tongue that means despair and pain and dying hope all in one. "I knew you were trapped, in torment, I knew there was nothing I could do to help you, nothing—" Ailanna broke off with a gasp.

"Hush, *cariad*, dear one, that's over now. Come, let me see you."

Our merged wills created a vision landscape, a copy of a very real forest grove in Cymra, just now very beautiful with the coming of autumn, touched with bright reds and golds and russets.

And my lady stood before me, or so it seemed. Lovely, so lovely she was in a simple gown of all the autumn colors, and one red leaf caught in the silken fall of pale golden hair! I must confess I nigh broke my vow then and there, nigh went flying home to her—

"Don't be foolish," she said.

"Foolish!"

"Dishonorable, would you rather?"

"No, I most certainly would not rather! Ailanna, I'm

no oath breaker, no matter how strong the temptation. And *och, cariad*, the temptation is very strong!"

"Don't you think I miss you, too?" Just for an instant her mind touch burned with passion, then slid, just as quickly, back into quiet. "But there's no getting around the fact of your vow. No matter how Estmere may think he feels about you, or you about him, you must, of honor, stay where you are till it is fulfilled."

"How?" I snapped. "How can he possibly 'need me by his side' when he thinks I killed his wife!"

"Did you?"

"Ailanna!"

"Well?"

Cursing Faerie pragmatism, I told her, "*Duwies*, no! At least . . . I . . . don't think so."

"What does *that* mean?"

"It means I'm . . . not quite myself yet. Nothing to worry you, *cariad*. Come, tell me how you're managing."

She stirred impatiently. "How do you think? This land is very empty without you. Aidan, when you say you're not quite yourself, what—"

"No, what I meant is, how are you living?"

Ailanna paused. "Sweet one, you *have* asked me that question before, remember? You do remember?"

A little chill ran through me. "I'm sorry," I admitted, "I . . . don't." There wasn't any way to avoid the truth. "I . . . have empty patches in my memory these days."

Mind-linked as we were, there was no need to explain why. Where a human might have gushed with pity, Ailanna merely . . . looked. But the intense love in those quiet Faerie eyes staring into my own spoke volumes. And promised endless misery to Bremor should he ever come within her reach.

But then Ailanna smiled the ghost of a smile and broke the spell, saying a touch too lightly, "No matter. No harm in telling you again: I have friends enough. They helped me build a neat little forest home for myself. And your own forest friends, those little sprites and such, have been falling over themselves to keep 'the fine Faerie lady' supplied with food and drink. Oh, and of course there's the magic to learn."

"Magic?" I echoed suspiciously.

"Forest magic. Yes, and human spells as well."

"What!"

"I can pass as a human woman when I wish. And the farmwives and their husbands are eager to share all their little folk charms with anyone who's polite and interested. Aidan, it's all so fascinating!"

"Is it?"

"Yes! It's so different from Faerie spells that I—why, Aidan! I think you're jealous!"

"I am not!"

"You *are!*" She laughed in delight. "If you can worry about me passing the time with human men, you can't be *that* badly hurt!"

"I'm not. But Ailanna, don't—"

"Love, if you can learn Faerie magics, why shouldn't I learn human spells?"

Why not, indeed? And Ailanna wasn't a naive little fool to get herself into difficulties she couldn't handle with a flick of her will. I yielded with a grin.

"Of course," Ailanna admitted with an answering grin, "it's not all song and laughter. No, I must bear Tairyn's naggings. He thinks I'm mad to deal with any humans, mad to learn anything not of Faerie, mad to wait! And he keeps threatening to drag me back to Faerie like an erring child." She shrugged, a fluid, graceful movement. "We both know he'd never carry out his threat. No matter what, I shall wait. And if *I* can endure it, *you* can endure it."

"My lady." I gave her my most gracious bow, and heard her chuckle.

"So-o! My country love has become a courtier! And will he still, I wonder, be happy in the simple woodland?"

I thought of all the tedious, tedious artificiality of the court, the gossiping, the backbiting, the nasty little games of power and prestige, and cried out, "He will, he will, indeed! When he's free to live as he would. But since I can't tell Estmere about you, about us—do thank dear Tairyn for that, won't you?—since things are the way they are, I'll settle for giving Estmere time to recover ... until the end of the period of mourning would be just, I think ... before I force either of us into any decisions about me."

"That seems only fair." She hesitated, then added softly, "Don't hate Tairyn too much, love."

"How can I not? He used me, dragged me off to Faerie to help him out of a problem he couldn't solve—" *a flick of guilt, I'd been glad to help when it meant rescuing that child and freeing poor, lost Lalathanai—* "and then, when I needed *his* help—"

"He did his best! Aidan, listen to me. Listen! Tairyn stayed with me all that time, working his strongest spells to free you. But ... there are Bans and Wards on that land. And n-neither of us could do anything at all—"

"*Cariad, annwyl,* dearest heart, it's all right. It's over. I'm safe. And I will have my revenge on Bremor, never fear."

"No! Oh no, don't!"

I stared at her, amazed. The Folk well understand the concept of revenge, and aren't bound by any human thoughts of mercy. "Why not?" I asked, but Ailanna shook her head.

"First swear to me you will not go after him."

"Ailanna, what—"

"Swear it!"

"The man tortured me! I was in his foul prison for two long months. His pet sorcerer may have permanently harmed my mind. And you would have me simply forget—"

"Not forget. I know you can't forget. But—swear it, please!"

The desperation in her eyes pierced through me. "If you insist. I ... will not go after Bremor to take revenge on him. My word on it. Now, will you please tell me why I had to compromise my honor?"

"When you were a prisoner," she said softly, "when I

was hunting wildly for any way at all to help you, I . . . managed a brief glimpse into the future."

"But I thought that was all but impossible!"

Ailanna sighed. "It nearly is. And the one vision I saw was misty and unsure. Yet of this much I am sure:

"Aidan, you will be Bremor's death—or he shall be yours!"

CHAPTER XXII

THE ASSASSIN

Now, of course things didn't settle down so easily, even after Estmere and I made our "good brothers, good friends" appearances. No, the buzzings continued throughout the next month. As I walked about the palace or worked with sword or knife in the courtyard, gradually building my strength back to normal, I was painfully aware of folks giving me nervous glances or falling suspiciously silent every time I passed. They didn't seem to realize I could *feel* the gist of what they'd just been saying: not a one of them knew for sure whether or not I'd had aught to do with the late queen's death.

If only *I* knew! The uncertainly, the frustrating gaps in memory, were making me every bit as edgy as they.

And then I chanced to overhear my old not-quite adversary, sly Baron Aldingar, whispering with two other courtiers. At first I wearily took it for more of the ditherings I'd heard from everyone else. But then I realized what Aldingar was actually saying and stood listening in sheer disbelief. What a nasty, filthy swamp of lies! No, not outright lies—those, at least, could be denied—but the subtle type of allegations that are so difficult to combat since they merely hint at sins. And what Aldingar was implying, never quite crossing the line into outright treason, was that there had been something more than kinship-by-marriage between myself and Clarissa, and that her death had involved something much worse than murder.

I sprang at him. The two courtiers to whom he'd been spewing his verbal garbage scuttled off into the shadows, but I ignored them, too intent on my prey. Trapping the baron in a corner, I hissed:

"So, my lord! You talk freely enough when I'm not around. Perhaps you would care to make your accusations to my face?"

I'm sure he saw his death in my eyes; *y Duwies* knows I was angry enough just then. I let him stammer out some tangled protestations, not listening to a word of them, then slammed him up against a wall hard enough to make him gasp, pinning him there, breathless and white-faced with shock, with my stare.

"Hear me, my lord," I growled. "Hear me well. If I learn that you have been spreading such vile lies about me, about my brother, about my poor late sister-in-law again, it shall be your last mistake. You shall *learn* what 'worse than murder' means! Do you understand me, my lord?" In my fury, I shook him like a child. "Well, do you?"

He was too terrified to do more than murmur, "Yes . . ."

"Then get out of my sight!"

I gave Aldingar a shove that sent him staggering down the corridor. But as the baron hurried off, I began to shake. *Damnio, damnio,* why had I done such a stupid thing? Using violence and threats—wasn't *that* a clever way to make folks stop fearing me? And Aldingar was a baron, a nobleman with who knew how many important connections—

No. The man would never confess to anyone how badly I'd frightened him. And at least no one else had seen what had happened.

Or . . . almost no one. Suddenly aware of another

presence, I turned sharply, and nearly groaned to find myself facing Father Ansel.

"What's this? Have you come to spread lies about me, too?" But then I rubbed a hand over my face. "Forgive me. That was a childish thing to say."

The shrewd gray eyes studied me without emotion. "I think, Prince Aidan," he said quietly, "we need to speak."

"*Och fi.*" I gestured helplessly. "Your chambers are closer than mine. Lead on, if you would."

Father Ansel's chambers reflected the man: quiet, neat, and serious. The emblem of his faith hung on one wall, and a small stand of books—presumably also related to his faith—proved that he, too, like Estmere, was literate. As I entered, I caught his quick, wry glance and gave him one of my own.

"No, I do *not* go up in smoke at the sight of holy symbols."

That roused a chuckle. "I hardly thought you did. Will it please you to sit, Prince Aidan? I assure you that what we say here shall not leave this room."

So formal. "Are you about to accuse me, too?"

"Have you done anything worth an accusation?"

I bowed my head to my hands. "*Och*, please. I am not in shape for word duels."

"So I see." He hesitated. "Are you quite healed?"

I straightened with a sigh. "As much as I'm likely to be. Tell me, Father Ansel, do *you* think I killed my sister-in-law?"

He never flinched. "No. I never did." At my startled stare, the priest added quietly, "The young man I've watched all these months, the young man who thinks nothing of his status but heals whoever is in need and worries about an injured pot boy, is not a murderer."

"I ... thank you. I needed to hear that from someone."

"But there is something I still must know. Prince Aidan, there is also the sin of guilt by omission. I know you aren't a murderer. But can you swear to me you had nothing whatsoever to do with the late queen's death?"

How I wanted to lie, to tell him blithely, *of course I didn't!* But between Cymraen and Faerie conditioning, I found myself answering honestly instead, "I pray not. I don't know for sure. My . . . my memory is not what it should be."

He sighed softly. "I see. I feared there might be some damage to your mind. So high a fever for so long. . . ."

So intense a sorcerous torment, I corrected wryly. "It *was* you at my bedside?"

He nodded. "We feared lest you die unshriven. But through God's mercy you have survived."

I was obviously supposed to make some holy response. "Amen," I said, and hoped that would do.

Father Ansel seemed satisfied. "I'm not going to ask who tormented you. If you haven't told your brother, there are surely good political reasons."

An unexpected flash of memory, of war, that raw, red horror . . . Bremor and Estmere at war over me . . . no, Duwies, no! Somehow I kept my face impassive. "There are."

"But surely you *have* told him of your lost memory?"

"No."

"No! Why ever not?"

Because I don't want his pity? Because I don't want him thinking I use memory loss as an excuse? Because I . . . don't want him thinking I'm lying to him . . . and that I really am guilty. . . . "I have my reasons," I said lamely. "I wish we could find a way to settle all questions, but . . . well . . ."

"We can't know till your memory returns. When or if it does is, of course, God's will."

"Of course," I echoed uncomfortably, and rose to leave.

"One moment more, please." Suddenly his voice was very gentle. "You don't have to be afraid. I know it must seem as though the whole world has turned against you.

But in truth, very few people here believe you any sort of monster."

"Why are you being so kind?"

He laughed shortly. "It *is* my job."

"No, really. Surely you know—"

"That you are a magician, and almost certainly not even of the faith?" He smiled at my start. "Prince Aidan, I'm not a fool. You've been very careful and very tactful, but there are hints for anyone hunting them."

"Ah. Particularly when I was too ill to properly guard my tongue."

"Exactly. I'll admit I have spent hours in prayer about you, and come to no clear conclusion. Were I to blindly follow the rules, I should be speaking out against you to the king and to my superiors."

Och fi. In my ... well, call it naivete it had never occurred to me that he might *have* superiors, that there might be a whole hierarchy of religious command in the world beyond Estmere's lands of which I knew nothing, that indeed Father Ansel's rightful title might be a good deal higher than merely "priest." As I stared at him in dismay, seeing in my mind wild images of heretics brought to the stake, he smiled at me and continued softly:

"But that poor little pot boy speaks in your favor, as does your love for your brother. You are as you are, and have broken no laws that either of us know about. Let us leave it at that for now."

"I'm sorry to have caused you so much trouble!" I said, and only half meant it as a jest; I was only now realizing how fortunate I'd been that Estmere's priest should be such a civilized man—and that I was a king's brother. With a polite bow, I turned to go.

"By the by," Father Ansel added casually, "did you know that one story wandering the palace has it you were in Hell for those missing two months, battling the Devil?"

"*What?*" It came out as an incredulous burst of a

laugh. "No, I hadn't heard that one! What's supposed to have happened?"

He smiled. "Why, you won, of course. God give you a good day, Prince Aidan."

Estmere glanced up as I entered the little audience chamber. "Ah, Aidan, here you are."

I bit back a sigh. After the almost warmth of Father Ansel, it hurt to see the unease still in Estmere's eyes. And I—I, who had been able to speak so openly to the priest, had nothing better to say to my brother than a lame, "You sent for me. Your messengers caught up with me just outside."

"I did. I'm leaving on a short . . . errand."

"Now? With the weather turning chill?"

"Oh, I'll be back before the first snow, never fear! You've heard me complain about Lyle and Westen?"

"Those two young hotheads? Of course I have!" They were both barons, both just itching for a chance to fight. And unfortunately for peace and quiet, their lands bordered each other. "What now?"

"It would seem that a small flood dislodged certain boundary markers."

"And of course it would never dawn on them to do the sensible thing and appeal to the proper authorities to restore them."

"Of course not. Word had it that they're taking up arms against each other. So," Estmere continued, getting to his feet, "I am going after them."

"You? I mean, you, yourself?"

"How not? I've warned them before. I've commanded that there be peace. But since they have refused to obey their liege lord's messengers, I do believe being faced by the royal presence might finally end their defiance."

"But it's not safe!"

"Nonsense. Lyle and Westen may be idiots, but they're not traitors. Besides, it's not as though I'm going alone! My personal guard will be with me, I assure you. And I will be wearing mail."

"But there's always mischance. A sword could slip, or someone accidentally loose an arrow—Estmere, I'm going with you, just in case—"

"No."

"But you—"

"Aidan, I will not have it look as though I am willing to settle things only through the force of magic."

"Odd. We've never had anyone accuse you of that before. In fact, up to this point, people have seemed rather pleased to see me with you, as though they're looking to you for honest judgment and to me to be sure everyone else is honest as well."

"Are you saying I'm not capable of making judgments on my own?"

"*Och*, Estmere. You know I didn't mean that."

"No. Well. At any rate, the situation is different this time. Lyle and Westen are too hot-blooded to be logical. They would not appreciate a magician's presence."

Sensible enough, I suppose. But the coldness in his voice hurt me. "Then why bother telling me about this at all?"

Why, indeed? He hesitated for so long a time I thought we might at last get to dealing with some of the trouble between us. "You *are* my brother," Estmere said at last, turning away. "You have a right to know what I'm about."

Dyri Uffern! But I couldn't think of anything useful to say either, and muttered a curt, "So be it." And, with an equally curt little bow, I left him.

The wind up here on the castle ramparts was sharp and cold, a northern wind bringing with it a hint of snow and the early changing of the season into winter. But it was also a clean wind, invigorating, at least to someone like myself who, unlike the sourly muttering guards, was out in the open by choice.

My head needed clearing after too much time spent peering into a magic-treated mirror, and the top of my own tower was too narrow to afford much satisfactory pacing. Estmere might be away, but it hadn't stopped me from keeping an eye on my brother, just in case.

And what I had seen:

Estmere had looked elegant and impressive, still in full mourning, but with mail, of course, hidden beneath the black garb. When he had thrown back the hood of his riding cloak, revealing the drama of golden crown and golden hair, I hadn't blamed the baron of Lyle, caught in the act of marching on Westen, for blanching. He had probably pictured his own head ornamenting Lundinia's Traitors' Gate.

With the Lyle men-at-arms sent meekly home again and their baron in royal hands, Estmere had gone on to Westen. Now, while it's relatively easy for a magician to see scenes from afar in a properly prepared mirror, it's difficult to catch the sounds that go along with those scenes. But it wasn't difficult to guess at the dialogue that followed when the baron of Westen had found his king at the foot of his castle.

"Ah . . . will you come up, sire?"

"No, milord baron. You will come down!"

I would have loved to hear what came next, with the two feuders before Estmere like two small boys before their irate father. His warning, I'm sure, was something like this:

"Be wary, gentlemen. My father created your titles. What he created, I can destroy."

Well. Quarrel resolved, peace firmly restored (and, I learned later, a quite regal fine imposed on both barons), Estmere was even now riding back in some personal triumph to Lundinia.

Aie, but it *was* cold up here! A knife-edged gust of wind cut right through my thoughts, and I ducked into the shelter of a watchtower, pulling my fur-lined cloak about me. (A princely gift, that cloak, literally, a present from Estmere in more comfortable days.)

Curiosity moved me to find out if my brother was close enough for me to sense his presence without the focus of the mirror. For a moment I located the familiar aura, even caught Estmere's image in my mind's eye—

And that saved my life. If I hadn't had my magical awareness so heightened, I might never have felt the sudden chill of danger. As it was, there wasn't time to do anything but desperately twist to one side—and then a heavy body was crashing into me and hurling me off my feet!

CHAPTER XXIII

NEW SORCERIES

Aldingar! He's getting his revenge—

For one wild, terrifying moment, I was sure my attacker and I were both going right out through one of the embrasures to the ground so frighteningly far below. But my desperate twisting brought me hard up against the side of the rampart instead. Pinned against the rough stone by the other's weight, tangled in my cloak and expecting a knife between my ribs any second, I called up a desperate, savage surge of Power that would sear right through my attacker—

But suddenly his weight was gone and I was staring up not at Aldingar but at a white-faced, horrified guard held in the determined grip of two others.

"Your Highness!" one of them gasped. "Are you all right?"

"Yes." Not trusting myself to say anything more just yet, I disentangled myself from the folds of my cloak and got to my feet, letting the fierce focus of energy dissipate back throughout my body and hoping I didn't look half as badly shaken as I felt.

Gallu nef, the man had tried to kill me! Estmere had

warned me that as his brother, I might someday be an assassin's target, but—he had actually tried to kill me!

Or . . . had he? There was something about the man's blank, uncomprehending eyes . . .

"Your Highness? Shall we take him for questioning?"

"No. Wait." I approached their captive, seeing sanity slowly flooding back into his face. The man stared at me with such complete bewilderment that I didn't need magic to know what had happened. "Release him."

"But, Your Highness—"

"Release him. He won't do me any harm."

They obeyed, very obviously ill at ease, now not so much afraid *for* me as *of* me (the man who had fought the Devil and won—*pw*, what nonsense!), plainly expecting to see my attacker struck down by some dark and deadly force.

The man must have been expecting the same thing, but he faced me bravely enough. "You don't remember what happened, do you?" I asked softly, and his eyes widened.

"No, Your Highness, I—I swear I don't! Last I recall, I was coming up to relieve Willim here, then the next I know, I'm being grabbed, and I seem to've done something wrong—"

"Something wrong!" hissed Willim. "You tried to kill the prince, is what!"

"No! I'd never do a thing like that, never!" He turned pleading eyes on me. "Not after you went and saved my Meg when she was so sick and— Please, Your Highness, I wouldn't ever try to hurt you."

"I know."

The other two guards stared at me, completely confused. "But, Your Highness . . ." Willim began weakly.

"No. I do thank you for your help, both of you. But what you saw was an innocent man used against his will."

There was a slight pause. Then Willim, a bit quicker than his fellow, asked, "It was drugs, wasn't it? Some coward gave him drugs so he'd attack you."

"A . . . good explanation." If not exactly accurate. "You

shall both be rewarded. But this is my affair, and I will settle it." Imitating as best I could Estmere's regal manner, I added, "You will say nothing of this matter to anyone. Now, leave us."

They did, and very willingly, too. I turned to their still shaken comrade, trying to remember his name (and, for that matter, the saving of his Meg). But it was one of the missing shards of memory that didn't seem likely to return, so I surrendered and asked, "What are you called?"

He didn't seem at all hurt that a prince hadn't remembered a commoner's name. "Hugh, Your Highness. Please, it couldn'ta been drugs, I didn't eat or drink anything different from the others. In the name of mercy, Your Highness, tell me what happened to me!"

"I . . . look you, Hugh, you were bespelled. *Och*, yes, go ahead, cross yourself; I'm no demon to be hurt by holy signs."

"But—but—sorcery—" His voice sharpened in new alarm as I raised my arms to his head. "What are you doing?"

"Nothing to harm you," I soothed, hands at his temples. "No. Stay where you are."

At first he shuddered under my touch like a frightened horse. But I overcame his fear and resistance easily: too easily. Just as some folk are so susceptible to mead they dare not risk one drink, so are some folk equally susceptible to the force of magic.

"Now, Master Hugh, I do think I'd best Ward you."

By now I was reasonably sure none of my spells had been affected by my unpredictable memory loss. I closed my eyes, calming myself, coaxing up the necessary focus of will, summoning a knowledge that wasn't on the conscious level. At last I felt my hand tracing certain Signs on Hugh's brow, and knew without having to look that each glyph glowed a pure, unsullied blue against his weatherworn skin for the briefest instant before vanishing.

As I traced the last of the Signs, I was suddenly aware

that my psychic hold on Hugh was slipping. Fine! That meant my shielding charm had begun to work, even against my own magic, and I opened my eyes in satisfaction.

"Wake up, Hugh."

He blinked and shook his head like a dog shaking off water, then looked at me in confusion. I gave him what I hoped was a reassuring smile. "You may go, Hugh. You're Shielded now. And don't look so fearful! All that means is that no one can work sorcery on you again."

"Uh ... I ... thank you, Your Highness."

"Go. Even," I added with a laugh, "to your priest, if you like."

But as soon as the man was out of sight, I let my mask of good humor fall. For one thing, I was feeling the aftereffects of the energy expended in my magic. For another, it was only now hitting home how narrowly I had escaped death.

"May the Darkness rend his soul!" I muttered in Cymraeth, and didn't mean poor Hugh.

Bremor.

By now his spies must surely have told him I was alive and reasonably recovered, and that Estmere wasn't going to war with him over me. But Bremor didn't know I wouldn't—I couldn't!—move against him myself, and so, *damn* him, he didn't dare let me live.

I suddenly realized I was gripping the edge of the rampart wall so fiercely that my hands hurt, and forced myself to let go, rubbing cold, reddened fingers as I began to pace.

Why hadn't Bremor tried a standard form of assassination?

No. The poisoned cup, the sly dagger, all that was so very chancy. If his assassin should fail and be caught, and be forced to confess all ... Such an overt act against the king's brother, virtually in front of the king, would certainly be grounds for war. And Bremor had as good as told me he wasn't yet ready for that. Instead, prudently waiting till Estmere was away, he had chosen a safer way to be rid of me, one that, win or lose, would leave no tangible evidence.

But . . . with Ybarre dead, how had Bremor managed any magic at all?

I stopped short, stunned, horrified, vaguely remembering Bremor boasting . . . saying . . . yes, saying he would rend my mind apart if need be to learn all I knew. Could he. . . ? *Gallu nef*, could he, somewhere in that dark, empty time, have done just that, torn the knowledge of magic from my brain? Was that the reason my memory couldn't heal?

Och, surely not. Any such violent rending of my psychic defenses wouldn't have merely damaged my memory, it would have left me quite mindless. . . .

My hands were shaking. Angrily I clenched them to keep them still. Of course Bremor hadn't stolen any magic from me! He had simply made use of some foul text or other left behind by the late, unlamented Ybarre. *And why couldn't Bremor have read the spell wrong, and blasted himself!*

But such ranting was foolish. At least it had been a clumsy attack, a wild snaring of the first mind he could reach, just what one would expect from a rank amateur.

Yes. Of course. And it had very nearly worked. The next time—but there wasn't going to be another time! Promise to Ailanna or no, I was not going to wait meekly for Bremor to try again.

I stormed to my tower, rage hot within me, refusing to admit just how shaken I still was. Working to channel my raw anger and shock into useable Power—no easy task, because it means holding fast to those emotions even as you're trying to keep yourself calm—feeling that Power burn like fire through me, I set the guarding Signs at door and windows, then brought mirror, brazier and certain herbs to the center of the room I used as my study.

"*Y Duwies* aid me in my work," I murmured in perfunctory prayer, then set about tracing in the proper sunwise manner, east to east, three concentric and precisely spaced circles about the items and myself. As I reached out with my will, blue fire blazed up briefly along the traced lines and as briefly was gone, and I nodded. The circle was complete, its Power activated, the vital aid to help me focus my magical sight. Considering the distance involved, it was going to take some focusing, indeed.

I started my brazier to burning, then cast onto it those herbs that intensify Sight, homely tansy and lavender and others I won't list here. It wasn't done without a qualm; that combination always leaves me with an aching head. But it would be well worth the headache to see what Bremor was about.

And, gradually emptying my mind of thought, emotion, everything but the memory of that one hated face, breathing in the mingled sharp and sweet scents of the burning herbs, I looked into my mirror. For long and long I saw nothing but grayness. . . .

Then, quite suddenly, quite sharply, I saw Bremor, seated alone at a table of dark, heavy wood, a great book, most certainly Ybarre's grimoire, lying open before him.

But Bremor wasn't reading. No, his head was thrown back against the high back of his chair, his eyes were squeezed shut, and on his face was a look of such intolerable anguish as to almost—almost!—move me to pity. But among my fragmented memories I could remember, far too well, chains and darkness and sophisticated, sorcerous torments . . . and at the sight of him, *y Duwies* forgive me, hot, savage joy raced through me.

"Fool!" I shouted, though of course he couldn't hear me. "You fool who thought you could control Power!"

His spell had been broken, after all; in Bremor's inexperience he'd lost his hold on Hugh even before I had gotten to my feet. And it was obvious the man knew nothing of the Threefold Law, because now he was suffering all the torment of unspent magic recoiling on him. Would it kill him, ahh, would it?

Bremor must have screamed, though I heard nothing, for suddenly there were servants about him. Even knowing painfully well of the sorcerous miasma fogging that castle, I was shocked by the terror and hatred burning in their eyes. What they might have done to their king with him so helpless before them, I don't know. But just then another man entered my limited field of vision. Judging from his richly bejewelled tunic and the respectful bows he was receiving, he was of high nobility. No. Of the Telessian royal family itself, surely. A cousin, perhaps? His face was fuller, more mature, but there was a definite resemblance to Bremor.

He had saner eyes, though. Surprisingly sane, because his life could not have been an easy one, not with Bremor's fear of trusting anyone, let alone a relative. Presumably only the king's need for an heir kept this obvious kinsman alive and unimprisoned.

Well, whatever rank he might be, the man was ordering Bremor to be taken from the room, presumably to the royal bedchamber, though the impulse must have been almost overwhelming to have him tossed from the nearest window instead. I drew back from the mirror, feeling pain already nagging at the edges of my mind. But I hesitated a moment more, wondering if there was anything more to be learned from this other, plainly honorable, member of Telessian royalty.

Then we both cried out in shock, he quickly crossing himself, as Ybarre's grimoire suddenly, spontaneously, burst into flame. I lost my hold on the scene, and the mirror instantly became no more than a mirror. But it didn't matter; I had seen enough. Quickly I broke the circle, discharging what energies might still be swirling within it, emptied the contents of the smoldering brazier into the fireplace, then collapsed gladly into a chair.

But despite a truly monumental headache, I was laughing.

Ybarre obviously hadn't trusted his master. He had set a Guardian Spell on his book to destroy the thing should anyone but he try to use it.

I leaned back in the chair, trying to summon enough will to banish the headache. But it was difficult to concentrate when all I kept thinking was:

Bremor, poor Bremor, your pretty book is gone! Poor fool, after that one moment of Power, you're nothing more than a poor, magickless little man again.

But in that moment of my mockery, trumpets blared, golden arrows of sound that pierced right through my aching head. Again they blared, telling all the world King Estmere had returned.

So much for my brief triumph. I set about in earnest banishing my headache, and this time was successful.

And with that, I once more took on the problems of everyday life, and went down from my tower to greet my brother.

CHAPTER XXIV

WINTER DARKNESS

As the year turned to an early, snow-filled winter, Estmere combatted the grief of his loss with revelry. The court rang out all that season with song and merriment, bright, shiny-green holly branches and fragrant pine boughs pinned up where once wedding banners had hung. And if Father Ansel thought that these winter revels touched a little too much upon paganism, the sorrow behind the mirth in Estmere's eyes must have moved the priest to pity, for he kept his silence.

What of me? *Och*, I went through the motions of enjoying myself, at least at first. But being joyous with my brother smacked too much of hypocrisy, particularly since Estmere resolutely pretended nothing was wrong between us even while he burned with unvoiced suspicions of me that I, with my maddeningly faulty memory, could do nothing to disprove.

Besides, that winter I had my own demons to fight.

They roused themselves into life the day a wagon overturned on the icy cobblestones, and crushed one of the castle laborers, a friendly, inoffensive man I knew only as Matt, beneath it. As I bent over him, heartsick, his

216

eyes, wild with pain, met mine, trusting, pleading, and I—I took one look at that poor, mangled body and knew there was only one mercy I could grant him. As Father Ansel (who, to give him credit, had come running almost as swiftly as I, with no thought at all to this being only a commoner beneath his dignity) performed the necessary rites of his faith, I gently bespelled away Matt's pain and heard him sigh softly with relief.

And then, just as gently, I stilled his heart.

When I got slowly to my feet, the *feel* of Matt's death aching within me, Father Ansel was watching me. He could only have known what I had done, and I straightened, nerves taut, thinking that if he said one word about murder . . .

But he must have seen from my face that just then I was dangerous as a wild thing, very close to losing control. And he said nothing.

All that day, the memory of poor Matt's trusting, anguished eyes haunted me. Even though, rationally, I knew there was nothing else I could have done, I couldn't stop mulling over what had happened, wondering if I had acted too quickly, arguing that surely there must have been *some* other course, finding none.

It wasn't as though I hadn't seen patients die before, even here at Estmere's court. The first thing any healer must accept is that he or she is not divine; there will always be illnesses too severe, injuries too terrible for even magical healing. Lalathanai—poor lost thing, there'd been little of her left, and no *feel* of her death to echo within me. But this time . . . *Duwies glân*, I had never taken a life by magic before!

Now, while I'd been recovering from Bremor's torments, I'd been very proud of myself for banishing nightmares, for blocking all thoughts of that dark, half-remembered horror: foolishly proud. It's an unfortunate fact that torture victims who seem fully recovered from their ordeal may be hit by the darkest despair long after the time of torment is past.

It had never occurred to me that I, too, might be such a victim.

But the night after Matt's death, the dreams began once more. And this time they refused to be banished. Ah, and they were dreadful things, distorted shards of darkness and pain, of hopelessness so strong it carried over into my waking hours. I began to wake each morning in despair, dreading the day, dreading my own inner night.

The healer in me knew that if I ever wanted my mind to recover, I should ignore missing memories, let them return if and when *y Duwies* willed it. But even so, I fought again and again to regain that lost time, somehow convinced that if I regained all my memory, despair would be vanquished, even though the struggle made my head ache fiercely. Even though the few memories I did regain were hardly those I would have chosen:

Ybarre's spells tearing at my mind and body, wrapping me in arcane fire that left no physical trace yet seared my every nerve while I lay chained in darkness, unable to fight, unable to move, unable to do anything but endure, endure, endure—

Ah, *Duwies*.

As the days grew shorter, as all my magic seemed powerless to shield me, I slid deeper and deeper into the darkness of my despair, afraid to sleep lest I dream, afraid to leave my tower, staying barred, alone, refusing food, refusing rest. . . .

Why didn't I go to Estmere? What could he have done? Clapped me on the shoulder and told me it was all in my head? Of *course* it was all in my head! But knowing this trouble was all of my own, overwrought brain's creating didn't help me to deal with it.

Why didn't I call on Ailanna for help? I don't know. I was past all logic by that point, convinced my Power was empty and unreal, convinced that any effort to save myself was futile.

And despair nearly won. For the first time in my life, I found myself considering ending that life. Body aching, eyes burning from lack of rest, I stumbled about my tower room wondering which potion might be quickest, surest, most fatal.

But before I could take any insane action, my legs betrayed me and let me fall. Exhausted and struggling against the darkness, I slipped helplessly away from consciousness. . . .

Someone was calling me. Someone was pulling me from true sleep into trance. I *felt* that careful mental touch that meant someone was opening a vision pathway between us, and murmured in vague confusion:

"Ailanna . . . ?"

"Hardly."

Tairyn. As the vision slowly firmed and grew clear, he stood before me in that dream-reality, as elegant and contemptuous as ever, hair a sleek fall of silver, cool, smoky green eyes looking me slowly up and down.

"Now, isn't this a ridiculous sight!"

For an instant he took what was left of my will from me, forced me to see myself through his eyes: unshaven, unwashed, clad in the same tunic I'd been wearing for . . . *y Duwies* knew how long. A flicker of anger stirred within me. Once . . . once before I had kept him out of my mind, and now I remembered Power enough to break his hold again and—

Yes. My will was my own again, and I snapped, "I'm pleased to see you, too!"

"Ah. He still retains some wit."

"Where were you? Where the *hell* were you?"

"Meaning what?"

"Why did you abandon me?" It was a shout of raw pain. Maybe my memories were shaky in all other things, but this, this I remembered. And there was no stopping the anguished flood of words. "I had just done your work for you, helped that child to live and that poor, poor woman to die! Why did you let me be lost after that? Was I no more than a tool? *Why did you abandon me?*"

Tairyn never flinched. "Listen to me. Come, listen. I did *not* abandon you. I am not omnipotent, human, nor do I pretend to hold a perfect view of the future. Had I known you would fly straight into the hands of a foe, yes, I would have done something to stop you. But I could not know. And after that, if I could have pulled you from your trap, yes, I would have done that, too. But I could not. Do you understand me? Can you?"

If he was trying to rouse me from apathy, he was succeeding. But I didn't particularly want to be roused; it hurt too much. "Tairyn," I managed, "I am honored you've contacted me, and all courtesies like that. But I'm not at my best and—"

"Fool."

I blinked in surprise. "What—"

"You heard me, human. Fool, I say, to let yourself be betrayed *by* yourself."

"I don't—"

"There are charms to bar this ridiculous self-torment from your mind. Listen. Learn."

With that, he proceeded to teach them to me, giving me no choice but to learn, waiting with—for him—remarkable patience while I struggled to commit those sleek, cool syllables to a mind that seemed far too worn to accept them. But at last I had them whole.

"Now use them," Tairyn ordered shortly. "You should be able to unlock their Power even in this sorry state."

I did. And of course the charms worked. As each was completed, I felt the inner darkness fall away more and more as a cool, wonderful peace settled about me.

And as I whispered the last spell, on the verge of sobbing like a child with relief, sanity returned in a rush. Yes, what had been done to me in Bremor's dungeons had been terrible; no, I would never truly forget. But that terrible time no longer existed. I could accept the past *as* past—and I would no longer let my mind keep me Bremor's slave.

"Tairyn, I am in your debt! I—I—"

"Enough." For an instant, I was almost sure I'd surprised something like sympathy in those opaque eyes. But then, lest I dare think he had softened in his opinion of me, Tairyn added in his usual cool voice, "Why Ailanna wishes to cleave to you is a mystery beyond my fathoming. But you would have been of little use to her dead or mind dead. Farewell."

With that, he broke the mind link and vanished, and I let myself fall into a sweet well of dreamless sleep.

Freshly bathed, shaved (after a brief self-debate I had decided the beard acquired during my . . . recovery made me look more villainous than sorcerous), and clad in blessedly clean clothing, I climbed down from my tower, feeling like some woods thing crawling out of its winter lair, and came face to face with Estmere on the stairway, looking as raw and worn and newborn as I felt.

For a moment we stared at each other in silence.

"I was just coming to see if you were still alive," he began hesitantly. "I assume you were engrossed in powerful magics up there all this while. I didn't want to disturb you. But the servants who'd been delivering food to you reported that the trays were going untouched and nobody was answering their knocks. I . . . was concerned."

"Thank you." I really must have been in a state of mental collapse; I couldn't even remember the last time I'd eaten, or heard anyone at my door. "I . . . let's just say I spent the winter exorcising demons."

After a startled moment, Estmere realized how I meant that, and let out his breath in a long, silent sigh. "So did I," he confessed softly. "Oh Aidan, so did I."

CHAPTER XXV

SPRING THAW AND SPRING PLOTS

The day was fine and fair, the sky unstained and richly blue as the pigment on a master artist's brush. I stood alone on the castle ramparts, cloak wrapped about me, breathing in the clean, clear air with something close to rapture, feeling like a man who has been given back his life.

The winter, the long, terrible winter, had finally ended.

Eh well, to be fair, it really hadn't been a terrible winter. Not for folk untroubled in their minds. The harvest had been a rich one, and the weather not unbearably cold.

As for Bremor—ah yes, he had survived his little excursion into sorcery; "the Devil," as people say, "looks after his own." But he hadn't been able to find himself a new sorcerer. Powerful ones are, after all, hardly common, and few are as foolish or as easily snared as Ybarre. Nor had there yet been any signs of military trouble out of Telesse.

By now I had almost managed to convince myself that my interest in him was strictly political.

And as for Estmere and myself ... what would you have me say? That our friendship had quickly returned to its former easy path? That in one little half-year all the fears and suspicions and mutual pain had been forgotten?

No. Though Estmere had proven that winter he still cared about what happened to me, though he never again openly accused me and we both fiercely pretended nothing was wrong, the gray uncertainty of Clarissa's death still hung between us like a never quite banished ghost. And I ... I still lacked the memories that might finally lay that ghost to rest. The period of mourning was nearly over now; it was time for me to face him and settle matters between us once and always. If I dared.

But how could I hold to bitterness now? Though the wind was still chill enough to make me shiver, it had lost the edge to its bite. And there was the faintest sweetness in the air, that wonderful scent so familiar to me from my childhood, telling me tales of thawing earth and the first new stirrings of vegetable life, a scent bearing the birth of hope within it. I stood for a time lost in a silent, heartfelt prayer of thanksgiving.

The most discreet of coughs brought me back to my surroundings. "Ah, Prince Aidan ..." said a tentative voice.

"Sir Verrin." I dipped my head a cool, polite fraction. "What are you doing up here?"

"A servant saw you climbing this way. I took the liberty of following. Please, Prince Aidan, if you would be good enough to spare me some of your time, I needs must speak with you. In private."

That surprised me. Sir Verrin, the king's seneschal, a solid, busy little man of definite abilities and scant humor, and if I haven't mentioned him much, it's for a very good reason: I don't like the man. That, in turn, is for an equally good reason: he dislikes (in a more flighty fellow I would have said fears) any hint of magic. And so, perforce, he dislikes me.

At least he'd had the sense to puzzle out that I'd been praying, and been courteous enough to let me finish. I glanced about the deserted rampart, intrigued. "None can hear us up here, Sir Verrin." A mischievous whim made me add innocently, "If you would prefer I cast *Sbel Dirgelwch,* the Spell of Secrecy, about us ... ?"

He turned a bit green at the thought. "Uh ... thank you, Prince Aidan, no. That ... will not be necessary."

"Well, then? Speak."

He took a deep breath, a man steeling himself for an ordeal. "Actually, it isn't just myself who needs speak with you."

"Ah?"

"No. But I—we—" Verrin shook his head. "Pray forgive me. What I mean to say is that we had no wish to intrude upon your privacy. But if it would please you to join us in the Rose Chamber?"

The Rose Chamber is one of the smaller audience chambers, so named for the roses—Anglic emblems of privacy—painted on the ceiling. "First name this 'us.'"

"None to harm you or betray his majesty, my word on it. Please, Prince Aidan ..."

Well now, perhaps it was foolish of me, but by now my curiosity was well and thoroughly roused. I followed the bustling little man down into the Rose Chamber— and stopped short. If this wasn't the entire flock of Estmere's advisors—that well-padded lot of velvet and fur—it was a goodly sampling. They stood as I entered, bowing with polite, unnerving precision. There wasn't a one of them who was less than a decade my senior, which was also a touch unnerving.

"Gentles," I said warily. "I hardly expected to see you gathered here. I thought you would be with my brother."

"No need, Prince Aidan," I was solemnly assured by Sir Randal, the very image of the somber graybeard. "As you know, your royal brother meets with the ambassador from King Wencin, and he did not wish us all there to ... ah ... 'unnerve the man.'"

That sounded like Estmere, indeed. "So instead you conspire here."

"No, no," Verrin cut in hastily. "We do nothing here to harm the king, I have already given you my word of that!"

They very obviously weren't going to tell me any more until I sat down in conference with them. "*Och fi,*" I muttered under my breath, and then, to all of them, "Before we go any further, gentles, pretty painted roses on the ceiling are all well and good, but I am going to cast *Sbel Dirgelwch*, The Spell of Secrecy in here. Don't give me that fearful look, Sir Verrin! I am *not* having someone think I'm conspiring against my brother."

Sbel Dirgelwch is one of those quiet spells that require nothing more from the magician than a certain amount of will and the properly twisting, hopefully graceful, gestures of hand and arm. Basically it isn't so much a forceful changing of anything but rather a simple entreaty to the air and walls and whatever else surrounds the magician to let none of his words pass beyond their boundary. Indeed, the less forceful the entreaty, the more likely it is to succeed. There really isn't anything for a non-magician to see, but I admit to adding a few melodramatic sparkles and gleams, just to keep these folk a bit off balance.

The spell slid smoothly into completion. I felt the air suddenly *soften* all around the edges of the room, absorbing all sound so none would escape. I sank into a chair to hide the fact that I was out of breath (even such simple spells aren't effortless) and waved the wary advisors all to sit. "Now, gentles, what would you?"

They glanced uncertainly at each other. Then Sir Verrin, the sacrificial goat, began: "Prince Aidan, the king your brother has been a widower now for a full half-year."

"I'm well aware of that."

"Of course." Verrin hurried boldly forward. "Surely you see the need for him to wed again."

I groaned. "Not you, too!"

"I beg your pardon?"

"Look you, all of you, I wasn't up on the ramparts merely to take the air; I was escaping people." I glanced about the room. "What, still no comprehension? I have already, within the past few days—within the past few hours—been approached by almost everyone at court! Each one of them has been transparently seeking to win my favor, because each of them, just as transparently, sees in me a shortcut to the royal ear—even as you do, gentles!"

"You misunderstand us," Sir Randal said.

"Do I, now? Do you mean to say none of you here is hoping for advancement? None of you here has his own candidate for queen? Ha, no, you can't swear that, can you!"

"But . . ." Verrin began warily. "Surely you see—"

"Sir Verrin, I am very well aware a king must have a queen. An heir. But what I can't see is the point of all this sudden rushing about. It's only been six months since my brother's wife died!"

Several advisors crossed themselves at that, several voices murmured, almost as though they'd rehearsed it, "God rest her."

"Indeed," I agreed. "But it doesn't look as though *you* are willing to let her rest."

Sir Randal sighed. "Prince Aidan, much as we all still grieve with His Majesty, the hard truth is that the period of mourning is over."

"Barely!"

"Ah yes, barely," he conceded. "But the fact remains, it *is* over, and we must think now of the future."

"Ah, wait. Don't tell me. You have a daughter, or some nice little niece or cousin you'd like to see advanced."

He gave me the look usually reserved for a parent faced with a rude child. "Please understand, none of us here are thinking of personal reward."

"Of course not."

Randal edged his chair a bit closer, leaning towards me. For a startled moment I thought he meant to give me a fatherly pat on the knee. But, just as surprisingly, he murmured, "I understand how you must feel, a powerful mage, a hero who's fought the Supreme Evil—"

"The Supreme—don't tell me *you* believe that ridiculous tale!" As I glanced around the room, I felt reality turn to mist. "You *do*, you all *do*!" I never *would* understand these folk, not if I stayed here till the stars ran cold! They could talk most rationally about the most mundane things and then suddenly turn around and believe something too fantastic for even the youngest Cymraen child!

"No need for modesty," Sir Randal said, and the others all somberly agreed.

"But I didn't—I never—look you, I'm not someone out of a—a wonder tale!" That wasn't getting to them at all. "Just how Powerful do you think I am?" I yelped. "If I'd been stupid enough to take on something as terrible as your Anglic Devil, do you really think I would have survived?"

Hands moved in hasty holy gestures. But obviously, they murmured, if I was here before them, I must have not only survived, but won.

This was like wading through cobwebs! "If I was the winner, what was I doing lying sick to death for so long?"

"You could hardly be expected to leave so terrible a battle with no wounds at all," Sir Randal said in a sensible tone.

"I wasn't wounded in battle, *damnio*, I was tortured!"

I hadn't meant to say that; what had happened to me was none of their affair. But even that dramatic proclamation didn't shake the advisors in the slightest. All they did was make the smallest shift in the story: of *course* I'd been tortured; that was what their Devil did to people. That I was now here and healthy *proved* there'd been a battle that I'd won.

Looking at all those totally sane, totally rational faces, I couldn't find a single sensible thing to say. "I give up. I just give up. Go on, Sir Randal. What were you saying before all this?"

"Simply that it must be difficult for you to leave the realm of great and terrible magic for the world of simple men."

"More difficult than I'd ever expected."

The sarcasm went right by all of them.

"Prince Aidan," Verrin said earnestly, "surely you must see that the sooner our good ruler weds and produces an heir, the sooner the royal line is safe. Why, if something should happen to the king today—which, of course, Heaven forbid!" He crossed himself hastily, and the others followed. "But if something *were* to happen, and he quite childless, there would be no one to take the throne except—"

He stopped aghast at what he'd almost said. Grinning, I finished for him, "Except the bastard son of a wild witch-woman. A hero, maybe, a great and terrible mage, but a bastard nonetheless. Most unsuitable."

The others murmured in disapproval, and Verrin all but squirmed in embarrassment. "Oh, Prince Aidan, I assure you, I didn't mean—"

"Oh, Sir Verrin, you did." My grin faded as I held him, as I held them all, transfixed by the force of my stare. "My thoughts about the throne have never been a secret. You know as well as I that I have not the slightest desire for the chains of kingship. You *do* know that, don't you? All of you?"

"Yes." It was a strangled gasp from Verrin. The others slowly nodded.

"So. Thank you."

As Verrin's glance squirmed away from mine, Sir Randal asked me quietly, "You agree, then?"

By this point I could hardly remember what we'd originally been discussing. "That Estmere must remarry?" I waved a helpless hand. "That's the way it's done in these ... civilized lands. But what has this to do with me? It's your job to find a suitable bride, your job to make all those complicated arrangements you people seem to find necessary."

"We have tried, Prince Aidan. *I* have tried. Believe

me, I have tried." Verrin's voice quivered with frustration. "But there are problems."

"And you're about to list every one of them, aren't you?"

He blinked. And proceeded. "Primus: There are no unmarried women of childbearing years in the direct royal line."

"True." Not that any noble would ever admit such a common comparison, but too many marriages of close kin had undoubtedly weakened the stock, just as is true in the breeding of animals. Poor, fragile Clarissa had been proof enough of that. "An unfertile lot, our royal folk!"

A few of the more sensitive advisors stirred at this unseemly jest, but Verrin ignored it, continuing doggedly, "Secundus: There are few enough available ladies of proper rank within the kingdom."

"*Och fi*, we wouldn't want him contaminated by a woman not of proper rank, would we?"

"Prince Aidan . . ."

"Yes. I'm sorry. I won't interrupt again, I promise."

He gave me a doubtful glance, but continued, "And tertius: Though a political alliance with some neighboring land would be the best thing for king and country . . ."

"Yes?" I stirred impatiently. "Come, out with it!"

Verrin reddened, glancing nervously about the room. "Tertius," he mumbled hurriedly, so softly I almost couldn't hear him, "your royal brother refuses to let me send out the proper inquiries, either within *or* without the kingdom."

"So-o! Continue, do!"

"He . . . absolutely refuses to even consider the question of remarriage, and . . . threatened to have my head if I ever mentioned it to him again."

Poor Verrin. I burst out laughing, I couldn't help it. "And so you are forced to come to me, the . . . ah, what was it you called me once? The 'dark sorcerer-prince,' was it?"

"Your Highness, I never—"

"*Pw*, man, don't perjure yourself."

He took a deep breath. "Please, Prince Aidan. For the sake of the kingdom, won't you—"

"Help you off the executioner's block?"

But even with my sarcasm, I was wondering, half in despair, *Why oh why do these people have to be so very sincere?*

Yes, they were ambitious; yes, they'd all probably said or done some questionable things during their years in royal service. But when it came to their love for and worry about their land, every one of them was most disarmingly honest.

You win, Randal. Maybe I'm not the spectacular hero you seem to think me, but my destiny does seem determined to dump me into this most mundane of situations.

Ah, well, not quite mundane. Not to Estmere. We were talking about his life, his future, after all. . . .

"Why yes, Sir Verrin," I said fiercely. "Since things are the way they are, I will see how my brother's mind really stands. Perhaps I will see if I can change said mind about remarrying. I may even help you find a 'proper' bride." There, that was devious enough to keep them wondering. "But remember this, all of you," I added with my most sorcerous glare, gratified to see most of them flinch. "Whatever I do, I do for Estmere's sake, not yours."

Triumph flashed in Sir Randal's eyes. "We can ask no more, Prince Aidan."

CHAPTER XXVI

DUELS

That unexpected and rather ridiculous meeting with his advisors had kept me from watching Estmere at his royal work: in this case, interviewing that ambassador from the court of King Wencin of Norrusk, one of our northern neighbors. Estmere hadn't actually requested my presence, so I didn't need to feel guilty about not having been there, but I generally enjoyed watching the game of diplomacy (even though that usually meant standing for hours at the side of my brother's throne or, if I was lucky, sitting on a formal but uncomfortable chair in an overcrowded room). There was something fascinating about those delicate maneuverings managed by folk without the use of magic.

There was nothing delicate about Wencin, though. An aged monarch, he, just a touch worn in the wits, with mental meanderings enough to infuriate my brother. A stubborn man, Wencin, too, with a stubborn ambassador whose temper couldn't have been improved by his party's having to wrestle their way along roads heavy with spring mud.

It must have been a fiery meeting. But now I found

the great audience chamber empty of all but a few busy servants and a psychic residue of anger and impatience, and went in search of Estmere.

I caught up with him in his private chambers. The guards gave me a somewhat uneasy glance, but they stood aside to let me enter; apparently their king hadn't quite commanded he not be disturbed.

I paused just inside the room as the door was shut quietly behind me. "Estmere?"

"Yes, yes," snapped an ill-tempered voice. "Come in."

He was slumped in a high-backed chair, legs outstretched, hands steepled, eyes dark and brooding.

"As bad as that?" I murmured, and Estmere glared up at me.

"I can't keep anything hidden from you, can I?"

"Don't take out your anger on me. I can hardly not sense that you're blazing with frustration."

He sat bolt upright at that. "Ahh, yes! Aidan, he is so hopelessly stubborn!"

"King Wencin?"

"Of course King Wencin! He just cannot or will not see that signing a pact of nonaggression doesn't mean he's signing away his freedom."

"And that fox-faced ambassador—what's his name? Gern? Master Sly-eyed Gern can't be helping things."

"He dares humor me." It was a growl. "As though I was still a boy in my minority. By my faith, were he not protected by his ambassador's status . . . But he is, and there's an end to it."

"And of course you can't let your temper loose."

"No! That would be the end of any hope of a treaty."

"I . . . don't suppose I could be of any help?"

Estmere raised a brow. "With your magic, you mean? Don't think I haven't considered it. But no, you know I can't have it said I use unnatural means of persuasion. *Damn* the man!"

"Gern or Wencin?"

"Does it matter? They've both earned me time enough with Father Ansel."

"Because you've ill-wished them? That's only human, Estmere."

He shot me a fiery glance. "That's also a mortal sin!"

"Why," I mused, "then Wencin's son must either be already damned, or a remarkably saintly man."

Estmere gave a sharp bark of a laugh, then winced, hand going to his head. "Or a remarkably patient one," he added in a subdued voice. "I will have that alliance, God willing, with enough patience. If only I can hold my temper long enough!"

That last outburst made him wince again, and me with him; the radiations of his pent-up fury were beginning to make my own head ache. Moving to my brother's side, I put my hands on his temples. Estmere started to flinch away from me, which hurt, then in the next instant changed his mind and stayed so rigidly still it hurt me the more.

Damnio, *brother, how I'd love to leave you to your own devices!*

But, healer that I am, I couldn't turn away from someone in pain, so I set myself to finishing what I'd started, and willed calmness into him, *feeling* that dangerous, inward-turning fury slowly fading. . . .

Estmere let out his breath in a long, relieved sigh. "Thank you. I can see why folks are eager to come to you for healing."

I let my hands drop and stepped aside. "I do what I can."

"Yes. That's what we all try to do, isn't it?" He stirred restlessly. "A healer must be a truly good person."

"Ha! I'm hardly one of your saints! Look you, I've tried to explain this before. It's not so easy to put this into Anglic, but . . . if Power is natural to you, illness or injury *feels* like a—a *wrongness* grating on your nerves. And you just can't be comfortable till you've done something to correct it."

He was staring at me. "You never seem to get angry."

"Not true."

"Then your control is far better than mine! I don't think I've ever seen you truly lose your temper."

My mind shied from partial, painful memories of Clarissa and that savage, embarrassing assault on Baron Aldingar. "I don't dare."

"Because of your magic."

"Precisely."

He was silent a moment, considering, I suppose, the nightmare of Power burning out of control, then raised a wry brow. "Can you really say you've never used magic against anyone? Never?"

"Estmere—"

"Oh, I don't mean for genuine harm. Still, all those little annoyances of daily life ... The temptation must be enormous to put down some bully or braggart with a flash of will."

Aldingar, again. "It is."

"So, now! You mean to say you have never, ever yielded to temptation?"

I had to grin. "Well ... once."

"Aha!"

"When I was very young and very proud of my new Power, a farmer's boy insulted me. And I ... ah ... conjured an illusion of worms into his bed. He hated worms. Unfortunately, my mother found out—but you wouldn't know about such things. No one would dare punish the royal heir."

"No?" He gave a reminiscent chuckle. "I might have been Prince Estmere, but my—our—father was King Estmere, and very determined to see I didn't grow up a tyrant." Impulsively, he added, "I wish you could have known him."

"So do I."

For a moment something of our old friendship trembled in the air between us. But then an uneasy Estmere turned from me.

"You didn't come here to share old memories. What would you?"

"The timing is terrible. If I speak my mind right now, I'm going to undo all my work of calming."

"I'll risk it. Come, brother, speak."

"As you will. I know my presence makes you uncomfortable these days."

"No."

"Yes. I . . ." *Damnio*. Much as I hadn't wanted to mention this, there didn't seem to be any way around it. "There is something I must tell you, and I hope you won't react too strongly. My ordeal during the two months I was missing left my memory . . . damaged. It never has quite recovered."

He looked at me in shock. "I never even suspected— Why didn't you tell me before?"

"Because I didn't want pity. I still don't. *Och*, look, it's not that terrible a thing; I can recall most of what I need to know and use logic to bridge the gaps."

"So *that's* why you looked so blank when I mentioned Baron Bernhart the other day. You didn't remember meeting him, did you?"

"I still don't."

"Oh, Aidan, I'm sorry. . . ."

"I told you, I don't want pity."

"But it must be so frightening!"

I sighed. "Not any more. Disconcerting is more the word."

"And your magic can't help you?"

"No. What caused the damage was sorcerous, not natural." I'd known that almost from the start. Memory loss due to shock generally affects only the patch of time surrounding the injury; these unpredictable blank spots and my headaches when I sought to fill them in could only be the result of Ybarre's failed attempts to steal my Power and break my mind. "As far as I know, there's no spell for— Estmere, please. The only reason I'm mentioning memory loss at all is because, frankly, I can't remember clearly enough about . . . Clarissa . . . to know if you have a genuine reason to be suspicious of me." I saw his face grow very still, and continued wearily, "I'm not using it as an excuse. I'm not trying to buy mercy."

"What, then?"

"Even though I can't prove my innocence, I had hoped you knew me well enough to trust me. I'd hoped that, one way or another, time would lessen your suspicion. But that doesn't seem to be happening. Come, be honest with me. Do you want me gone from court?"

"You're not my prisoner. If you would leave, I won't hold you."

"That doesn't answer my question."

"Why is my answer so important?"

"Because you're my brother. Because you were my friend."

"I still am!"

"Are you?"

His eyes glittered. "I've warned you before: don't play games with me."

"See now, there it is. You back away from answering me."

"If you want to go, go! If you want to stay, stay! In the name of God, what more do you want of me?"

"Pretentious as it may sound, I want you to be happy. I want *me* to be happy. Do you want me gone from court?"

He stared at me, frustrated. "Sometimes I find it very difficult to believe we share any blood, because sometimes I swear I don't understand you at all. Why do you persist?"

"Because I need an answer. Do you want me gone from court?"

Estmere let out a wordless, maddened cry. "*No*, dammit, I do *not* want you gone! Whatever you might have done, you are still my brother! And you are still the only person in all this castle who dares be honest with me, the only person I can trust, and I—I need you by my side. Now let the subject drop!"

He had no way of knowing he'd just hurled the very words of my vow back at me. Now I was truly bound. "So be it."

"God's blood, man, you look as though I'd just sentenced you to death! Didn't you really want to stay?"

"I must. And pray don't ask me to explain, because I won't."

Estmere shook his head. "Why do I feel as though I just participated in some arcane rite? Clarissa would have said—"

He broke off abruptly, and I winced. "You still can't speak of her without pain, can you?"

"No." His tone warned me I was treading on perilous ground. "What of it?"

"Nothing. It's just that I know what it's like to lose a loved one."

"Ah. Your mother." His glance flicked to mine, flicked away almost guiltily. "Of course."

I studied him warily, unhappy at what I'd seen in that moment's contact, unhappy at what could still be *felt*. And I said, very delicately, "I also know that even when that first terrible anguish of loss fades, it doesn't quite go away. But, *brawd*, surely after six months, the edge of grief must be at least a little blunted. *Y Duwies*—all right, then, the Creator, whatever Name you prefer, That One never meant for us to bear more than we can endure."

"What's this? Turning priest? I get enough words of comfort from Father Ansel."

I grit my teeth. "Very well, then. I'll be blunt. And if the truth hurts, I'm sorry for it."

"Go on. I never yet executed a man for speaking truth."

"Estmere, Clarissa is dead. I regret it for her young sake and yours. But regret isn't going to change things. She's dead and you're alive, and it's time to stop using grief as a shield against—"

"Don't." There was a world of warning in the word.

"Look you, I said I didn't want to hurt you, and I don't. But you know I'm telling the truth."

He turned angrily away, but I moved to face him

again. "Listen to me! I'm sick of being used as an excuse."

"Now what does *that* mean?"

"Would you imprison one of your people on a charge of It Might Have Been?"

"Of course not."

"Exactly! You'd suspend judgment till you had some tangible proof of guilt. But—*dyri Uffern,* you're not showing me the same justice! I told you, I don't know if I could have prevented Clarissa's illness, I may never know—*Duwies glân,* you don't know how often I've prayed for proof that I didn't abandon her!" I stopped sharply. "That wasn't what I meant to say."

"What was?"

"*Och, brawd,* be honest with yourself! You're uncomfortable with me not because you think I'm a—a criminal, but because I remind you of your own guilt—"

"No!"

"—about Clarissa and—"

"*Enough!*" Estmere's eyes blazed into mine. "How dare you speak like this?"

I froze, choking on pity and rage. Rage won. I could argue with my brother, not with the king. Remembering how he had flinched from my touch, I said something under my breath that would have shocked prim Sir Verrin, bowed my most formal bow and, in defiance of all courtly etiquette, turned sharply to leave.

"Wait." A heartbeat later, most surprisingly, "Please."

"Well, my liege?"

"Stop that. I know you don't mean to hurt me. And I don't mean to hurt you, either, truly I don't. But before God, there are times when you infuriate me!" But the fire of royal anger was already fading, and all at once Estmere gave the ghost of a chuckle. "I do suppose it's good for me."

"I beg your pardon?"

"As Father Ansel says of you, no matter what you may be, you do keep me from the sin of pride."

I forced a smile. "You mean the man actually said

something complimentary about me?" Which was, of course, doing the priest an injustice, but at the moment I couldn't think of anything sensible to say.

At any rate, it got a true laugh. "Believe it or not, he likes you. Albeit reluctantly."

Silence fell. We stood looking at each other for what seemed a very long time, and I think we were both aching to be as we once were, though neither of us knew how to take the first step.

But then we were distracted by a most respectful servant, most tactfully reminding his king that the royal presence was overdue in the Council Chamber.

And with a quick, almost apologetic, glance at me, his king left.

CHAPTER XXVII

FEARS AND DREAMS

That wasn't the end of it, of course. The next day brought a visit to my tower rooms from a bemused Estmere.

For some time, my brother roamed through my study, which just then, flooded with sunlight as it was and green with pots of herbs, couldn't have looked less magical. I saw his restless gaze go from herbs to my shelves of salves and potions to the mirror I use for my scrying (I think he was disappointed to see only his reflection in it)—in short, acting very much like a man not at all at his ease.

"Estmere? Nothing here bites, I assure you."

He gave an embarrassed little laugh. "No. I hardly thought so."

"Let's see now, how do the proper phrases run? Hmm . . . you do me great honor, my liege, in gracing my humble abode with your royal—"

"Oh, no more of that, Aidan, if you please."

"Less formally, then, how is it a king comes to a prince rather than the other way around?"

"There's more privacy here," Estmere said frankly.

"Men may eavesdrop even at a king's door. No one dares spy on a magician."

"Save another magician. Wait, I'll guarantee our privacy."

I set my guarding Signs at door and windows, very much aware of a not quite comfortable Estmere watching me.

"I thought you said magic wasn't easy."

"What, that? That takes no more energy than bolting a door. I traced the initial Signs the first day this tower became mine, so that by now all I have to do is touch them with my will to spark them into life. Of course, if I was setting High Wards instead—but you can't possibly know what I'm talking about. *Brawd*, what did you come here to say?"

My brother turned uneasily away, pretending to study the lush greens of the herbs. He touched one plant with a gentle forefinger. "Vervain?"

"Vervain. Good for treating headaches and fevers. Also for magical purifications, among other things. Estmere . . ."

"I've been thinking of yesterday's debate." His voice was very carefully neutral. "You claim I've been using my bereavement as a shield. Suppose you tell me against what."

"You know I wouldn't spy on you."

"You're hedging. Tell me what you see in my heart that I presumably can't see for myself."

"Fear," I said bluntly, and he started. "Fear and . . . loneliness."

"Now what might that mean?"

How could I answer? How tell him—

"Aidan, come! What would you say?"

That Clarissa wasn't the right mate for you, and, somewhere within you, I think you know it, too.

No. I couldn't say that.

That underneath it all, so deeply buried it's almost impossible to read, you're secretly relieved to be free. And your guilt over that relief is what's making grief all the sharper.

Och fi, I certainly couldn't say that!

And all this while, my poor, tormented brother, the gentle, romantic self so rarely revealed cries out in the night for What Should Have Been. . . .

No, no, no, I couldn't say any of what I was thinking! Instead, I tried for once to take the tactful way out. "Deny this as you will, *fy brawd,* but you deeply need someone at your side: a wife. A true, loving wife."

Maybe it wasn't so tactful at that. My brother's eyes lost whatever softness they might have held. "So. And here I thought you were just genuinely trying to be kind. You've been talking to Verrin, haven't you?"

"Well, yes, but—"

"Stay away from his politics. They don't become you."

"I couldn't care less about Verrin's politics! I don't *like* the man! But, much as I hate to admit it, he has a valid point about the need for your remarriage."

"God's blood, it's only been six months! The official period of mourning is scarcely over."

Exactly what I'd tried, and failed, to argue with the advisors. "I know. I'm sorry." I hesitated, studying him, all at once wondering, "What do you fear so much?"

He gave me a glance like iron. "What foolishness is this?"

"This isn't merely indignation or a refusal to be pushed. You shy like a frightened deer at the very mention of marriage. You weren't like this before, not even at your most nervous before . . . Clarissa. What do you fear? It . . . can't be that you loved her so much you can't bear to put another in her place."

Estmere grew very still. I thought that surely he was about to strike me, I even half-raised a hand in defense, because there was suddenly a very keen tension in the air between us.

The tension faded as swiftly as it had come. I saw my brother's shoulders sag, and all at once pitied him with all my heart. Defeated, Estmere murmured, so softly I almost couldn't hear him, "Oh, Aidan. Why do you have to be so damnably perceptive?"

He looked at me in misery. "I did love Clarissa. Though I never really understood her, I suppose, nor she, me. I did love her."

There are different depths to love, and all of them quite real. "I never doubted it."

My brother nodded, straightening, very obviously forcing himself back under regal self-control. "I know perfectly well I must remarry. Unless I get an heir, the royal line dies out. Except for you, of course."

Sheer panic must have flashed in my eyes, because Estmere laughed aloud. "Come now! You don't really think I'd be so heartless to you or—to be frank—to my kingdom as to leave you the throne."

"Not that anyone would accept me, anyhow."

"Ah . . . no. So. I must marry again. I will. But I—I must have more time."

Time. That's a luxury monarchs aren't permitted. I pictured Estmere cornered by his advisors as I had been, Sir Verrin might have acted like a blustery, panicky little partridge, but that had only been because of his fear of me. Put him in his proper setting in audience hal or chamber with no terrifying magic about, and he could be quite calmly ruthless. As could the others, all those ambitious, strong-willed, oh-so-cunning advisors. Granted, Estmere was far more experienced than I in matters political. But, strong and kingly clever though he was, my brother was still too young not to be cornered by their older, slyer minds, tricked and overcome by their long years of political cunning before he knew what had happened, forced into a second marriage not of his choice but theirs—

There was only one way to outmaneuver them. "Estmere," I said carefully, "isn't there anyone you've seen on whom you could look with some favor?"

He raised a brow at my archaic turn of phrase. " 'Look with some favor?' You jest. Surely by now you know all the court candidates as well as I."

"Well . . . yes."

"Have *you* seen anyone even vaguely suitable?"

"There are other lands. Verrin wants to send out official queries—"

"That's a waste of time."

I blinked. "How can you be so sure?"

"I can."

"*Brawd*, that's ridiculous. You can't possibly know every noblewoman out there."

"Are you doubting my word?"

"*Och*, don't bristle. All I'm suggesting is letting Verrin send out—"

"No!"

I stared at him, seeing nothing behind his eyes but despair. "What in the name of *y Duwies glân* is so frightening?"

He stared right back at me, challenging, "Do I dare be honest with you?"

"I should think so!"

"That's not enough. Swear to me that what I tell you will go no further than this room."

"*Brawd, brawd*, don't be so dramatic. Of course it won't. My word on it."

"That's not enough! Swear—"

"Not enough! Look you, if you can't trust me by now, you have no business being in this room alone with me!" The insulted words came tumbling out almost faster than I could order them. "You know vows are sacred to me—I just gave you my word! How *dare* you mock it!"

Estmere's mouth tightened in anger. "Walk warily, brother," he said very quietly, and I remembered belatedly that he was, after all, the king. So I bit back my outrage as best I could and said with great, if somewhat sarcastic, restraint:

"I didn't mean to offend you."

"I know. And I—I didn't mean to insult you, or your beliefs. It's only . . . I . . ." Estmere took a deep breath, like a man about to plunge into danger. "You read me too well. I *am* afraid. You like frankness, so I'll try to be as frank as possible:

"I was fortunate in my marriage to Clarissa. More

fortunate than I ever dared hope. But, as I told you the day when you counselled me so kindly before that marriage—remember? When I was so nervous? You ... don't remember, do you?"

No, I didn't. Yes, I knew he'd been nervous, yes, I knew I must have said *something* back then, but what? What? My struggle to remember must have been obvious to Estmere, because he clasped my shoulder and told me softly:

"Never mind. It's not important. I only wanted to point out that though Clarissa and I were technically strangers, we were still kinfolk; we had both heard enough about each other over the years for there to be at least a tenuous bond between us. And we had enough family memories in common to help us be at ease. To help us find what was turning into love ..."

He shook that off. "You were right. I suppose I have been using my loss as a shield, trying to fend off the inevitable. Love isn't going to enter into whatever new marriage I form. Of course not. I'll be firming an alliance, or—or guaranteeing a trade route. What a pity Wencin doesn't have a daughter, or maybe a sister who isn't so old she couldn't give me a son in exchange for a treaty. After all, it wouldn't matter what she looked like, or acted like, or thought, as long as she was fertile and of the proper royal blood—"

"Enough," I broke in. "Come, sit." Taking him by the arm, I virtually pushed him down into the chair, standing over him to keep him there. "That's better. I have mead in the next room, or if you prefer, I can probably manage to conjure it into wine that's no worse than what you usually drink."

Estmere glanced up at me with a weak laugh. "I forget; you're used to treating hysterical patients, aren't you? I promise: no more hysterics." He stirred impatiently. "I know, I'm not supposed to worry about such things as love. A king isn't required to love his queen. He need come to her only for the creation of heirs, and as for ...

anything else, why, a king is expected to take as many mistresses as he pleases.

"But I can't be like that. I don't know why. Maybe my nurse told me too many romances when I was a child!" Estmere hesitated, eyes fierce with distress. "I know it's a weakness in me. But I just can't rid myself of the vision of a true, loving wife—I just can't be properly cold-blooded."

Now I was truly baffled. "But surely that's to your credit. I don't see what—"

"Don't you? I don't know what the custom is in Cymra, but here marriage can only be broken by death."

Yes, Estmere, I do know that. But I wasn't about to interrupt.

"Whatever politically correct and ... fertile wife I'm forced to accept," Estmere continued, "whether we chance to like or tolerate or l-loathe each other as much as King Arngrim and Queen Gerda, there just won't be any escape. We'll be forced to go on together, sharing, whether we will it or not, every moment of our lives down through all the years to come." He smiled bleakly. "But at least the succession will be assured. Aidan, you look as though I told you something unbelievably blasphemous."

"You did." That slipped out before I could stop it, and now there was nothing to do but continue, "Forcing two people into the most sacred of intimacies, conceiving a child in hatred or indifference instead of love—that's against all the harmonies of the world."

"Ah well, I suppose it is, at least to you of the old religion." Estmere laughed, a soft, humorless little sound. "Now can you see why I wanted privacy? What I've told you, these secret and ... unkingly fears, I cannot, I will not, tell to anyone else." He paused, chewing on his lower lip, then continued, "I'm not commanding you. I'm asking you, brother to brother, not to let what I've told you leave this room."

"You already have my word," I reminded him gently. "But don't be afraid. The future isn't going to be like that for you. I give you my word there, too."

He gave me a quick, almost amused smile. "Don't foreswear yourself. You can't fight royal obligation with swords or even magic." Estmere got to his feet. "Look you, I'm sorry I said even as much as I did. Forget it. In the end I will do what I must for my people's sake, just like every other king before me."

"If you were willing to start the search for a new queen . . ."

"Aidan."

"I know, I know, I'm only asking. If you *were* willing, how would it go?"

He frowned slightly. "Didn't Verrin tell you? He would send out messengers to those of our allies with eligible daughters or sisters, and if said allies agreed, I would in time receive firsthand reports and pretty little paintings of the ladies in question, together with descriptions of their royal dowries, so that I might better make a decision."

"So I thought."

Estmere stiffened. "Now I *do* command you. As your king, I forbid you to mention this conversation to Verrin."

"We already established that."

"Don't interrupt! I forbid you to give him or any other authorization to send out messengers. And I most firmly forbid you to send out those messengers yourself!"

I returned his regal stare tranquilly. "I had no intention of doing anything like that."

He let his fierce gaze drop. "Of course not. Aidan, I must leave."

I suddenly remembered the Sign on the door. "Ah, wait! You won't be able to get out."

As I negated the Sign's Power for him, I heard Estmere's inward-drawn breath as he realized that up to this moment he had been virtually my prisoner. I opened the door for him and said sweetly, "Good day to you, *fy brawd.*"

"And . . . to you."

As I watched him leave, I was smiling to myself. *Och*, Estmere, I had tricked you, and you never even knew it!

With all your careful bans, you still hadn't forbidden me to do exactly what I had intended.

First, though . . .

I replaced the guarding Sign on the door, then settled myself in a chair, eyes shut, concentrating. I felt another consciousness brush my own almost at once, felt a vision pathway opening and growing firm. "You heard?" I asked.

"Every word. Love, when did you realize I was listening?"

"Not till the end. Ailanna, *cariad,* dearest one, you shouldn't have spied."

"Why not?"

"Because . . ." As well scold the wind as lecture one of the Folk on human morality. "Because," I finished lamely, "spying on a king is a dangerous thing to do."

That got the laugh it deserved. "Dangerous for whom? Me? Don't be silly! You? Hardly. Besides, he loves you too well for that." I felt her mood shift with Faerie swiftness. "The poor man." If it wasn't quite said with pity— Ailanna was too much of Tairyn's blood for that—at least sympathy quivered behind the words. "They're always after him, aren't they? All those foolish, ambitious courtiers, prodding him to remarry." She paused thoughtfully. "Though from what I've seen of your brother and what you've told me, he really would rather be married, wouldn't he?"

"If he had any say in the matter, yes. If he was allowed to take his time and fall in love."

"Ae, such fools! Why can't they admit their king is only flesh-and-blood?"

"Because then they have to admit he's fallible as well."

She shook that off impatiently. "You humans just will *not* accept that love is as necessary as food and air."

"Some of us accept it, Ailanna." I felt her mind touch mine at that, gentle as a caress, and I smiled. "*Cariad,* something must be done for Estmere."

"Indeed." Impatience swirled through her thoughts. "Especially if we're ever to be free to lead our own lives.

I can't see any way out of your vow unless he does wed that one perfect-for-him mate. Or," she added with true Faerie coolness, "unless he dies."

"Y *Duwies* forbid!"

Ailanna sighed. "Even so, that would leave *you* as his heir, wouldn't it?"

"Not that anyone would support me, but yes, it would."

"Ae-ye, what a pity your brother can't just go out and find himself his own wife!"

"Nice thought, isn't it? But I'm afraid a human king can't very well up and abandon his throne, even temporarily. *Cariad,* wait, don't get so upset! I have a plan."

I told it to her, and she laughed. "But didn't he forbid—"

"Did he?"

She retraced the words with Faerie accuracy, then laughed again. "Why, no, he didn't! Ah, my clever love, may your plan succeed—and swiftly."

Ailanna enfolded me in a sudden wave of love and longing, then was gone, leaving me breathless. After a time I reluctantly opened my eyes, abandoning lovely visions for the solid world around me.

Who knew Estmere—that inner, gentle, music-loving Estmere—better than I? For that matter, who here at court loved Estmere better than I?

So. I wouldn't mention remarriage to my poor brother again. Not yet. Somewhere out there must be a lady who would be more than some pathetic little pawn in the game of court intrigue. She must exist, I *felt* it, that lady who was clever enough, intelligent enough, to understand court politics yet forget personal gain. That lady who would wed Estmere simply because she loved him. That lady who, for all our sakes would be his mate, his partner, his true and joyous heart's delight—

And I, searching all alone and unabetted (and therefore outside my brother's ban) would find her.

CHAPTER XXVIII

HUNTING

Ambitious, wasn't I? Ah, but surely we're allowed such well-meant conceits by the One who watches over us, call that One what you will, surely we're allowed to use our Powers to help those we love.

I told Estmere merely that I had some private business to attend. He didn't pry; he who was allowed so little privacy of his own generally respected mine. Which was fortunate, because otherwise I would have had to overcome scruples and attempt a lie he almost certainly would have seen through.

As it was I set out unchallenged from my brother's court, once more on the back of my tawny griffin friend, whom I'd coaxed out of Faerie with amazing ease (he did seem to enjoy our outings together), to begin my princess quest.

In the days that followed, I saw princesses and duchesses and ladies enough. *Och*, yes! I'd never dreamed there'd been so many women born of noble birth! But nowhere in all that time of searching did I find the one I sought, the one who could mix love and wisdom, the one who could be Estmere's joyous bride and friend.

Dejected, I sat me down on a grassy hilltop and thought, while beside me the griffin preened his yellow wings and snapped playfully at butterflies. The sight of such a powerful predator using his curved sword of a beak (the beak that could, I knew, easily tear a deer in two) to act so—so *trivially* made me squirm with impatience.

"This is stupid," I told him. "Stupid! I feel like one of those wispy little minstrel-tale princes who run around on idiotic quests! I ask you, griffin, am I using my powers for good? Am I doing anything wise or clever or heroic? No! I'm *bride-hunting*! *Pw*, what a farce!"

The griffin wasn't impressed by my theatrics. He reached about to delicately work a wing feather into place, then sneezed. "*Benedith*," I told him drily, and the griffin tilted his head towards me, blatantly inviting a petting. "Now, if life was as neat and easy as it is in those minstrels' tales," I continued, reaching up so I could scratch behind the furry ear he was offering, "Estmere would simply ride out one day, fall madly in love with a beautiful country maid, and live happily ever after."

But in the real world happy couples really do need to have something in common. And kings and country maids never wed. No, my tedious, ridiculous, so very infuriatingly mundane search must continue amid royalty.

"But where?"

Of course the world was far wider than I had ever suspected back in Cymra. Even with griffin wings to help me, I could hardly search it all, let alone bring back some truly foreign bride. Gloomily, I sat and conjured an illusion map before me of those regions I could, in all reality, reach, letting each image land fade as I realized I had already visited it. Surely there must be one....

"Ha, yes!"

The startled griffin stared at me, and I laughed at him, reaching out a hand to rub his furry neck. "More fool I! There's one kingdom so close to home I overlooked it."

King Adland's realm, it was, a small land but an

important one, not so much for its pretty, rolling hills and fertile fields but for its location: it lies trapped between the kingdoms of Estmere and Bremor.

Bremor. For a moment, a chill, chill shadow seemed to steal over me, leaching away hope and joy. . . .

But then I straightened, and made a very rude Cymraen gesture. *"That* for Bremor!" The griffin made a sound almost like an approving chuckle, and I grinned at him. "Now if my memory serves me, King Adland has a daughter. A young, hopefully still unmarried daughter. I think she's called Rosamonde, 'Rose of the World.' "

Despite its size, her land was certainly of enough strategic importance to satisfy the court. And Princess Rosamonde's lineage was surely proud enough to make even prim Sir Verrin happy.

"Forget Verrin. Let us pray only that Rosamonde and Estmere can make each other happy!" Getting to my feet, I added, "Come, my furry, feathered friend. Let us pay this Rose of the World a visit."

Of course I didn't want my presence in King Adland's realm known. For one thing, I was acting very much without my brother's authority. For another, I wanted the chance to judge the Princess Rosamonde honestly. So I left my griffin, cast my invisibility illusion about myself, and entered on silent, unseen feet into King Adland's squat and heavily fortified castle. (Truly, that was a tale in itself, since I had to wait till they'd lowered the drawbridge for someone else, then hurry in after him before I could get squashed.) Once inside, I searched warily, trying not to get lost, listening to servants' gossip for clues, till I finally located the king and his daughter together in a small, sunlit chamber.

Now, I really had planned to be quite cold-bloodedly efficient about the whole thing: Faerie practical, as Estmere would have put it. But from my first glimpse of the princess, I forgot efficiency, because surely my search was finally ended.

Though she looked nothing at all like Ailanna (and,

therefore, lacked just a tiny bit to my biased eyes), there was no denying that the Princess Rosamonde was lovely. Tall and slim and, yes, sweetly formed as a woman out of Faerie, with long, thick plaits of richly honey-dark hair falling past her waist and nothing of Clarissa's too-inbred delicacy about her. Rosamonde's face was strong rather than pretty, saved from severity only by the smooth curve of cheek and the hint of humor in lips and eyes. Those eyes were the deepest blue I had ever seen in a human, and bright with intelligence. I could picture her at Estmere's side, I could!

Don't be naive! I snapped. *You don't know anything about who she truly is.*

Here was a tricky little moral dilemma: I had to learn *something* of who and what Rosamonde was—the true, inner Rosamonde—yet I could hardly pry into the young woman's mind or soul; that would be too akin to rape even if she never learned the violation had taken place.

So I compromised and took a less sure, less safe road by catching the gaze of those lovely eyes and letting my mind lie passively open to what might be behind them. It was not done without a qualm, believe me! Passive searching meant running the risk of being flooded with the fear and jealousy of another Clarissa, or the bitter darkness of a Bremor. . . .

But what brushed my mind was . . .

Power? Magical Power?

Magic it was, given her by some fluke of breeding or Dame Fortune, but no more than the slightest touch, not enough to truly be developed; I doubt the princess even knew she had anything more than the intuition tradition grants to women. That tiny touch of magic, though, meant no one would fool this lady! She would see through deception as easily as I, and have the wisdom to deal with it. If she sat at Estmere's side at meetings with advisors or ambassadors, what a wondrous help to him she'd be!

A little shiver of delight raced through me. For look, yes, look, the princess was more than mere cleverness, more than wit, she had what poor Clarissa had lacked—a sense of the wonder and joy that is life. And yes, yes, yes, now I *felt*, I *knew* that she and Estmere *fit*. They must be happy together, they must belong together—

Wait. As I drew my mind shut again, sealed my senses back within myself, I found myself wondering a bit. Such diffuse sensings as I'd just worked aren't always quite true. Had I read her rightly? Or was I so eager for a happy ending I saw only what I wanted to see?

Och fi. I would have to find a way to meet the princess and her father ... mm, and without revealing my true identity ... tricky ...

My unannounced visit had been brief enough to be measured in heartbeats (magician's sight, of course, takes no longer than a magickless glance), hardly qualifying as an intrusion, but I could hardly justify spying on them at length. If I stole carefully past King Adland, I should be able to be out the door without them thinking me anything more than a sudden gust of wind.

As I tiptoed past her, I saw despair flash in Rosamonde's eyes, and paused, realizing that up to now I hadn't been aware of a word of what father and daughter had been discussing. It wasn't really my affair, I really shouldn't stay to listen.

But then Rosamonde said, "There's no chance of it. I will not marry him." And I came starkly alert.

Marry him? Marry whom? *Gallu*, was Rosamonde already betrothed? An Anglic betrothal was as legally binding as a marriage—had Estmere already lost his rightful wife without even meeting her?

I glanced hastily from princess to king. Preoccupied with Rosamonde as I'd been, I had barely noticed her father, save as a pleasant-looking man of middle years, graying of hair and running somewhat to fat. In that quick dismissal, I was doing Adland an injustice—but I'm racing ahead of my story. At the time, all I knew was that worry (and fear?) was blanching his face, shadowing his eyes.

"Rosamonde, don't be hasty. Oh aye, I'll grant his

father was a cruel man, but a son doesn't always take after his father."

"Yes, but—"

"No, no, I'm not finished. You must admit he's young and well-formed, not at all ill-favored."

"Oh, yes!" Rosamonde spat out. "The devil wears a pleasing shape!"

"Rosamonde!"

"Father, please. You know I'm not a coy, silly little girl. I wouldn't reject a suitor just on a whim. But why do you keep harping on my accepting his suit? Are you *that* fond of him?"

King Adland wouldn't meet her gaze. "Ours is a very small land, my love," he said softly. "If it lay anywhere else, no one would even know it existed. Yet here is a rich and powerful king asking for your hand." He glanced at her hopefully, but the shadow of overwhelming worry loomed behind the hope. "It would be a very good match."

"A good match! You can't think the man's mad for love of me! He needs an heir, that's all."

"What's so very wrong in that?"

Rosamonde stirred uneasily. "Nothing, if that was his only motive. We both know if he captures me, he captures our land as well. How very . . . convenient."

"My dear, don't worry about such things."

"But you raised me to worry about them! You encouraged me to think for myself—"

"I know, I know. It was wrong of me to force you to be my heir—"

"What else could I be? I'm your daughter!"

"Exactly. I never should have given you a *prince's* education. I should have married again after your poor mother died (God rest her), I should have tried to get a son. But I . . . loved her, I couldn't . . . No. That's not the point. This is a highly valuable offer of marriage, and I'll not have you refuse it out of some childish whim."

"Father, please, *please*, listen to me! I told you this isn't a whim!"

"Well?"

The princess took a deep breath. "I'm not objecting because the man's a stranger. Of course I must marry, and of course my bridegroom will be a stranger. That's the way life is! I assure you, I long ago grew out of wanting to run away as a knight errant." Rosamonde glanced down at her undeniably feminine self and added with a glimmer of wry humor. "I doubt anyone would believe I was a boy, at any rate!"

"Daughter, I . . ."

"Don't give me that pitying look. I'm quite happy with who and what I am. Even if it means I must sit here and wait like a d-damned poppet— Sorry," she added hastily before her father could object. "I didn't mean that. But I repeat, I'm not a silly little girl. My husband doesn't have to be handsome, or heroic, or even young. If he's a kind, honest man who cares for his people and . . . me . . . why, I wouldn't even object if you married me to be a heathen if he—"

"Rosamonde!"

This time it was an outright shout. The princess winced, but continued bravely, "I wouldn't object to a heathen if he followed the Light. A man doesn't have to worship in our chapels to choose Good over Evil."

I gave her a silent, heartfelt salute.

Her father, though, was clearly scandalized. But before he could manage to sputter out more than a word, Rosamonde added hastily, "I'm sorry, I didn't mean to shock you. I was only trying to make a point—"

"I don't see—"

"Please. Let me finish. Father, the man to whom you'd give me is worse than any heathen. I cannot and will not marry anyone who freely worships Evil. And such a man is King Bremor of Telesse!"

Bremor! In my shock, I nearly lost my hold on the invisibility illusion. But fortunately father and daughter were so distressed they didn't notice me fading in and out like some conjurer's trick.

Bremor.

Of course. Before he could risk anything as dangerous as conquest, his advisors would insist on an heir. No matter how much a *cythraul-slav*, a demon-thrall, he might be by now, Bremor would still be king enough to agree. Particularly when the only other choice for heir was that sensible-eyed relative I had seen in my mirror— *och*, no, Bremor certainly wouldn't risk his life by naming an almost certainly more popular man his successor! He would definitely want a child, an heir of his body. And naturally he'd be delighted at the thought of gaining a kingdom along with a wife.

His Patrons would be even more delighted at the *war* potential of that kingdom just happening to border Est-mere's own. . . .

So engrossed in unhappy thoughts was I that I almost failed to see King Adland pacing nervously in my direction. He had me cornered! I glanced about for a table, a tapestry, anything under or behind which I could hide—ah! Just in time I leaped silently up onto the window sill. It was so close a thing that his sleeve brushed against my leg, and I held my breath, expecting an out-cry, but he never noticed.

"Daughter, daughter, that's a harsh accusation."

"It's true."

"You can't be sure of that."

"Oh, I can."

Of course you can, I agreed silently. *Your touch of magic would be just enough to let you sense the bitter coldness of him.*

As though she'd heard my thought, Rosamonde shud-dered. "I know he didn't mean me to see it, but Bremor wears the sign of his foul pact about his neck. I'm no student of magic, but I do know the difference between a 'good' pentagram and an 'evil' one."

Adland drew back in horror. "I should have supervised your studies more closely! First heresy, now sorcery—"

"But Father, it isn't—"

"No! I'll hear no more about it! And I never should

have let you be so blunt about refusing Bremor. Even his messenger was furious!"

To me, Adland's anger seemed a bit too blustery to be real. Rosamonde must have been thinking the same thing, because she corrected softly, "Not furious. Merely terrified of bearing the brunt of his master's wrath when he . . ." Her voice trailed into silence as she studied her father. "There's more to this marriage proposal, isn't there? Something's very wrong. No, don't deny it. Please, let me help."

"It's nothing." But fear glinted in the man's eyes, and after a moment he confessed, "Ah, I can't say that. My love, today I received a new message from Bremor."

Rosamonde bit her lip. "I thought as much. What did he say?"

King Adland turned sharply away. "Simply: if I didn't give you to him, he would pull down this castle and take my life."

"And *that's* the man you would have me marry? He sounds like a small boy hitting out because I hurt his pride!"

"I wonder."

"How can he possibly hurt us? Bremor hasn't got an heir or anyone he really trusts; that much he let slip. He can't afford to leave his throne untended long enough to mount a siege. Even if he could, our castle is built strongly enough to outlast any siege." Rosamonde laughed without humor. "Besides, whatever else he is, I doubt Bremor's a fool. He has to know we have a powerful ally to the north."

"King Estmere." Adland sighed. "I've never had cause to call on him, or his father before him, and I pray I never shall. He's an honorable young man, but even if he did send help immediately . . . Rosamonde, love, you miss one point: *we* might be safe behind our castle walls, but what of the commons? For all our border defenses, ours is such a little land. Before help could reach us, dear Lord preserve them, what Bremor could do to our poor people!"

Rosamonde's hand clenched as though it longed for the hilt of a sword. "If only I could *do* something! Take up a weapon, fight him, send him shrieking down to his d-dark master—"

She turned away with a stifled sob, staring blindly out the window. That meant of course that, though she couldn't see me (or, fortunately, have sufficient Power to sense me), we were virtually staring into each other's eyes. And *och*, how it hurt to see hers all bright with unshed tears!

"If I must marry Bremor to save my people," Rosamonde murmured in resignation, more to herself than her father, "then I shall." But, so softly even I almost couldn't hear her, she added, "They say King Estmere is young and fair and kind of heart. Why couldn't *he* be the one seeking me?"

Why, indeed? Of course I couldn't speak for Estmere, of course I couldn't command his heart. But if my brother could look at her and not be captivated, then he was even less human than he thought me!

I longed to materialize then and there to tell Rosamonde that. And wouldn't *that* have been a foolish thing to do? Instead, I contented myself with sending a message to her with all my will:

I think that may come to pass, Rosamonde, I truly do.

She started slightly. Hoping she just might have heard me, I continued fiercely:

And this much I can promise you, come what may: Bremor shall not have you!

CHAPTER XXIX

BROTHERLY LOVE

Wind sprites, those glittery little mostly transparent beings, aren't as powerful or perilous as their high cousins the Air Elementals; they're smaller entities, more capricious than dangerous. But they can be helpful enough if the whim suits them and the magician calling to them is persuasive enough.

I was. Our return flight to Lundinia was so swift it left both me and my griffin friend gasping. Sending him once more free on his way (he was so worn from our journey, poor beast, he virtually dove back into Faerie!), I hurried down into the palace in search of Estmere.

I found my brother in his chambers, alone for once, head bent over some old scroll, hair a mass of burnished gold in the candlelight. For a long moment I hesitated to disturb him. But:

"Estmere?"

He looked up with a start. "Aidan! I'd begun to wonder if you'd abandoned us."

"Ah . . . no."

"Business finished?"

"Yes and no." This was ridiculous. I had entered full

of confidence, sure he would welcome news of the lovely Rosamonde, yet now I was as uneasy as—as—

As an erring subject before his king? Ridiculous!

"*Fy brawd*, I have something to tell you. But frankly, I'm not sure how you're going to accept it."

He stared at me. "Good Lord, you haven't killed someone, have you?"

"No!" Enough hesitation. "Do you remember our conversation some days back about the need for you to remarry?"

His hand tightened on the scroll so fiercely I heard the old parchment crackle. "Yes." Suddenly aware of what he was doing, Estmere very carefully put the scroll down on a little table by the side of his chair. Not yet looking at me, my brother asked softly, "What would you tell me?"

A cold weight seemed to suddenly settle in my stomach. *Dyri Uffern*, why hadn't I realized this before? If I told him about Bremor, Estmere wouldn't accept the news on a personal level. No, no, he was a king, he could only take the idea of Bremor seizing Rosamonde as a military threat. *That cruel flash of memory repeating: that war, all that ugly, pointless dying* . . . It wasn't a threat, I told myself desperately, not yet, not if we acted in time. But how could I word this safely and not—

"Aidan! What would you tell me?"

Panic. "I was bride hunting for you." *Damnio!* That wasn't at all what I'd intended to say.

"You *what*?" Table and scroll went flying as he sprang to his feet—

And the next moment, the room was full of guards who'd heard the crash, their weapons at the ready. "Sire?"

"It was nothing," Estmere told them rigidly. "An accident. Leave us." As soon as we were alone again, he whirled to face me. "How dare you defy me?"

The force of his rage staggered me. "I didn't—"

"The devil you didn't!"

"You told me not to send out messengers. *Gwych*, splendid, I obeyed you! I went myself and—"

"Stop twisting my words! Aidan, curse you, I wasn't jesting. I gave you a command not to meddle in my affairs—and that command was not from your brother, but from your king!" As I stared, open-mouthed, Estmere continued in a softer, deadly voice, "I assure you, had anyone else at court dared defy me like this, interfered as you've done, I would have had him banished."

"Now just a moment! I didn't do anything so dreadful that—"

"Damn it, Aidan, are you such an innocent you don't realize what your meddlings have done?"

"Suppose you tell me what—"

"To go off to other courts—you, the king's brother—announcing to all and sundry that King Estmere is searching for a wife, to stir up all manner of political waves I did not wish disturbed—"

"Will you *please* let me finish just one sentence?"

"Well?" His hand tapped impatiently at the side of his chair. "Speak."

"I am not anywhere as naive—as stupid—as you think me! Look you, if I wanted to be petty, I could give you a list as long as my arm of all the noble fools who've tried to buy me. *Pw*, the court is full of a hundred little intrigues! But have you ever known me to be tricked into even the most subtle of them? Well? Have you?"

"Don't lecture me, Aidan."

I sighed, thinking, *Estmere, sometimes you are a true test of a magician's patience!* "No lectures. Yes, I went looking for a prospective bride for you. No, I did not involve you in anything you might not wish to handle."

"Meaning?"

"Meaning, *fe damnio*, that I made very sure, by magic, that no one knew I was there!"

That stopped my brother for a moment, waves of thwarted anger swirling about him. Then Estmere muttered, "Thank God you've *some* sense."

"And thank *you* for some small measure—"

"Silence!"

I fell silent, but only because rage was choking me.

Was *this* why I was living in exile? Was *this* why I was torn from my own dear one and—

And what? I knew my brother's fears. I knew the whole sensitive subject had cried out for tact. Yet instead I had come blundering in like the country lout he thought me.

"Aidan." It was said with visibly forced control. "I'm sure you meant no harm. But ... stay with the things you know. Tend your sick peasants. Work your healing arts. Don't meddle in the king's affairs again. Because I promise you this, Aidan: despite our kinship, if you ever dare to flagrantly disregard a royal command again, I swear before Heaven I'll exile you. Now, leave me."

What could I do? We were both too angry for honest speech. So I did the only thing I could:

Raging silently, I left.

Well now, that gives you some idea of how the week went. True, it never came down to the two of us shouting at each other again. How could it? Every time I tried to simply mention the name of the Princess Rosamonde, my most royally stubborn brother would neatly elude me, pleading sudden, urgent business elsewhere.

What could I do? Call him a liar?

How dare he treat me like a child?

He dared. He was the king. More to the point, he was my brother, who knew I wouldn't use magic against him.

Won't I? Duwies glân, *but it's tempting!*

It would be so easy to catch Estmere in a net of enchantment, to bend his will to mine, force him to listen to me—

Just as there had once been a stag snared and helpless in the net of my will, the storm of his terror flooding me and, worse than the horror, the shame of having knowingly done Evil ...

Gallu, no! Controlling Estmere like that, mind and body, against his will, no matter how briefly—I couldn't do that.

I couldn't just forget the whole thing, either. When

I'd first set out on my bride hunt, Rosamonde had been nothing but a name. Now she was real to me, a living, despairing human soul in need. My dreams were of her and Bremor, dreams filled with such ugliness that every night I woke wild-eyed and shaken—

Prophetic dreams? Not if I had any say in the matter.

So I finally cornered my brother, quite literally, in an alcove not far from the royal apartments, trying to ignore the guards hovering nervously behind me, trying to ignore their half-drawn weapons as well.

Even with his back to the wall—again, quite literally—Estmere didn't lose his dignity. He signalled almost casually to the guards to draw back, then studied me with cool, appraising eyes.

"Springing at me like that is a good way to get yourself killed, Aidan. If the guards hadn't recognized you in time . . ."

He was quite right. "I wasn't thinking. I apologize."

"You obviously want to speak with me. Of what?"

"You know very well of what."

"Oh, Aidan, not again! Just because you've seen some pretty little lady who's taken your fancy—if you find her so charming, *you* marry her."

"Don't mock me, Estmere."

"I wasn't mocking. You're a bachelor of the blood royal, after all, a fine catch for—"

"Will you stop being so *damniol* civilized and just hear me out?"

"No." His voice was flat. "I will not. I have no intention of playing one of your odd little elfish games."

"I'm not playing games! I'm not even asking you to do anything. But Estmere, you *must* know—"

" 'Must'?" There was the faintest hint of ice to the word. "No. The subject is closed. Stand aside."

"Why won't you listen to me?"

He sighed. "People are always after me, trying their cunning best to persuade me, influence me, push me. You know that. I allow you liberties I'd allow no one else, surely you know that, too. But I will not be pushed, even by you." Estmere's voice sharpened just a bit on those last words, and I saw the guards tense. "Now, stand aside!"

Did he mean to have me forcibly moved if I didn't obey? I *felt* Power stir, knew I could stop the guards easily enough—

And frighten them. And anger my brother even more. No. It wasn't worth the trouble.

Raging silently yet again, I stood aside.

So. Here we were sitting in my brother's hall, Estmere and I, Sir Verrin and the rest, all of us "a-drinking ale and wine," as the song goes, unofficially celebrating the news that had just reached the court:

There had been a forced (if reasonably gentle) abdication on the part of our northern neighbor, poor, addled old King Wencin: apparently his middle-aged son had finally reached the end of filial patience. And said son, now king, would seem to have taken a hard look at the size and strength of his neighbor to the south, because he had quickly sent a very subdued Ambassador Gern with word he would gladly sign that pact Estmere had been seeking these many months.

Reason indeed to celebrate.

Well, at least most of us were celebrating. I, for one, wasn't in a singularly festive mood.

Someone else wasn't celebrating, either. I could feel the advisors' eyes on me, sharp as daggers. I had been deliberately avoiding the lot of them this past week—and so, it would seem, had Estmere—since the last thing I wanted them to do was learn of my visit to Rosamonde before I was able to discuss her with my brother. If they knew about that visit, they would almost certainly push my brother so hard he never would agree to meet her. But now I knew they were all aching to know when I planned to broach the subject of a new bride to the king.

When, indeed?

It was no longer only a matter of healing my wounded pride. Not after what I had seen in my mirror just before being summoned here to my brother's hall. For I'd been watching Bremor. . . .

He stood alone in his own dark chapel. The sight of that plain little room sickened me with such a painful, unexpected surge of memory I was almost physically ill. And I admit to being terrified, too. Dry of mouth and damp of palm, I almost broke contact there and then, wondering wildly, *What if They sense me here, what if They know I'm watching?*

But of course the *cythrauliad* couldn't. There's a limit even to demonic Power. The only way They could know of my spying would be through Bremor.

And Bremor was—what? Not demanding; not even a king makes demands on Them. I certainly won't call it praying. Beseeching, then, most fervently beseeching his Patrons for power, for dominance over his foes.

And, I realized with a shock, for help in winning the Princess Rosamonde. Even though I couldn't hear him, I clearly saw her name on his lips, and for a doubtful moment wondered if Bremor, in his own corrupted way, might actually be in love with her.

No. I didn't misread what he was offering his Patrons, quite calmly, quite regally:

It was a pact. Let Them insure a son and heir for him from the Princess Rosamonde—and he would grant Them her life and soul in exchange.

Gallu nef, Gallu nef, he didn't even see it as wrong! His Patrons had already warped his mind so badly he thought it only one more royal treaty!

And he was all but ready to march on King Adland.

Dizzy, sickened, head aching most foully, I had broken contact at that moment, silently swearing a vow. Now, here in Estmere's hall, I silently repeated it:

Estmere will learn about Rosamonde, no matter how I must arrange it. And between us, we will keep her from Bremor's pact.

Fine words. Now let me do something about them. It

was too late by now for any rational private debates. But here, with all the nobles about us . . .

So be it.

As soon as there was a moment's silence, I said, with a boldness very much feigned, "Tell me, *fy brawd*, when will you think of taking a new wife? A queen at your side would gladden us all."

There was a murmur of surprise and no little approval from the gathered nobles. Estmere stared at me. I don't want to ever see again what was in his eyes, the shock and anguish at this . . . betrayal on the part of the one person he'd thought would never turn against him. In that moment, I think he truly must have hated me.

But what could Estmere do? All the nobles were awaiting his answer in suspense. My brother turned away from me and answered with a false heartiness, "Oh, I don't know that there's a lady in all the land free to marry me."

I was ready for that, of course. "King Adland has a daughter, *brawd*, the Princess Rosamonde. She's said to be as beautiful as spring, and as wise and witty as she is beautiful." Which was true, even if I was the one, right now, to say it. "Why, were I king here in your stead"— *which* y Duwies glân *forbid!*—"that princess might be my queen."

'Might,' Ailanna. Anything might *come to pass.*

Under his breath, Estmere muttered in fury, "God's blood, how I've misjudged you!"

"No."

"Yes! Tell me, Aidan, who bought you? How much did it take?"

"Don't talk like a fool. I can't be bought."

And I let fire flicker from my fingertips, an illusion for his eyes only, to remind him, *I am a magician, I have no need for silly coins.* That took Estmere as aback as I'd intended, and I let the illusion fade and continued quickly, "I'm sorry I had to trick you. But you know full well that otherwise you'd never have listened to me."

"And why in God's name *must* I listen to you?"

"Because the Princess Rosamonde is every bit as charming as I've said. I'll stake anything you like that you'll agree."

"Our friendship?" he asked darkly. "Or what you may be leaving of it?"

"Look you, *brawd,* I'm not asking you to marry her. I wouldn't presume so much even if you weren't king." I took a deep breath, because there wasn't any way around the next thing I must say: "But if you don't do something, Bremor of Telesse will."

Ha, that surprised him! Plainly the royal spies had been lax. Estmere snapped, "You're sure of this?"

"I am." Grimly I added, "I doubt you want Bremor as a neighbor."

For a moment my brother just stared, struggling for words. "You *have* maneuvered me, haven't you? As neatly as Verrin himself." Estmere glanced at the assembled nobles, all of whom were watching us with wide-eyed fascination, and I heard him give an almost inaudible, "Damn!"

But there wasn't any excuse or explanation he could make to them, so Estmere straightened royally and called out, "Sir Verrin."

"Sire?"

"Sir Verrin, find me your most worthy messenger to send to King Adland's court, so I may have a true picture of this"—he shot a deadly glance at me—"wonder of a princess."

I didn't want that. "No, *brawd.* Many a man has been deceived by secondhand reports. No matter how honest and loyal the messenger, his judgment is still going to be colored by his personal tastes."

"Well?"

"Far better to go to King Adland's court and be your own judge. I'll ... go with you if you like."

The flat coldness of his eyes made it quite clear that he didn't care for the thought of my company just then. "*Och,* Estmere," I said, very softly, "what harm in simply going to look?"

He frowned. "I never could understand you, Aidan. And I don't know what game you're playing now. But . . . I can't believe you're my enemy. I'll go. I can't very well refuse now, can I? Yes, Aidan, you are most definitely going with me. And, dear brother, the Princess Rosamonde had best be every bit as wondrous as you say."

CHAPTER XXX

VISITS

"So, now." The crisp words cut into my sleep.

"My Lord Tairyn. Am I dreaming you, or have you slipped me into trance?"

He ignored that silliness. Of course this was trance; I'd be a poor magician if I couldn't tell it from mere dream. "And is this not a foolish situation?" the Faerie lord said with his usual cool, quiet mockery. "You may be a human, but you *are* a wielder of some Power. Yet look at you, wasting that Power, acting as your brother's slave—"

"I am not—"

"—running his errands, hunting for a wife for him."

"Is that what's bothering you? Tell me, my Lord Tairyn, haven't you figured out yet why I've been doing it?"

Silence. By now I'd come to realize that whenever Tairyn didn't have an answer, he slid back into that inhumanly cool quiet, that *I am too wise for mere humans* pose. But no matter how much I itched to shake that calm, I knew better than to push him.

"My Lord Tairyn," I said gently, "the sooner I find

Estmere someone who can stand by his side in my place, the sooner I am free to leave. To return to Ailanna."

More silence, this time definitely tinged with disapproval.

There's no pleasing you, is there? I thought. *Either I annoy you by "wasting" my time and Power among humans, or I annoy you by rejoining Ailanna.* "My Lord Tairyn," I added, "like it or not, I *will* fulfill my vow. I *will* return to her."

"If you live," Tairyn said shortly, "if your foe does not slay you," and was gone.

And I, of course, was left wide awake and uneasy.

Why, thank you, Tairyn!

Now I couldn't help but keep thinking of Bremor, and the fact that everything I was doing seemed to be pushing me closer to a confrontation. A small, childish voice deep within me cried out in sudden panic, *I don't want to die!*

Nonsense. Ailanna had said only one of us would die. Foolish to think that one was I . . . foolish to think the future could be read at all.

Foolish to let Faerie slyness bother me! What *had* Tairyn been about? Had this visit been sparked by curiosity? Malice? Was this another trap? Or, *y Duwies* help us, could this possibly be Tairyn's way of showing concern?

Impossible.

At last, towards morning, I told myself that any human who tries puzzling out the workings of a Faerie mind is a fool, and settled down to get some sleep.

By that time, of course, it was already too late.

Groggy though I was from lack of sleep that morning, I was all for flying Estmere and myself directly to King Adland's castle on the back of my griffin friend the next day.

"Nonsense," Estmere told me. "I am *not* going to turn up on another king's doorstep like a beggar. We are going to do this ridiculous quest properly, with a full, brave contingent of guards and courtiers."

"But that's going to take too long!" I protested.

"No more than a few days.

That didn't seem so terrible a delay. "Fine. Then let's start choosing which—"

"Not so fast, Aidan! First I must send out a messenger to Adland, asking his permission."

"Why bother? He'll be thankful to see you!"

Estmere sighed. "I imagine boundaries don't mean too much to magicians. But I can hardly march into another monarch's sovereign territory without that permission."

"*Och.* Right. Of course not." I really *was* still sleepy. "But I can see that a message reaches him far more swiftly—"

"What *is* the matter with you? All this panicky haste—I thought you knew your geography by now. Bremor's capital is half again the distance to King Adland of Lundinia. Even if the man started preparing at the same moment we do—and you've assured me he isn't—we'd still reach Adland a good seven days before Bremor."

We compromised. Estmere began putting together the crowd he wished, while I charmed one of our messenger pigeons so that it would fly straight to King Adland, and sent it out on the wings of the wind sprites.

Sure enough, we received a reply, borne by a bedraggled, very weary pigeon, within three days. As I'd predicted, King Adland, though he was a bit puzzled by Estmere's vaguely worded request (deliberately vaguely worded, just in case some harm had befallen the pigeon), quite happily granted us permission to cross his borders.

When Estmere makes up his mind to do something, things happen swiftly. In less than two days, a party of courtiers, guards and victualers was ready to ride. In a bit more than a week we had passed from one kingdom to the other (without more than a few token and very polite questions from Adland's border guards), and had arrived without incident at King Adland's castle, Estmere and I and our royal escort, all of us quite elegant in regal red and gold. Whatever Estmere's private thoughts on the matter—and he wasn't sharing them with me—he was at least willing to make a brave show of it.

What of me? *Och*, I was most certainly torn between guilt that I'd had to maneuver my brother and anger at him for doubting me, between worry for the Princess Rosamonde and about Bremor—and about whether relations between Estmere and myself would ever return to normal.

Surely they would, I assured myself. If we reached Rosamonde in time. If Estmere actually did take to the princess, and she to him. If I hadn't been mistaken about the whole thing and—

Pw. If, if, if.

I glanced at my brother. No matter what he might be thinking, there was no denying that Estmere looked nigh as proud and handsome as any Faerie Lord, and his hair blazed more brightly in the sunlight than gold. It wasn't surprising that the castle porter should stare at us all, most particularly at Estmere, but the man freely bade us enter.

Which meant, to my relief, that we *were* in time.

King Adland himself met us in the Great Hall, poised and self-controlled as though he hadn't a worry in the world. "Welcome, King Estmere, in God's name, welcome," he began formally, then stopped and laughed, with eyes as well as mouth. "Ah, but look at you! When I last saw you, you were only a very little prince, not even reaching your father's waist. Now here you are, grown into a fine, tall young man, the very image of your sire, may he rest in peace."

I had never stopped to think they might know each other. Then Estmere might already have met—no. If he had been little more than a toddler when he'd visited King Adland, Rosamonde must surely have still been a babe in arms.

There was genuine warmth in Estmere's smile as he returned Adland's greeting. "You were ever a friend of my father. And it's good to see you again, indeed."

Adland hesitated. "The message I received was so very mysterious."

"For security reasons."

"Of course. But might I ask why you've come? Was it for pleasure, or have you some business with me?"

"Both," I said, and the two kings turned as one to me. Suddenly feeling as awkward as a child performing in front of strangers, I continued as calmly as I could, though I wasn't very comfortable with the stiff words of protocol, "King Adland, you have a fair young daughter, the Princess Rosamonde. King Estmere fain would meet with her and, if they are both willing, would court her."

Adland was staring at me. "I didn't know you had a brother, Estmere."

"Half-brother," I told him, giving a polite little bow. "Aidan ap Nia, at your service."

"And at yours," he replied politely. But then what I had said about his daughter registered, and he turned to Estmere in dismay, self-control slipping an uneasy bit. "I'm afraid you're here in vain. Yesterday two weeks King Bremor of Telesse was here to ask for my Rosamonde's hand. She said him nay, and for all I know, she'll say nay to—"

"Bremor is a foul suitor!" The words shot out before I could stop them. I was aware of Estmere staring at me, no doubt wondering at the force of my hatred, but it was too late now not to continue, "And I blame the princess not at all for refusing him."

"But grant me this, I pray," Estmere cut in smoothly. "King Adland, grant me but a sight of your fair daughter."

"Oh, indeed. I shall send a message up to her where she sits with her ladies, and bid her come down to us."

"Bid?" I thought wryly. From what I'd seen of the Princess Rosamonde, "ask"—and politely, too—would be a far better word! If Estmere expected a shy little fawn of a girl, he was in for a surprise.

I only prayed it would be a happy one.

* * *

King Adland, for all his unquestioned maturity, was curious as a child about me and my magic. Though, to be honest, I suspect he would have welcomed any diversion from his worries about Bremor. At any rate, though, as I've said, I detest performing like some marketplace conjurer, I did little tricks of shaping and illusion to help pass the time. I glanced at Estmere and saw a faint, amused smile on his lips. But my brother's vague gaze showed he wasn't really paying attention to me at all. And I knew why:

Despite the fact he hadn't wanted to come, despite his resentment of my ... meddling, now that he was actually here, all Estmere's thoughts were only of the Princess Rosamonde. Willy-nilly, she would seem to have intrigued that secret, romantic self within him. And, though he never would have admitted it, my brother was nervous.

He wasn't the only one.

What if the princess simply refused to come down to us? She hadn't struck me as the sort to be at anyone's beck and call.

No. She would come. The hope of escaping Bremor would bring her to at least meet Estmere. Besides, didn't she harbor that tiny hope of him courting her?

But what if she and Estmere just didn't like each other? What if I had been blinded by my own longings and read them both completely wrong? *Duwies glân*, what if they actually hated each other? I had a sudden miserable image of Estmere so enraged he really *would* exile me—but with my vow still binding me, how could I possibly let myself be exiled and—

Then, down into the Great Hall came the Princess Rosamonde and her pretty little handmaidens, with pages, squires and knights as their escort.

I don't think Estmere saw any of that procession. From the first, his gaze went to Rosamonde. Ah, how fair she was, clad most sweetly in deep, clear blue, her honey-dark hair streaming unconfined down her back. Her head was encircled by a little coronet of crystal flowers, and a ring of that bright crystal shone on her hand.

So, the Princess Rosamonde. Softly she descended, eyes downcast in what I knew must be a wild mingling of fear and hope, and I thought, *Ah, Rosamonde, look up! His heart is all but in his eyes—Rosamonde, look up!*

Whether she heard my silent plea or whether she felt the weight of Estmere's entranced gaze on her, Rosamonde did glance up at that moment. Their eyes met for the first time—

And I forgot all my fears. I had been right, *Duwies glân* thank you, I had been very right! She was for him, he was for her, and with my magician's eyes I saw the wonder flash all pure and bright and golden between them, heart to heart, soul to soul, the oldest, truest magic, stronger than the strongest spell of wizardry.

While the two young people, royal titles forgotten, stood transfixed and silent, faces innocent and defenseless and beautiful with the awe of what had passed between them, King Adland bustled about—proving he'd been nervous, too—making introductions and conversation until I gently steered him aside. And all I said was:

"I doubt she'll say nay to him, King Adland."

CHAPTER XXXI

THE LOVERS

Estmere and Rosamonde had no eyes for anyone else all that day and night. Not that they ever quite forgot again that they were king and princess. How could they, having both grown up as royal heirs? I chanced to overhear one of their conversations as they strolled together through the palace gardens blissfully hand in hand (oblivious to the courtiers trailing after) and realized the two of them were seriously discussing politics—politics, of all things! And yet somehow, for all their regal earnestness, they managed to make even that unlikely topic hopelessly romantic.

True love, no doubt of it.

That garden intrigued me. Like Estmere's palace gardens, it was meant for use more than pleasure, and was more herbs than flowers. Along with the plants I knew were some of the more southern herbs familiar to me only in their dried state. The next morning found me (a little weary of Estmere's perpetual wide-eyed wonder and glad to temporarily escape him) down on my knees by an intriguing patch of what I thought must be arnica, an herb not native to Cymra (a deadly herb to taste, but good, it was said, for treating sprains and bruises). As I warily touched a leaf, wondering if anyone would mind if I snipped off a sample, a woman's voice asked:

"Prince Aidan?"

There was no graceful way to turn in that awkward position. Steadying myself with a hand against the ground, I blinked up into sunlight at the dark outline of a feminine shape. Puzzling out more by magic than sight that it was Princess Rosamonde, I got hastily to my feet, brushing earth from my knees. "Your pardon. I didn't realize anyone was watching."

I can't say Rosamonde looked radiantly lovely; like Estmere, she very blatantly hadn't been getting enough sleep lately. But a quiet joy enfolded her, more beautiful than any bland, perfect prettiness.

Her smile included me in that joy. "Estmere . . ." She said the name as a caress. "Estmere has told me you're a healer. Please feel free to take whatever plants you wish."

"A healer? That's . . . all he told you about me?"

Rosamonde straightened slightly. "Prince Aidan, I already know you are a magician, if that's what you're worried about."

Remembering poor, frightened Clarissa, I asked warily, "You're not afraid?"

"Should I be?" Her gaze was steady. "From everything I've heard from Estmere and your courtiers, you are a follower of the Righthand Path, which means there's nothing of Evil about you."

"So!" She really *had* been given a comprehensive education!

"Besides . . ." Her wonderstruck smile broke out again. "You are his brother. Nothing you are could frighten me." But then Rosamonde shook her head impatiently. "Listen to me. I sound like some romantic little idiot."

"Hardly. Just like someone in love."

There must have been a certain wistfulness in my voice, because deep blue eyes studied me thoughtfully. "You know about such things, too, don't you? You have a lady of your own."

"Yes. I ..." But then Tairyn's *damniol* spell clamped down on me again, and after a brief, futile struggle, I had to add ruefully, "I'm sorry. I ... can't say anything more."

I think she suspected, with her tiny touch of magic, that I meant it quite literally. "No matter." Her voice was polite, her eyes suddenly impatient. "Prince Aidan, I ..." But then Rosamonde glanced back over her shoulder to where her curious ladies clustered nearby, and bit her lip. "There are no secrets in a castle."

"Don't I know it!"

"Couldn't you cast some manner of secrecy spell?"

"Not without it looking terribly suspicious to everyone who would see but not hear us."

"Ah. That *would* be awkward." She gave me a sudden, bright, false smile and chirped for her ladies' benefit, "Come, Prince Aidan, will you not walk with me?"

Rosamonde held out her hand. I bowed over it, and we strolled together, her hand resting ever so lightly on mine, like any courteous, casual couple, moving seemingly by chance further and further from curious ears.

"They can't overhear us now," I said after a time. "What did you wish to discuss?"

She never hesitated. "Bremor of Telesse."

"Ah."

Rosamonde glanced at me sharply. "You don't want to talk about him, do you?"

"Your pardon, no." But I couldn't ignore the worry in her voice, so I added, "He's not a magician of any sort, if that's what concerns you."

"But he does worship Evil."

It wasn't a question. "I—yes."

"I see." Rosamonde paused thoughtfully. "It was you sending me a message about him, some days back, wasn't it?"

"By magic, you mean?"

She nodded. "It was an odd sensation, something like a ... a brushing at the mind."

"I hope I didn't frighten you!"

"No. I didn't know who or what you were," Rosamonde said with a wry little laugh. "For a moment I even thought you might be something supernatural. An angel, perhaps. Or," she added with a sly little sideways glance, "a devil. But whatever, I knew you meant your words kindly."

"I'm glad. *Och*, look you, don't be afraid of Bremor! As I promised, Estmere and I will shield you. We won't let any harm befall you."

She stopped short. "Oh, thank you." The words dripped sarcasm. "And I'm supposed to wait in my tower like a helpless, dutiful little princess while you heroes save the day."

"I didn't mean—"

"Please don't patronize me, Prince Aidan. I've heard enough soothing words from my father lately."

"I'm sorry."

After a moment, she murmured, "So am I. I didn't mean to snap at you. But after all these years of being raised *not* to be passive, *not* to be submissive ... God, I can't just sit back and do nothing!"

"How maddening it must be for you! I wish there was something I could do to help."

"You mean that, don't you? Those aren't just ritual words." Rosamonde hesitated a moment. "Thank you."

I held out my hand. She placed hers atop it, and we started forward again. "You're from Cymra, aren't you?" Rosamonde asked.

"My accent's still so thick?"

She gave me a sweet flash of a smile. "Still so musical, I would have said. But is it true Cymraen women are the equals of their men?"

"Particularly by your people's standards."

"My people." She let out her breath in a weary sigh, and all at once I saw *princess* overwhelm *woman*, just as in Estmere the king must always be dominant over the man. "Yes," Rosamonde said flatly. "That's what it comes down to, doesn't it? They *are* my people, as much as my father's. You may not believe this, but I haven't been worrying about myself these past days so much as I have about them. Our little kingdom lies in such a precarious position, balanced as it is between two greater powers."

"I won't lie to you. Bremor is a very real threat, magic or no. And I wish I could do something to remove him. Believe me," I added savagely, "nothing would please me more. Unfortunately, I . . . can't. But I can't see Bremor being foolish enough to challenge Estmere." *No matter how much his Patrons might prod him.* "You will almost certainly be safe. Particularly if you form an alliance."

Glancing out of the corner of my eye, I saw Rosamonde redden. She laughed softly, nervously. "With your brother, you mean?" Suddenly the princess pulled her hand free, turning sharply away. "I d-don't know," she said after a moment. "This has all happened so quickly. . . ."

I waited. And at last Rosamonde turned to me again with a smile joyous as springtime. "But . . . I . . . think such an alliance may come to pass, Prince Aidan, I truly do."

As Estmere's brother, I had been assigned a room to myself, Adland having graciously yielded to my "peculiar" love of solitude. Although it had no door, which meant little genuine privacy, the room was comfortable enough, holding a smotheringly deep feather bed and the ubiquitous clothes chest, and with walls covered by innocuous tapestries of wood and field. Just now, the night was cool enough for a fire to be pleasant, warm enough for that fire to be more a luxury than a necessity, and I sat before it and stared moodily into the flames.

Adland's castle was far enough south for its architects to have been influenced by southern styles, which meant that the living quarters faced inner courtyards and had luxuriously wide windows (a major problem to heat in the winter, but so nicely dramatic in summer). My room overlooked the very romantically moonlit garden. And in that garden wandered Estmere and Rosamonde. They were chaperoned—of course they were chaperoned—but

I doubt either of them was aware of anyone else in the world but the other.

I was delighted for them, no doubt of that. But on this lovely evening, watching them together in the garden while I was alone . . .

More than a little jealous and missing Ailanna passionately, I sat before the fire, studying the flames as though they might escape. After a time, the temptation to play with them became too strong. Ailanna had once taught me that minor Faerie Art, and now I began to hold and form the flames with my will, shaping fantastic castles and spires and forests of that most malleable of mediums. Of course the pretty red-orange-yellow pictures faded as quickly as they were formed, but they were amusing enough until I found myself creating image after image of a certain slim and lovely Faerie woman . . .

"How charming," said a sudden voice, and I whirled, half rising from my chair, ready to take fire in my hand and hurl it—

"King Adland!"

I caught my breath and got to my feet with a polite bow, straightening to receive his apologetic smile.

"I fear I startled you."

"No harm done." I wasn't about to confess how close he'd come to a singeing. Quickly I glanced at the fire, relieved to see it had died properly back down to normal.

Adland followed my gaze. "A lovely art."

"It was nothing. A little trick of shaping. No real skill to it."

"Still, it was lovely. Prince Aidan, may I speak with you?"

"But of course! This is your castle."

I offered him the chair, but Adland stood looking out over the garden and the happy couple, and after a moment I joined him. "They look well together," the king murmured, like any plain, non-royal father, and I had to smile and agree, "They do."

"More, they seem to suit each other." Gaze never leaving the garden, Adland continued softly, "I never dared hope. My daughter is very dear to me. I must admit, it always troubled me that her marriage would, perforce, be nothing but a . . ."

"A business arrangement?" As Adland glanced at me in surprise, I nodded. "I feared the same thing for my brother." I smiled. "No danger of that now."

"Amen." But Adland's answering smile faded as swiftly as it had come. "There's only one thing I would know, Prince Aidan: how is it that you and your brother are here so opportunely?"

"I don't see your point."

"I think you do. How is it your message and arrival come so hard on Bremor's departure?"

I didn't know how to answer that. "I . . . must confess I had something to do with it."

"Bremor is your enemy, isn't he?"

I started. "Your pardon, but I would rather not discuss that."

He snorted. "In other words, he is. And for reasons of your own, you don't want your brother to know."

"King Adland, you do amaze me!"

"Be that as it may, why are you here now? To thwart Bremor's proposed . . . ah . . . annexation?"

"Not merely for that. I really do want to see my brother happy, and your daughter, too, for that matter."

"Ah." There was a world of skepticism in that syllable. But then the king sighed wearily. "It's not that I'm not truly grateful to see you here, please understand that. Bremor, as you surely know, can be very free with his threats, but I don't doubt there's a real menace behind them."

"There is."

"My daughter thinks that he—that he worships—" He shook his head. "But you would know the truth of that, white wizard that you are."

I could feel my face reddening. "Please. I'm a magician, no more, no less. But I can guess what you want to ask me. And . . . yes. Bremor really does worship Evil." Adland looked so sickened that I almost found myself

telling of my invisible visit. Just in time I said instead,
"I think I understand your situation, King Adland, and I
sympathize—if you don't think I'm being too
presumptuous."

"No. Go on."

"I fear you've been a man torn several ways these past
weeks, between love for your daughter, for your people,
for . . . ah . . . sheer self-preservation."

"Too true!" he murmured.

"But you don't have to worry any longer."

"Ah, the certainty of youth." There was the faintest
hint of paternal amusement in his voice. "You *are*
younger than your brother, aren't you?"

"By nearly two years."

"Don't look so wary. I'm not insulting you." He gave
me a sideways glance. "And I do think you know more
about all this than you've confessed, oh Prince Magician.
But . . ." The king turned to face me fully, and the warm
relief in his eyes was very plain. "Whatever your reasons,
you and your royal brother—ah, but I'm glad you're
here!"

CHAPTER XXXII

PREMONITIONS AND PLOTS

It was a warm, clear night sweetly scented with healthy greenness, and no hardship at all for our royal party to camp in the pretty glen we'd found a day's journey out from King Adland's castle. We were on our way back to Lundinia after a very joyous week. And a very painful parting, Estmere from Rosamonde. But part they must, of course; he must return to kingdom and throne.

Not that they would be parted unbearably long, *y Duwies* willing. First, of course, there must be the formal acknowledgement of their betrothal. Then the news must be spread throughout the two kingdoms and their allies (which lengthy process I intended to speed along in any way I could). And then at last would come the preparations—and the royal wedding itself.

All about us was activity, horses being picketed, fires being lit, but I don't think my brother noted any of the mundane details of setting up camp. Since the night was so warm and fair, he'd had servants place our two chairs (uncomfortable little folding stools, actually) just outside the royal tent, and now Estmere sat staring blindly out into the deepening twilight, looking very much like some moody hero out of a minstrel's romance, his eyes dark with memory, his thoughts so turbulent I could *feel* their confusion from where I stood. Sensing my eyes on him, my brother looked up, then gestured to me to sit beside him. As I did, I heard him murmur:

"Aidan, Aidan, what is this that's happened to me?"

I chuckled. "Can't you guess?"

Estmere smiled faintly at that, a smile at once as young and old as the dawn. "I love her," he said softly, as though trying out the words. "I never thought to say that again, but . . . I love her." He shook his head impatiently. "It's more than that with Rosamonde. . . . Bah, I don't even know what I'm trying to say."

"She lets you forget who and what you are?"

Estmere's glance was sharp. "No. Never that. Rosamonde is every bit as aware of royal obligations as I." Then, more gently, "But together we find ourselves able to—to accept what we are. Or doesn't that make any sense at all?"

"It does."

But he wasn't finished trying to explain. After a time of helpless floundering, Estmere said simply, "With Rosamonde I feel I have come home. I would give my life for her."

"*Y Duwies* prevent!" I sketched a quick protective Sign in the air. "Love is a joyous thing, or at least it should be. Why are you brooding?"

"Because I don't understand myself."

"Why not? You're permitted to fall in love just as common folk do!"

"That's not what I mean. How can I possibly feel what I feel so quickly?"

"It happens." I smiled, remembering my first, wonderstruck sight of Ailanna. "It does happen."

"But . . . so soon. Not even a year since . . . Clarissa . . ." He shook his head again, more bewildered with himself, I sensed, than grieved or shocked.

"*Fy brawd,* there's no time boundary for love. I don't know if this will be a comfort to one of your faith, but remember that Death and Life are simply two parts of a whole."

"The ... what do you call it? The ever-turning Wheel of Life? The pattern of birth and death and rebirth in which nothing's lost, nothing's wasted?"

"Something like that."

"Your Goddess does sound like a most practical lady. Oh, don't bristle, Aidan; you know I didn't mean it as an insult." He snorted. "And if it will set your mystical Cymraen mind at ease, I'm really not 'melancholie as a hare,' nor hopelessly brooding over Clarissa and—and what might have— Never mind."

There was a long, long silence. I watched the evening darken about us, listening to the murmurs and jestings of our men gathered about the campfires, to the occasional stampings and snortings of our horses, to beyond our civilized little circle, the thousand small songs of a spring night.

Estmere stirred. "It's the suddenness that bothers me," he murmured. "One short week ago I didn't even know sweet Rosamonde existed, and yet now I don't think I could live without—oh God, *no!*"

Startled, I turned sharply to him. His eyes burned into mine, so bright with suspicion and fear that they seemed almost to glow. "Aidan. You forced me into this journey."

"Well yes, but—"

"You were so incredibly insistent I meet Rosamonde. Why?"

Taken by surprise, I could only stammer, "Why—why, because I thought you could be happy together."

"No other reason? None at all?"

"I didn't want her trapped by Bremor. Estmere, *brawd,* what's the matter?"

"You arranged—you *forced* my meeting with Rosamonde. Please, tell me you didn't arrange something more."

"What in the—"

"Please! Tell me that what I feel isn't just the result of your magic. In God's name, swear to me you didn't force me to fall in love!"

I stared at him, stunned. "Why would you ever think something like that?"

"I don't know! Magician, elf-friend—I don't know how your mind works!"

Shimmering faintly just behind his eyes was the specter of Clarissa. And as ever, that vital last memory of her taunted me, almost within my reach, then gone when I would grasp it, leaving me crying out in sudden fury, "What a wonderful excuse!"

"What—"

"It's so much simpler, isn't it, to say, '*Och*, well, he's alien, I don't have to understand him,' so much simpler than struggling to see things through someone else's eyes. 'He's alien' explains it all, and you can piously accuse that 'alien' of—of—" But I just couldn't mention Clarissa's name. "Of whatever crimes you wish!"

"I didn't mean that."

"Didn't you? Once and for all, I am *not* one of the Faerie Folk, I don't *think* like one of the Folk—"

"Aidan, hush."

"And, *Gallu nef*, you go too far when you suggest I would ever, ever perform such sacrilege as interfering with the holiness of love. . . ."

I floundered to a stop under the weight of his cold, regal stare. "Are you quite finished? Or perhaps you want the whole camp to hear you?"

I glanced quickly about, reddening to see our men staring at me in astonishment. At that range, they couldn't have quite made out my words, only my tone of voice, but even so . . . "No," I muttered. "But, Estmere, to accuse me of such a crime . . ."

His steady gaze suddenly wavered and fell. "Forgive me. Things really have been happening too quickly for me. I still cannot believe—"

"Estmere. Any further discussion right now is only going to lead to us shouting at each other. The One granted you and Rosamonde a wonder. In your heart you know that's true. I had nothing to do with it. Accept it. And now, good night!"

With that, I turned my indignant back on him and entered our tent to try settling down for the night. My insulted anger faded bit by bit as I relaxed.

Poor Estmere. He really hadn't realized the blasphemy of his words. And I supposed the suddenness of love *was* difficult for his ... civilized mind to accept....

How much simpler if Tairyn's cursed spell wasn't on me and I could tell him of my own dear one....

I drifted off to sleep with a vision of Ailanna warm in my mind.

But as I sank deeper into slumber, my dreams changed, growing darker, troubled and distorted. And at last I began to dream horrors I'd thought banished. Once more I was back in Bremor's dungeon. Once more I was lost in that despair and anguish while he taunted me, calling my name mockingly over and over....

"Aidan.

"Aidan!

"Aidan, wake up!"

My eyes shot open. Gasping, shaking, I tried to strike out—

"Hey! Gently, brother, gently."

"What ... Estmere?" I rubbed an unsteady hand over my eyes. "It ... was only a dream, then."

"Yes." Estmere waved away the alarmed guards who had gathered in the tent's entrance. "A singularly foul one, I would guess."

"*Gallu*, yes." Still dazed, I stared up at Estmere, trying to marshal my thoughts, reassured by the warmth of concern in his eyes.

"Aidan? Are you all right? Yes? You're sure?"

"Do I look that badly shaken?"

"You do. Do you want some wine?"

"No. Thank you." I sat up, shaking my head to clear

it of the last haze, glancing at Estmere, who was watching me with a curious alertness.

"What is it, *brawd*?"

"Can you talk clearly now?"

"Yes," I said warily. "What?"

"In your sleep you kept shouting a name: Bremor."

"Oh." *Damnio*.

"Don't try to evade me. When King Adland mentioned Bremor, I saw true hatred flash in your eyes."

"I . . . have no love for the man."

"That time when you returned to me in such sore distress, when you refused to name the one who'd tormented you—it was Bremor, wasn't it?"

I sighed. "Yes."

"But why? Why would he risk—"

"*Och, brawd*," I murmured wearily. "He hardly expected me to escape. Let's just say he envied me my Power, wanted it, and didn't much care what was done to me to steal it."

Estmere's eyes widened. "He didn't . . ."

"Succeed? No. I'd be dead if he had. Please. My memories are shattered enough. I would rather not have to remember that time."

"Of course not." His hand was warm on my shoulder. "But can you just tell me why you refused to name him? Did you—oh." Estmere sat back on his heels. "Were you afraid I would do something foolish? Like perhaps sending an army into Telesse in retribution?"

"*Duwies glân*, yes. I—I—I saw *war* in Bremor's mind once, horror, ugly horror, mindless killing . . ." I swallowed hard. "We have nothing that foul in Cymra; we don't even have a word for it! And I c-could not let that horror happen because of me."

"It wouldn't." Estmere's shoulders sagged. "Not even for you could I so endanger the realm."

As I gave a shaken sigh of relief, he glanced fiercely my way. "You could have trusted me, though. Even if you didn't want to avenge yourself with magic for some arcane reason—that Threefold Law, I suppose—you still could have come to me. After seeing what Bremor had done to you, I would gladly have helped you plot some other revenge." He smiled thinly. "No matter how much time it cost me with Father Ansel."

"No." I remembered the vow sworn to Ailanna, and the fear sharp in her eyes. "I cannot seek revenge."

"Cannot!"

"Ask me no more, *brawd*." I got to my feet, driven by a sudden surge of unease. "I shouldn't have had that dream. I had set my mind against any nightmare memories. *Mor a mor . . . was* it only a dream? Or was some unsleeping sense trying to send me a warning?"

Estmere tensed. "Of what?"

"I . . . think I do sense something . . . a vague shadow. *Damnio!* I've lost it." As my brother watched me anxiously, I sought after that elusive psychic thread, only to shake my head in frustration.

"I'm sorry, Estmere. Much as I hate sounding like some cheap village seer, I just can't put it any clearer than that." Our glances met. "Now, I'm not sure," I said carefully. "I may well be wrong. But I do think it best that we return."

"To Rosamonde?" His hands clamped painfully down on my arms. "Tell me! Is she in danger?"

But try and try though I would, I just couldn't answer that.

We hadn't ridden far into the pale gray coolness of early dawn before I spotted a small shape running unsteadily towards us. I caught a flash of yellow hair and thought for one foolish moment, *Arn?*

"That's one of Rosamonde's pages!" Estmere gasped.

We leaped off our horses together, more quickly even than the guards, and were just in time to catch the boy as he fell, exhausted. He glanced wildly from one of us to the other, trying desperately to find enough breath to speak.

"Couldn't . . . get to my pony . . . horses all watched . . . had to . . . had to run all night . . ."

"Never mind that, lad." Estmere signalled to a soldier, who brought a flask of water. The boy drank thirstily, then tried again:

"Sire, my . . . my lady, the Princess Rosamonde . . . my lady sends her love, but . . . oh, she is in sore peril."

"What peril? Tell me!"

As the boy struggled for coherent speech, I put my hands on his temples, willing calm into the frantic mind and a little bit of my strength into the exhausted body. After a moment, the page took a deep, steadying breath and sat up. With a grateful glance at me, he began, "It was no more than a half-day after you had left, Sire, that King Bremor entered our land—"

"Bremor!" Estmere and I cried in unison.

"Yes. He—he swore so convincingly that he had come in peace our king opened the castle gates to him."

I groaned. From what I had seen of Adland, he never would have been so foolishly trusting, not without sorcerous persuasion from Bremor's dark Patrons.

Estmere glanced from me to the boy. "Go on, lad. What then?"

"We were tricked, Sire. King Bremor had full many fighting men with him. And our own soldiers seemed so helpless . . . almost as though they'd been bewitched."

"Indeed," I muttered.

A shudder shocked the slim form. "And now Bremor holds the royal castle, Sire, and s-swears that this very day he will wed my lady, and—and tomorrow carry her away."

"Now, by my faith, this he shall not do!" Estmere sprang savagely to his feet, me with him, and the wave of raw rage and horror and fear for Rosamonde blazing from him nearly knocked me over. I caught my balance and his arm.

"Are you planning to boldly rush in and singlehandedly cut down all Bremor's men?"

He looked at me with fierce, despairing eyes. "What else am I to do? Abandon Rosamonde? Go meekly home? Aidan, there's no time to gather an army!"

Even if there were, openly attacking Bremor would be declaring outright *war* on Telesse. *Och fi, och fi,* what were we to do?

With a surge of will that must have been equal to anything summoned by a magician, Estmere forced his emotions under control. In a voice that was almost level, he commanded, "Counsel me, brother. Use your magic. How may I rescue Rosamonde?"

How, indeed? "Give me a moment to think, I pray you."

I glanced about the glen, pretending to be searching for something but actually just stalling for time while my mind insisted only on reliving those fragmented, unwanted memories of Bremor, and darkness, and chains. Useless! Worse than useless!

Come, come, think! You can't abandon Estmere, nor Rosamonde—think!

But I couldn't turn my mind from the darkness, from lying helpless at the mercy of a merciless man. Whatever I did, it would mean confronting Bremor. . . .

Was *this* the reason I'd agreed so quickly not to seek revenge? Was it not for sweet Ailanna's sake, but because, secretly, I was glad of the excuse not to face him again?

Was I afraid to face him?

"No!" I said fiercely, and told myself it was the truth.

So be it. We couldn't fight him, not with our small party. So we must use guile. A disguise—but surely Bremor or his Patrons would see through any disguise.

Save . . . a magical one?

Pw, but it had been difficult enough to shape-change when I'd been in peril of death in Ybarre's storm. I would never manage that spell again without aid.

Aid? And my odd, distorted memory brought an image to mind of a spring meadow, and my mother and I gathering herbs, me trying to memorize the use of every planet, including one . . .

I glanced about that glen in earnest. The time of year was right, the vegetation seemed right, too. Now, if only the herb grew this far east and south. . . . Blind to the rest of our party, I set out in an ever-widening circle, hunting for that one strange, homely little plant.

And *y Duwies* was with me. All at once I bent and plucked two small, dull green little herbs from the clump I'd found. "Yes, yes, *yes!* Listen to me, *fy brawd,* and I'll show you how to set your lady free!"

I hurried to his side. "See these? I've just found a way for us to enter Adland's castle unhindered. Wait. Estmere, it has to be just the two of us."

There was a great uproar from our party at that. What, their king go alone into an enemy camp? It wasn't wise, it wasn't safe!

They were right, of course; it *wasn't* safe. But it was the only chance I could see, because the herb's power was limited. Besides, any group of strangers larger than two begins to look suspicious to a suspicious mind.

But if I'd had any doubts about the sincerity and intensity of Estmere's love for Rosamonde, they vanished there and then, because for once my brother abandoned ingrained royal caution (and, some might say, common sense as well). Eyes blazing, he held up a hand for silence, commanding me:

"Continue."

Brushing the earth from the roots of the herbs, I had a bizarre little flash of memory: an Anglic ballad Estmere had once taught me. Right now it was so singularly appropriate I couldn't resist quoting:

" 'My mother was a westerne woman,
    And learned in gramarye,
    And when I learned at the schole,
    Something she taught it me.' "

"Yes, yes, Aidan, I'm sure your mother taught you herb-magics, and all the rest of 'gramarye,' too! But—"

"Here. Swallow."

For all his impatience, he eyed the herb dubiously. "What, roots and all? What is it?"

"In Cymraeth: *cyfnewidiwr*. Now, are you the wiser. Trust me, *brawd*. If you would rescue Rosamonde, swallow."

He did, grimacing at the taste. I waited, smiling as I *felt* the tingling of Power growing, surrounding his being like the faintest of heat hazes, just as it was supposed to do. . . . Yes. Now.

It was easy, surprisingly easy, thanks to that odd little herb legend says first grew in Faerie. Estmere heard his followers gasp, saw them draw back, amazed and frightened, some crossing themselves, some grabbing at weapons, and he whirled to me in horror.

"What have you done to me?"

"Nothing so very alarming. See?"

As he stared transfixed at his reflection in the little mirror of polished tin, I swallowed the second herb (understanding his grimace; *och*, bitter!) and prepared for my own transformation.

Cyfnewidiwr means, you see, "the changer."

And so, to all outward seeming, Estmere was now a stranger, dark of hair and eye, weatherworn of skin, while I let the Power in the herb lighten my black eyes and hair to a nondescript, mousey hue, let it seem to make face and form younger till I looked no more than a boy barely come to manhood. Feeling the herb's magic heightening my own (as though I'd drunk some rich, rare wine), I worked an invisibility illusion over our two swords. Turning to a stunned archer, I took the bow from his unresisting hands and sent my will deep within its wooden self, altering the patterns of its shape slowly, delicately . . . till I held a fair little harp, sweetly strung by a bowstring transformed into a fine seeming of bronze and silver.

Estmere just stared, as frozen with shock as any of his men. I smiled. "Don't worry, *fy brawd*. All this is but illusion, to change back to rightful shape at the slightest flash of will."

And ignore the fact that I'm going to collapse as though hit by an axe when all this energy is used up!

"I . . . see."

He stopped, shaken anew by the sound of an unfamiliar voice coming from his lips. Before he or his men could panic, I added calmly, "Go ahead, cross yourself if you wish. Speak holy names. The spell won't be harmed, because this is never devil's work."

Estmere straightened. "Of course it isn't."

"*Gwych*, splendid. To business. You are already truly skillful with a harp, no magic needed there. And musicians are always welcome at a royal court."

"Normally, yes."

"Then let us hope Bremor wants to keep up the appearance of normality, because you shall be a harper . . . mm, yes, a wandering musician come down from the north countries to try your luck at a more urbane court. Ah . . . do you think you'll be able to act the part?"

Estmere smiled grimly. "I shall. And you?"

"Why, I shall be your apprentice, the singer to your harping."

My brother let out a fierce bark of a laugh. "By my faith, you're a clever man!"

"Mm. Save your praises till we see if this works."

"But what happens once we're inside Adland's castle?"

What, indeed? The wine-sharp Power of the herb was fading, and all at once I wasn't so sure of myself. *Och fi*, and this was the king I was leading into danger! If something went wrong, if something happened to him—

But Estmere, this once in his life openly romantic and foolhardy, wasn't about to turn back. "Come, what's your plan?"

I ran my hand down the harpstrings, rather astonished and pleased to hear from the pure trail of sound that I'd conjured the thing already tuned. But I couldn't think of a single clever thing to say, except, "Why, to go boldly ahead, trust in the . . . ah . . . the One and, as the harpers say, simply play it by ear!"

CHAPTER XXXIII

HARPERS

So it was that the two of us alone, most unregally clad in clothing we'd borrowed from two of Estmere's grooms—such well-worn garments as travelling musicians a bit down on their luck might wear—rode back towards King Adland's castle. I glanced at my brother (a little unnerved myself by that unfamiliar face), marvelling at his apparent composure and wondering if he was at all afraid; I know I was going through every self-calming spell in my possession.

"Aie, Estmere, don't look so proud! You're supposed to be a harper now, not a king."

He gave me a wry smile. "Every harper I ever saw considered himself a king. Don't worry. I won't betray us." The smile faltered. "But what about you?"

"Me and Bremor, you mean?"

He'd hit on my greatest worry: that I, not my self-possessed brother, would be the one to destroy us. *Gallu nef*, would I be able to face Bremor without anger? Or . . . fear?

"I'll manage," I said grimly.

Pity flickered in his eyes, but all Estmere said was, "That's fortunate, because here we are."

We were stopped at the castle gate by Adland's porter, who eyed us most suspiciously. "Who are you? What's your business here?"

"We're harpers," I answered, trying to keep my voice properly innocent and boyish, "come down from the north countries. We've heard that there is to be a wedding here, a fine, proud, royal wedding. And so we've come to entertain with our music."

But all the while the porter was studying Estmere. I remembered how thoroughly he had stared at my brother before, and suddenly was very uneasy, wondering if the disguise was, after all, sufficient.

"Now, if your hair was yellow," the porter said softly, "if your skin were fairer, I would say you were none other than King Estmere."

My brother didn't panic. Smoothly he slipped a gold ring into the man's hand. "We are but harpers, fellow. Do us no harm."

The porter looked long and hard at Estmere, he looked long and hard at the gold ring.

Then he shrugged, and opened the gate to us.

We rode boldly straight into the Great Hall itself, which of course isn't exactly an unheard-of thing for even a minstrel to do—though if you think I might have used a touch of magical persuasion to smooth our way, you're right. But that persuasion didn't stop the hard-eyed guards from slamming the doors shut behind us, making our horses shy. And I nearly did some shying of my own when the bolts were slammed into place.

They know—no, no, of course they don't know. Bremor is merely being wary.

That wasn't exactly a comforting thought.

A grand feast was prepared in that hall. Banners brightened the grim stone walls, and sweet-scented rushes carpeted the floor. All the long tables were set out, from the foldable everyday trestles to the heavy, solid, priceless High Table with its royal canopy. All were covered from top to floor by fine white linen, and nearly sagged beneath the platters of meat and bread and sweetmeats piled upon them. Elegant, jewel-set goblets and ewers glowed softly silver in the extravagance of torch and candlelight, and I caught hints of brightness from that new delight of the wealthy: golden plates.

Not a seat was vacant about those tables, and I thought absently that no doubt things were arranged as they were in Estmere's court, noble folk in the preferred spots closest royalty, above the massive, ugly, expensive saltcellars, commons below. But just then, I noted the crowd merely as one great blur of color, because my attention was shooting straight to one man:

There in the place of honor sat Bremor, King of Telesse.

And I—felt no fear. Whether from shock or desperation or sheer emotional exhaustion, I felt nothing at all, nothing save a mild contempt.

There was certainly nothing contemptible about his appearance. Bremor was proud and fiercely handsome as ever, very elegant in a dark red velvet tunic, richly embroidered with gold thread and gems glinting with every breath he took. A spotless white cloak trimmed with the royal ermine was thrown casually back over his shoulders. His face was a cool, finely chiseled mask.

But his eyes were haunted. And I *felt* hints of a terrible fear not quite hidden behind that mask.

The rewards of sorcery, I thought, then caught myself. Sorcery? No wielder of Power can hide from another, not at so close a range, and yet I was willing to swear there was no sorcerer in that hall. Except . . . Bremor? *Impossible.*

Estmere distracted me with the softest of gasps. For Rosamonde sat at Bremor's right hand. I winced, but fortunately my brother had the self-control not to cry out to her.

Most charmingly the princess was clad in pale rose samite—priceless stuff—her pretty crystal beads gleaming at neck and wrists, shining from the circlet binding her hair. Despair burned in her lovely eyes, and with it, a certain unconquered fury that boded ill for Bremor should she get her hands on a weapon. Wisely, he wasn't trusting her with so much as a little meat knife.

King Adland sat at Bremor's left. And I almost didn't recognize the man, for all that I had been at his side just a short while ago. He looked . . . pathetic, unbearably weary and sad, on his face the utter hopelessness of a man who has lost everything in the world that matters to him. *Och*, it hurt to see that shrewd king and loving father so reduced.

Worse, I didn't doubt that Bremor meant to see that in due course Adland simply vanished. After all, once Rosamonde was safely wed, and her kingdom firmly in her new husband's hands, there would be no need to keep a potentially dangerous father-in-law alive.

I glanced warily about the hall, trying to separate friend from foe. And for the first time I realized, with a growing chill, that none of the folk here were mere courtiers. For all the bright and festive garb, all, save for one sad-eyed, miserable priest, were fighting men, weapons hidden at their sides.

Bremor's men. And only his.

Invader that he was, the king of Telesse wasn't taking unnecessary chances. Estmere and I, two apparently harmless and unarmed minstrels, had been allowed to enter; Bremor was probably glad to see us, looking to us to provide a much-needed lighter tone. But once we were within the hall, as I've said, the door had been bolted fast behind us. Now I saw that all the other doors to the Great Hall were barred as well, and smiled grimly to myself. Clever Bremor! King Adland's men had quite literally been barred from the feast, presumably till after the wedding was safely, legally, concluded.

Estmere and I were two against a small army.

This, I suppose, would have been a very sensible time to be afraid. Instead, a bold madness born of sheer panic seized me. I took our two horses and, before any of the guards could stop me, stabled the animals right at the High Table, so close to where Bremor sat that when my steed snorted, the froth lit most satisfactorily right in the king of Telesse's finely trimmed beard. He cried out in fury, and turned on Estmere, roaring:

"What is the meaning of this?"

Estmere, to my delighted surprise, played his role beautifully. He must have been wondering what I was about, but my brother smiled beatifically at Bremor and asked innocently, "The meaning of *what*, Sire?"

"Don't play games, fool!" (His accent, I noticed irrelevantly, was heavy, but he seemed more fluent in Anglic than I'd been in his tongue.) "Your horse belongs in the stable, not in a royal hall!"

Two meek servants came to lead our animals aside. Estmere ignored them, his smile never wavering. But there was a world of delicate mockery in his voice as he said, "Oh, my lad is so headstrong. He never does what's fitting or proper."

"Then he shall be taught manners." Bremor signalled sharply to one of his men, commanding in his native tongue, "Go down there and beat me that lad. And when you've done, beat me that insolent harper as well!"

Disguise or no, I certainly wasn't going to allow that! The soldier came up to me menacingly, and a coarse-faced, powerful fellow he was, too. But I caught his glance with mine. And I willed terror into his mind, just as I'd once done with a wild boar. The sending of fear is even easier with a reasoning target, and almost instantly I saw wild panic blaze up in the man's eyes. White-faced, he hurried back to his place.

"What ails you?" Bremor hissed at him.

Gallu, was that dawning suspicion in those hard eyes? Estmere must have been wondering the same, for he quickly raised his harp as distraction and began to play.

And ah, the sound of that harping! Despite our peril, a shiver of sheer delight raced through me, for if Estmere's music had been silvery fair before, now it was a flame of beauty, keen enough to make one weep with wonder, for his very heart was in it. All within that hall, down to the lowliest servant, grew still, listening entranced.

But Estmere played only for the Princess Rosamonde. I think she suspected who he was almost from the beginning. For when Estmere had first spoken, even though his voice was as disguised as his face, the princess had given a little start, as one who can't quite believe her ears. Now, as Estmere harped and gazed at her, Rosamonde gave a small, involuntary laugh, as one who dares hope anew.

Well now, they do say love pierces all disguises. Besides, more logically, she did have that touch of magic to help her.

Bremor couldn't help but notice what was happening. I thought, *Brawd, brawd, be careful,* and wondered: Bremor was no trained magician to see through illusion, and yet . . .

Our charade must end soon. I caught Estmere's eye and sent him as clear a silent message as I could. He nodded.

But at that moment, Bremor said, "The lady would seem to be quite taken with your music, minstrel. Sell me your harp."

"For what fee, Sire?" Estmere's voice held just the right touch of greed.

Bremor laughed in contempt. "Would you bargain with a king?" He made an extravagant sweep of his arm. "For as many gold coins as there are men in this hall!"

Estmere's fingers never faltered on the strings. "And what would you do with my harp, Sire, if I did sell it to you?"

"Why, play a sweet tune for my wife when we are alone on this our wedding night."

Innocent words. But I glimpsed cruel mockery in Bremor's eyes: he knew full well to whom he spoke!

But Estmere was saying, his voice lightly insolent, "If I sell my harp to you, you must sell me your bride." There were angry murmurings throughout the hall at that, but my brother continued smoothly, "As many coins as there are men in this hall? Miser! For this fair lady I would pay more coins than there are stars in all the reaches of Heaven."

The disapproving murmurs grew louder. Only Bremor showed no sign of anger. But I saw his hand slip smoothly down to the hilt of his sword, and at last something broke free within me and I could feel emotion: a cold, pure, clear fury unlike anything I had ever known.

If he does but the slightest harm to Estmere, he shall die, I thought, and wondered at my calmness.

And I knew, with a quiet, dreadful certainty, that nothing I could have done, no vow Ailanna could have had me swear, would have changed this moment. I would not be breaking that vow; I would not be seeking anything as small as revenge. Bremor had freely chosen the Lefthand Path, I, the Right, and it was surely fated that we face each other in battle.

It was surely fated that one of us must die.

But Bremor, all unaware of Fate, was saying to my brother, "And why should I sell so beautiful a prize to so filthy a beggar?"

The contempt in his voice was finally too much for even Estmere's self-control. "Because even a beggar is a finer mate for a princess than you, Bremor of Telesse!"

With that, he drew from his harp the wild, fierce music we had chosen earlier as a signal. And I sang:

> "Oh lady, this is thine own true love,
> No harper, but a king!"

And again I sang, though this time the words weren't those we had planned:

> "Oh, lady, this is thine own true love,
> As plainly thou mayest see—
> And I'll rid you of that foul, false king
> Who parts thy love and thee!"

With those words, I let illusion fall. Amid gasps of wonder, Estmere and I regained our proper forms. I know my brother wanted to be the one to face Bremor, but that wasn't the way it must be. Before Estmere could move, I had pushed him unceremoniously aside. And something fierce or fatalistic in my eyes kept him from protesting.

So I confronted my foe at last, Faerie sword bright in my hand.

Only Bremor showed no amazement at my sudden transformation. "I was wondering if you would ever dare meet me again," he purred. "You make a fine entertainer, princeling. Even as you did in Telesse, writhing in your chains, screaming like a beaten slave."

There was a hiss of fury from Estmere, but I waved him sharply to silence. *Words,* I told myself, *only words, they have no power to harm.* "No chains bind me now, Bremor."

He shrugged. "But now I have no use for you. So I shall kill you."

What he did next truly startled me. For he cried out three sharp, ugly Words of Power and shouted, "I call a Spell of Holding on this company!"

All motion instantly ceased in that hall, as though everyone, down to the two horses standing forgotten in a corner, had been turned to stone.

Everyone save me. With the first Word Bremor shouted, my Power roused, and his spell slid from me as harmlessly as water.

Bremor smiled. "I didn't think it would affect you. Good. Now none shall interrupt our little play."

"Must you always be so *damniol* dramatic?" But how had he ever managed ... *och.* "You persuaded your Patrons to lift the Guardian Spells from what was left of Ybarre's grimoires."

"Clever princeling. I did."

But where was an untrained sorcerer getting his magical stamina? Those Words of Power alone should have drained him.

Unless, of course, Bremor was drawing on the all but inexhaustible strength of his Patrons? Yes, of course he was! And did he realize the danger? Did he know that even a trained mind can die from an overflow of Power. An untrained mind could only be helplessly intoxicated by that endless flood, wildly drinking in more and yet more of Power far beyond all mortal bearing until . . .

For a moment I suppose I really was thinking like one of Faerie, which is to say, quite without that most human of emotions: pity. For a moment I considered simply shielding myself and letting Bremor strike futilely at me again and again till at last he overreached himself. The backlash of demonic Power would very literally burn out his brain, and I would watch him writhe in anguish as he had once watched me—

No! Morality aside, such Powerful wildfire would destroy everyone in the hall!

Ah well. Decided, I smiled thinly. "Despite your Patrons, you're still very much an amateur. We both know it. You wouldn't stand a chance in combat with a true magician."

"Such as yourself?" he mocked. "You were my *slave*, princeling, remember that. You were my *toy* to torment as I saw fit."

He was trying his best to weaken me with terror or shame. But I ignored his taunts, overwhelmed by the fierce eagerness building within me. "I don't want to murder even such as you." I also didn't want to risk taking on the infernal magics of his Patrons. "So let this settling of accounts be a test of iron, not Power."

He grinned, throwing off his elegant cloak. "Agreed."

With one lithe bound, he had cleared the table, theatrical even in his moves. His sword flashed out.

And our long overdue battle was joined.

CHAPTER XXXIV

BATTLES

We fought in silence. Leave the gallant words, the mocking jests, to minstrels' tales; in true combat you have no breath to spare for them. There was only the wild, cold song of blade on blade, the faint rustle of our feet on the treacherously shifting rushes, as we cut and slashed and lunged, all before the eyes of that motionless, helplessly entranced assembly, beneath those bright, incongruous banners.

But we were much of a height, much of the same reach and skill; Bremor knew the shieldless style of fighting as well as I. Time passed: too much time, I thought. Trying not to pant, I began to realize it might well be Estmere's fickle Dame Fortune or simple exhaustion that determined the winner. My sword already seemed painfully heavy, and perspiration was stinging my eyes and what small cuts Bremor had managed to inflict.

But wasn't he ever going to tire as well? Though I knew I'd cut Bremor a few times, darkening that elegant red velvet here and there, the wounds hadn't been important, not enough to weaken him. For all that his hair was now as sleekly wet as mine, the man's stamina seemed inhuman.

Inhuman? Demonic, perhaps?

Gallu, no, if I started letting myself believe I was fighting something more than a man, I was lost. But by sheer ferocity he was driving me back and back—

Dame Fortune laughed. My foot landed on something round—a dropped goblet. It turned under my heel, and I went sprawling, cushioned by rushes, clinging to my sword and twisting desperately to avoid Bremor's savage downward stab. His blade crunched into the rushes, so close to my head I lost a lock of hair. Before he could pull the sword free, I scrambled to my feet, trying to slash at him even as I struggled for balance. Bremor sprang back out of my reach with a contemptuous laugh—

Dame Fortune pointed. Bremor's fashionably high heel caught on the trailing edge of the High Table's linen covering. Bremor, the linen, and a spectacular rain of gold and silver vessels went thudding down.

I didn't play the gallant, not in a death duel: I did my best to spit him while he was still wrapped in linen. But Bremor freed an arm and slashed at my legs, keeping me at bay till he was untangled. Teeth bared in a silent snarl, the man came lunging up at me with such speed I only just parried his attack in time, feeling the shock of blade against blade shoot up my arm to the shoulder. Gritting my teeth, I braced myself, unable to get back on the offensive, catching slash after slash on my sword, blessing the strength of Faerie metal. A particularly savage blow made me stagger—*Damnio!* I wasn't going to let myself be driven back any further.

Praying I wouldn't land on any more goblets, I sprang backwards to give myself some room, hastily took a deep breath, then pressed forward with all my might, sword beating and beating at him. And now, to my fierce delight, it was Bremor who was off balance and forced to give ground. The High Table was just behind him, and I drove him back and back again, trying to trap him

against it. But Bremor glanced quickly over his shoulder
and realized his danger just in time. He twisted like a
cat and rolled right up onto the denuded table, springing
to his feet again, silently mocking me.

I should have been sensible. I should have cut at his
feet, or just waited out of reach till he came down again.
Instead, like some brainless *hurtyn*, I followed Bremor
up there. In the next moment, I was wishing I hadn't
been so impulsive. A bare, slippery, half-cluttered table
was a stupid place for a duel.

But Bremor wasn't giving me a chance to jump down
again. As he forced me down the length of that table,
somehow never slipping or stumbling, his eyes began
to burn with a terrible, exquisite cruelty: he was looking
forward to a slow, painful kill, cut by small cut. And
in that horrifying moment, I remembered the pathetic
shell that had been the Faerie woman Lalathanai, and
knew that whatever Bremor once might have been—
honorable king in his own hard way, honorable man—he,
like she, had been corrupted beyond rescue. He had all
but passed beyond the limits of humanity. If I died here,
so, more terribly, would Estmere and Rosamonde and
their people after them—

Y Duwies, no! I swung my sword, two-handed, with
all my strength. And, with a sound like a woman's silvery
laugh, that bright Faerie blade sheared right through
Bremor's sword, leaving him holding only the hilt and a
jagged hand's breadth of blade.

For a heartbeat's time, we both stood astonished. Then
Bremor cried out like some great hunting cat, and hurled
the hilt at me with all the power in him. I sprang aside
to dodge the jagged thing—

And I fell right off the *damniol* table. As I fell, my
head cracked against one corner with such force there
wasn't even any pain. I suspect a magickless man would
have been killed outright; innate Power, refusing to dissipate, fought to hold spirit and body together. I—I was
where? Crumpled in the rushes, clinging with fading
strength to the shreds of my life, but I was also *where*?

Seeing from nowhere and everywhere Bremor standing over my body in grim delight ... feeling nothing but a dull resentment that now he was going to slay what was left of me. ...

"No," I heard the man mutter. "Magician that you are, I've a more fitting death for you. One to properly impress these fools."

It didn't really seem to matter. But then I heard Bremor begin a sharp, savage chant, and horror dragged me back to awareness:

The king of Telesse was welcoming his Patrons here to deal with me.

No, Bremor, you hurtyn*! Without binding Star or Circle, They're not going to obey you! You're giving Them freedom here—and They'll destroy us all!*

No. My thoughts couldn't have been that coherent. Desperate, I made the mistake of trying to rejoin *self* and body, and only then discovered how badly I'd been hurt. Such agony slashed through my injured skull I fell helplessly back to the rushes, drifting once more *elsewhere*, this time unable to return. ...

"*No.*"

Someone was swathing me in a cool, sheltering embrace: Lalathanai, healed now, sane now, Lalathanai come from wherever the Folk are sent after body death, Lalathanai holding me, blessing me, forcing me back towards *self*. ...

But the pain in that injured *self* was too great, the cool softness of *elsewhere* was so comforting I slid free of Lalathanai ... she was gone, and I ...

"*No, Aidan, please, no!*"

Estmere? He drew me to him by our kinship, close enough to see him fight in vain against the Spell of Holding, able only to breathe, to blink. I felt his fierce, desperate eyes on my body, *felt* the force of those pleading thoughts:

"*Live, brother, live and fight!*"

But of course no mind unschooled in magic could hold such an intense focus for long. And I ... just couldn't guide him. There was a limit even to a magician's strength, and I was slipping helplessly away from light and sound and pain. . . .

And then a second mind touched my own. A skilled, sure, so-familiar presence barred me from that final crossing. Dazed, I thought I saw a vision of Estmere— but with him, another, more vaguely sensed, a fine-boned, lovely other, with eyes of vibrant green:

Ailanna! My sweet lady, there in spirit with Estmere— But how could this be? I heard his silent plea:

"Help him, lady, I pray you!"

"I can't, not at such a range, not alone. You must help me!"

Somehow, I knew, Ailanna must join their strengths, merge their two most dissimilar minds. But it could never happen. Estmere still doubted me. Deep within him, he blamed me for Clarissa's death. He would never be able to drop his guard. Clarissa . . .

Ah, did it matter? I was already dead . . .

. . . and it seemed to me the past was present. I was once more within the royal chapel, once more kneeling at Clarissa's tomb. Strange, strange, this time my emotions seemed so clear: pity for that young life ended too abruptly, and guilt—

No. Not guilt over her death. What I felt was nothing more than a helpless, very human regret that I had never liked my brother's wife, that my last words to her had been angry ones, that I hadn't been there to help her, that I hadn't even known she was ill—

I hadn't even known!

The mind is such an odd, odd thing. Whether from shock or injury or the nearness of death, the missing memories were rushing back to me like water on the flood.

But it was more than my ebbing strength could bear. The world was fading, and in the distance was Clarissa . . . and I wondered with a vague sadness, Is this finally death?

But my brother's thoughts wouldn't let me escape. *"It's*

true. God help me, Aidan, it's true. You didn't *abandon her. Oh, my poor brother, how I've wronged you. No longer!"*

And, though it must surely have been one of the most difficult things any king has done, Estmere let fall all his ingrained defenses. Human mind and Faerie mind freely joined. That doubled strength reached out to me, that doubled love enfolded me like a blessing.

And love, though skeptics mock, really is one of the strongest powers in the world. Surely those two most dear to me summoned more healing strength than could ever have been contained within them. Surely *y Duwies* Herself let them draw on the very Force of Life, because an incredible surge of Power blazed through me.

And when I could think again, I found *self* and *self* rejoined, quite healed.

There was no time for thanksgiving. To my astonishment all that seemingly endless time of near-death had taken only a few moments of reality, but Bremor still stood poised on the table, chanting—

And it was already too late to stop him. No human eyes save mine could have seen the sudden Something, the not-quite mist swirling about Bremor. And ... It knew me. It sent me a wordless, savage greeting in the form of a memory flash of a dark, featureless room and myself huddled helplessly within it.

That was only the beginning. My newly healed mind was assailed by wave after wave of mockery, crueler than honest hate, distorting my senses as They had in Bremor's chapel, tearing me from the fabric of reality, and I—

—had slain Estmere. We had fought over Clarissa's death, and I had lost control of Power. Estmere lay dead before me—

"Illusion!" I cried in silent defiance. *"I will not believe it!"*

But I couldn't fight demonic strength. That cold, cold mockery was all around me and—

—there were chains about me, an iron stake harsh at

my back. I had been condemned for my brother's death, and now I saw Father Ansel staring grimly back at me as the hooded executioner lowered his torch to the wood heaped about me. Fire blazed up around me; I could feel the heat scorching my skin, feel my clothing smoldering, and the strands of my hair—

"I will not be tricked! This is only illusion!"

But then, most cruelly of all—

—I was in Bremor's dungeon. The chill, foul darkness was about me and cruel chains chafed my wrists. Then ... the escape and all that had followed had been only a desperate dream. *This* was reality. I would be trapped down here, alone, despairing, to be endlessly tormented. . . .

And that very nearly broke me. But dimly, dimly, I was aware of a mocking Other presence—

"Illusion!" I screamed. *"Damn you,* cythraul, *I will not believe!"* There was the heart of it: no demon can truly possess you unless you allow it, and now I fought back with every scrap of will within me, shouting, *"Illusion can't hurt unless I accept it—and I do not! I reject this—*and I reject you!"

It was as simple as that. The psychic bonds slipped from me (shuddering, I *felt* them as chill, slimy rope dissolving at my feet). So suddenly I staggered, the reality of the Great Hall was about me.

But in those few moments of illusion, I had run out of time. Bremor's Patron was becoming part of him—*no, not like Lalathanai, worse than she*—and in his sickness, the man saw that merging as the most desirable of things. Eyes blazing with power lust, Bremor was actually welcoming it. I had a sudden horrifying vision of the future as it well might be, of Bremor's armies, dead in soul, surging forth from a sterile Telesse, their very touch sapping will from any who opposed them, of true death-in-life spreading out and out, worse than any plague, and behind it, the immortal, invulnerable thing that had once been a mortal man. . . .

What last shards of humanity lingered in Bremor died

at that moment. His Patron stared out at me through Bremor's eyes, filling the handsome face with an obscene ecstasy of Power strong enough to hurl Ailanna's exhausted spirit back to her body so far away in Cymra, leaving Estmere defenseless, and me— As what had been Telesse's king shouted out the last phrases of his chant, as the final strands of Binding began to slip irrevocably into place, I was nearly crushed by the pressure of Power-saturated air. Gasping, lungs aching, I fought till I nearly burst my heart, trying in vain to raise my arms, trying to take one step, just one little step forward— Useless, I would never reach him in time. For all my magician's will, there was a limit to what a human form could do. The Bremor-thing was already calling out the final Word, and it was too late for anything except—

Except for the last thing I would have expected: Tairyn, there in a wild roar of stormwind (*och*, the Power, the incredible Power of the man, to cast open a Gateway and himself through it in one wild moment). He stood behind me, risking a roomful of iron, hands on my shoulders, encircling me with his own magic, so cold and clear it shook me to the bone, so alien it was almost beyond bearing. In the next moment, the Faerie Lord was gone again; that roomful of iron must have meant agony for him. But he'd freed my arms.

I didn't stop to think. "*Y Duwies* guide me!" I screamed, and hurled my Faerie sword as though it was a spear. Like lightning, that slim blade, that thing of purest magic, blazed across the hall—

And it sheathed itself in Bremor's heart.

Ah, what a cry he gave, human, inhuman—the sound haunts me still. Bremor crumpled across the High Table, his gaze on me, so fierce with hatred I made sign against sign to ward off evil. *Duwies glân, Duwies glân*, was he never going to die?

But then the hatred faded. Bremor's Patron lost Its hold on our world, and with one last flash of impotent rage, vanished, leaving behind only what was left of Bremor's human hatred. I *felt* one flash of sheer, anguished frustration from that shattered mind at the failure of his dream.

Then that, too, was gone. Bremor, King of Telesse, was dead.

A second later, so was the Spell of Holding. The hall was plunged into turmoil as each man discovered his body was his own again, as those at the end of the hall ducked the hoofs of the two frantic horses.

Then shocked silence fell. Bremor's men stared at the limp body before them. Maybe his people had feared and hated him, but he had, after all, been their ruler.

And one man shouted, "Traitor! Murderer! You've killed our king!"

He hurled himself at me. I would have died right there, but Estmere sprang to my defense, just barely catching the descending blade on his own in time. As I struggled to free my Faerie sword (not without a shudder), I heard the soldier fall. And that sparked a true battle. Back to back Estmere and I stood, ringed round with foes eager to cut us down.

And cut down, we would have been, two swords against twenty, no matter what the stories say. Nor is it true I cast Power on our blades: by that point I was too weary to cast even the simplest of spells.

But no one had thought to guard the Princess Rosamonde. And it was she who saved us, racing door to door of the Great Hall, casting aside all those heavy bolts with a strength born of fierce will. And that was how King Adland's own men-at-arms could rush in to our rescue. *Och*, that hall became a true battlefield then.

Not for long.

And when the brief battle was done, we were the victors.

CHAPTER XXXV

DISCOVERIES

The backlash from those ... shall we say ... adventures with Bremor and his Patron, and from my near death, kept me in drained sleep for a full day. But just before waking, I touched thoughts with Tairyn by accident; I had actually been reaching for Ailanna. But *och*, the Faerie Lord was worn, so worn I would have pitied him if I hadn't known how human pity would have insulted him.

"Why?" is all I asked. "All that iron—you nearly killed yourself for me. Why?"

His answer was slow and weary. "Lalathanai returned from *elsewhere* for you. Ailanna nearly drained her life for you." Then, just when I was finally expecting to hear some sign of liking for me from him, Tairyn added coolly, "I will never understand why they bothered. But after all their efforts, it would have seemed a waste to let you die. Now leave me alone, human."

"Are you all right?"

"Of course I am. But I have tired myself out in your behalf, and I wish to sleep."

He broke the contact. And I—I chuckled so much

over Tairyn, stubborn, obstinate, honorable Tairyn, that I woke myself up.

What I woke to was a feeling of being thoroughly healed of any harm, and a sense that I was being watched. I opened a wary eye to find King Adland beaming down at me paternally.

"Ah, at last! I was beginning to worry about you, Prince Aidan, though your brother—poor young man, he was almost as weary as you; I wouldn't let him watch over you but sent him to his own bed—your brother told me it was perfectly normal for a magician to sleep so long after—" He stopped short, grinning with embarrassment. "Ay me, I sound like a gossiping fool."

I laughed. "No. Just like someone who's very, very relieved."

"Ah God, yes. Believe me, I am eternally in your debt, you and your royal brother both. If there is ever any favor I can render, anything at all, pray don't hesitate to ask."

"*Och*, well, there is." My body was complaining it wanted new energy, and quickly. "King Adland, I will be in *your* debt if I can just have one thing: food!"

While it was being brought to me and I was temporarily alone, I reached out with my consciousness again, suddenly frightened I wouldn't receive any answer. My poor Ailanna, working magic from so far away . . . but at last I *felt* our minds touch. And for a time we were too lost in the plain joy that we were both alive and unharmed for any rational conversation.

"*Cariad*, I have only one question," I said, just before we were about to break contact. "How did Estmere ever know how to reach you?"

"Your brother is a truly amazing man," Ailanna teased.

"Yes, but how—"

"Truly amazing."

"But, Ailanna . . ."

She was already gone, leaving me with only the echo of her laughter bright within my mind.

I devoured my breakfast of fruit and hot, buttered

bread with scarce concern for manners, then let a determined group of servants dress me. It wasn't easy to shake
my devoted following, but at last I used my invisibility
illusion to elude them and went down into the garden
for some much-needed sunlight. There I found Estmere
and Rosamonde together, so radiantly happy their linked
auras fairly glowed. I would have left them alone, but
Rosamonde waved to me and Estmere signalled me to
join them. We made polite conversation for a time, but
at last I couldn't keep from asking:

"Estmere, *brawd*, how in the name of all the Powers
did you know to call to . . ." Here I paused, waiting for
Tairyn's spell to clamp down on me. But, wonder of
wonders, nothing happened. Evidently the spell had
finally died of exhaustion (or else, circumstances being
what they were, Tairyn had finally relented), and I was
free to finish, "to Ailanna?"

He grinned at me. "I had guessed you had a lady for
some time."

I could feel myself reddening under Rosamonde's
amused eyes. "How?"

"My dear brother, I may not be able to read emotions,
or whatever it is you do, but there was certainly more
than mere homesickness, your . . . *hiraeth*, in your eyes
whenever you spoke of Cymra."

"But I never mentioned—"

"That gave me the clue. Why would you, who've
always been so" —his grin broadened "—disgustingly
honest never mention that lady? Ha, it was obvious: you
were bespelled."

"What?" asked Rosamonde. "A magician?"

"Yes," I ceded ruefully. "Even a magician."

Estmere was looking hopelessly smug. "The stories do
say the Folk won't let humans discuss them. Not even a
human who speaks their language and carries a Faerie
blade. Therefore, I decided, your love could only be one
of the Folk herself!"

"Logical," Rosamonde murmured. "But that still

doesn't explain how you knew to summon help from her."

"Oh. Well. I didn't doubt that a lady whose very blood is magical would be watching over my brother here in some arcane way. At least, so I prayed." The humor faded from Estmere's eyes. "So, when Bremor had us trapped, and I thought you were ... dying, yet couldn't move a finger to help you, I tried calling to her."

"Mentally. *Gallu nef, brawd*, do you know how difficult that is? Particularly for someone untrained in Power?"

He gave me a pitying look. "Yes, brother. I do know. I did it, remember? I hadn't the vaguest idea of what to do, or how; I just kept yelling in my mind, praying she would hear me." Estmere chuckled. "It's amazing what one can do under the whip of sheer terror! God's blood, I don't know where you magicians get your stamina. I thought my brain was going to burst. But—I did reach her!" He paused. "Now, I have only one question for you, Aidan. Who was that fierce, splendid, silver-haired fellow who appeared behind you for a moment?"

It was my turn to be smug. "*Och*, that was merely a Faerie Lord," I said, and grinned.

Plans for a royal wedding went through with truly remarkable haste: "It's either that," Estmere warned his court once we were home again, "or you're going to find your king has eloped!"

Rosamonde made an exquisite bride. And if a fragile, blue-eyed ghost watched the proceedings, she did not linger.

Now, two months later, little remains to be told. My mind seems totally healed; what few small gaps of memory remain are hardly worth concern and will almost certainly vanish with time. As for the fact that a king died on my sword—

Do you recall that sensible-eyed member of Telessian royalty I'd seen in my mirror? Merhaut, his name is, cousin and perforce heir to the late king: in short, he's now King Merhaut I of Telesse. What with no sorcerer in residence there—and none ever likely to be!—the gray hopelessness is fading from that land. Judging from the courteous message of congratulations he sent to the newlyweds, with polite, wary greetings added to me, Merhaut bears me no grudge at all for taking him out from under Bremor's threat and placing him on the throne!

Estmere and Rosamonde, of course, are radiantly happy together, so obviously in love that even prim Sir Verrin beams when he sees them. My brother never did learn of the vow that held me at his side, and I see no reason to enlighten him.

And what of me? Can't you guess? Now that Estmere no longer needs me by his side, now that he's truly happy, I can find my own happiness. I'm returning to the land that's always been my true home. I'm returning to Cymra—

And to Ailanna.

END

GLOSSARY

Aidan's Cymra is, of course, loosely analogous to
Wales, though the geography of that and other lands
is hardly the same as our own Western Europe.
Most of Aidan's Cymraeth exclamations should be
obvious to the reader, but a list of translations fol-
lows for the curious.

a ....and
anfoniad ....literally, sending. In
                          magic: a sorcerer's
                          mindless creation, sent
                          to destroy an enemy
annwyl............................dear
bachgen ....boy
bachgennyn.....................little boy (used
                          affectionately)
barddi............................bards
blin ....weary, tired
brawychu ....frighten, terrify
brawd, fy brawd ....brother, my brother
cariad ....love, sweetheart
chwaer............................sister
chwi ....you
cryfder............................strength
cyfnewidiwr ....literally, change. In
                          magic, an herb that
                          assists shape-shifting
cythraul,
   cythrauliad................demon, demons
cythraul-slav ....demon-thrall
damnio, fe damnio.......damn, damn it

damniol ....damnably
datguddiad ....revelation
datguddio ....reveal
Duwies, Duwies
   glân............................Goddess, holy Goddess
Duwies diolch...............Goddess be thanked
dychrynu ....frightened, terrorized
dyri Uffern....................literally, thorn of Hell (a "shorthand" oath, short for: "May it be rent by the thorns of Hell!" Cymraeth is full of similar exotic curses).
fflam ....flame
gallu...............................power (capitalized, it refers to magical Power)
Gallu nef ....Power of heaven
golau..............................moon
grym ....strength, energy
gwych ....fine, splendid
hiraeth...........................roughly, a bittersweet longing, nostalgia or homesickness
hurtyn ....idiot
llyfr-dwin ....literally, book-sorcerer, a contemptuous phrase for a magician without innate Power
Mawr Cyfanfor ....Great Sea, analogous in our world to the Atlantic
mor ....so
och, och fi.....................all purpose Cymraeth exclamations, meaning (depending on the situation)

	anything from "oh my," to "alas!"
pw!	bah!
sbel	(magic) spell
Sbel Dirgelwch	Spell of Secrecy
Sbel Drysu	Spell of Entanglement
swynwr	magician
Uffern	Hell
unig	only
ysblennydd	splendid, elegant

MERCEDES LACKEY

The Hottest Fantasy Writer Today!

URBAN FANTASY

Knight of Ghosts and Shadows with Ellen Guon

Elves in L.A.? It would explain a lot, wouldn't it? Eric Banyon really needed a good cause to get his life in gear—now he's got one. With an elven prince he must raise an army to fight against the evil elf lord who seeks to conquer all of California.

Summoned to Tourney with Ellen Guon

Elves in San Francisco? Where else would an elf go when L.A. got too hot? All is well there with our elf-lord, his human companion and the mage who brought them all together—until it turns out that San Francisco is doomed to fall off the face of the continent.

Born to Run with Larry Dixon

There are elves out there. And more are coming. But even elves need money to survive in the "real" world. The good elves in South Carolina, intrigued by the thrills of stock car racing, are manufacturing new, light-weight engines (with, incidentally, very little "cold" iron); the bad elves run a kiddie-porn and snuff-film ring, with occasional forays into drugs. *Children in Peril—Elves to the Rescue*. (Book I of the SERRAted Edge series.)

Wheels of Fire with Mark Shepherd

Book II of the SERRAted Edge series.

When the Bough Breaks with Holly Lisle

Book III of the SERRAted Edge series.

HIGH FANTASY
Bardic Voices: The Lark & The Wren
Rune could be one of the greatest bards of her world, but the daughter of a tavern wench can't get much in the way of formal training. So one night she goes up to play for the Ghost of Skull Hill. She'll either fiddle till dawn to prove her skill as a bard—or die trying. . . .

The Robin and the Kestrel: Bardic Voices II
After the affairs recounted in *The Lark and The Wren,* Robin, a gypsy lass and bard, and Kestrel, semi-fugitive heir to a throne he does not want, have married their fortunes together and travel the open road, seeking their happiness where they may find it. This is their story. It is also the story of the Ghost of Skull Hill. Together, the Robin, the Kestrel, and the Ghost will foil a plot to drive all music forever from the land. . . .

Bardic Choices: A Cast of Corbies with Josepha Sherman

If I Pay Thee Not in Gold with Piers Anthony
A new hardcover quest fantasy, co-written by the creator of the "Xanth" series. A marvelous adult fantasy that examines the war between the sexes and the ethics of desire! Watch out for bad puns!

BARD'S TALE
Based on the bestselling computer game, *The Bard's Tale.*℗
Castle of Deception with Josepha Sherman
Fortress of Frost and Fire with Ru Emerson
Prison of Souls with Mark Shepherd

Also by Mercedes Lackey:
Reap the Whirlwind with C.J. Cherryh
Part of the Sword of Knowledge series.
The Ship Who Searched with Anne McCaffrey
The Ship Who Sang is not alone!

Wing Commander: Freedom Flight with Ellen Guon
Based on the bestselling computer game, *Wing Commander.*™

Join the Mercedes Lackey national fan club! For information send an SASE (business-size) to Queen's Own, P.O. Box 43143, Upper Montclair, NJ 07043.

POUL ANDERSON

Poul Anderson is one of the most honored authors of our time. He has won seven Hugo Awards, three Nebula Awards, and the Gandalf Award for Achievement in Fantasy, among others. His most popular series include the Polesotechnic League/Terran Empire tales and the Time Patrol series. Here are fine books by Poul Anderson available through Baen Books:

FLANDRY • 72149-6 • $4.99 _____

THE HIGH CRUSADE • 72074-0 • $3.95 _____

OPERATION CHAOS • 72102-X • $3.99 _____

ORION SHALL RISE • 72090-2 • $4.99 _____

THREE HEARTS AND THREE LIONS • 72186-0 • $4.99 _____

THE PEOPLE OF THE WIND • 72164-X • $4.99 _____

THE BYWORLDER • 72178-X • $3.99 _____

THE GAME OF EMPIRE • 55959-1 • $3.50 _____

FIRE TIME • 65415-2 • $3.50 _____

AFTER DOOMSDAY • 65591-4 • $2.95 _____

THE BROKEN SWORD • 65382-2 • $2.95 _____

THE DEVIL'S GAME • 55995-8 • $4.99 _____

THE ENEMY STARS • 65339-3 • $2.95 _____

SEVEN CONQUESTS • 55914-1 • $2.95 _____

STRANGERS FROM EARTH • 65627-9 • $2.95 _____

GRAND ADVENTURE
IN GAME-BASED UNIVERSES

With these exciting novels set
in bestselling game universes,
Baen brings you synchronicity at its
best. We believe that familiarity with
either the novel or the game will
intensify enjoyment of the other.
All novels are the only authorized
fiction based on these games and
are published by permission.

THE BARD'S TALE™

Join the Dark Elf Naitachal and his apprentices in
bardic magic as they explore the mysteries of the
world of The Bard's Tale.